BELLAMY WESTBAY

REVELATIONS

The INFINITY Series, Vol.1

www.bellamywestbayauthor.com

ISBN: 0-9996065-0-6
ISBN-13: 978-0-9996065-0-6

Artwork by Ana Grigoriu at books-design.com

Editing by John Fox at BookFox

The Nephilim were on the earth in those days—and also afterward—when the sons of God went to the daughters of humans and had children by them. They were the heroes of old, men of renown.

Genesis 6:4

PROLOGUE
Gwen

The world is such a twisted place, I mused as I slid to the floor. Never in a million years would I have imagined I'd die like this – at the hands of someone I trusted.

I took my last shuddering breath and absorbed everything about the moment. Hannah's silky black hair falling across her eyes, Jasper's battered face, Alexander's clenched jaw and angry expression, and Ky's strong voice in the distance.

Funny, you never know who you can really trust.

CHAPTER ONE
Gwen

I dug my feet into the white sand as a flock of seagulls sailed over the ocean. I closed my eyes and wiggled my toes, enjoying the gritty feel of the sand sliding between them.

Where was he?

I released an impatient sigh. He'd be here soon enough. Every night for the past four years, he'd met me here in my dreams, I just had to be patient.

I leaned back on my elbows and gazed out at the water. Everything was so vivid. The violet sky, the breeze on my face, and the taste of salt in the air made it almost impossible to believe I was dreaming. But the crashing waves had no roar, and the seagulls made no sound. The complete and absolute silence destroyed the illusion of reality.

His warm hand on my shoulder caused my heart to leap with excitement.

He wore the same board shorts as always, and my eyes soaked up his incredible physique and bronzed skin. My heart raced as my gaze slid up his lean body. Tight washboard abs made way to broad shoulders, accented by his defined biceps and chest. I felt the familiar twinge of disappointment as I gazed up at his face. For some ungodly reason, in this beautifully vivid place, his face was a blurry muddle of color, as if the universe had censored it out. I should have been used to it by now, but the disappointment hit me full force.

His fingers twined around mine and tugged me forward.

What would we do tonight? Sometimes we had an adventure, other times we played in the waves. There were nights when all we did was lie in the sand holding each other's hands. Every single night was amazing.

I followed closely behind him and enjoyed the view. Tanned skin pulled tight over the lean, well-defined muscles of his back.

He was absolutely flawless, with the small exception of the oddly shaped birthmark behind his right ear. That birthmark was his only imperfection and the only thing about him that seemed real.

Without warning, he turned and pulled me into his arms.

His blurry lips moved, and though I couldn't hear the words, I knew what they were.

I smiled.

My dream man had always been there for me. On my hard days, when I started college, when my friends let me down, he was always there.

I found myself mouthing the words, "I love you, too."

Warmth washed over me, and a smile stretched across my face. I knew no matter what happened, my dream man would always be there.

∞∞∞∞∞∞

"Ugh! I hate the heat," Hannah whined from the backseat. "Why are we riding in this hunk of junk? It doesn't even have air conditioning."

I silently agreed with Hannah. Even with the windows down, it was suffocatingly hot in Florida this time of year. As if to prove my point, a drop of sweat slid down my face and onto my shirt.

I wasn't sure how much more of this I could take.

"Come on, Hannah. It's not that bad. Besides, your car is in the shop."

"Yeah, but why didn't we take your car?"

I shrugged as I loosened my seat belt and leaned forward.

"Can't you at least try to enjoy the fresh air?" I motioned toward the open window. The hot outside air blew my hair back and almost took my breath away as it dried the sweat on my face.

I glanced over at Ky. His chocolate brown eyes stared straight ahead behind his sunglasses. His face was covered in sweat, and his tousled blonde hair was plastered to his forehead. He was ignoring our conversation.

Or he seemed to be. But I knew better. He'd worked his butt off the last few months to save up for this car, then just days after purchasing it, the air conditioner had gone out. I looked to where his hands gripped the steering wheel. His clenched fingers and tight jaw proved what I already knew to be true.

I shook my head. When it came to Hannah, it didn't take much to piss him off. From the very start, those two hadn't been able to stand each other.

"Hannah, are you going to your dad's fundraiser next week?" I asked, changing the subject to defuse the tension between them. I saw Hannah's expression change as a broad smile transformed her eager face.

"Of course," she exclaimed. "Daddy even promised he'd take me out to eat before the event, just the two of us!" Hannah continued gushing about the evening she had planned, down to the smallest detail. It wasn't until we entered Veridian Hills and pulled up to her driveway that she quieted.

Hannah grabbed her purse and slid out of the car. "You are coming, right?"

"My dad's not giving me a choice."

"Good." Hannah slammed the door and sauntered inside.

Ky relaxed the moment Hannah was out of the car, and for that I was thankful. We spent the rest of the drive in amicable silence. I leaned my head back on the headrest as sweat poured down my face, making me wish we had taken my car this morning. But if we had taken my car, Ky wouldn't have been able to ride with us. And besides, I wanted to enjoy this time with my friends. When I found a job, I'd have a lot less time with them. I already had a few interviews lined up, and hopefully one of them would work out because I needed the income. And I needed something to put on my resume when I finished my degree.

"Gwen?"

A quick glance around told me I was in my driveway, and Ky was watching me expectantly.

"Sorry."

"It's okay," he replied, a smile playing at the corner of his lips. "It wouldn't be the first time you zoned out on me. I just wanted to say I'm sorry for getting pissed off back there."

"Don't worry about it. It's understandable when Hannah gets like that."

"You mean when she's acting like a bitch?"

I laughed. "You said it, not me. So are you coming to the fundraiser with us?"

"No, I've got to work. Beverly and Hannah will be there to keep you out of trouble, or at least keep you from being bored out of your mind."

"Hey, if anyone needs babysitting, it's not me."

"That's true," he retorted with a laugh. "Are we still on for tonight? Is Beverly going to be able to make it?"

"No, her flight doesn't come in until late. It's just you and me tonight."

"Oh," he paused. "All right."

I undid my seatbelt, got out of the car, and waved goodbye as Ky sped off down the street.

When I opened my front door, the cold blast of air sent goosebumps up my arms. The relief from the heat was almost painful. I shook my head as I pulled my phone from my pocket.

Me: Lets take my car 2nite

Ky: Y?

Me: bc when ppl say im hot i dnt wnt it 2 b bc of the sweat dripping off my nose

Ky: OK

Me: and dnt txt n drive!

Ky: i stpped car 3 min ago

I sighed.

Sometimes Ky was too serious. I couldn't tell if he was angry about my text or just agreeing with me. I'd tried to make it funny, but maybe I'd failed.

I reread my text and didn't see anything wrong with it. I'd see him tonight and apologize if he seemed off. He was one of my best friends, and I trusted him, but he really needed to loosen up.

Twenty minutes later, I'd showered and was ready to go. I passed the remaining time watching Netflix and playing with Spyder, the black kitten Ky had given me as a late birthday present. Spyder was a feisty little thing, always attacking my fingers and toes. The ball of fur seemed to think he was a ferocious tiger. I had fallen in love with him almost instantly. He was the perfect companion.

∞∞∞∞∞∞

Going to dinner and a movie with Ky was always a safe bet for a fun night out. He was great company, and we enjoyed the same movies. Tonight's choice was Ky's, and he'd opted for *Devil's Fury*, a horror flick that was completely out of character for him.

We walked out of the theater arm in arm as Ky laughed at my

trepidation.

"Nothing's going to jump out and get you, I swear."

I glanced up into his mirthful eyes. "You did that on purpose."

"Did what exactly?"

"Picked a scary movie. I think you enjoy hearing me scream."

His head dropped back, and a loud laugh boomed from his lips. "You have no idea."

My eyes met his for a moment before glancing away. "I can't believe their family stayed in that house."

Ky shook his head. "Yeah, me neither."

"It was crazy, right? I'm so glad my family's not that insane. I mean, we have our moments, but-"

"Wait," Ky interrupted. "Your family? Crazy? They don't even come close. Your mom and dad are the tamest people on the planet."

"Are not!"

"Are too. Come on, a campaign manager and a political strategist? They are the very definition of tame and boring."

"They let loose and have fun sometimes," I protested.

"Oh yeah? Like when?" Ky smiled teasingly. "Give me one good story about your parents."

"You first," I replied without thinking. My hands weren't fast enough to stop the words as I slapped my mouth shut. My eyes darted to Ky's. "I'm sorry. I didn't mean to-"

"It's okay," he replied stiffly.

"Ky, you know you can talk to me, right? It's been eight years since they passed, maybe it would help to talk about them. And we've been friends for two years. I just want to finally understand."

"There's nothing to understand. They're gone. That's it." The finality in his tone startled me.

His eyes softened. "I'm sorry, Gwen. I just don't like talking about it."

"But I want to know about your past, Ky. Couldn't you tell me something? Anything at all? Like where you grew up?" I didn't like pushing, but his hesitancy always frustrated me.

Ky's jaw clenched. "I said I don't want to talk about it."

He turned and strode away from me toward the parking lot.

Damn it. We were having such a good night, and I ruined it by pushing him. I should have known. He'd never wanted to open up to me before, why would he start now?

I shook my head as I walked to the car where Ky waited for me. We rode to his apartment in silence. The moment I shifted the gears into park, Ky's hand gripped the door, flexing his forearms.

"I'm sorry about this. I'm just not ready to talk about it."

"Okay." I did my best to sound patient, but on the inside, I was growling in frustration.

I drove home rehashing our conversation. His need to hide his past baffled me. Ky's parents died in a car accident when he was fourteen. He lived in foster care afterward because he had no other living relatives, and that was everything I knew about his past. I had no idea where he had lived in foster care or where he had grown up. I didn't know if he'd ever played football or joined any clubs. That was all he'd ever given me, and he told me more than anyone. I could understand why he wouldn't want to talk about his parents, but why not the rest of it?

By the time I got home, I hadn't made any progress in figuring it out. I brushed my teeth and distracted myself by thinking about Luke. Luke was the name I'd given my dream man. I didn't know why, but something about that name seemed right. By the time I'd put my pajamas on, I'd completely forgotten our argument and was almost dancing with anticipation. Too much anticipation, apparently, because I was too excited to fall asleep. I rolled my eyes at the irony. I was so excited about a dream that I was too hyped to sleep.

Hilarious.

I leaned over my nightstand, popped two melatonin in my mouth, and laid back down.

Thirty minutes later, I was laying in the sand, cuddled next to Luke. The warmth from his muscular body radiated into mine and melted away all my worries. I was content to lay in his arms for eternity. He was the sun that my world revolved around. He was my shelter in the storm. I wished I could stay in this dream forever.

His arm nudged me.

"I'm okay." I pulled myself up on one elbow to look down at him. Oh, how I longed to see his face. I bet it was as beautiful as the rest of him.

I traced my fingers across his chest while I stared into his face. Desperately, I tried to force his blurred features into focus. I wasn't surprised when it didn't work. It wasn't the first time I'd tried. Discouraged, I looked down at his beautiful chest. An intricate golden tattoo covered the entire right side and wrapped down his shoulder. The gold reflected and shimmered in the light. I'd never seen anything like it; the only things that came close were the temporary tattoos done at that kiosk by the beach. I traced my finger over the image. It was dazzling.

His skin was smooth and warm beneath my fingertips. My finger tingled where I traced over his tattoo, the image glowing wherever I touched.

I leaned down and placed a kiss in the center of his chest before I pressed my cheek against it. His heart strummed comfortingly against my ear.

Luke's warm arms wrapped around me protectively, and I snuggled in.

∞∞∞∞∞∞

Class had just finished when my phone buzzed.

Beverly: Scooter's?

I smiled. Did she even have to ask? I never turned down happy hour at Scooter's.

Me: B there 15 min

I threw my books into my backpack and headed out the building. Opening the door to the parking lot was like opening the door to a furnace. The heat hit my face, and sweat instantly popped out on my skin. I couldn't wait for summer to be over.

I sat in my car and put the air conditioner on as high as I could get it, then turned the radio up.

I should have taken the summer off. Somehow, Beverly had convinced me that taking summer classes was a great idea. It was, but it would have been a lot nicer if I could have spent the summer laying on the beach. My tan had seriously faded over the winter months, and I could have used a little sun.

In typical fashion for this time of day, Scooter's was packed. I scanned the room and found Beverly sitting in the back corner at our usual table. The instant she saw me, she began waving furiously and signaling the waiter.

I dropped into the chair next to her just as the waiter arrived.

"Three strawberry margaritas," Beverly ordered, then brushed her pale blonde hair behind her ear.

"Hey, girly. I've missed you." She threw her arms around me and squeezed harder than you'd think a five-foot-two, hundred-pound girl was capable of.

"Can't breathe," I squeaked.

Beverly chuckled and released me.

"How was your trip?"

She sipped her drink and told me about her family trip to Spain and Italy. "Gwen, I wish you could have come with me. It was so much fun, and there were so many hot guys there."

I rolled my eyes. Of course, that was what she'd focus on.

She caught my expression. "You know, it wouldn't hurt you to hook up with someone once in a while. Might loosen you up a bit."

She laughed when I stuck out my tongue out at her.

"So how long are your parents going to stay overseas?"

"Till the end of summer. Dad somehow persuaded the board to let him conduct their meetings via Skype. This is the first real vacation he's had in years. Mom was thrilled. I honestly don't think I've seen her that happy before."

Mr. and Mrs. Shultz were like a second mom and dad to me. I'd spent more time with them than I had my own parents, but Mr. Shultz did work a lot. I was happy they finally made some time for themselves.

"So where's Hannah?" I asked as I scanned the restaurant. Just as the words escaped my lips, I saw her. She was at the bar, her black hair smoothed into a sophisticated ponytail, surrounded by a bunch of guys as usual. One very handsome blonde had his muscled arm around her waist. I squinted and leaned forward. Was that Devin? He was a linebacker on the football team, all brawn and no brain. He was a good-looking guy, but definitely not my type.

Beverly spotted Hannah just after I did and yelled for her to join us. Hannah told the guys goodbye. Devin's arms snaked around Hannah and refused to let her go until she planted a kiss on his cheek. Freed, Hannah strutted over to our table and swayed her hips as the guys' eyes followed her.

Beverly slid Hannah her margarita and smiled.

"Beverly, you know I can't drink all this," Hannah motioned to the fishbowl-sized glass. I had to agree, Hannah was kind of a lightweight. But then again, so was I.

"That's okay. I'll finish it off for you," Beverly said with a smirk. "Remember I'm half Irish. We're a drinking people."

I rolled my eyes at her.

Beverly was definitely a drinker, but she never did anything stupid. In fact, I'd bet she took a cab here tonight so she wouldn't have to worry about leaving her car.

Hannah's eyes swept over me. "Gwen, you look like crap."

I scowled.

"Your makeup has melted off, and your hair is sticking to your face." She pulled a limp strand of hair off my cheek with a disgusted look. "Why do you do this to yourself?"

"You don't have to be such a bitch, Hannah," Beverly retorted.

"I'm not a bitch. Seriously, I have no idea how she has Ky wrapped around her finger the way she does. You smell like a sweaty guy. You know, you should put your hair up in a ponytail so you don't sweat so much. Would that really be so bad?"

"Wrapped around my finger? What are you talking about?"

"Nothing. And stop changing the subject. You look like a drowned rat."

My hand subconsciously patted my hair against my ears. "I like my hair down."

Beverly rolled her eyes again. "Leave her alone. She can't help that she has Vulcan ears."

"I do not." Again, I patted the strawberry blonde hair that covered my ears. They weren't that bad; they just stuck out a little. In kindergarten, all the kids laughed at me. They said I looked like Dumbo the flying elephant. After a few years, the rest of my body caught up with my ears. They looked mostly normal now, but I still couldn't stand the thought of people looking at them, so I never wore my hair up.

"*Whatever*. I'll be back in a minute." I finished my drink and went to the bathroom. Standing in front of the mirror, I wondered if I really looked that bad. My face was dirty and sweaty, and my hair was plastered around my face and neck.

Hannah was right. I looked like hell.

I pulled my hair off my shoulders and away from my face. I turned my head left, then right. I studied my face and decided I wouldn't look bad with a ponytail. It made my soft, heart-shaped face look cute. Then my gaze shifted to my ears.

I lowered my eyes.

My ears didn't stick out anymore, but I just couldn't do it. I released my hair and touched up my makeup.

When I returned to our table, Beverly and Hannah were already squabbling. No surprise there.

"What are you two arguing about now?"

"I was reminding Hannah that this was supposed to be a girls' night, which means no guys."

"Well, if a guy starts talking to me, I can't be rude."

"You had no problem being rude to Gwen a few minutes ago," Beverly countered.

I knew I'd better stop their bickering before it reached full-blown smackdown levels. "So did y'all see the chick Jasper was with at Brodie's party?"

That got their attention. An intense interest in hot guys was about the only thing they had in common, and Jasper Mills was just that. He'd enrolled at VBCC almost a year ago and had been the hottest thing on campus ever since. With short blonde hair that framed his chiseled face, full lips, and luminescent blue-green eyes, he looked like a cross between Brad Pitt and Channing Tatum.

Beverly's eyes lit up. "Yeah, wasn't that Tatiana Yurogi, the Russian model headlining Victoria's Secret lingerie campaign?"

"Yeah," Hannah scoffed. "But I hear she's a complete slut."

"Jealous much?" Beverly taunted.

Oh hell, not this again. Jasper was a complete player. He'd hooked up with half the girls on campus but wouldn't give Hannah the time of day, which only made Hannah want him all the more. And Beverly was constantly giving her shit about it.

I sighed deeply.

It was going to be a long night.

∞∞∞∞∞

"What do you think? The black dress or the green one?" I asked, holding both up against my reflection in the mirror.

"Definitely the green one. It really makes your eyes pop,"

Beverly exclaimed.

I hung the black dress back in my closet. It was a relief to have a friend whose judgment I could trust. Beverly and I had been best friends since my family moved to Verona Beach when I was in third grade. She was honest, trustworthy, and loyal. She was the sister I had always wanted.

"Gwen, you've got to cheer up. It's not that bad. At least it's an excuse to dress up," she said as she smoothed her straightened hair over her shoulder.

"You know how these things are. Just a bunch of suits schmoozing each other for more money. I've been to hundreds of these fundraisers, and they're all the same. Boring, boring, boring." I knew how whiny I sounded, but *oh God*, how I hated going to these ridiculous fundraisers every few weeks.

"Come on. There'll be music to dance to. Screw everyone else. It'll be just the two of us having a blast on the dance floor. Besides, we could always entertain ourselves by watching Hannah hit on all the rich old men in the room."

I couldn't help but smile. That would be *so* Hannah. She'd show up in the skimpiest outfit imaginable, but still manage to look like a supermodel instead of a hooker. She'd know it too. That girl loved attention.

I couldn't count the number of times she had scooped up guys I'd had my eyes on. Never intentionally, but whenever a good-looking guy was around, her natural instinct was to flirt shamelessly with him until he was hers. No guy could resist her charms. Still, a part of me resented her for it. I never had much luck with guys. They noticed me, and I saw the looks I got when I walked down the street, but somehow I always ended up the friend and never the girlfriend. Beverly claimed it was because I was too friendly. She said I needed to "let my inner slut out," whatever that meant.

Who was I kidding? I knew exactly what she meant, but I had absolutely no idea how to be sexy. Every time I'd tried flirting with a guy, I ended up making an utter fool out of myself. It was humiliating time and time again.

I smiled at Beverly. She was right. Tonight would be fun.

"Come on, let's get dressed! We're gonna rock this shindig."

"Hell yeah!"

∞∞∞∞∞∞

Beverly had been right. We were having a blast. The DJ's music selection was restricted to the 80's and 90's, and I knew all the words. We were on the dance floor swaying to "Truly, Madly, Deeply" by Savage Garden when Hannah sashayed up to us.

"You trying to pick up a man tonight, Gwen?" Hannah questioned with a laugh and a slight slur.

I blanched at her strange question. "What are you talking about?"

"You look like a million bucks," she said, slurring again. "You must be looking for a man."

"Hannah, are you drunk?" I couldn't hide my surprise. "Since when do you get plastered?"

"Since dear old dad stood me up this afternoon for a business associate," she replied sullenly. "Sometimes it's like he forgets that he even has a daughter."

Hannah paused a moment, then dropped her head. "Sorry, don't concern yourself with me. I'm fine. I may have had a few too many glasses of wine tonight, but I've reached my limit. No worries."

"Are you sure you're okay?"

"Yeah, it's not like anything has changed. Dad's always been like this. I could burn down half the house, and he wouldn't notice. He's always too busy trying to raise money for his campaign." Her face brightened. "Speaking of fundraising," she leaned in conspiratorially, "I heard that Eli Prescott was going to be here tonight!"

She paused for dramatic effect, then rolled her eyes. "*Seriously*, neither of you know who Eli Prescott is? The billionaire and entrepreneur? He's the CEO of Prescott Tech." She looked at us incredulously. "*Peoples'* Sexiest Man Alive?"

Recognition lit Beverly's icy blue eyes. "Oh my God! I read an article about him recently. He's a genius. He came up with some super hi-tech inventions, started his own company, and made his entire fortune in just the last seven years, and he's only, like, forty-two."

"Where is he?" I asked, curious to see how he looked. I found it hard to reconcile the conflicting images of super-nerd and hottie that flashed through my mind.

Hannah scanned the room for a few moments before her eyes lit up. "He's over there." She glanced back at us. "How do I look?"

Before I could answer, Hannah was already making her way across the room toward an incredibly handsome older man.

"Guess we can't laugh at Hannah tonight," Beverly quipped as we watched Hannah introduce herself.

"Oh, how I wish I had her self-assurance," I couldn't help but say out loud. She looked like a beautiful heroine from a movie as she placed her hand on his arm and smiled.

Beverly and I continued to watch with rapt attention as a petite Greek goddess walked around Hannah, pulled Eli in close, and kissed him passionately.

We both gasped.

Hannah discreetly turned around and retreated back to us. "That's his *wife*," she whispered, head down, wiggling her ring finger at us. Beverly and I nearly fell over each other with laughter.

Hannah's cheeks reddened, then she rolled her eyes and stalked off to find other prey.

I glanced at Beverly. "You were right again. Coming tonight was *so* worth it!"

CHAPTER TWO
Alexander

What am I doing here? I'd been asking myself the same question for two hours. Like Zane, I should've had the sense to stay home. There was nothing here for me, just a room full of power-hungry politicians and lobbyists.

"Sir, can I interest you in some wine?" a waiter inquired.

"No, thank you."

That was it. I was done. I'd hung around long enough to say I'd tried. As I walked toward the exit, I removed my tie and glanced down to unbutton the top buttons of my shirt.

Suddenly, my heart started racing, my body froze, and my feet planted on the floor. I had the overwhelming sensation that leaving tonight would be a mistake.

Always listen to your intuition, Father's sound advice echoed through my mind.

Father was always right.

I turned and drifted back toward our table to join Eli. He stood alone, looking dapper in a tailored black suit and holding a glass of champagne.

If anyone had it worse than me, it was Eli. I hated the responsibility that had been thrust upon his relatively young shoulders. It was a necessary evil that weighed heavily on him. He'd spent the previous few years cultivating the contacts we needed to complete our mission. Tonight, we were finally in a position to tie up loose ends before we went home.

When the world looked at Eli, they saw a handsome, successful, and charismatic businessman. No one saw the weariness in his eyes, the rigidness of his shoulders, or the tightness in his lips. I hated seeing him like this. I was so thankful this charade was almost over.

As I watched Eli, a beautiful woman approached him. Though I couldn't see her face, I could see that she was stunning. It was evident in everything about her, from her silky black hair to her manicured nails to her long shapely legs. She walked with a sultry confidence that drew my eye.

Who was this beauty? Something about her seemed eerily familiar.

I slowly circled the room.

"An hors-d'oeuvre, sir?"

"No," I replied as I leaned around the waiter in an attempt to get a better view.

The path between us cleared. My heart nearly stopped. Light illuminated her heavenly skin, large honey-colored eyes, and full pouty lips. Shock froze me in place as my world shifted beneath me.

Was that...*Eva?*

I watched as she flirted shamelessly with Eli. I snatched my phone from my pocket and texted Ariel.

Get out here. Now!

Within seconds, Ariel rounded the corner and pulled Eli into a passionate embrace. For the first time since arriving, Eli's body relaxed. The love between Ariel and Eli was undeniable. His body lit up like a Christmas tree when she touched him. His skin shimmered with a mild glow. His happiness was palpable. I cleared my throat loudly as I walked toward them.

The last thing we needed was for people to notice we were different. Especially now that we were so close to our goal.

Ariel smiled at her husband, then indulged him with another quick kiss.

I scanned the room, searching desperately for Eva. I must have imagined her face. She couldn't be here. It must have been an illusion.

My eyes finally caught her at the other end of the room. She leaned seductively over a middle-aged gentleman in a blue pinstriped suit. I cringed as she whispered in his ear, then attempted to climb into his lap.

Impossible.

I turned and headed for the door. I'd only taken a few steps when I realized I couldn't leave — I *needed* to know if that woman was my Eva.

I strode toward her, dodging waiters and other attendees as I went.

Suddenly, all obstacles cleared between us, and her eyes met mine, widening in surprise before narrowing into a look I knew too well.

Desire.

A seductive smile spread across her oval face as I closed the distance between us. *Not Eva.*

"Hello. Do we know each other? I swear I've seen you somewhere before." I reached my hand out for hers. "I'm Alexander Prescott."

"Hannah Kinsley," she replied, slipping her hand into mine. "And no, we haven't met." She batted her eyes and smiled. "If we had, trust me, you would remember."

"I'm sure you're right." I laughed, then motioned toward the dance floor. "Would you like to dance?"

Her smile broadened as she grabbed my hand and led the way, swaying her hips as she went. I enjoyed every second of it.

When we reached the middle of the dance floor, she turned to eye me seductively.

"If we're going to dance, you're going to have to get a little closer." Her voice slurred on the last word.

Is she drunk?

I pulled her against me and began to move to the beat. I leaned in close, then recoiled when I inhaled the overpowering smell of wine on her breath. I hoped that wasn't something she made a habit of. It was very unattractive.

As we danced, I took a good look at the woman who had stolen my attention. My hand rested on her lower back, and her body was pressed flush against mine. We were as close as two people could be in polite company, yet despite how much she looked like Eva, and despite how beautiful she was, I felt nothing.

Well, nothing other than the physical reaction to having a beautiful woman pressed against me. Which would have been fucking fantastic if I hadn't been expecting something more. Sadly, this perfect doppelgänger to Eva was, in reality, nothing like her. But despite my lackluster response to her, she was obviously the reason I was meant to be here tonight. How else could such a coincidence be explained?

I needed time to think.

I remembered a side door near our table that led outside. Maybe some fresh air would help clear my head and give me answers.

"Hannah, thank you for the dance. It was a real pleasure." I bowed, pressed my lips to her hand, and walked off the dance floor and through the side door.

The temperature outside had finally dropped, and the mild breeze was refreshing. I took a deep breath and thought about the night.

Hannah was drunk. Her voice had been slurred, her eyes glassy, and her behavior inappropriate. But when I'd pulled away from her, I'd seen a flash of sadness in her eyes. There was more to her than I had thought.

There was no way I could let my Eva get away again, but

spending time with Hannah tonight was a bad idea.

She'd said her last name was Kinsley. Was she Senator Kinsley's daughter? I'd come up with an excuse to visit their home soon enough. Then I would take the time to know Hannah better.

Until then, I ought to have some fun. Maybe I could pull a 'Zane' and pick up a random chick to take home for the night.

Yeah, I could do that.

I returned to our table and scanned the room. There weren't many attractive women here. None my age, anyway.

I noticed two brunettes in their early thirties over by the DJ. They were giggling and staggering around the dance floor.

No, thank you.

My eyes skimmed the room until they settled on a strawberry blonde beauty. Her sparkling sea green dress and emerald eyes contrasted beautifully with her tanned skin.

How had I missed her? How had I not zeroed in on her the moment she'd arrived?

I wasn't the only one who noticed. Every guy here was sneaking looks her way when their wives' backs were turned. For a moment, I forgot my ploy to find a one-night stand. *I want her for more than a night*, I thought as my eyes slid over her curves.

No.

One night only. That was all I had time for. After that, I'd set my focus on Hannah.

CHAPTER THREE

Gwen

I couldn't believe how much fun we were having. As predicted, Hannah was the source of copious amounts of laughter. At that moment, she was flirting with Senator Andrew Jones. Apparently, she was unaware that Senator Jones had no interest in women.

She was performing what Beverly and I call "The Hannah." It was this perfect move where she touched the helpless guy's arm, pushed her chest out to give him ample view of "the goods," and then whispered in his ear. Neither of us had any idea what she said to them, but whatever it was, it must have been good.

"Do you think-" I started, then turned to get Beverly's attention. The toe of my shoe scrubbed the floor, and I stumbled forward into a pair of strong arms.

Damn heels, I thought as I gripped the muscled shoulders of the man whose arms held me up. Heat flooded my cheeks. I slid my gaze over his firm, masculine chest up to the most beautiful eyes I'd ever seen. Luminous, Mediterranean blue eyes framed by long, thick black lashes stared just inches from mine. I lowered my gaze to his lips, swaying forward as an irresistible urge pulled me toward him. Desire heated my veins as I pressed into his chest.

He cleared his throat.

My arms jerked, and my brain began to function again.

What was I doing? I was in a stranger's arms, staring unabashedly at him. And I'd almost kissed him. I shook my head and positioned my feet to regain my balance. *Damn*, on top of everything else, I probably looked drunk. I felt the blood rush to my cheeks. Of course I looked drunk. I'd clumsily tripped over my own two feet and was standing there staring up at this stranger like an idiot. *Real smooth, Gwen!*

I summoned the courage to look up and apologize.

The man before me was sexy as sin. His luxurious black suit accentuated his tall, muscular physique. The hypnotic eyes that had captured my attention were made only more striking in contrast with his perfectly bronzed skin, thick black hair, and strong angular face. Even in my wildest dreams, I'd never imagined someone so smolderingly sexy.

"Are you okay?" he asked with a smirk that revealed both amusement and concern.

I breathed deeply, and against my body's wishes, I took a step back from him.

"Y-" I shook the fog from my head again. "Yes."

He towered over me. The heat from his body lingered on my skin. My heart raced at his proximity. I couldn't think.

Flustered, my words came rushing out. "Sorry about that. I may have been having a little too much fun with my friend, and I wasn't paying attention to where I was going, and I was laughing too hard at my other friend..."

Oh my God, someone please tell my mouth to stop talking.

"I was about to tell Bever-"

He stopped me with a hand on my arm. "You looked like you were having so much fun over here, I came over to join in. If you'll have me?"

Our eyes met.

"Sure," I replied, my thoughts jumbled. "I'll have you anytime."

The moment the words were out, I snapped my mouth shut and

averted my gaze.

His lips twitched.

"That's not what I meant."

A sexy lopsided smile spread across his amused face. "It's not?" He raised an eyebrow.

"Yes...no. I mean, um..." my voice rose in frustration, "...you know what I mean!" I finally exclaimed, laughing at myself and relaxing as he laughed with me.

"Where's your friend?"

The moment I'd fallen into his arms, I'd forgotten all about Beverly. Where was she? I scanned the room and spotted her at the bar talking adamantly with Hannah.

"That's her over there," I pointed for....

What was his name? Had he mentioned it earlier? Damn it. I should have been paying attention.

All thoughts stopped short when his dimpled smile reappeared.

"Doesn't look like she's coming back anytime soon. That leaves just you and me." He stepped closer and lowered his voice to a whisper as his eyes dropped to my lips. "So would you like to 'have me' on the dance floor?"

The air crackled with tension. My lips parted. My heart jolted to a stop.

When his eyes met mine, the hint of a teasing smile formed on his taunting lips.

Breathless, but trying to play it off, I replied, "Oh, you think you're funny, huh? I misspoke earlier, that's all."

His playful laugh made it clear he didn't believe me.

"Stop it! That's not what I meant, and you know it." I smacked his arm.

"Surrrrre," he replied with a twinkle in his eyes and a huge smile on his face.

I couldn't stop the grin that spread in response.

"May I?" He held his hand out for me to take.

Surprised by his sudden seriousness, I placed my hand in his and allowed him to lead me to the dance floor. Tingles flowed from his hand into mine and across my fingertips. How could holding someone's hand feel so intimate? And how was it possible I'd never noticed that before?

He turned to face me, pulled me into the warmth of his arms, and swayed to music I suddenly couldn't hear. Nothing else existed in that moment. The dance floor, the people, the music disappeared. All that was left was us.

Our eyes met. He lowered his face to mine and gazed into my eyes.

"What is your name?"

"Gwen Adams," I answered shyly. "And you?"

"Alexander Prescott."

No way.

Prescott? He must have been Eli Prescott's son. They looked so much alike I was surprised I hadn't noticed the resemblance sooner.

I thought about the gorgeous older man. Despite his salt and pepper hair, he couldn't have been a day older than forty, despite what Beverly had read. He must have had Alexander when he was really young because the man before me was at least twenty-four. If they hadn't looked so much alike, I would've assumed Alexander was adopted.

Why am I having this conversation with myself? I should be focused on the incredibly handsome man in front of me. I glanced back up, determined to set my focus where it should've been the whole time.

Alexander's eyes met mine and never strayed as we danced, hip to hip, swaying to the rhythm. Another slow melody filled the air. He pulled me closer, erasing the small distance between us.

His expression changed as his eyes slid over me. His heated gaze met mine once more, and then he leaned forward, his intent clear.

Those intense blue eyes were fierce and full of passion. My body hummed with desire. I yearned to feel his lips on mine.

"Mr. Prescott." An eager male voice shattered the moment.

Alexander's arms remained wrapped around me as his gaze shifted to the gentleman.

"Yes?"

"My name is Dale Roshman. I'm an associate of Senator Kinsley. Could you spare me a few moments of your time?"

Alexander stared at the man, then his gaze fell to mine and softened. His hands lingered at my waist. Regret colored his eyes as he leaned in and pressed his warm lips to my cheek.

"I'm sorry, Gwen."

He turned and walked away.

My eyes followed his retreat. I pressed a dazed hand to my cheek, where I could still feel the warmth of his lips, and wondered if I would ever see him again.

∞∞∞∞∞∞

"I saw you dancing with him Friday night," Hannah announced. That was Hannah, always straight to the point when she wanted something. "Do you like him?"

"Well, he seems like a nice guy," I replied. "Why do you ask?"

"He danced with me too, and I've gotta say, there were definitely some sparks! So, since you don't seem interested, I'm going to go after him," she squealed.

"I never said I wasn't interested. And I see sparks with everyone."

"Do not! Come on, Gwen. I saw you flirting with Jimmy the other day," Hannah whined.

Hannah then proceeded to give Beverly and I her "plan of attack." She'd apparently begun concocting a well-thought-out plan to win Alexander last night after she'd spent hours researching him and his family. Luckily for her, the Prescotts had a beachside mansion two lots down from hers. They bought the property months ago but only recently moved in. Apparently, there were some behind the scenes deals brewing between her father and Alexander's. According to Hannah, Eli Prescott had made multiple trips to her home over the weekend. The internet also mentioned an older brother, but Hannah was unable to get any info or pictures of him.

"I bet he's in prison," she mused. "Every family has that one member they wish they could hide. The 'black sheep' so to speak."

As she droned on, I reflected back to her earlier comments and her complete dismissal of my feelings. My anger instantly returned. Sometimes Hannah really pissed me off, and today was one of those days. I just loved how she conveniently ignored what I tried to tell her. I rolled my eyes.

Here we go again.

This was the fifth time she'd done this to me. Though to be honest, I wasn't positive Alexander was into me like that. His "flirting" was probably a combination of my overactive imagination and his good-natured humor. Besides, why waste my time competing with Hannah? No guy in his right mind would choose me over her. People like the Prescotts and Kinsleys always ended up together.

"What's with the sour face?" Ky's voice stole my attention. My eyes shot open to see him standing over me, his eyes filled with concern.

"Nothing."

"She's fine," Hannah interjected. "You know how she gets sometimes."

The look Ky gave me clearly asked, "Why are you friends with her?" and for a moment, I wondered the same thing.

"Oh, come on." Hannah trailed a hand up Ky's arm. "You know I'm right."

His eyes narrowed.

"Fine," Hannah huffed.

Ky extended his hand to me. "You want to get out of here?"

"Thought you'd never ask," I replied as I took his hand.

Ky pulled me to my feet. I grabbed my bag, grateful to be leaving

Hannah behind.

∞∞∞∞∞∞

I was glad it was the weekend. I had every intention of lounging around in my pajamas all day, watching movies, and reading books. I'd slept in late that morning and was snuggled up on the couch with a bowl of cereal, watching old-school cartoons on Netflix. When I was a kid, my parents had convinced me that things had been much better in their childhood. They made sure I heard all the old hits and watched all the great films. Mom's most recent persuasion was *Animaniacs*, and it was hilarious. She'd persuaded me to try it out last night when she and Dad got back from Seattle.

"Good morning, honey. You're finally awake." I heard Mom's voice behind me.

"Morning, Mom." I motioned toward the television. "You were right about this show, these guys are insane!"

She rounded the couch, sat next to me, and tucked her knees underneath her. We watched in silence, occasionally laughing at Yakko's antics. It was nice being together. Mom and Dad worked for Senator Kinsley, and due to the upcoming election, they were constantly on the road to campaign in one city or another. In fact, this was only the third time I'd seen them this year.

"Honey, we'll be heading out in a few minutes. Your dad needs you to run some documents over to the Senator's house. I hope that's okay."

"Won't you see him whenever you get where you're going?" I knew it sounded like I was trying to get out of it, but I couldn't help it. I'd just wanted to stay home this weekend.

"Not this time. Don't you remember? We have a week-long break in the campaign. Your father and I are going on a mini-vacation to Jamaica. We need some time alone. You understand, don't you?"

What about me? Don't you want to spend time with your only daughter?

If I'd said what I was thinking my mom would have reminded me of how much she and my dad loved me, but ultimately, they would still leave me behind.

Yeah, my parents loved me, but I had been an accident. They had never wanted kids.

I smiled and adopted a pleasant tone. "Yes, of course. I just forgot. I don't mind delivering them. Where are they?"

I followed my mom into the study and waited while she sifted through the papers strewn across the desk before she stopped abruptly. "Oh, what was I thinking?" She opened the filing cabinet and retrieved a manila envelope. "Here it is."

She handed me the bulky package. "Make sure you hand deliver this yourself. Do not leave it with his secretary. Poor Gretchen, she's more disorganized than your father." She shook her head and laughed.

Less than an hour later, we said our goodbyes, and my parents headed off to the airport. I stood as they drove away and wondered bleakly when I'd see them again. Our home was small, but it was so quiet and lonely without them.

I knew I had no reason to complain. I had parents who loved me and were supportive. They may have been overprotective at times, but that was their way of making up for being absent so often. I had no right to be bitter. Poor Hannah didn't have anyone. Her mother had died when she was born, and her father was away more than mine. Senator Kinsley never took an interest in his daughter. She was more a fixture in his life. Ornamental. Only wanted when she was needed at parties or for pictures with the media. She'd been encouraged at a young age to flirt with wealthy benefactors to secure more funding for the campaign. Sadly, Senator Kinsley, or Jim as he continued to insist I call him, didn't recognize how much he neglected Hannah. He was too wrapped up in himself and his career to see clearly. Conversely, he was always kind and generous to his employees and their families. It was only his daughter that was an afterthought.

One great thing about Jim was he couldn't care less how I showed up at his house. I could run these documents over then get right back to my couch without having to change clothes. I found a scrunchy, pulled my wild hair up in a bun, grabbed Jim's documents, and headed out the door.

CHAPTER FOUR
Alexander

I had been sitting in the family room outside of Senator Kinsley's office for twenty minutes. I'd come over to attend a business meeting with Senator Kinsley and Eli but was unceremoniously kicked out so the "adults" could talk.

Wow. I should have seen that coming, so instead of going home, I was waiting in hope that Hannah would pass by.

Our chance meeting the other night had really thrown me for a loop. I had thought that after all these years I'd finally found Eva, and the excitement that had coursed through me had been unreal. Even after the disappointment of realizing she wasn't Eva, I recognized our meeting was destined.

I knew I had to do everything in my power to know her. Anything to get a part of my Eva back, even if that included sitting outside Senator Kinsley's office all day, watching the news on the huge flat screen on the opposite wall while wearing an uncomfortable suit.

"Good morning, Gretchen. Is Jim in? I need to deliver some documents to him." I heard a soft feminine voice behind me. I glanced back to the secretary's desk to see a completely unexpected sight: a petite blonde in fuzzy pink pajamas, her hair pulled back haphazardly, the golden strands flying everywhere. She had her back to me and was conversing with Gretchen like they were old friends.

"Oh, I'll make sure he gets them. You can leave them right over there, honey," Gretchen replied with a bright smile.

"Come on. You know how paranoid my mom is. She made me promise to hand them over myself." Gretchen and the woman laughed together. They chatted casually about Gretchen's new work schedule and the new twists in the campaign. Their conversation didn't interest me, and I should have turned around, but damn, Pajama Girl had a hot body. My eyes roamed up her toned physique, taking note of her full curves and beautifully tanned skin. She had great skin, the kind that looked rich and luxurious, the kind I'd enjoy putting whipped cream on and licking off.

Wtf?

I jerked back toward the television and tried to forget the girl, reminding myself that I was here to see Hannah. I couldn't get distracted by some random hot body.

I forced myself to focus on the screen. The newscaster's voice droned on about Hurricane Wilma crossing the Atlantic and how strange it was to have a hurricane this early in the season. That category four storm was creating quite the buzz. Forecasters predicted a direct hit to the Jacksonville area with billions of dollars in damage.

Boy, were they wrong. Wilma would turn and head north, causing mild wind and stormy weather up the East Coast, but nothing more. The humans were getting all excited over nothing.

It wasn't that I was psychic or anything. I'd designed a forecast algorithm that was accurate within 0.0001 percent. It was foolproof. Unfortunately, it was one of my creations we'd decided not to share with the world due to the many negative applications it could be used for.

"I guess I'll wait on the couch until he gets out," Pajama Girl sighed. Her bunny slippers shuffled along the hardwood floors, then came to a sudden halt.

I was stunned to see that Pajama Girl was Gwen, the hottie I'd danced with at the fundraiser. All thoughts of Hannah were suddenly wiped from my mind.

"Hey, stranger," I quipped.

Gwen, clearly shocked to see me here, gave a little wave with her hand, then sat on the far end of the couch. She pulled her feet under her, scrunched her body into a ball, then angled her flushed face away from mine and stared dutifully at the television.

I watched her for ten minutes. She didn't move a muscle other than to self-consciously pat the hair above her left ear.

Weird.

Her shoulders were rigid and every muscle tightened. She must have been well aquatinted with the Kinsley's to show up in her pajamas. Few women could pull it off, but with a bright, clean face and wild hair framing her features, Gwen was breathtaking.

"Gwen?" I waited until she glanced in my direction. "I—"

"Hey, Gwen," Gretchen spoke loudly behind us. "Something's come up with my granddaughter. Would you mind taking over for me? There's nothing going on. He has another meeting in three hours, and you can leave when it starts. I've already turned the phone volume up so you can stay on the couch. It's really important."

Gwen nodded without speaking, and Gretchen took off.

"You work here? Is that how you know the Kinsley's?"

Gwen flinched. "I've worked here a few times," she replied. "Mostly to help out Gretchen. I've never been paid to be here though. My parents have worked for Senator Kinsley for years."

"What do they do?" It was possible I'd met them.

"My father is Jim's campaign manager. My mom is one of his political strategists." She shifted in her seat.

I looked her over once more. She had a flawless beauty. Wavy blonde hair, dazzling emerald eyes, full lips, and a perfect heart-shaped face. A cute smattering of freckles was sprinkled across her high cheekbones. I couldn't look away.

I also couldn't stand seeing her so uncomfortable. I took in her posture and expression. She was tense as hell and stiff as a statue. If she didn't loosen up, she'd be sore for days.

I removed my tie, stood, and started removing my jacket when she finally turned her head toward me.

I ignored her and continued. I unbuttoned the top few buttons of my shirt, untucked it, and rolled up the sleeves. As I kicked off my socks and shoes, her bewildered voice finally inquired, "What are you doing?"

"Just trying to get comfortable," I responded with a shrug. Then I sat on the couch next to her, my thigh brushing hers. I propped my bare feet up on the coffee table and crossed my arms behind my head.

She stared at me like I'd lost my damn mind.

I waited and tried like hell to keep a grin off my face. I leaned over, my face inches from hers, then asked as seriously as I could, "Mind if I change the channel?"

Her laugh was music to my ears. It started as a high-pitched giggle that she tried to stifle, but after a few seconds, she gave up and laughed heartily. It was exactly what I was after. The muscles in her neck and shoulders relaxed, and the stress in her body melted away.

"Turn around." The words flew from my mouth, and I was shocked when she complied.

Not sure why I felt compelled to do it, I began kneading her sore shoulders and neck.

Compelled wasn't a strong enough a word for what I felt. I *had* to have my hands on her. There was no thought involved. Just a strong undercurrent of emotion, an uneasiness that the world would never be right unless my hands were touching her skin. I'd felt it since she'd arrived. It was like an itchiness that twitched just beneath the surface.

I inhaled deeply as I dug my fingers into the soft curve of her neck. The faint scent of honeysuckle and vanilla filled my senses, and my mouth watered.

The feel of my fingers gliding over her supple skin and taut muscles sent electricity sizzling up my fingertips and down my spine. Her skin was absolute heaven beneath my hands. I couldn't get enough of her. I reached beneath the soft fabric of her top, gliding my thumbs in small languid circles above her hips.

A soft moan escaped her lips as her muscles relaxed.

I needed more. My hands slid further up her back, caressing her smooth skin.

More.

Desire flooded my veins like liquid fire. Nothing would ever be enough when it came to her.

I jerked my hands off her.

Fuck. What the hell am I doing?

I was here to see Hannah. I couldn't have it both ways, couldn't pursue both Hannah and Gwen.

I had to get the hell away from this temptress.

"I've got to go," I blurted and jumped off the couch.

The hurt, bewildered look on Gwen's face almost stopped me. It was a look that I knew would have me feeling guilty late into the night.

I grabbed my jacket and tie, threw on my shoes, and practically ran out of the house.

∞∞∞∞∞∞

I wasn't wrong about the guilt I'd feel. Every time I closed my eyes, I pictured Gwen's hurt expression.

I rolled onto my back and stared at the ceiling.

Damn it. Why was doing the right thing always so difficult?

I closed my eyes, took a deep breath, and tried to relax.

I pictured the island in my mind. Saw the waves crashing against the shore. Heard the distant caw of the seagulls. Slowly, I drifted into a fitful sleep....

I hung my head thinking of the compatriots I'd lost today. They had been some of my best warriors. Their loss was a massive blow to our cause, yet their sacrifice was not in vain. The souls of an entire universe were saved from a darkness that had threatened to consume them. Though the people of Venturi would never know of my warriors' sacrifice, would never know of the countless battles waged on their behalf, they would now be allowed the freedom to choose their own fates. Their destruction, if it came, would be their own doing rather than thrust upon them by outside forces.

As Vice Commander of Heaven's army, I was responsible for the well-being of every soldier. I sighed as I stepped through the portal into the throne room. The pain, weariness, and negativity I felt were washed away by the atmosphere of Heaven. The presence of God saturated the air and seeped through my skin into my bones. My whole being vibrated with euphoria. The harshness of the battle in the Venturi universe quickly became a distant memory.

With a lightened step, I strode to the palace blacksmith to leave my damaged armor for repair. When I rounded the corner to Farrar's shop, I was surprised there wasn't a line. The last few times I'd visited I'd had to take a number and return.

"Be with you in a moment." The voice was beautiful, melodic, and female. Definitely not Farrar's old raspy voice, but one unfamiliar to me.

Moments later, a tall, beautiful angel approached. She slowly circled me, her rich honey-colored eyes studying my busted armor.

"Looks like you took quite a hit," she stated quietly. "It's going to take a few days for such extensive repairs. Are you sure you wouldn't rather order new equipment?"

"No. I've worn this in every battle. It's my lucky armor."

"No such thing as luck," she murmured with a smile, still studying my equipment. "You're going to need help removing that." She pointed out the dent at the shoulder of my chest plate. "Follow me."

I nodded, then followed her past the armory and down a long narrow corridor. I couldn't help admiring the image before me. Her elegant form was draped in a flowing white gown that shimmered in the light. Her long glossy black hair accentuated her tiny waist and curvy hips. Her ethereal image contrasted sharply with the harsh metallic surroundings.

"Where's Farrar?"

"Farrar is my father. He's been training me as his assistant for years and decided he needed a vacation. So here I am. Don't worry, I know what I'm doing. My father taught me well."

When we entered a small, dimly lit room at the back of the shop, she spun around and met my eyes for the first time. Surprise flashed fleetingly across her face. "What is your name, soldier?"

"Alexias Lukas Prisco. But please, call me Alex."

"Hmmm...*defender of mankind....* I like that," she muttered. She grabbed a tool off a nearby bench and took a step toward me. Her breath brushed my neck as she worked to loosen the clasp on my armor. Her oval face was tight with concentration, and I couldn't help but laugh at her serious expression.

Her eyes darted up to mine, and her ivory skin flushed. Her pink cheeks highlighted the beautiful eyes that were engrossed in her work.

"There, all done." The clasp popped loose as she stepped back.

"What is your name, daughter of Farrar?"

"Eva." She motioned for me to follow her. "You may pick up your equipment in three days."

Her clipped tone and sudden abruptness indicated that our meeting was over.

As she slowly walked away, the air began to shimmer. The light around her slender figure took on a hazy appearance. Her black hair gradually faded to a beautiful strawberry blond.

"Eva?"

She whipped around, and her large emerald eyes pierced mine. Electricity rocked through me as Gwen stood where Eva had once been.

∞∞∞∞∞∞

I woke to the peaceful sound of waves crashing against the shore. I closed my eyes, holding on to the memory of the dream that had already begun to dim. So many years had passed that Eva's memory had faded, even if my love for her hadn't. Meeting Hannah must have stirred those memories from my subconscious.

I sat up and recreated the night in my mind. I understood how it was possible for Hannah to resemble Eva so closely. The right combination of human DNA could result in an exact replica of Eva. It made perfect sense. What I had a difficult time wrapping my mind around was the premonition I had when I almost left the fundraiser and then the coincidence of meeting Hannah moments later. The probability was astronomically small, and yet it *had happened.*

And what about that dream?

I shook my head. Meeting Hannah must have shaken that memory from my mind. Why else would I dream about something that had happened so long ago? And why had Gwen been in the dream? She had not been part of my memory of Heaven. In my memory, Eva had continued walking away from me.

I got out of bed and crossed the room to the balcony doors I'd left open. I enjoyed the cool gentle breeze against my bare skin. It was refreshing compared to the stuffy suits I was forced into on a daily basis.

Never again, I swore to myself. After this mission, I would never again wear one of those confining things.

I breathed in the salty air, stretched my arms wide, and blinked into the sunlight.

I cringed when my stomach growled and decided to put off brushing my teeth until after breakfast.

The smell of bacon assaulted my senses as I rounded the corner to the kitchen. Eli hovered over a skillet while Ariel sat on the counter beside him. She trailed a hand through his greying hair, and he looked up at her adoringly.

The bacon sizzled and popped.

"Back to work," Ariel reprimanded him with a quick peck on his lips.

I grabbed a plate and waited as Eli finished preparing our breakfast.

I enjoyed watching Eli and Ariel. Their love never ceased to amaze me. Even after all these years, their eyes shone with a passion that never faded, and their skin radiated with the brilliant golden glow that signified their love.

Eli offered me a plate of bacon. I grabbed a few pieces and waited for them to join me.

"It looked like you met someone at the fundraiser," Eli said. When I didn't reply, he continued, "That girl you were dancing with, you know, the blonde in the green dress? You seemed pretty taken with her."

He was, of course, referring to the beautiful Gwen.

I shook my head. "No, it was just a dance."

"It didn't look like just a dance to me," Ariel teased.

Unfortunately, Ariel was right. I *had* felt a connection with Gwen. There was something about her that drew me in, and I hadn't wanted to leave her that night.

But then there was Hannah, who looked so much like my Eva I couldn't ignore her. It wasn't coincidence we had met, and I couldn't sabotage my one chance to have her in my life again.

"No, it really was just a dance." I paused, trying to decide how much to reveal. "I did meet someone else. You met her, her name was Hannah Kinsley."

Eli frowned. "The one with the long black hair?"

I nodded.

"Kinsley? Is she related to Senator Kinsley?" Ariel asked.

"Yeah, she's his daughter."

Eli shrugged. "Well, I guess it couldn't hurt to date the Senator's daughter. It would make him more likely to help us."

"It's not like that." Irritation at the idea turned to anger. "We do not do such things. Just because we can't go back to Heaven doesn't mean that we are fallen. We do not take advantage of humans like that."

Shame colored Eli's face. "Yes, sir. It won't happen again," he responded as Zane entered the room.

Zane smiled widely at Eli. "In trouble already this morning? What did you do to upset His Highness this time?"

"Shut up, Zane."

"Whatever." Zane shrugged and strutted into the room wearing only pajama bottoms, his white wings flared out behind him.

Eli rolled his eyes. "Could you stop strutting around like a damn peacock?"

"At least I've got wings," Zane retorted. "Jealousy does not suit you, brother."

I sighed in exasperation.

The fact that they'd had hundreds of years to mature had done nothing to alleviate their childish sibling rivalry. That we'd been able to convince the world that Eli was our father was only a testament to our superior acting skills. But behind closed doors, the two argued like twelve-year-old boys.

A mild chime notified me that someone approached our home. The image of a woman shimmered in the air in front of me. I watched as Hannah reached the door and adjusted her clothing before ringing the bell.

I waved my palm over the image, making it disappear.

"I'll get it," I told them as I left the kitchen. I reached the foyer a moment later and opened the front door.

"Hannah," I feigned surprise. "What's going on?"

I had no misconceptions about her intent. Her choice of clothing and the alluring look I'd seen her practice before I'd opened the door told me everything I needed to know.

Her eyes lit up and smile widened as she took in my apparent state of undress. "I figured I'd come by to welcome you to the neighborhood. I thought you'd like a tour of the area. How about it?"

"Yeah, that'd be great. Just give me a minute to find a shirt and brush my teeth," I answered.

I led her through the foyer and down the hall toward my private suite.

"This is a nice place. You have this entire side of the mansion to yourself?"

"Yeah, my dad and Ariel are gone most of the time, so they let me have the master suite."

"Why do you call her Ariel?"

Damn. I hadn't meant to let that slip.

"My mom died giving birth to me," I lied smoothly. "Ariel is my stepmom."

I quickly turned the conversation away from myself, asking about her life and aspirations. From what I could tell, Hannah was your average woman other than her wealth and beauty.

"Where do you go to school?" I asked as we got into her red convertible.

"Right here at Verona Beach Community College," she answered. "And before you say anything, I know what you're thinking. You're wondering why I'm going to a local community college when I can afford to go to any university I want, right? My dad wondered the same thing. See, the thing is, I have no idea what I want to do with my life. The only thing I know is that this is where Beverly and Gwen are."

My ears perked up. "Are those friends of yours?"

"Yeah." She lowered her eyes. "Actually, you met Gwen at the fundraiser. I believe you danced with her."

I shrugged. "I danced with a few people that night. Your friend could have been one of them, but I don't remember."

A bright smile lit up her face. "You remembered me."

I laughed and shook my head. "Yeah, I guess I did."

CHAPTER FIVE

Gwen

For the first time in my life, I enjoyed taking an English course. In fact, I would go so far as to say I loved it. My accounting degree didn't require it, but after Beverly told me how much she enjoyed the new professor, I figured I'd give it a try. Besides, I had a few electives left and there was nothing else I wanted to take.

Beverly was right. Mr. Mills was a fantastic teacher. He was new to VBCC, temporarily replacing stuffy old Mr. Jenkins. Mr. Mills was passionate about literature and preferred to act out poems and plays in class. That wasn't the intent of the course, but no one bothered to stop him. Out of all my classes this semester, his was the one I enjoyed most.

I walked into Intro to Literature and sat in my usual chair.

"Hey, Gwen. How was your week?" Mr. Mills asked.

"I was forced into another fundraiser. But it could've been worse."

"Your mom and dad back in town?"

"No, they left again. I'm not sure when they'll be back."

Mr. Mills glanced at his watch. He was nothing if not prompt, and it was exactly ten o'clock. I pulled out my book and prepared to read my lines.

"Let's get started. Ky, you'll be reading Romeo's lines. Gwen, you've got Juliet. We're starting at page thirteen."

I quickly found our spot and began. Our lines went smoothly. Our voices easily matched the emotion the words conveyed. I loved reading lines with Ky. His obvious skill made the lines flow effortlessly. Unlike most guys in the class, he took his part seriously and delivered his lines with passion. He was a fantastic Romeo, and with dirty blonde hair, sparkling brown eyes, and an athletic build, he already held the hearts of the majority of the VBCC female population. Unfortunately for them, Ky didn't seem interested in dating. For a short while, I'd entertained the idea that he was gay, but when I confronted him about it, the look on his face told me I was way off base. Apparently, he was very interested in women, just not any at VBCC.

Ky opened his mouth to deliver his line when he was interrupted by a loud knock and the sound of the door opening. Alexander strode through the door with Hannah at his side, her hand draped possessively over his arm.

"Mr. Mills, this is Alexander Prescott," Hannah's voice beamed with pride. "He enrolled this week, and since our families are friends, they thought it would be a good idea for me to show him around." Hannah could barely contain herself. She was acting like a damn teenager; this was college, did he really need an escort?

"Welcome to Intro to Literature. I'm Mr. Mills. You can take the empty desk over here." He motioned to the desk immediately behind mine.

"But, Mr. Mills," Hannah responded hastily, "I'm supposed to be showing him around. It only makes sense that he should sit with me." Hannah looked at the professor sweetly and smiled.

Instead of succumbing to her charms, he politely informed her that there were no unclaimed desks on her side of the room. "Besides, I'm sure he'll be all right on his own for the short duration of this class."

Hannah's eyes widened a moment before narrowing, and then

she stomped to her desk, dropping sullenly in her seat.

Alexander leisurely crossed the room, arms relaxed, eyes lowered to the phone in his hand.

I couldn't take my eyes off him. He looked so different from before, and yet so much the same. His previous suit was gone. That incredibly sexy, James Bond aura had vanished, and what stood in its place was mouth-watering. Thick black hair framed his angular face and perfectly shaped lips. He wore designer jeans and a pale green t-shirt that stretched tight across his chest and torso. The hint of a tattoo snaked around his tan bicep and peeked below the sleeve of his shirt.

His azure eyes slid up and peered into mine through thick black lashes.

I stopped breathing. My heart fluttered weakly in my chest.

His eyes blazed with an intense blue flame that glowed against his bronze skin. The ferocity of his gaze confused and excited me. It made me want things I shouldn't want and imagine scenarios that'd never happen.

Why was he looking at me like that when just days ago he couldn't get away from me fast enough? He had been charming, even though I'd looked like a homeless hag. And when he'd touched me, I swear I'd seen stars. But then, without a word, he'd just run off.

A lopsided grin spread across his face.

My cheeks heated, and I averted my eyes from the intensity of his stare.

He took the seat behind mine and leaned forward. His warm breath tickled my neck as he murmured in my ear. "Hey, stranger."

"Hey," I whispered. A traitorous smile threatened at the corners of my lips.

Ky had turned from his seat and was eyeing me strangely. I smiled nonchalantly and pretended that my heart wasn't galloping away in my chest.

"No more distractions," Mr. Mills began. "Ky, the next line is yours..." And with that, class re-commenced.

As soon as class was over, I grabbed my books and ran out the door. I needed to get away from Alexander as quickly as possible.

"Gwen?" Ky rushed to catch me.

Damn.

I was in such a hurry I'd forgot Ky.

"What was that about?" Ky asked as we walked toward the parking lot.

"What do you mean?"

"That guy in there." He gestured back toward the classroom. "Do you know him?"

"We've met."

"And?" Ky's brown eyes stared into mine with an intensity I was unaccustomed to.

What was with him today? Why would he care if I'd met Alexander before?

"We met at the fundraiser the other night."

His inquisitive eyes bore into mine, questioning me before he shook his head. "Never mind."

"There's nothing to tell." I adjusted the strap on my backpack.

"Okay," he replied with obvious disbelief. "Want to go to Applebees for lunch?"

"Sounds good. I'll text Beverly and Hannah to meet us."

I sent the text and got prompt replies.

"They both say they'll be there."

"Great. Hannah's coming," Ky remarked sarcastically, then asked, "Ride with me?"

I cringed. I didn't want to spend the rest of the day covered in sweat, but I refused to hurt his feelings.

We walked to the parking lot and found Ky's beat up Toyota Corolla. The blue paint was faded and cracked. The back tires needed air added every other day, and the air conditioner didn't work, but it was all he had.

He opened the door for me before rounding the car and starting the engine. Inside the car, he turned toward me expectantly.

"What?"

His eyes held mine. A smile spread across his face, highlighting the faint scar that ran down his chin. "You don't feel it?"

"Feel what? What are you—" The cool air blowing across my face finally registered. "Holy crap! You fixed the AC."

Ky grinned triumphantly. "Figured you'd like that."

"I love it. But why would you do that? You should have used that money on bills."

"This was important too. I couldn't have my best friend refusing to ride with me."

My chest warmed. I knew what a sacrifice this was for him. It couldn't have been a cheap fix. And he'd done it for me, of that I was certain. Ky would have suffered the heat if he were only thinking of himself. He was too good a friend to me.

Lunch was uneventful. Thankfully, Alexander didn't show up with Hannah.

Ky and Hannah took swipes at each other the entire meal while Beverly and I laughed about Beverly's blind date from the night before. Apparently, it hadn't gone well.

"Why in the world do you keep going on dates with guys who are all wrong for you?"

"I told you it was a blind date. I didn't pick the guy, Jenny did. She said we were perfect for each other. Apparently, she doesn't know me as well as I thought."

"You trusted Jenny? What were you thinking? No more blind dates for you unless I pick them, you hear me?" I pointed my finger at her.

"Yes, ma'am! So what do you suggest?"

I scratched my chin thoughtfully. "First of all, no more idiots. You need a guy with some brains in his head. Secondly, you need someone who's not a pushover. Someone who can put up with your shit."

"And third?"

"Third," I paused, furrowing my brow in concentration, "he's got to be hot."

"Damn straight!" Beverly's laugh bubbled over. "Well, whenever you find this nerdy, badass hottie, send him my way."

"For sure."

Moments later, when the food finally arrived, we were deep in conversation about this year's play.

"Yeah, I heard it was written by a student," I told them.

"Not surprised. Have you read the synopsis? It's going to be pretty racy," Beverly added. "Not sure if I'd want to be the female lead until I knew who the male lead was."

Of course that would be the first thing Beverly thought about.

"I mean, if the male lead were someone like Jasper Mills, oh yeah, I'd be all over that," Beverly smirked.

Hannah nodded in agreement.

"I'd have to agree. Although Hannah would lose her shit if you got to make out with him and she didn't," I said.

"Would not," Hannah's indignant voice rose above the roar of the crowd.

"Don't lie. We all know it's true. But," I continued, "I agree with the sentiment. If Jonah Jones got the part, I'd totally have to quit."

Jonah was a year behind us. He was a chain smoker who didn't bathe regularly and smelled like a sweaty ashtray. I hated using him as an example, but he fit the bill perfectly. I'd never let him kiss me, acting or not.

"What about me?" Ky asked.

"What do you mean?"

Hannah rolled her eyes and stood. Without a word to us, she went to the bar and ordered a drink.

"What if it were me in the lead role? Would you be okay with it?" Ky's eyes met mine. For the first time, I felt something shift in our relationship. My foundation moved beneath me.

I didn't know what to say. What to think.

"Ky, I-"

My shaky hand dropped spaghetti noodles onto my chest.

Ky laughed.

"What?" I asked as I struggled to avoid his bombshell of a question.

"I can't figure out why you always order that stuff when you know you'll end up making a mess."

I looked down at my ruined blouse. Bright red spaghetti sauce stained my white shirt.

I sighed.

Why did I do this to myself? Why did I always order the messy meals?

"I'll be right back."

Beverly started to get up, but I raised my hand to stop her. "Don't. I'm fine. Finish eating, I'll be back in a minute."

I had to get this out before it stained. I rounded the corner, rushed past the men's room, and pushed the women's door open with a loud bang.

"Sorry," I apologized to no one in particular.

I got some paper towels and wet my blouse, rubbing quickly to remove the stain.

No, I thought when my efforts caused the stain to spread. The once small red spot was now a sizable reddish-orange stain. I rubbed more, but no amount of coaxing seemed to pull the sauce from my shirt.

I stood under the hand dryer and waited, and knowing I had a few minutes to kill, I considered Ky's question.

It could have been innocent. Ky was a talented actor. There was a good chance he'd get the lead role. Maybe he wanted to ensure it wouldn't affect our friendship. I could see how that would be awkward and uncomfortable for him. So uncomfortable that it could ruin our friendship. Maybe he hoped I wouldn't try out for the lead. But the idea of kissing him.... In a moment of indulgence, I let myself imagine gazing up into Ky's soulful brown eyes, his hands pulling me close as he brushed his lips against mine.

My face flushed.

The image was much more enticing than I would have thought. Ky was gorgeous and so completely out of my league that I'd never allowed myself to think about him that way before.

I shook the tempting image from my head. I shouldn't have entertained the idea. Ky was my friend. One of my best friends. I already cared too much for him. I couldn't complicate those feelings with physical attraction. The idea of opening myself up to that kind of pain again was more than I could bear.

This whole thought process was ridiculous. Ky wasn't interested in me. Right?

Besides, I needed Ky. He was one of the few people in my life I could count on. I couldn't afford to lose him, so as conflicted as I felt about it, I mentally erased those alluring images from my mind.

There, I thought smugly. *Gone forever.*

I would never jeopardize our friendship with that silliness again.

Peering down, I saw my shirt had dried.

I took a deep breath and walked back to our table.

"I'm ready to go. Ky, would you mind driving me back to my car? I don't want to stay here like this." I motioned to the stain on my shirt.

"No problem. You know, I have a t-shirt in my car. It'd be loose on you, but you could wear it for the rest of the day."

I knew I was overreacting, but I just wanted to go home. "Ky, please. I really want to leave."

He nodded.

We paid our bill and left the restaurant. Surprisingly, Beverly remained quiet through our entire exchange. She sat there with her lips sealed and an amused expression on her face. I was sure whatever crazy thoughts she was having, I'd hear about them soon enough.

∞∞∞∞∞∞

Finally, some alone time.

Mr. Mills' class was canceled, and I was forced to endure Hannah's gushing about all the fun she had with Alexander over the weekend. I was overloaded and needed some peace and quiet.

Wow, I thought as I looked around. I couldn't believe my luck. This was the first time in weeks the beach was empty, and on a bright summer day, no less. I spread out my beach towel, removed my cover-up, and pulled out my newly purchased book. I was ready for some good ol' me time.

The book was a recommendation from my cousin. She'd never read a book in her life until she got hooked on these crazy romance novels. I shook my head and laughed; this was *so* not my thing. I was more of a sci-fi girl.

But she'd insisted, and I wanted to encourage her new addiction.

I laid back on my towel and enjoyed the sun's heat and the sound of the waves crashing nearby. The temptation to close my eyes and enjoy the peaceful bliss almost consumed me. Instead, I opened the book to the first page and began reading what I fully expected to be a complete waste of time.

Not thirty minutes into the book, I understood what my cousin had been raving about. It was embarrassing to admit how right she had been. This book had me breathing heavily and so turned on I could barely see straight. The words on the pages faded away as I was transported into the scene. I felt phantom hands stroking over my skin, touching places no man had touched in a long time. My body flushed and overheated as the scene progressed. I ached for that intimacy. I was lightheaded and drunk with desire.

"What are you reading?"

"What?" I jumped at the sound of a sexy male voice. Heat

flashed through me as my eyes met Alexander's vibrant blue gaze.

My breath caught in my throat, and my jaw went lax as my eyes traced over Alexander's bare chest and down his lean torso. His bronzed skin glistened with beaded water that streamed from his broad chest, chiseled abs, and down to that muscled v where his board shorts hung off his hips.

His eyes twinkled, and a wicked grin spread across his lips. "Oh, this must be good!"

I shoved the book under the edge of my towel, but Alexander dropped to his knees, and before I could stop him, he grabbed the book and flipped it open.

"Let's see here ...*Beauty and the Bastard.* Oh, yeah, I've got to read this for myself. What page are you on?" His eyes darted to mine, and my heart slammed to a stop.

I grabbed for the book, missed, and fell clumsily across his lap. The heat from his bare skin warmed my already sweaty palms as I scrambled to pull myself upright.

"Just can't help falling for me, can you?" He winked.

I straightened and pulled my hands back. My heart pounded so loudly in my chest I was sure he could hear it.

Jumbled words flew from my mouth, "Look, it's not my book. Well...it is my book, but I didn't pick it out. My stupid cousin wanted me to read it. So there's no reason for you to look at it. It's just a silly book, not at all...."

Lord, help me! All kinds of craziness flew out of my mouth whenever he was near. His smile grew the longer I spoke, showing off white teeth and sexy-as-hell dimples. When I couldn't stand it any longer, I grabbed for the book again. Alexander jerked it just out of my reach. With a playful smirk, he opened the book to where I'd been reading. The smile on his face faded away as his eyes skimmed the page.

The silence between us thickened. I flicked my eyes to Alexander's face, both curious and fearful to see his response.

He swallowed forcefully before his smoldering gaze locked on mine. "You dirty girl."

My eyes dropped to my hands. My face burned crimson. I couldn't breathe.

Alexander shifted closer. His eyes studied me so intensely I couldn't bear to return his gaze.

His callused hand reached up to caress my cheek a moment before cupping my jaw and forcing my eyes to his. A thoughtful expression passed over his features as he watched me.

"You may not have chosen this book...but you *like* it." His seductive voice pulled me under its spell. "You're off balance...your breathing is shallow...your eyes are dilated." His eyes lowered to my lips. "You are absolutely drunk with desire."

My breath caught as he dipped his mouth to mine.

"Alexander!" A familiar female voice yelled in the distance.

Alexander dropped his hand and leaned back, but his eyes never left mine. Animalistic desire was instantly replaced with guilt as we both recognized who was calling for him.

"Alexander!"

The voice was closer, more insistent. He squeezed his eyes closed and shook his head.

Just then, Hannah came into view. The moment she recognized me, a shocked expression crossed her face that was instantly replaced with a determined, yet confident smile.

Hannah jogged over, grabbed Alexander's hands, and pulled him to his feet.

"Come on. You promised to teach me how to find sand dollars, remember?"

Hannah smirked at me, then turned and skipped toward the ocean, fully expecting Alexander to follow.

I've got to get the hell out of here.

I stuffed my book into my beach bag, rolled up my towel, and was sliding on my sandals when Alexander's hand grasped my wrist.

His lips parted to speak when a look of confusion crossed his face. He turned my arm over and looked down at the jagged scar covering my left wrist.

"What the hell?" His eyes shot to mine. His face was a mask of shock.

"It's not what it looks like," I mumbled.

"How did you—"

"It's nothing. It looks worse than it is." I jerked my arm away from him.

"Alexander," Hannah called across the distance.

Resignation and regret swam in his eyes as she called him to the shore.

"Gwen?" A war was waging behind his luminous eyes.

Behind him, I saw Hannah in her yellow bikini splashing as she skipped into the waves. She was so beautiful, her silky black hair billowing around her perfect figure.

Unexpected emotion clogged my throat as I clutched my bag to my chest.

"Sorry, I've got somewhere I have to be." I forced the words out and rushed to my car. I took the stairs two at a time, but for some unknown reason, maybe a subconscious desire to torture myself, I turned back to look out over the beach. Alexander and Hannah were standing waist deep in the ocean. The gentle waves lapped against their perfect bodies. Orange light reflected off the dark blue water. The sun had begun to set, and seagulls flew low in the distance. Before I could turn back and save myself further torment, Alexander took Hannah's hand to his lips and kissed it.

I had been a fool to turn around. I was also a fool for thinking he could possibly want me.

Everything in me hated the idea of them together. And no matter how much I knew it wasn't true, I couldn't shake the feeling that it should have been me on the beach with him.

∞∞∞∞∞∞

Find the position of two bodies over time given their masses, initial positions, and velocities. The Kepler Problem, which we'd been studying in my Intro to Astronomy class, had been kicking my butt for the last hour. I ran my hand through my hair and sighed.

I was so thankful I had Beverly to explain this shit to me. I figured when I signed up for an astronomy class, we'd be looking through telescopes and discussing the stars. I assumed it'd be an easy A.

No such luck.

"Beverly, I need you," I whined. "Explain this to me, please. I can't even understand the questions right now."

Beverly raised her eyebrows. I understood the look. Usually, Hannah was the one who needed help studying. But today, I couldn't get my head on straight. It was like someone had replaced the wording in my textbook with Greek, Aramaic, or some other unused and indecipherable language. I had read the last sentence at least five times and still couldn't remember a single word.

"What is it?" she asked, dropping her pencil and looking over my shoulder. She scanned the pages I was looking at, grabbed a blank sheet of paper, and began scribbling equations across the page.

"Okay, I've got it. This is what it's saying – if you know where two objects start out, and you know where they're going and how fast, then you can calculate where they're going to end up." She scribbled another equation on the page. "This is the simplified version of the equation you need to use."

Too bad this equation couldn't be used on people. I could just plug in where Alexander and I met and our trajectories, and voila, I'd have the solution. There would be no guesswork. I would know without a doubt if we were meant to be together.

"What happens to the equation if you add in another object? Something massive with a lot of gravity like a star?" I asked, thinking of Hannah.

"Depending on its proximity to the two original objects, it could completely negate the results of the original equation. It would be impossible to predict their destination without performing a new, modified equation."

"So what you're saying is, the star getting involved would throw everything else to shit."

Beverly laughed. "That's not the technical term for it, but accurate nonetheless."

Beverly returned to her studying. I tried to resume mine but found it to be impossible. My mind kept straying to less important things.

"Beverly, what's the deal with Hannah and Alexander? Are they together or not?" I drummed my pencil on the table. "I see them out all the time, but then I see Hannah with other guys too. She was making out with Dane Snyder at the theater the other night. What's up with that?"

Beverly looked up from her chemistry homework and gave me a knowing look. "First, admit why you want to know."

My silence earned me a smirk.

"Yeah, that's what I thought. Gwen, that passive-aggressive crap with Hannah from the other day has got to stop. You're going to get hurt. You need to be honest with yourself and with Hannah."

"Don't know what you're talking about." I looked down at my book, unable to meet her gaze.

"Gwen, I'm not telling you anything till you fess up. You know that, right?"

Yeah, I knew it. But I'd be damned if I was willing to admit it.

I closed my book, leaned back in my chair, and stared at the ceiling. Maybe the reason Hannah always got the guy was that she never gave up. While I, like the damn fool that I was, always gave up. Maybe if I had half the confidence Hannah displayed, I'd have no trouble with guys. It wasn't like they didn't notice me. Sophomore year, Beverly and I had made a game of it. We'd meet downtown dressed for the clubs, and we'd compete to see who got the most "Damn, girl's." Once, Beverly even had a guy so distracted watching her that he tripped off the sidewalk and almost got hit by a car. Hilarious! We'd almost spilled our drinks trying to look away and not laugh.

That night had been the best, but things hadn't been the same since. That was the night Beverly brought Hannah and I together. It was the night my confidence slowly begun eroding away, chipped away piece by piece as every guy I took an interest in was sucked in by Hannah's allure. She was flawless in their eyes, and next to her, I was invisible.

The sound of a door opening drew my attention. Hannah strutted in, looking fabulous as ever in a pink sundress and strappy sandals.

"OMG! Alexander is so amazing. Being with him," she spun around once and flopped into her chair, "it's like being in heaven." Hannah sighed and looked up at the ceiling in awe.

It must be liberating to be so blissfully unaware of others' feelings.

"Shhhhh...keep it down," I admonished her, exaggeratedly looking around the library. I just wanted her to stop. Her words felt like daggers piercing into my chest, making it hard to breathe. I didn't want to be bitter and upset. I didn't want the pain in my chest or the inappropriate emotion coloring my voice. I wanted to forget about Alexander the way I had all the others.

Why can't I forget about him?

I lowered my head. Deep down, I knew I was as infatuated with Alexander as Hannah was.

"Are you guys going to talk about him all day? He's hot, but damn, neither one of you really know him. Get a grip." Beverly rolled her eyes in amusement.

"Whatever." Hannah cut her eyes at Beverly and took a bite of her deli sandwich. Even so, there was a small smile on her face.

"Wait," I questioned, "what do you mean by 'you guys?' I haven't said one word about Alexander, that's all Hannah."

"Oh, please. What was all that crap earlier about then, if not him? And when have you ever needed my help studying anything? I know I'm smart, but I'm not you, Gwen. And the calculations you needed my help with today, you can do those in your sleep, so stop bullshitting me." Beverly crossed her arms over her chest.

I stared at Beverly, wondering what game she was playing. Why would she bring this up now in front of Hannah?

"What the hell is she talking about, Gwen? Is there something you're not telling me?" Hannah's eyes narrowed, and I knew she hadn't forgotten how close Alexander and I had been on the beach. She must have had an idea of what had almost happened.

"I have no idea." I shrugged innocently.

"Bullshit. You know exactly what I'm talking about, so just tell her. This is nothing like the times before. You will lose your friendship if you don't speak up for yourself *now*!" Beverly raged. Her sudden anger rendered me speechless.

"What the hell is going on?" Hannah's voice rose. "Would somebody explain to me what she's talking about?"

A quick look around made me realize we were attracting an audience.

My face flushed. "It's nothing," I hissed. "Beverly's just her usual worrywart self."

Beverly shrugged with a look that seemed to say, 'suit yourself,' then turned to Hannah. "Gwen has a crush on Alexander."

The emotions that flickered across Hannah's face fluctuated between shock, anger, and sympathy, before settling on the original shock.

"Hannah, I love you, but you need to start paying attention to your friends. This isn't the first time you've set your sights on someone Gwen wanted."

"When? Who?"

I lowered my head in embarrassment as Beverly listed them off. "Let's see. First, there was that cute soccer player. I think his name was Eric. Then there was Garrett Henderson, Shane Baker, that guy that worked at the physical therapist's office...and now Alexander." She smiled. "In every case but one, Gwen had met the guy first before you swooped in for the steal."

"Oh, please," Hannah huffed. "She wasn't interested in any of them. And it wasn't like I tried to steal them away from her. They pursued me. That's not my fault. Besides," she shrugged, "she wouldn't have liked them anyway, so if you think about it, I was doing her a favor."

Hannah shifted her gaze toward me, and for a moment, I wanted to punch her in her perfect teeth.

"But I am sorry. I had no idea you felt that way. If I had, I would have backed off, I swear." Hannah seemed sincere, but I could see she was holding something back.

"But," she continued, "it's different with Alexander. I met him before you did. Alexander and I have a lot in common. He pays attention to me and not just to get into my pants. He's such a gentleman." She laughed. "He hasn't even tried to kiss me yet."

Her eyes widened, and a shocked expression appeared on her face. She lowered her voice, leaned forward, and became more serious than I'd ever seen her. "Do you think maybe he's...gay?"

Complete silence followed.

Beverly and I caught each other's eyes and burst out laughing. Hannah looked at us with concern, still waiting for an answer. Of course, Hannah would think that was the only explanation.

"Totally not possible," Beverly explained. "He's too hot. It just wouldn't be fair."

Hannah was determined. "Gwen, how about we just let things happen however they're going to happen? Whether Alexander ends up with you or with me, we'll remain friends. What do you say?"

Before I could nod my head in agreement, Beverly objected. "No, no, no! Oh, no you don't. Don't you dare try to turn this into a competition. I've known you my whole life, Hannah. This will not end well."

"It'll be fine, Beverly. Hannah and I aren't going to fight over a guy. And we're certainly not going to compete for one. Let's let this conversation go, I think the subject has been thoroughly discussed. Agreed?"

"Agreed."

"Agreed," said Beverly, reluctantly, before she changed the subject. "So, any big plans coming up?"

Hannah reminded her of the huge party being thrown at her house in a few weeks. As Hannah and Beverly began discussing the upcoming party, I allowed my mind to drift.

I wished I could stop thinking about Alexander. It was beginning to border on obsession, but when he looked at me, everything faded away, and nothing else existed.

Did he look at Hannah like that?

Stupid question. Of course, he did. I saw him on the beach at sunset kissing her hand. What other proof did I need?

I needed to forget about him. He was so far out of my league, we might as well have been different species. Besides, no one had ever turned down Hannah. It was best if I stopped wasting my time.

∞∞∞∞∞∞

I hated the heat.

Why is it always so friggin' hot here? I wiped the sweat from my brow and climbed the steps to my last interview of the day despite being tempted to turn around and go home. Mercury Technologies hadn't even made the top ten on my list of job choices, but they'd been bought out by a large corporation that had decided it was time for new blood. There were quite a few full-time positions available and one very appealing part-time position that had persuaded me to apply. It was perfect for someone going to college full-time and in need of experience. It was an assistant position with flexible evening hours, no more than a twenty-hour commitment a week.

"Hi. I'm Gwen Adams, I have an interview with Mr. Grimes at noon," I informed the receptionist at the front desk.

"Please have a seat, Miss Adams. It'll be a few minutes," she replied distractedly, shuffling papers across her desk. I found a spot across the lobby, pulled a napkin from my purse, and attempted to pat my sweaty skin dry. *Good Lord*, it must have been over a hundred degrees outside.

I look hideous, I thought, pulling a mirror out of my purse and glancing at my reflection. *Oh yeah, I'm wasting my time here.*

I spent the next few minutes attempting to revive my hair and makeup.

"Miss Adams," the receptionist called loudly, "Mr. Grimes will see you now." She motioned at the door to her right, then resumed her work.

I stood and straightened my skirt before walking through the door she'd indicated to find Mr. Grimes, a sweaty, balding man in his mid-fifties. Like the receptionist, he was so consumed with work that he barely lifted his head from his strewn papers to address me.

"Miss..." he shifted more papers and found my resume, "Adams. Just a few questions. Are you available to work evenings four p.m. to eight p.m.?"

"Yes, I-"

"Are you proficient using Zodiac software?"

"Yes-"

"Can you occasionally work weekends?"

"Yes."

"Are you prepared to travel, if need be?"

"I'm taking college classes most mornings, but I can travel on weekends," I said in one breath.

"What about evenings?"

"Yes, I could travel evenings."

This was by far the strangest interview ever. He had yet to look up from his desk.

"The pay is thirty dollars an hour. You start a week from today. Four p.m. sharp. The days will vary from week to week."

"Excuse me?"

He abruptly removed his glasses and looked at me. "Congratulations. You've got the job. That is, if you want it?"

"But-But *why*? You haven't asked me anything yet. I could be a...a...a serial killer, and you wouldn't have a clue." I found my composure before continuing. "Why are you offering me this position?"

He rubbed his balding head. "Let's just say you've got great recommendations."

He looked back down at his work, indicating the interview was over.

Daddy!

I seethed as I turned on my heel and left the small office. I should have known my dad would pull this crap. This wasn't the first time he'd called in favors for me, but he'd promised he wouldn't do it again. Though part of me understood that this was his way of taking care of me, it didn't matter. The fact that he was parenting from a distance again only pissed me off more.

When my parents got back in town, I would definitely have a long talk with him.

CHAPTER SIX
Alexander

Gwen.

Since running into her at the beach, I couldn't stop thinking about her. I kept replaying our meeting in my head over and over. I couldn't help but smile at the look on her face when I'd asked about that book. The way her cheeks had flushed, the pitiful way she'd tried to hide it ...*priceless*. When I'd asked, I had assumed it'd be... well, quite frankly, I'd assumed it'd be pretty damn boring. I couldn't have been more shocked when I'd read what was on that first page. What a fucking turn-on. I had been ready to take her right there on the damn beach. Then I'd glanced up from the book to her face. There'd been crippling embarrassment, for sure, but also something else.

Before I could stop myself, I'd grabbed her and studied her carefully. Obvious desire had been written all over her body – not just an effect of the book as I had initially assumed, but because of me. *For me.* I'd leaned forward, testing my theory, hoping she wanted me as I did her. The pull of my lips to hers, like gravity, grew stronger as I closed the distance between us. Our lips had almost touched, and I'd paused to savor the moment, stopping close enough to feel the warmth from her breath.

If only we hadn't been interrupted.

I shook my head as I remembered touching her wrist and feeling that familiar indent. I couldn't believe my eyes as I'd flipped her arm and saw the thick scar that ran four inches up her wrist. How did she get that scar?

That scar could only have come from a very serious wound, possibly even a fatal one.

What the hell had happened to her? Certainly, she wouldn't have done that to herself.

"What are you thinking about?" Hannah's big eyes stared into mine.

I sipped my coffee and thought about how to answer. And...I came up with nothing.

"Nothing."

"Oh, well, do you want to know what I was thinking?" she sang. "I was thinking about dancing. What do you say? I know the best place. We'll have so much fun, you'll love it!" She squealed like a sixteen-year-old girl instead of the twenty-three-year-old woman she was. She smiled and bounced in her seat, waiting on something from me.

"What?" I asked, widening the smile on my face to match hers.

"So, will you go with me?" Her wide eyes were pleading.

"Allllright," I answered, trying to sound reluctant but winking at her as I said it.

She squealed again and clapped her hands together a few times before she replied, "Yay! This will be so much fun."

I'd like to say her overexcitement annoyed me, but truthfully, it was adorable. I didn't know what it was about her; it wasn't attraction, but there was definitely a connection. A connection that made me want to keep her happy. I was pretty sure she felt it too, but I was also sure it wasn't nearly as platonic on her end.

"Just not this weekend," I told her. "I've got a few things to take care of."

We both stood to leave. I threw my arm over her shoulder as we walked through the mall. "Are you done shopping?"

She shrugged. "I need to buy a new outfit for the club and some new shoes." She gave me a hopeful look.

"Lead the way."

The day went well. We spent a few hours shopping, during which Hannah insisted on trying on every revealing dress in the store and prancing around in front of me. I certainly didn't mind the free show, and I enjoyed her company. In fact, it was quite refreshing to have someone other than my family to talk to. Ever since we'd gotten here, Eli, Zane, and Ariel had been all I had, and Zane had only recently joined us.

I was beginning to believe that was a mistake. Zane was much too young and immature for this mission. Add the fact that he had no duties, and he turned into a ticking time bomb. I'd had to bail him out of jail twice in the last six months and pay off several witnesses and reporters to keep the scandals out of the news.

The last thing we needed was bad publicity. To get what we needed and complete the mission, our image had to be squeaky clean. Especially Zane's. His role would come much later, in a few years, actually, and his record and reputation had to be beyond reproach. In the meantime, I needed to give him some responsibilities, something to keep him busy and out of trouble. It also wouldn't hurt for him to start building up the backstory for his future.

"Hey, Hannah, when will your dad be back in town?"

Hannah's back stiffened, and her eyes narrowed. "I should have known," she mumbled, so low I knew she thought I couldn't hear her. *Damn*, I felt like an asshole.

Hannah regained her composure and plastered a phony smile across her face. "He'll be back this evening. We're supposed to be having dinner together over at Armand's." She looked at me. "You know, the new French restaurant that opened downtown?"

I hadn't heard anything about it, but I had to find a way to talk to Senator Kinsley again. Maybe I'd show up at the restaurant tonight. I debated asking Hannah what time they'd be there.

"Hey, why don't you come to dinner with us? I could finally introduce you to my dad. You know, since we've been spending so much time together and all." She batted her eyelashes.

Well, that worked out well.

"Sounds like fun. What time?"

"Seven o'clock. That means we need to get you some new clothes for tonight!"

I chuckled. "Oh, no. I've got plenty. I'm done shopping for the day."

"Come on. You at least need to get new shoes." She looked up at me, and a smile formed on her face as she realized she was about to get her way again. "It will only take a few minutes."

"Damn it, woman. I'll be broke by the time you're done with me."

She stuck out her tongue.

"All right," I caved. "Let's hurry. I've got things I need to get done before I can go out tonight."

Hannah grabbed my hand and dragged me to the nearest shoe store. As we entered, Hannah wrapped her arm possessively around mine, then somewhat loudly said, "Okay sweetie, what size do you wear?"

I noticed the guy behind the cash register flinch.

"Size fourteen."

Hannah turned to the guy and proceeded to tell him to bring out a few pairs of shoes for me to try on. Hannah smiled sweetly and rubbed her hand up and down my arm.

After the guy walked away, I turned to her and frowned. "What was that about? Who is that?"

"Oh, he's nobody. I just want to make sure you have nice shoes for tonight." She batted her eyelashes innocently.

I narrowed my eyes. "Yeah, I don't think so." I crossed my arms. "Look, I'm not cool with you using me to make another guy jealous. I don't need new shoes anyway. I'm out." I turned and walked away.

"Wait!" she cried after me. "I wasn't trying to make anyone jealous." She scrambled to get in front of me. "Why would I? I want to be with you. Why would I care about some stupid retail clerk anyway?"

"About that....Look, Hannah, I don't feel-"

"It's okay Alexander, I forgive you. Let's go." She grabbed my hand and pulled me out of the store before I could respond. "Oh yeah, I meant to ask. Are you planning on trying out for Mr. Mills' play? I'm hoping I get the part of Beth, the heroine. I know if you try out, you'll get the part of Nathan. There's no way we won't get those parts. We look too good together, don't you think?"

Hannah chatted nonstop as she pulled me along behind her.

∞∞∞∞∞∞

Damn, it was early. Why the hell Mr. Mills set auditions for six in the morning, I'd never understand.

But it wasn't like I had anywhere else to be. Besides, the only reason I was even here was for Gwen and Hannah. Mostly Hannah, I thought. Hell, I wasn't even sure anymore.

"Are you nervous?" Hannah bounced up and down in the passenger seat beside me. "I am so nervous. I have to get the part of Beth. I just have to."

I didn't bother answering. Hannah hadn't wanted to know if I was nervous. She was like a child who thought the world revolved around her. The only feelings she was aware of were her own. It was a very selfish way to go through life, yet that was Hannah. Surprisingly, I didn't hate her for it. Something about her childishness was sweet and endearing. She had become very important to me, the pull I felt toward her growing stronger every day.

I breathed a sigh of relief as the auditorium came into view. The drive had seemed unusually long this morning. I maneuvered the car through the parking lot to the very back.

"There are plenty of spots closer to the front. Why are we parking all the way back here?" Hannah grumbled.

"I don't want people parking next to my car and dinging up the paint." I told the lie with a straight face.

The truth was, there had been a lot of odd coincidences lately. It was as if someone was out to get me, so I parked where the best security cameras were. If anyone took this opportunity to mess with my car, I'd hack into the cameras and find out who was so interested in my family and me.

The inside of the auditorium was packed. There were people milling about everywhere, but a guy at the door pointed us toward the registration table. I filled out the registration form and checked the box marked 'All' for the parts I wanted to try out for.

The next part was a bit trickier. There was a stack of excerpts from forty different movies. I was informed to pick a manuscript to memorize while I waited in line to audition. This could be difficult. I had watched my fair share of movies the last few years since we'd returned to the mainland, but nowhere near as many as everyone else who'd had a lifetime to watch them. I flipped through the different scripts, most of which I had never seen and a few that I'd seen but had no interest in acting out, when I finally came across one that caught my attention. It was from an old movie, but I had only recently watched it. It was a monologue by Robin Williams in the film *Good Will Hunting*. It was an exemplary speech, and one I was sure I could pull off. I grabbed a copy and joined Hannah, who had finished and was waiting in line.

"Which manuscript did you pick?" I asked as soon as I was close enough to be heard.

Hannah jumped. "Sorry. I'm getting nervous." She took a deep breath. "I picked the script from *10 Things I Hate About You*."

It was one of the movies I'd never seen, so I had no idea how to respond.

"You haven't seen it, have you? I guess it's kind of old. Hey, would you mind helping me with my lines?"

"Sure, no problem."

She handed me her manuscript and began. "I hate the way you talk to me, and the way you cut your hair. I hate the way you drive my car...."

Holy crap. For someone so good at pretending in real life, she sucked as an actress. Or maybe this was how it was supposed to sound? It wasn't like I'd seen the movie to compare. I watched her, trying hard to keep my face passive and not laugh.

"...the fact that you didn't call. But mostly I hate the way I don't hate you. Not even close, not even a little bit, not even at all." She sniffled and whimpered dramatically, then finished with a timid smile. "So, what do you think?"

What do I think?

I couldn't answer that honestly, but I also couldn't ignore her.

"That was amazing. You did the entire scene without looking at the paper. How did you memorize it so quickly?"

She smiled and blushed at the praise. "Actually, I didn't have to memorize it. I've seen that movie so many times I could quote it in my sleep." Her eyes suddenly focused on something behind me.

"Beverly! I thought you changed your mind about trying out."

I turned toward the line forming behind me, and my eyes instantly met Gwen's. She looked fantastic. Tight jeans hugged her curvy hips, and her full breasts strained against the snug blue v-neck she wore. Her wavy blonde hair fell to her lower back and framed her beautiful face.

She was perfect.

I felt my blood surging through my body. I stepped forward, only to be jerked harshly back. Hannah's nails dug into my arm and made me realize I was staring. I almost brushed Hannah aside to remind her we weren't together, but I stopped myself because that was my ultimate goal, wasn't it? To be with Hannah?

I tore my eyes from Gwen to see who was with her. Beside her on one side was Beverly, who I'd met when I was out with Hannah the other day. On the other was one of the guys from our class. Hannah waved them over to stand with us. As they approached, I realized that the guy from our class was the guy from the shoe store.

He stood back and tapped his foot impatiently. He didn't seem particularly happy to be here.

Unable to stop myself, my eyes shifted back to Gwen. She didn't seem that thrilled to see me either. She had a smile but refused to meet my eyes or even speak to me. Was she angry? I tried to figure it out while we waited in line.

It wasn't long before Hannah and Beverly started laughing at some joke one of them had told.

I glanced at Gwen. Her eyes shifted away from mine.

Had she been watching me? I pretended to pay attention to Hannah and Beverly's conversation while I watched Gwen through my peripheral vision.

There. She did it again. The moment my eyes moved toward her, she looked away.

I was wrong. She wasn't mad at me. But why was she avoiding my gaze?

"Alexander and I will make a great Beth and Nathan. Don't you think?" Hannah looked at Beverly and Gwen. "What parts were you guys hoping to get?"

Beverly answered first. "I want the part of Josie, Beth's evil best friend. She's described as being a real bitch. I figure that's the perfect role for me."

Everyone laughed.

"What about you, Gwen?" I asked quietly.

The guy with Beverly huffed and crossed his arms.

Gwen's eyes flitted to mine for a split second before darting away. She seemed to think about it a moment, then commented nonchalantly that it didn't matter.

Didn't matter?

I didn't know why, but her answer annoyed the shit out of me. Did she really have no preference at all?

Hannah squeezed my hand and pulled me closer. The conversation lulled as everyone turned their attention to the manuscripts we were supposed to be memorizing. I lifted mine, read through it once, then played it through my mind the way I planned to say it. *"...Because the doctors could see in your eyes that the term 'visiting hours' don't apply to you. You don't know about real loss, 'cause it only occurs when you've loved something more than you love yourself. And I doubt you've ever dared to love anybody that much..."*

I recalled how moved I'd felt the first time I'd heard this intense speech six months before. I remembered how much I'd yearned for the pain of loving someone that much, how I'd wished to love someone to the point of suffering.

"Alexander," Beverly said, getting my attention, then motioning to the guy next to her. "Have you two met yet?"

I shook my head.

"This is Kyle Harper. Ky, this is Alexander."

I extended my hand. "Nice to finally meet you. We have Intro to Literature together, right?"

The guy pursed his lips and stared at my hand. Beverly elbowed him and growled his name under her breath.

His eyes rolled, but he grudgingly took my hand. "Yeah, I just can't figure out what you're doing in that class."

"Trying to get an education like everyone else," I answered smoothly, despite his rudeness.

He snorted. "Yeah, right."

What the fuck is this guy's problem? Is he intentionally trying to piss me off?

Beverly shoved Ky and glared at him.

"What?" he questioned, as if he couldn't fathom what he'd done wrong.

The line had been slowly shuffling forward, and we'd finally reached the front.

"Next!"

I looked to Hannah, about to push her forward, until I saw the terrified look on her face.

"Are you okay?"

"No, I need a few more minutes to practice. Take my place and go next, please?"

"Sure, no problem."

I squeezed her hand for encouragement, then walked through the door and onto the stage.

∞∞∞∞∞∞

Auditions were over, and everyone was waiting outside for the results. Hannah was absolutely certain she'd nailed it and was bouncing up and down with excitement. I dreaded seeing Mr. Mills return with the cast listing. Hannah was going to be so disappointed.

Just as I had the thought, the door to the auditorium opened, and Mr. Mills' assistant emerged with a stack of papers in his hand.

"Who's that?"

It was Beverly who answered. "That's Jasper, Mr. Mills' nephew. He's a student here, but I heard he's the one who wrote the play."

"He wrote it?"

"Yeah, and he's directing it too. Mr. Mills is giving him full responsibility for the entire production."

Jasper taped the papers to the door and strode away without a word.

Hannah dashed toward the results. Beverly and Ky followed closely behind. I sneaked a look in Gwen's direction to find her looking my way. She didn't avert her eyes this time, and for a moment, her wide emerald eyes held nothing back. Pent-up desire and passion blazed uncontrollably. Without conscious thought, my legs closed the distance between us, and my eyes dropped to her parted lips.

I didn't even know her, but I was irresistibly drawn to her like a moth to a flame. No understanding. No reasoning. Just pure unadulterated lust.

The logical part of my brain shut off. I didn't care who was around to see. I wanted her. I took the remaining step that separated us, eager to taste her lips, desperate to feel her skin beneath my hands again.

I brushed by thumb across her flushed cheek. Her soft pink lips parted with an audible gasp.

Fuck. I lowered my mouth to hers, desperate to capture that vulnerable softness-

The fire was suddenly doused from her eyes. She took a frantic step back and glanced around. Her gaze avoided mine as she ran shaky fingers through her wavy blonde hair.

What the fuck just happened? It was like watching someone flip a switch. One minute she was on, the next she was off. Had I done something wrong?

Hannah's frosty voice drew my attention from Gwen as she stomped toward us. "You got the part of Nathan. Let's go!"

Ah. That was why Gwen had reacted the way she had. She'd seen Hannah approaching.

Hannah didn't wait for a response. She grabbed my arm as she stalked by and dragged me along with her.

"What part did I get?" Gwen mumbled as Hannah passed.

Hannah halted abruptly, and I stumbled into her, almost knocking her down. She turned, looked Gwen in the eye, and practically spat in her face. "Beth!"

Hannah then turned and stormed toward the car, dragging me along with her.

Hannah's reaction had a sobering effect. What the hell had I been thinking? That I was going to kiss Gwen? Right here in front of half the damn school? With Hannah not fifty yards away?

I shook my head in disgust.

I was such an ass.

∞∞∞∞∞∞

"I thought we could go on a picnic today," Eva commented as she finished up her work.

"My only goal is to make you happy. If it's a picnic you want, a picnic you shall get." I started to stand but froze as a sly smile stretched across Eva's face.

"Good. Because I've already packed one for us."

I grinned.

It was amazing how quickly I'd fallen in love with Eva. It was only two weeks ago that I'd dropped my armor off at her father's shop, and already I couldn't go a day without her. I couldn't do without her smile, her humor, or her beautiful honey eyes that looked at me adoringly.

"Where do you want to go?" I asked, but it didn't matter. There was no choice that wouldn't be perfect. No place that wouldn't be beautiful. Even after a century's time, your eyes never acclimated to the wonders of Heaven. The colors were as vibrant after two millennia as they had been on Day One. There were snowy mountain tops, pristine beaches, awe-inspiring canyons, waterfalls, jungles, and the most beautifully colored skies in all the multiverse.

The only thing it lacked was the night sky. Microscopic gold-like particles saturated the air, reflecting God's light and bathing Heaven in a golden glimmer. These particles made it impossible for darkness to exist. Thus, no shadows and no night sky.

"Come on." She glided across the room and pulled the picnic basket she'd hidden out of the cabinet. She smiled playfully as she strapped it to her back. "I already have a place picked out. However, you'll have to find it," she taunted.

She leaned in close and whispered a hint in my ear. "Find me if you can." She grinned then raced out the door.

I knew the place the moment she'd given her hint. It was an exquisite location and a fantastic choice. After giving her a few moments head start, I leapt to my feet and took off running.

I darted around the marble buildings and crossed the busy streets until I came to the edge of the city where the jungle began. I walked along the edge and pushed the massive leaves aside. When my hand brushed the velvet petals of a lavender banana flower, I knew I was close. I pressed the leaves back, and there it was: the faint path that led to the hidden lake a mile from town. Few angels knew of it, and those that did kept its location a secret, so I did my best not to call attention to myself. I discreetly turned to make sure no one saw me, then leapt onto the path and raced into the shelter of the jungle.

Within moments, the glittering turquoise lake came into view. Its deep blue-green water stretched as far as the eye could see. I raced forward and dove beneath its sparkling surface. I swam deep and fast, searching for the mouth of the underwater cave I knew was close. The crystal formation came into view quickly, as did Eva.

Her slender legs fluttered delicately as her white gown billowed out behind her. She glided gracefully through the water no more than a hundred yards ahead of me.

I raced to catch her, pushing myself as fast as my arms and legs would move.

I darted through the mouth of the cave, and within seconds, she was within my reach.

Eva swam languorously and blissfully unaware of my approach. I held back, biding my time, waiting until just the right moment.

She swam up toward the massive air pocket that existed within the cave and just as she surfaced, I grabbed her foot and pulled her under a split second after her startled scream echoed through the cave.

I released her and watched as she splashed out of the water and scrambled on to the nearest rock.

"Alex!" Her voice lashed out at me. Her face blazed crimson as she refused to meet my gaze.

I couldn't help it – I laughed.

She crossed her arms and turned from me, her head held high and her back ramrod straight.

I should've felt guilty for scaring her, but that scream and the indignant look she'd given me were even more amusing than I'd imagined.

When she still refused to meet my eyes, I moved to stand in front of her.

"Eva?" I crooned, unable to remove the grin from my face. "You know it's funny."

She harrumphed, but a smile played at the edges of her lips.

I knew all I had to do was wait her out.

Her lips twitched.

Just a few more seconds.

Then there it was; the smile that spread across her face was as bright as the brightest star. Rainbows cast from the iridescent ceiling above glittered against her cheeks.

I laughed and smoothed a wet strand of hair behind her ear, but then the colorful light shimmered and slowly began to blur. The room suddenly began to darken.

"Eva?"

The temperature dropped, and my surroundings took on a fuzzy, unreal quality that unnerved me.

"*Eva?*"

My vision blurred. I couldn't see her anymore, just blurry splotches of color where her body should have been.

My voice became frantic as I yelled her name.

What was going on? Was she okay? Her disappearance had transpired so fast my mind couldn't decipher what was happening. As the darkness closed in, I saw Eva's blurry figure walk toward me. Her face suddenly appeared just inches away, eyes bright as emeralds meeting mine.

"Gwen?"

I was astonished. How was Gwen here? Where was Eva?

Gwen reached out and stroked my cheek.

I closed my eyes and sucked in a breath as her touch did unspeakable things to me.

I wasn't supposed to want her. I wasn't supposed to dream about her.

I stood mesmerized as she brushed her thumb across my bottom lip. "Stop fighting it, Alexander. It's me you really want."

She pulled my face to hers and touched her soft lips to mine.

"No!" I yelled as I was jolted out of bed. My heart thundered in my chest. My breaths came out in ragged gasps.

"What the hell?" I whispered as I rubbed my head with my hands.

Where were these dreams coming from? And why were my memories being distorted this way?

I slowed my breathing and tried to relax.

Calm down and go back to sleep, I told myself. *It's Hannah you're supposed to be with, not Gwen. Get that through your stubborn head.*

It was just a dream.

CHAPTER SEVEN

Gwen

"What do you think about this one?" I held up a blue dress suit.

"Absolutely fantastic if you want to look like Hillary Clinton," Beverly responded cheerfully.

"I'm shooting for a young, yet competent, professional look, not a seventy-year-old politician with bad hair." I shot her a glare. "Come on, Beverly. I need an outfit for my new job, and I want to look the part."

I browsed through the suits, but my mind was elsewhere. I couldn't figure Alexander out. Some moments he was totally into me, and at others, it was like he wanted Hannah.

Maybe he's a player, the nasty thought popped into my head. Just because he seemed like such a nice, responsible guy didn't mean he wasn't a player. Players could be nice guys too, right?

"Beverly," I bit my lip, hating myself for even asking. "Are Hannah and Alexander together?"

She glanced up, her piercing blue eyes nailing me with a knowing look. "I'm not sure. They're together a lot, but Hannah has been dating other guys." Beverly shrugged. "She's always all over him, but it doesn't seem to go both ways. You know what I mean?"

Memories flashed through my mind. Hannah wrapping her arm around Alexander's. Hannah rubbing her hands up his arm. Hannah grabbing his hand and pulling him across the parking lot.

But then again, Alexander had kissed Hannah's hand when we were at the beach.

I shook the image from my mind.

"He doesn't look at her the way he looks at you," Beverly continued.

For once, Beverly was wrong. "I think you're confused."

She laughed. "Yeah, right. Every time he looks at you, it's like he wants to rip your clothes off."

"He looks at everyone like that."

"Hell no, he doesn't." She shook her head. "Only you."

Was that really how he looked at me? I was flattered, but at the same time, I wasn't sure I liked it.

What a freaking lie. I loved it. But I knew I shouldn't. I should have been offended, right? He should have wanted me for my personality.

Not that he'd gotten to see much of it.

Oh hell, what was wrong with me? I wasn't looking for a relationship anyway.

"Should I forget about him?" I asked as a skimmed through another rack.

"I don't know, hon. I can tell you like him, but he needs to decide what he wants. Don't wait around for him to make the right decision. You've got plenty of other options." She raised her eyebrows meaningfully.

"What do you mean?"

She began sorting distractedly through another rack. "Oh, nothing. You know me, always saying something crazy."

She suddenly held a skirt up in the air and yelled, "Found it! Try these on." She shoved the skirt and a silk blouse against my chest. "I think if you pair these with a few accessories, you'll have the young, competent, sexy look you were hoping for."

"I never said sexy," I reminded her as I headed to the nearest dressing room.

"Just because you didn't say it doesn't mean you didn't mean it," she called as I pulled the door closed.

Later that night, I still hadn't stopped thinking about Alexander. I'd kept everything locked up in my head for far too long. I felt like I might explode. Beverly knew I had a thing for him, but not nearly the extent of it, and I wanted her to know everything.

But did I really want to compete with Hannah for a guy? Despite how often she'd done the same to me, I just didn't know if I had it in me. I closed my eyes and tried to focus on the movie we were watching.

We were having a girls' night, and Beverly had rented a few chick flicks. Our only plan was to watch movies, paint our toenails, and give each other facials. Hannah was supposed to be here too, but she'd backed out at the last minute.

She and Alexander were going on a date, and she'd had the audacity to ask me to wish her luck. I found myself wondering once again why I was friends with her. She was such a bitch sometimes.

I'd known Hannah since my parents took a job working for her father years ago. She was a selfish and bratty child. Hannah always had to have her way and pitched a fit when she didn't get it. I'd never liked her and complained when our parents forced us to be together.

That was until the night Beverly persuaded me to meet Hannah downtown.

"Come on, Gwen. I know she's a bit of a handful, but you'd be surprised how much you two have in common if you'd take the time to know her."

And because Beverly was always right, I'd agreed.

We'd been sitting at the bar, the night almost over, when Hannah had finally made an appearance. She'd stomped up to the bar, sent a pointed glare toward Beverly and huffed. "You didn't tell me she would be here."

At the sound of her arrogant voice, I'd almost snapped, but when she'd plopped onto the stool beside me, I'd seen the faint sheen of unshed tears in her eyes.

It took some coaxing, and an awful lot of drinks, but Hannah finally had confided in me.

She was lonely.

She had grown up alone, with no one but nannies to care for her.

It had finally made sense. The way she acted out all the time. The way she threw herself at men.

She just wanted someone to show her some affection, and if not affection, then at least some attention.

It was that night, for the first time, that I'd understood her.

It was also the night that Hannah and I had finally become friends.

But that friendship didn't mean that I had to let her walk all over me. Again.

I shook my head. Tonight was supposed to be about fun and relaxation, so I did my best to ignore my irritation and focused on the movie.

It was probably the hundredth time we'd watched *She's the Man*.

It was definitely one of our favorites. Me, because I was a huge fan of Amanda Bynes. Beverly, because she was a huge fan of Channing Tatum without a shirt.

We both sighed as Channing entered the scene wearing nothing but loose jogging pants.

I could have stared at him for days.

Hmmm... Something about the actor suddenly seemed familiar. "Hey, he reminds me of someone...."

"Yeah, that would be Channing Tatum. Figured you'd know that by now."

I threw my pillow at Beverly. "Very funny, I meant he reminds me of someone we know. I just can't figure out who it is."

"Well, when you figure it out, please point me in his direction. I want me some Magic Mike." Beverly giggled and threw my pillow back at me.

"I'd have to agree, but I think I'd prefer a little Jacob Black instead."

"Taylor Lautner? He *is* sexy, but Channing has all the right moves."

"Yeah, I guess I could go either way." I paused, then answered honestly. "Actually, I'd rather have them both."

"I can't believe you said that." Beverly glanced around like I was hiding somewhere. "Where have you hidden my best friend?" Beverly laughed again before continuing, "You know Hannah would totally pick Channing. She's always had a thing for blondes."

Beverly's comment reminded me of something. Ky was blonde. He was also tan, built like a bodybuilder, had gorgeous brown eyes with eyelashes to die for, and was one of the nicest guys you'd ever meet. So what was Hannah's problem? Why was she always so determined to piss him off instead of pursuing him like every other hot guy she knew?

Beverly pointed the remote at the television and paused the movie.

"What is it, Gwen? I can see the wheels in your head turning. Whatever it is, just spit it out."

I sighed. "Okay, so I've kinda got more than just a thing for Alexander." I continued, telling her all about the night we'd danced and all the times we'd almost kissed. I was shocked when I realized how much time had passed since we'd met. I couldn't believe I'd waited so long to confess my feelings.

"I guess I'm finally admitting my obsession. Happy?"

"Oh, yeah. Admission is the first step to recovery," Beverly grinned.

"What does that mean? It doesn't even make any sense."

She laughed. "I have no idea, it just kinda came out. It was funny though, right? I don't know, after what that boy's been doing to you, you may actually need rehab!"

She wasn't wrong, but I rolled my eyes anyway. The smile that I'd been trying to hide spread across my face. "He sure does make addiction look tasty, right? I may not want rehab!"

We laughed then drifted into a comfortable silence, both of us sorting through our private thoughts as we stared silently at the darkened television screen.

"They met about a year and a half before you and Hannah became friends," she started softly.

I turned my eyes solemnly to hers.

"It was love at first sight, at least for Ky. Hannah and Ky met at a football game, rival teams. I don't know how much of this you know, but here it is. Ky's parents died when he was fourteen, and the foster care system was not kind to him. He begged the courts to grant him emancipation when he turned sixteen, and they granted his request. Since then, he's been living off the small fortune his parents left him and working part-time to supplement his income."

"He was working the concession stand the night of that football game. He told me, the moment he laid eyes on her, he knew she was the one. He said it was like looking at an angel. Well, an angel with an attitude, at least. Ky was so nervous he forgot her ketchup and gave her the wrong drink. And boy, did she give him an ear full. Afterward, he asked around and found out her name and where she lived. A month later, he enrolled in our school and got an apartment two miles from her home. Don't say anything to Hannah. She still has no idea that he moved here for her. Anyway, it didn't take long for Ky to win her over, no surprise there. I mean just look at him. What was a surprise was how much Hannah adored him. Everyone knew those two would end up married one day."

"What?" I couldn't hide my shock. How had I not known this? I'd had no idea they'd even known each other before Ky and I became friends.

"So what went wrong?" So far, it sounded like the perfect love story.

"It's a mystery. Hannah saw him driving off with a beautiful blonde. Ky disappeared for three days, and he didn't answer his phone or his texts. When he returned, Hannah's heart was broken. I mean, she was literally a mess. Ky swore nothing happened and begged Hannah to take him back. But he absolutely refused to tell her where he went, who the woman was, or why he did it."

"Do you believe him?"

"I don't know. Maybe. He was so distraught when he lost her. It was evident in his eyes that it was killing him not to tell her the truth."

"Wow."

What secret was so important that Ky'd give up the love of his life to protect it?

"That's so strange. You think she'll ever forgive him?"

"I don't know. You should have seen her when it happened. It's the only time I've ever seen her without makeup. Hell, she was so upset she wouldn't even see me for the first two weeks after it happened because my blonde hair reminded her of the blonde in his car. She got pissed off every time she looked at me."

"Wait, so Hannah knows how Ky feels about her? So when she treats him like dirt one minute, then flirts with him the next, she's intentionally torturing him?"

"Something like that. The thing is, Hannah won't forgive him until he tells her about that night. It must be pretty important because despite how in love with her he was, Ky's lips are sealed."

"Was in love with her? Past tense?"

"Gwen," Beverly rolled her eyes. "You are so blind. Ky stopped being in love with her the minute he met you. Why do you think he follows you around everywhere? And why Hannah's always stealing your dates?"

∞∞∞∞∞∞

I wiped the sweat from my face as I loaded the last box into the truck. Whew, was I glad that was over. I sat down on the curb and took a few deep breaths.

"Gwen, dear," Mrs. Johnson called.

"Yes, ma'am?" I stood and walked over to the elderly lady.

"I wanted you to know how much we appreciate what you do for our little charity," she squeezed my hand tightly. "You have been such a blessing."

"Thank you, Mrs. Johnson. I just want to help."

"Oh, sweetheart, you have been so wonderful to us. We couldn't thank you enough. There aren't many youngsters your age willing to give up so much of their free time."

I forced myself not to remind her that I was twenty-two now. I knew in Mrs. Johnson's eyes I'd always be the nine-year-old girl who'd joined her small church so many years ago.

As if she could read my mind, she continued, "Haven't seen you at church in a while. Is everything okay?"

I smiled. "I've been really busy with school. I'm sure I'll be back soon. Don't worry about me, Mrs. Johnson."

"Of course, I'll worry about you. And I'll pray for you too. I love you, dear, just like one of my own grandbabies. Now, give me a hug, it's about time for me to go." She leaned forward and squeezed my neck with more strength than a little old lady should have been capable of, then turned and walked to her green Cadillac.

I sat on the curb thinking about all the good times I'd had at Mrs. Johnson's house. My cousin and I used to pick blueberries and bring them to her house. We'd spend hours picking those suckers and eat about half of them as we went. Then Mrs. Johnson would make the best blueberry pies you've ever eaten. She'd open her windows while she baked, and you could smell them a quarter mile down the road. We used to ride our bikes to her house every weekend to see her until my aunt and cousins moved back to Georgia.

A gentle breeze blew my hair from my face, and out of the corner of my eye, I saw a sleek red car pull over and park on the opposite side of the road.

The driver got out, and my eyes widened at the thick black hair and broad shoulders.

It was Alexander.

Courage, Gwen. Be brave. Don't chicken out.

"Alexander," I yelled across the street. My cheeks burned with embarrassment.

His head shot up, and his eyes met mine.

"Hey." I waved him over, doing my best to overcome my shyness.

He stared directly into my eyes for a moment, his blue eyes distant and cold, then turned and walked away.

What the hell?

If my cheeks had been burning before, they were certainly an inferno now. I discreetly looked around to see if anyone else had seen us.

Nope. Still alone.

Maybe I'd been wrong about him. I couldn't figure out what his problem was. Was he bipolar or something?

And hell, he'd almost kissed me at auditions. I hadn't imagined that. And now he was completely ignoring me.

Again.

Was he screwing with me? Was he trying to see if he could get under my skin? Whatever his game was, I refused to play it anymore.

A loud roar interrupted my thoughts. Apparently, I wasn't as alone as I'd thought.

A black motorcycle pulled to a stop beside me. The rider smoothly lowered the kickstand and turned the engine off before removing his helmet. Thick blonde hair fell against a chiseled face.

Jasper Mills.

"Hey, Gwen."

He knows my name? We didn't have any classes together and certainly didn't hang out in the same circles. As far as I knew, Jasper Mills wasn't in anyone's circle. He was a big hunky mystery to everyone.

My mind flashed to the last time I'd seen Jasper in town. He'd been seated in the corner of Level Seven. The dark shadows of the club had barely concealed the fact that he was making out with three different chicks at the same time. He'd had his tongue down one girl's throat, one hand sliding up the skirt of another, and girl number three was kneeling on the floor between his legs, pawing at him. And while everything about that should have disgusted me, it hadn't. What did that say about me?

"Hey," I responded weakly.

His aquamarine eyes sparkled in the sun, and his lips twitched as he suppressed a smile. Looking at Jasper Mills was like staring at the sun. He was impossible to look at for too long.

I averted my eyes and licked my lips.

Jasper eyed the charity truck and chuckled.

"What?" I crossed my arms over my chest.

"Do you really buy into this crap?" He motioned toward the truck's logo.

"Helping the less fortunate? Of course, doesn't everybody?"

He shook his head in disbelief. "You are so naive. You're going to have to toughen up if you're going to be the star in my play."

"What's that supposed to mean?"

Jasper shook his head, then looked to the sky. "You haven't even read the manuscript yet, have you?"

I hesitated. It couldn't be that bad, could it? "No."

"Read it. Tonight. It's not for the faint of heart." He motioned to the truck. "And stop letting places like this take advantage of you. It's a scam. They all are."

He slid his helmet over his head, revved the engine, and took off down the street.

Knowing I didn't have time to waste, I got in the truck and headed for the church.

CHAPTER EIGHT
Alexander

It is such a beautiful day, I thought as I walked around downtown. The cloudless sky and gentle breeze were a nice reprieve from the scorching heat we'd been subjected to recently. This was also the first time I'd taken the opportunity to walk around. More of a large town than a small city, Verona Beach, with its cobblestone streets and quaint businesses, was a rather charming place to live. It almost felt like home.

The thought surprised me. When had I started feeling nostalgic for a place I barely knew? Why was it that even though I knew we'd be going home soon, my heart rejected the idea of leaving?

The loud roar of an engine caught my attention just as a T12 Massimo motorcycle sped up the street from behind me into the parking lot to my left.

Beautiful. With its sleek black design, 230 horsepower, 999cc four-cylinder engine, it was my dream bike. But its 300,000-dollar price tag and the fact that it wasn't street legal made its purchase impractical. I had to know who the owner was.

I approached the bike as the rider got off and pulled the helmet from his head.

"Jasper?"

Jasper glanced over his shoulder at me, then continued securing his gear to his bike.

"I'm Alexander Prescott. We go to school together."

"I know who you are. I chose you for my play."

"I thought Mr. Mills did that," I replied.

"No. He videoed all the rehearsals, but I picked the cast."

Well, that was surprising.

"This yours?" I motioned toward the bike.

"Yeah. It's a present from the old man. You know, as a pat on the back for finally taking responsibility or some bullshit." He yanked open some snaps and fished through the pockets. "Hold up." A few more snaps later, Jasper finished with his gear and turned to face me, cigarette in hand.

"Want a smoke?" he offered.

"No, thanks." Before I could stop myself, I asked, "What kind of responsibility was worth three hundred grand?"

A sarcastic chuckle escaped his lips. "My dumbass father seems to think this whole deal with the play is about starting a career. So he bought me this bike."

"How the hell did you get the license plate for it? These things aren't exactly street legal."

A cocky grin spread across his face. "I know someone. Why? Are you looking to buy?"

"Can't buy one, my dad would kill me. I've always wanted to ride one though."

I looked at the bike longingly. The damn thing called to me. Maybe I'd get one before we went back home.

"Why not now?" Jasper tossed me the key.

I was sure my face showed my surprise.

"Don't get too excited. It's just for a quick drive. Meet me back here in twenty minutes." Jasper blew a puff of smoke to his left. "And don't even think about scratching the paint."

"Sure thing," I responded before mounting the bike with anticipation.

I shot out of the parking lot and outside the city limits. At the first straight away, I floored it, the jolt of power that rocketed the bike forward sending pure adrenaline coursing through me. Together, the bike and I flew across the asphalt, and before I knew it, my twenty minutes were up.

Damn it.

I returned to the parking lot where Jasper waited. I parked and sat on the bench next to him.

"Thanks, man, that's a pretty sweet ride."

"No problem," Jasper responded. "I've got to ask..."

"What?" His sudden intensity unnerved me.

"How are your other classes going? You know, other than the one my uncle is teaching?"

"Your uncle is Mr. Mills?"

"Unfortunately. Why do you think he's using the play I wrote? It's all my dad's doing. So...you never really answered my question. How are your other classes going?"

I shook my head and smiled. Despite knowing that eventually someone would ask, I hadn't put much thought into answering that question. I couldn't tell people the only reason I'd signed up for college courses was to get closer to Hannah, and I hated lying any more than I had to. "I'm not taking other classes." I stared straight ahead and hoped he wouldn't ask.

"Why the hell would you only take one class? What's your major?" Obviously, Jasper was not going to let this one go.

"No major. I was bored, so I figured I'd take a class or two. I've already got plenty of money. What would I need a degree for?"

"Fuck, man. We're at the beach, why the hell would you spend your free time in a classroom when you could be hanging on the beach with some fine ass girls? If you don't need the money, why do it?"

"Like you're any better. If your family can afford that bike, why would you even need a degree? Why aren't you on the beach?" I asked, attempting to take the spotlight off myself.

He threw his head back and laughed.

"Because my dad's a twat. He insists on the degree, so I'm majoring in performing arts. Mostly because it comes easy to me, which leaves me plenty of free time. And I've got plenty of game with the ladies, I don't need the beach."

He wasn't joking. He was the only guy I'd ever seen get more women than Zane.

I looked across the street and noticed more and more people entering the church. I nodded. "What's going on over there? It's not Sunday."

Jasper laughed and shook his head. "Just a bunch of do-gooders. People drop off food and whatnot for charity."

He shook his head and flicked his cigarette onto the road. "Follow me. Someone ought to show you how pathetic this town is."

Taking him up on his offer, I followed him across the street.

He nodded to his left. "We have to go in through the side entrance."

I followed him up a small trail that led to a glass door on the north side of the church. I turned, pushed the door open for us, and raised my eyebrows at him as he passed.

"People are fucking gullible," he mumbled.

The room was filled with the gentle roar of dozens of echoing voices. It was split into two sections. The left side, the side where we stood, was set up for drop-offs. Not much to see on this side, just two large tables for donations with a volunteer stationed nearby to help. It was the other end of the room that was the source of the noise. Based on the number of people in line to pick up food, distribution must have been done on a weekly rather than daily basis.

I was amazed it was so crowded. People of all ages filled the room. The scant supplies were disappearing fast as volunteers worked frantically to keep the line moving. My eyes scanned the line. I could do something about this. I could make a difference in these peoples' lives. My eyes reached the front and homed in on an unexpected sight.

Gwen.

She must have driven straight here after I'd seen her earlier. I felt like shit for ignoring her the way I had, but that was the way it had to be from now on.

I couldn't take my eyes off her. She was radiant with her wavy blonde hair and a bright smile across her beautiful face. She worked quickly but made an effort to greet everyone before they left. She chatted and laughed with them. It was impossible to look away. She was breathtaking, and not just because of how amazing she looked, but because of the kindness and compassion on her face.

"Got a thing for Gwen, huh?" Jasper asked as he walked up beside me.

I looked down at my hands. I must have been staring longer than I'd realized. "No, of course not." The words flew out of my mouth a little too quickly.

"Yeah, right. I saw the way you two were eye-fucking each other after auditions." He hesitated a moment before continuing. "It was pretty obvious."

"You need to get your eyes checked."

"Dude, you've got it bad. You do have one little problem though."

"Yeah, and what's that?"

"I think she's got a boyfriend. He's a pretty decent guy, too. His name is Kyle Harper. They're almost always together." As soon as he said that name, a few missing pieces fell into place. It explained so much. "Also, in case you don't know, he plays the part of your best friend in my play."

"Sounds like pretty stiff competition."

"Yeah, I'd say so," Jasper agreed.

"Guess it's a good thing I'm not interested in Gwen then," I replied.

"Right." His sarcasm was too thick not to notice, but I decided to ignore it.

Gwen was officially off limits. Well, good for her, cause I wasn't interested anyway.

With a wave, I left Jasper and headed back to my car, deciding I needed some time alone.

∞∞∞∞∞∞

My memories of Eva had been visiting me every night, and last night had been no exception. Each dream was full of the yearning and desire of forbidden love.

My sweet Eva, how desperately I had wanted her. A love so innocent and pure and yet the cause of so much destruction. I never had so much as kissed her, and yet, the repercussions of our love sent shock waves through the multiverse.

If only things had been different. Before we'd met, Eva had fallen in love with another angel and performed the ceremony that would unite them forever. I hadn't known of her union, so after I dropped off my armor, I stopped by Farrar's shop every day with a different excuse to see her. I knew she enjoyed my visits. Her eyes sparkled every time I entered the shop. Each day I spent more and more time with her, determined to do things right. Even that beautiful day at the lake had been innocent. Each day we had together, our attraction grew stronger, and our skin shone with a golden glow that announced her betrayal to any who may have spied us together.

It didn't take long for someone to notice. Just weeks after our first meeting, Eva came to me. A huge grin spread across my face as I opened the door, then dropped the moment I took in her tearstained face.

She grabbed my hands and explained that she'd come with bad news. She informed me of her union with another then begged me to forgive her.

She no longer loved him. He was arrogant, took her for granted, and made her feel worthless. She pleaded with me to run away with her and professed her love for me with earnestness.

Pain crushed my chest as grief ripped my heart apart. I yearned to be with her. I wanted to forget all she'd told me and pretend it wasn't true.

But I couldn't do it, despite how I loved her. What she'd asked of me was wrong and selfish.

So I refused her.

Then, when I didn't think I could take any more, she destroyed my world.

She was pregnant with his child and didn't know what to do. She begged me to reconsider. Begged me to run away with her.

Though it almost killed me to do it, I sent her away. It was the hardest thing I'd ever done.

That day, someone must have seen her standing on my doorstep and noticed the golden glow of love radiating off our skin because the following day, my life changed forever.

I was in the courtyard of the palace when I saw my best friend approaching me. Between his responsibilities at the palace and mine on the battlefield, it had been over a hundred years since we'd last seen each other, and I had missed him.

Lew was my oldest and most trusted friend. If ever there were someone I could confide in about the turmoil in my heart, it was him. I was relieved to finally see him.

Something was wrong. The emotion evident on Lew's face was one I'd never seen before. In the following moments, I would find that the emotion I was viewing was rage. The moment he was within range, Lew's fist shot out to strike me squarely on the jaw, sending me flying and landing heavily on my back.

Here, my subconscious warped my memory. Instead of having the shit beat out of me by my former best friend, darkness swirled around me, and then my vision was filled with a close-up of Gwen's perfect face.

Her voice strained with urgency as she stared deeply into my eyes. "Alex, be careful, danger is coming."

"Alex," her voice echoed, "danger is coming!"

"Alex!"

I bolted out of bed.

What the hell?

∞∞∞∞∞∞

I loved my work. That was not something many people could honestly say, but I could. Well, maybe not what I was doing right now, which was working as the technical advisor for our newly acquired company, Mercury Technologies. Basically, I was nothing more than glorified tech support most of the time.

Eli Prescott may have founded Prescott Tech, but my research was behind all the cutting-edge technology the company developed. Every billion we'd acquired was a direct result of my work, and I couldn't even give them my best inventions. The most innovative technology in the world today, I'd designed centuries ago. My newest ideas were so many light years ahead of human technology that they'd be seen as witchcraft. But this job was my choice, just as Eli was my choice. I would do whatever it took to get the resources our people required back home. In just a few short years, we had acquired enough wealth to sustain us for the next century, and soon we would liquefy a majority of our assets and return home. All that was left was to aid Senator Kinsley in his re-election bid and in exchange obtain some much-needed help with U.S. Customs.

But the job I was doing now was pointless. The company didn't even need me at this point. We could pay someone to do the work I was doing.

Idiot, I thought to myself, *it was your idea, you're the one who said you were bored.* I decided I'd tell Eli to find a replacement for me when I got home.

The ten-minute ride to work flew by uneventfully. I parked the car, entered my building, and rode the elevator to the top floor.

"Mr. Prescott." Bonnie strutted over. "There's a problem at the

Atlanta office, they'll be expecting you in two hours. Oh, and your new assistant is here. She's waiting in your office."

"What's her name?"

No one told me I'd be getting an assistant. This would cause nothing but problems. The last thing I needed was another female in this office.

Not my problem, I reminded myself. Someone else would be doing this job soon enough.

"Gertrude...Gabby...I don't know, something Adams. She's in there waiting." She hesitated a moment, then fluttered her eyelashes at me. "Is there anything I can do for you before I leave for the day, Mr. Prescott? Anything at all? I really don't mind staying late," she finished, licking her bottom lip seductively.

I wanted to roll my eyes.

I didn't bother answering Bonnie. Seriously, how many times did I have to shoot her down before she'd give up? I wanted her out of my hair, but she was too good at her job for me to fire or transfer. I'd have to continue ignoring her advances. Hopefully, this Mrs. Adams would turn out to be a ninety-year-old prude with cataracts and a walker.

"Good afternoon, Mr. Prescott," Emily purred as I hurried past her desk.

"Good afternoon."

I increased my pace as I turned the corner and flung open the door to my office where I was greeted by a completely unexpected sight.

Holy shit.

Next to my desk, looking sexy as hell in a black pencil skirt, high heels, and sexy librarian-style glasses, sat none other than Gwen Adams.

Damn it. That last name, Adams, how had I not picked up on that? The stunned look on her beautiful face probably matched mine. She was the last person I had expected to see.

Why did she have to be here? What were the chances that she'd be the one they hired? I had to get the hell away from her. She was too much of a temptation.

But she probably needed this job.

Fuck.

I'd just have to keep my distance. I could do that without being a complete asshole to her, right?

She adjusted her clothing self-consciously. "W-What are you doing here?" she questioned, a confused look spread across her angelic face.

"The door does have my name on it, so what do you think I'm doing here?"

A fire flickered behind her eyes. "I don't know. As far as I can see, the only thing you're doing here is being an arrogant ass," she snapped.

Her cheeks instantly heated, and her eyes dropped to her hands. "Sorry," she muttered.

I ran a frustrated hand through my hair.

She was right. I was an asshole.

I glanced at my watch.

Unfortunately, I didn't have time to apologize. And besides, it was better if she hated me. It would make avoiding her so much easier.

But damn it, there was a part of me that didn't want to avoid her.

It pissed me off that I was struggling so much with something as trivial as physical attraction. I'd never been this...Hell, what was it?

Undisciplined?

Maybe. Whatever it was, I didn't like it.

"Grab your stuff. We'll be flying to Atlanta shortly."

I turned and walked out the office, glancing over my shoulder to make sure she was following. I passed the elevator and headed straight to the stairway where I held the door for her and noticed the confused expression on her face. I led us up the last set of stairs to the roof.

"We're taking a helicopter to Atlanta?"

"No, we're taking a helicopter to a private airport, then boarding a jet to Atlanta."

I walked her over to the chopper and opened the door. The step was low, and she didn't need my help. Hell, a blind cripple could have boarded this thing alone, but even so, before she could get in, I wrapped my hands around her waist and lifted her up.

Fuck, I needed to keep my damn hands to myself.

"Grab that handhold to your right," I told her as I lifted her petite body up into the helicopter. She stumbled and fell into her seat. I hopped in immediately after her and strapped her in.

"Where's the pilot?"

"You're looking at him," I answered tersely, doing my best to limit our interaction and focus on anything but her.

CHAPTER NINE

Gwen

After listening to the engineers in the Atlanta office, it was evident there was a serious problem. The technical details were beyond me - over my head by a mile, actually. But Alexander listened patiently and asked a few questions.

Did he know enough to ask the questions properly? Did he even understand what was going on?

I assumed Alexander was given his position because his father owned the company. I would never have guessed someone my age could attain the level of expertise that he exhibited. Within minutes, he responded with a coherent solution, then drew up detailed schematics by hand for the project engineers, leaving the engineers and myself astonished. As Alexander explained, they nodded thoughtfully, occasionally asked questions, then shook their heads in amazement at his answers. The man was absolutely brilliant. I couldn't help but wonder why he was attending a community college in Verona Beach. From the looks on the engineers' faces, he should be teaching at VBCC, or more likely, at one of the more prestigious engineering universities.

My mind wandered back to earlier this evening. Talk about a shocker. When Alexander had strutted through that office door in a sleek black suit, he'd looked more like a male model off a Paris runway than a technical advisor.

Then he'd turned into a complete asshole. How was I supposed to know it was his office? The daytime secretary had led me there and told me to wait. She'd completely ignored my questions and hadn't bothered to tell me anything. It was only natural I'd be completely caught off guard when he showed up.

I rolled my eyes to the ceiling. Of all the people in Verona Beach, what were the chances I'd end up working with him?

For a moment, I entertained the idea that my father hadn't gotten me this job. Maybe Alexander had. Maybe he'd wanted an excuse to spend time with me.

Yeah, right.

Alexander hadn't known I was looking for a job. He hadn't known me when I'd interviewed. Besides, the shocked look on his face when he'd entered the office told me everything I needed to know. If Alexander had wanted to spend time with me, he must have suddenly changed his mind.

I gazed across the room. Alexander was immersed in conversation. His muscular frame was bent over the table as he explained the new plans. Black hair fell across his eyes. His sensual lips curved into a smile as the engineers finally understood his design.

I absently nibbled on my lower lip as I watched him. Jerk or not, it was impossible not to admire his handsome profile.

As if he'd heard my thoughts, Alexander turned and met my gaze across the room. His expression was unreadable, but his eyes blazed with fire.

My heartbeat quickened.

Was it anger or something else? Had I done something wrong?

His strange mood swings made me uneasy. I didn't know where I stood with him. Frustration, anger, and worry swirled around my insides, but beneath it all was a simmering desire.

I ripped my gaze from his and busied my hands in my purse.

How was it he could still do that to me? Even cold and uncaring as he'd been, he still got me flustered. God, I'm so screwed in the head.

I pulled out my notepad and started taking notes, determined to distract myself. Instead of trying to figure out what they were talking about, I kept a running log of who Alexander spoke with and any specifics I was quick enough to pick up. In all honesty, I didn't think anything I did was of value, but at least I had something to show for those few hours.

Shortly after midnight, we started the silent flight back. The entire evening had been awkward, and I couldn't wait to get home.

Frankly, I couldn't wait to be in the company of someone who actually wanted to be around me. I'd never felt so unwelcome in my life. Alexander hadn't been cruel; he just gave off this really cold vibe like he wished I'd crawl off and disappear.

Well, screw him. I'd rather spend time with my cat than his frigid ass.

I lifted Spyder from the floor and got into bed. His furry little body squirmed and wiggled until he found the perfect spot. I quickly fell asleep to the soft sound of Spyder's purring.

∞∞∞∞∞∞

Three days had passed since my first day at work, and I still bristled when I thought about how rude Alexander had been to me.

I was just glad it was the weekend, and I didn't have to go to work.

I took a deep breath and attempted to forget Alexander and enjoy the evening.

I watched as the sun dipped under the horizon, its fiery orange rays fading to blue as the vibrant neon lights of the fair flickered to life around us.

I shivered.

Ky shrugged off his jacket. "Here, put this on."

I slipped my arms into the sleeves. The heat from his body

saturated the jacket and brought me instant relief. I snuggled in, loving the combination of warmth and Ky's woodsy cologne that engulfed me.

A sharp whip of wind blew me forward a step, my feet faltered, and I stumbled onto one knee.

"Come here." Ky pulled me up and put his arm around my waist.

Before Beverly's revelations, I would have thought nothing of it. But now, with his arm wrapped around me protectively, I felt confused. I'd never had these feeling for Ky. Never let myself. But as warm waves of attraction crashed over me, I felt the underlying anxiety bubble to the surface.

I shifted uncomfortably.

"What were you thinking dressing like that?" He nodded at the tank top and shorts I wore.

"I was thinking that I don't watch the news and had no clue it would drop twenty degrees in under an hour."

Ky rolled his eyes. His arm tightened around me and he leaned over and kissed the tip of my nose. "What am I going to do with you?"

My heart rate skyrocketed. This was much too intimate.

I wasn't sure how I felt about this new development, so I deflected. A grin spread across my face as the idea occurred to me. "You could race me."

He raised an eyebrow but remained silent.

"You know, on the go-carts!" I saw the grimace on his face before I'd even finished my sentence.

"That's not a good idea, Gwen. You're already freezing, do you want to catch a cold? Why don't we ride the Ferris wheel instead?"

I shook my head. I'd come to the fair for the excitement and adrenaline rush. I didn't want to ride the Ferris wheel. I didn't even like the Ferris wheel, but there was no point in arguing with Ky. His mind was made up, and no amount of pleading would change it. I tried to squelch the growing resentment in my chest. I told myself I should be grateful he cared enough to look out for me. Maybe I needed to be more responsible, like Ky.

I glanced up at Ky's face. I could immediately tell that he'd caught my expression.

"I'm sorry. You know I just don't want you to get sick, right? I'm not trying to tell you what to do or anything. Under other circumstances, I'd do whatever you wanted. I'd follow you to the moon if you asked," he paused and smiled. "But you're already shivering. The last thing you need is to be racing around in the cold wind."

"I know." It was the only reply he'd be getting. I couldn't help it. The rebellious spirit I'd had since childhood was rearing its ugly head. Regardless of his intentions, I didn't want to be treated like a child. I could make my own decisions.

"You ride the Ferris wheel. I'll ride the go-carts by myself." I maneuvered out of his grip and walked away.

"Gwen, you're being childish."

Childish?

I whirled around to face him. My unjustified anger got the best of me. "I'd rather be childish than resign myself to an early grave. We're in our twenties for God's sake, but you act as if we should be on social security. I don't want that. I want to be young. I want to enjoy life. So what if I'm cold? So what if I get sick? The sniffles aren't going to kill me. But going through life by always taking the safe route, always holding back and being so damn gentle all the time, that's not living. Damn it, you don't have to handle me with kid gloves all the time. That's what's killing me."

Oh hell. We even sounded like a couple. How had I missed this? The dinners, the movie dates, hanging out at my house, just the two of us. Despite the lack of intimacy, we were basically a couple.

Ky's face became incredulous. "I'm killing you?" He paused and rubbed his hand roughly down his face. He shoved his hands in his pockets and paced in a small circle once before finally meeting my eyes. "I'm killing you?" he repeated, anger seeping into his voice. "You are killing me!"

I was shocked into silence.

Not noticing the surprised expression on my face, he continued, "Let's pretend for a moment that I actually believe this bullshit. First of all, where I come from, gentle is how you treat a woman. Especially the one you care about. You cherish her, protect her, take care of her. What do you want from me? Do you expect me to abuse you or take you for granted like all the other assholes out there?" He took a deep breath. "I have been patient. I have been there for you every minute you've ever needed me. I fucking love-" His mouth snapped shut. His chest rose and fell as he fought for control.

"I know all about your past with Wesley. So I've been patient and tried to take things slow with you. And just when things seemed to be moving forward between us, that rich bastard shows up."

How did Ky know about Wesley? That was years ago. Beverly couldn't have told him. She wouldn't break my confidence like that. God, just hearing Wesley's name put a stake through my heart. The guilt and heartbreak I'd been ignoring for years came back full force.

"I don't get it. He's constantly back and forth between you and Hannah. And both of you eat it up like he's some kind of god or something. What is it? Is it the money?"

I could barely hear him anymore. A single tear slid down my cheek. Everything about that night with Wesley came flooding back. The cold rain soaking through my clothes. The fear and utter helplessness of being trapped. The loud crunch of metal crashing around me. The flashes of crimson splashed everywhere. It was too much to bear.

Silent tears spilled down like rain across my cheeks and over my lips.

Ky stared up at the sky, unaware of my inner turmoil. "I feel like I'm losing you. And I don't even really have you yet."

Ky finally looked down at me. His sorrowful eyes took in my

tear-stained face and misunderstood.

I didn't see it coming. One moment we had been talking, and the next Ky had pulled me into a warm embrace. His soft lips pressed against mine, his large calloused hands cradled my face, and the hard length of his torso flattened against me. He kissed me with a skill I hadn't known existed. My earlier pain was forgotten, and all I could feel was the intense passion coming from his lips.

His hands slid to my waist as he deepened the kiss. When his lips lowered from mine, lacing soft kisses down my neck, I returned to my senses.

The moment Ky looked into my eyes, he knew. "I made a mistake kissing you, didn't I?"

How do I answer that? I didn't even know myself.

"Yeah, it was a mistake." Ky nodded to himself.

"No, it's just-"

"It was a mistake doing it tonight because you haven't quite figured it out yet."

"Figured out what?" I mumbled.

"You haven't figured out how much you care about me. That you're in love with me but aren't ready to admit it," he paused, making eye contact, "yet."

His eyes pierced mine with a cold determination.

"Gwen, you've got to get the idea of Alexander out of your head. He's not a good guy. You'll figure that out soon enough." He paused and extended his hand to me. "Until then, we've got some go-carts to ride."

I wiped the tears from my cheeks and grabbed his hand, thankful for the change of subject. "Really?"

"Yep. I learned recently that sniffles aren't fatal. Who knew?" Ky shrugged his shoulders nonchalantly.

A boyish smile spread across Ky's handsome face, and his eyes lit with mischief. A familiar warmth filled my chest as I admired the wonderful man before me. Ky was so good to me. He was hardworking, kind, and loyal. He radiated everything that was good in the world.

And he wanted me.

It was then, under the moonlit sky and sparkling lights, with the man who would always be there for me, that my heart finally began to thaw.

"Ky?"

I stepped slowly toward him, watched as his smile faded and his eyes trailed over my face.

He dipped his chin as he towered over me. His broad chest brushed mine with every shaky breath. Confusion mixed with barely restrained desire as his eyes lowered to my lips.

"What is it, Gwen?" His words were soft and hesitant.

I slid my hands up his warm, muscled chest, and caressed his face.

"Ky," I whispered. "It wasn't a mistake."

Powerful emotions flashed through Ky's eyes as he gazed down at me.

With slow, deliberate movements, his right hand cupped my jaw as his left wrapped around me in a tender embrace.

My breathing hitched as Ky's soft lips lowered to mine.

Deliberately slow, drugging kisses weakened my knees. His lips seduced me with soft, sweet caresses. Desire flooded my body as the sweetness of his kiss heated and elicited a yearning deep inside me.

I moaned, and his grip tightened in response. His hand slid to the back of my neck, holding me possessively as he parted my lips and tortured me with the toe-curling strokes of his tongue.

I couldn't breathe. I couldn't think as the world tilted around us.

He pulled back and rested his forehead on mine as he held me in his arms.

Then, under the star-filled sky, with his adoring eyes staring into mine, he whispered, "I love you, Gwen."

∞∞∞∞∞∞

"Earth to Gwen."

My eyes darted to Beverly's, and my shoulders slumped. I had been caught daydreaming again.

"Damn, girl. Where are you, in la la land?" She grinned.

I looked at my notebook.

"It's blank," Beverly stated blandly. "Nothing on the page. Now, tell me what's going through your head."

I glanced at Hannah, who was silently filing her nails.

"I was thinking about Ky."

Hannah's hands froze.

"Well, how's it going? I saw you two at the movies on Friday night. You looked pretty cozy."

I shifted uncomfortably in my seat and glanced toward Hannah meaningfully. Why was Beverly doing this with her here? Especially with what she knew about Hannah and Ky's past. Hannah may have been a bitch most of the time, but rubbing our relationship in her face wasn't right.

"I'm going to touch up my makeup." Hannah shot out of her seat and stomped away.

"What the hell, Beverly?"

"She needs to get over herself. She gave Ky up years ago, and it's not like she even wants to take him back. Besides, she went out with two different guys last weekend and slept with both of them. I hardly think she's worried about Ky."

That didn't sound like Hannah. Yeah, she was something of an attention whore, but she never slept around.

"That doesn't sound like her. Are you sure?"

"She told me so herself. Hell, she even seemed proud of it."

"Maybe I should talk to her-"

"Gwen, that's not a good idea. You're not exactly her favorite person right now."

Well, that was true. I was the last person she'd open up to. But why would she be fooling around with other guys if...

"What about Alexander? They never got together?"

Beverly eyed me suspiciously. "They've been out a few times. But as far as I know, they're not a couple."

My shoulders relaxed.

Why was I suddenly relieved? I didn't want anything to do with Alexander. He'd been nothing but rude to me the last few weeks, like the way he'd stormed out of the office in the middle of our conversation yesterday. Or how he'd jumped back and looked at me in disgust when my arm brushed his while I was filing paperwork. All of that unjustified animosity had me wondering what had attracted me in the first place.

But then images of his smoldering eyes and ridiculously hot body flashed through my mind. Yeah, I knew what attracted me.

"So, tell me about Ky." Beverly leaned forward. "Have you two, you know?"

"What?"

Beverly rolled her eyes. "Had sex?"

I almost choked on my gum. "*No.* What is wrong with you? It's only been a few weeks."

"Yeah, but you've been friends for almost two years, so it's not like you've got to get to know him first. You're already so close. What's the problem?"

I lowered my voice. "There's no problem."

Beverly closed her eyes. "Damn, he is hot. You're seriously not going to tell me?"

"We haven't done anything," I replied emphatically, then ran a hand through my hair before continuing. "Not that he hasn't tried."

"What?" Her eyes flashed open. "So why hasn't he succeeded? I mean, damn, girl, just look at him. Why would you ever turn him down?"

I shrugged. "I don't know. I just can't do it."

Beverly's tone became harsh. "It's not those archaic beliefs of yours, is it?"

"No."

Her tone softened. "Is it because of Wesley?"

"I don't know. Maybe. But Ky keeps trying, and I don't know what to tell him. In one breath, he says he'll be patient, then in the next, I've got this guilt trip put on me." I paused a moment to catch my breath. "I take that back. He's not trying to make me feel guilty. I'm doing that to myself. But either way, it's stressful."

"I'm sorry. I don't know what to tell you, girl."

"It'll be okay. I can't be the only twenty-two-year-old virgin out there. Right?"

Beverly didn't even bother answering that one.

CHAPTER TEN
Gwen

This is not how I planned on spending my weekend. I watched the countryside fly by even though I was supposed to be at a beach party with Ky.

"Where are we going?"

"Miami." Alexander's answer was curt, polite, and completely emotionless. The same tone in which he'd talked to me all morning.

"I know that," I snapped. "I mean, what facility? And what will I be doing?"

"It's our microprocessor plant, and I won't know what I need you for until we get there."

Stupid jerk.

I rolled my eyes and wondered what I'd done to piss him off this time.

I lifted my drink to my lips and resigned myself to staring out the window for the rest of the trip.

By the time we reached the Miami plant, I was sure something was wrong. Not once in the remaining six-hour drive did Alexander speak to me. He hadn't even looked in my direction. It appeared that Mr. Pissy Pants had woken up on the wrong side of the bed.

Alexander deftly parked the car, then reached behind my seat to grab his briefcase. "Let's go."

He got out and slammed the door behind him. I grabbed my bag, swung the door open, and almost fell out of the car trying to catch up. His long strides had me scrambling to keep pace. When we finally reached the conference room, I was out of breath, and my feet were killing me.

We were greeted by a handsome older man with a deep tan and a Hispanic accent. He shook Alexander's hand and nodded respectfully toward me. "Mr. Prescott, my name is Calderon Garcia, but please call me Cal."

"Mr. Prescott is my father's name." He nodded politely. "My friends call me Alex."

Well, wasn't that interesting? He'd never mentioned that to me.

Alexander turned as if to take a seat when Cal spoke again.

"Alex, who is this lovely young woman?" Cal inquired.

"That's my assistant. She'll be taking notes of our meeting."

Cal cleared his throat. Apparently, I hadn't been the only one to think Alexander's comment was rude.

Alexander shook his head. "It's been a long drive. I didn't mean to offend."

If Cal had noticed Alexander's apology was directed at him and not me, he didn't show it. But then again, Alexander was the boss. A pretty intimidating one at that. Gone was the carefree guy from the beach. The man in front of me today was a cold, driven asshole.

I extended my hand and winked. "My name is Gwendolen Josephina Adams. But my friends call me Gwen."

Cal laughed and shook my hand.

Alexander scowled.

Cal's smile widened. "Sassy. Gotta love that in a woman."

Cal offered me his arm and led me toward the facilities while Alexander followed closely behind.

"Gwen, let me tell you about why you're here today. It seems we've had a series of security breaches. We didn't notice the breach until yesterday morning. Our senior IT tech decided to run diagnostic scans on all our operating software even though they weren't scheduled. These particular scans are only performed once every twenty-four months because they stop production for a minimum of thirty minutes. However, we had a small electrical fire that shut us down, and it was only two months till the next scan, so Mike decided to run the tests early. It's a good thing he did because the scans found something. Someone infiltrated our security system and input tiny flaws into multiple systems throughout the plant. It would have been a catastrophe. Every single processor would have been corrupted, and we wouldn't have had a clue until people bought and used them. Our stock price would have dropped like a rock, and we'd all be out of jobs." Cal glanced back at Alexander. "That's why we need your help. We can't figure out how it was done, or who did it."

Alexander nodded. "Where do you keep your servers?"

"In the Service Annex. Follow me."

Cal lead us around the facility, pointing out different buildings and equipment and explaining their uses. He kept his arm out for me and led me around like a gentleman. It was something no one had ever done for me. I didn't know how to feel about it. Part of me thought I should be offended, the other part felt honored to be treated with such respect.

I glanced back to find Alexander glaring at me. His eyes burned into mine. What was his problem? His unwarranted dislike of me was really pissing me off.

We walked into a small building and down to the end of a long corridor. Cal swiped his badge through a scanner, and the thick glass door slid open. Without speaking, Alexander headed to a terminal and began flipping switches.

"Alex, will you need Ms. Gwen for anything?"

Alexander glanced up from his work, confusion written all over his face. "Why?"

"I figured if she weren't needed, I'd keep her company. Maybe show her more of the facility."

"No. I need her here. You can get back to work now, Cal. I've got this."

Cal looked at me with an apologetic smile and held out his hand. "It was very nice to meet you, Gwen."

"You too, Cal."

We shook hands, then Cal silently left the room.

The whirl of the server fans and the occasional electronic beep were the only noises filling the silence. I glanced at my phone. One o'clock. What exactly was I doing here? Alexander was steadily clicking away at one of the dozen or so computer keyboards in the room while I had absolutely zilch to do.

"Is there anything I can help you with? I don't mind."

"Just sit there. When I need help, I'll ask for it."

I slammed my purse onto the table.

Stupid, impossible jerk. Why did he have to be like that?

I huffed and dropped into a nearby chair.

I opened my laptop to do some research. The least I could do was learn a little more about the company I worked for. I opened a browser and began a search on both Mercury Technologies and Prescott Tech manufacturing divisions. Within moments, I was inundated with results. The two companies had facilities in almost every major nation of the world. The amount of capital held by Prescott Tech alone was obscene.

I stared at the numbers.

Holy shit. When Beverly had said the Prescotts were rich, I hadn't realized the extent of it. These people could quite literally buy their own country and then fund it themselves for many years. How in the world did one company amass that kind of wealth?

I glanced at Alexander as he typed furiously into a terminal. It amazed me that this man had that level of power in this world. Yeah, he had nice clothes, fancy cars, a helicopter, and probably servants to boot. But despite all the trappings, he seemed like a normal guy.

Brilliant, but normal.

And a complete pain in the ass, I reminded myself as I glanced at my watch.

Four hours had already flown by.

I looked back at Alexander. He was putting some equipment into his briefcase and seemed to be cleaning up.

"Are you done?" I asked, praying he'd say yes.

"Yeah. I just finished up. Get your stuff, and let's go."

Not wanting to argue, I did just that. I threw my laptop into my bag and scrambled to my feet. "I'm ready."

I thought I saw the faint hint of a smile before it disappeared. "Come on."

In fashion with the rest of our day, we returned to the car in silence.

If the drive down had been bad, the drive back was miserable. We had gotten only five miles down the road when we were hit with a torrential downpour that forced us from a happy eighty mph to a sluggish thirty-five. Things only got worse when we exited the interstate and found ourselves on the back roads. The sun was almost on the horizon, but the sky was already dark and gloomy. Rain poured onto the windshield in sheets. The *thwack-thwack-thwack* of the windshield wipers and the loud beating of the rain roared in my ears.

There was nothing to do but think, and all I could think about was what had changed between us. There had been a time that I had thought Alexander liked me. He had been charming, flirty, and kind. But now my presence clearly irritated him. He couldn't stand to be near me. He constantly snapped at me. And yet, he'd insisted I come with him today, even though he sure as hell hadn't needed me here.

I didn't understand.

"Alex-"

The car suddenly fishtailed and slid across the slick asphalt, drifting uncontrollably to the left.

Fear gripped my throat, and my heart raced.

The next few moments were a blur.

Lightning crackled across the sky, illuminating Alexander's clenched jaw as he jerked the wheel in the direction of our spin.

The car jolted harshly to the right as the tires regained traction just a second too late. A massive tree rushed toward us. The impact was unavoidable.

A loud boom sounded as I was flung forward in my seat. My head whipped forward, then slammed back into the headrest.

Lightning flashed across the sky and blinded me. In a moment, everything was gone. Alexander had disappeared, and in his place, crimson streaks were splashed across the car's interior. Blood poured down my hand, off my fingertips, and into a puddle beneath me.

I was dying.

Oh, my God.

I was going to die here.

I couldn't contain the horror as a terrified scream built up in my throat.

It was then, in my panicked state, that I glanced over to where his lifeless body lay. His blonde hair was matted with blood that had already begun to dry. His arm was torn and ripped from its socket.

No.

This couldn't be happening. He couldn't be dead. He just couldn't be.

I reached for him, hoping if I could just shake him, he'd wake up. He couldn't be gone. I loved him too much. The scream I'd been holding back felt like it would burst through my chest when his brown eyes flipped open.

"It's your fault, Gwen."

Another bolt of lightning flashed brightly across the sky, followed instantly by a loud boom that shook the car.

Alexander sat looking at me strangely.

"Are you okay?"

Confused, I patted my trembling hands over my arms and wrists, which were definitely not bleeding.

I could barely think past the loud beating in my chest, but managed a shaky, "Yeah, I'm fine."

"There's no cellphone signal here. The nearest town is a little over ten miles away. Wait here. I'll be back with a tow truck." Before I could argue, he jumped out of the car and walked away.

No, no, no, no.

I leapt out of the car, not caring one bit about the rain that instantly soaked through my clothing. "I'm coming with you."

"Like hell you are. Get back in the car," he replied with an air of authority I'd never heard from him.

There was no chance in hell I was getting back in that car.

"No."

"Damn it, Gwen. It's dangerous out here. Get in the car. Hopefully, I'll come across a house, and someone will give me a ride to town. You won't be out here long, I'm sure of it."

His reassurances did nothing for me. I didn't care if it was ten hours or ten minutes. I couldn't stay here by myself, not after the flashback I'd just had.

"No. I'm going with you."

His stubborn gaze bore into mine, studying my determination. The haunting blue of his irises glowed against the dreary backdrop.

"Fine. Suit yourself." Then he walked away from me like I wasn't even there.

Only three steps into our ten-mile hike, I realized what a horrible mistake I'd made. I couldn't go back to the car, but with every single soggy step, my heels sunk into the ground.

The sun had finally set, and the only lights illuminating the endless forest were the constant flashes of lightning that blazed across the sky. I trudged along, keeping a good five paces behind the moody Alexander and doing my best to avoid the ever-growing puddles. Water streamed down my face and into my stinging eyes. Every minute it got harder and harder to see, but I had to keep going.

I knew I should try to distract myself from my current misery, but the farther we trekked, the angrier I felt until I just couldn't ignore it anymore.

"What the hell have I done to piss you off so badly?"

He kept walking, for all the world as if I hadn't spoken.

"Alexander!"

Again, he ignored me.

"Damn it, why won't you look at me?"

He didn't turn, but his booming voice lashed out at me. "Because I can see through your fucking shirt, Gwen."

I glanced down at my drenched white blouse just as lightning flashed. Sure enough, my lace bra wasn't the only thing clearly visible through the fabric. Oh, my God. I quickly wrapped my arms across my chest.

Heat burned my cheeks as I realized how I must have looked, alongside the fact that he couldn't stand to look at me. He wasn't being a gentleman – if that were the case, he wouldn't be so angry about it. Apparently, my barely covered chest offended him.

"Why are you being so mean?" I knew it was childish, but I couldn't help it.

He followed the road to the left. The rain beat down on his proud shoulders as he walked away from me.

I stomped through the sludge intent on grabbing his arm when my shoe sunk lower into the ground than I expected. A sharp pain shot up my leg as my ankle rolled. My body twisted as it fell, and a pair of bright headlights drifted into my field of vision, not six feet from my face.

Strong hands gripped my waist and flung me toward the grass. Time slowed as I drifted toward the ground.

I watched in horror as Alexander's body shifted directly in front of the oncoming car.

No!

The loud impact of the vehicle slamming into his body, the graphic crunching of bone, and the whine of skidding tires never came. The car floated through him like an apparition.

What the-

Bam!

An explosion went off inside my head as I slammed into the ground. Everything went white for a moment before complete darkness enveloped me.

∞∞∞∞∞∞

I groaned as I laid face down in the mud.

"Gwen?"

Alexander rushed to my side. He rolled me onto my back and ran his hands slowly down the back of my neck. He then grasped my arm with his warm hands and slid them toward my wrists.

Mmm, this feels nice.

My foggy thoughts tried to make sense of Alexander's actions. His hands glided smoothly over my skin. It was just a whisper of a caress and such an odd thing to do, but-

Wait a minute, he was checking to make sure I hadn't broken anything.

I could feel myself blushing. Here I was, thinking how sweet it was he was trying to comfort me, and he was just trying to make sure I hadn't broken my neck. I was such an idiot.

He made the same circuit down my other arm, then both my legs down to my knees. He put one hand on my face and stared into my eyes. For the first time that day, his eyes were warm and caring.

I winced.

The pain throbbing in my head was almost worth it, just to have him looking at me like that again.

"God, Gwen," he paused, his thumb gingerly brushing across my cheekbone. "Are you okay?"

Am I okay?

I was speechless. His thumb brushed lazily back and forth across my cheek. My eyes lowered to his lips. A single raindrop slid across his broad cheek and dropped to my mouth.

Intensity flared behind his eyes as he lowered his lips toward mine.

A loud roar followed by the spray of water against his back broke the moment as a car sped by. Alexander searched my face, then he bent over and pressed his lips to my forehead.

"Damn. That was probably our only ride to town."

I pushed myself onto my elbows and groaned from the strain.

We sat side by side in silence as the rain continued to pour. The lightning had let up some, but that just meant it was almost impossible to see anything.

It didn't take long to realize the pain radiating behind my eyes had quickly dissipated. I could barely make out Alexander's profile in the darkness, just the blurry outline of his stiff posture as he stared ahead.

I almost didn't hear him when he murmured, "I'm not angry."

"What?"

"I'm not angry at you. I just can't be around you." He lowered his head between his knees.

I pushed myself up and tried to digest what I'd just heard. "Wha-"

"We need to go." He stood and pulled his shirt over his head. "Here," he said, shoving his soggy shirt in my direction.

I struggled to pull the clingy fabric over my head but managed after a few embarrassing moments.

Alexander grabbed my hand and pulled me upright.

I hissed.

"What's wrong?"

"It's my ankle. I twisted it when I fell." I leaned on my left foot.

"Can you walk on it?"

I shifted my weight and gritted my teeth. "No."

I closed my eyes as I breathed in pants.

My eyes flew open in panic as my legs were suddenly swept out from under me.

Alexander held me with one arm under my legs, the other around my waist. "Put your arms around my neck."

I stared at him in shock.

"Just do it."

I did as he asked, but I knew he wouldn't be able to carry me the remaining six miles to town.

It finally hit me just how bad our situation was.

"Unless somebody stops, we're in pretty bad trouble here, aren't we?"

"We'll be fine. Just lay your head down and go to sleep."

"Go to sleep? Are you crazy?" I looked around incredulously at the shit storm around us. "You expect me to sleep through the thunder and lightning, the pouring rain, and the insane temperature drop? Not possible. Besides, there's no way you'll be able to carry me the whole way to town. We're screwed."

"We are not screwed. You'll be fine, just close your eyes. And trust me when I say I could carry you a lot further than six miles if I needed to, so stop worrying."

I closed my eyes and laid my face against his warm neck. His whole body was warm. I shuddered as the heat soaked into my freezing limbs. I snuggled into him. The heat was wonderful. I hadn't realized how cold I'd gotten until that moment as warmth radiated off his bare skin.

The heat and the steady swaying from his smooth strides relaxed me. A strange peacefulness washed over me even as the rain streamed down my face. My eyes fluttered closed, plunging me into darkness as I was slowly rocked to sleep.

A flash of memory jolted me, and my eyes flew open.

"Alexander?"

"Yeah." His voice vibrated through my body.

"What happened back there?"

"What do you mean?"

"I know this is going to sound crazy, but I swear that car was going to hit you."

"Guess I'm lucky it didn't then."

I was almost afraid to say the next words, but I had to. "It did hit you. I mean, I saw you and the car in the same space. How is that possible?"

He laughed. "You're joking, right?"

"No. I know what I saw, even if it's impossible. I saw that car drive right through you."

"Gwen, the car missed me. It was a close call, but as you said, what you saw was impossible. And don't forget, you hit your head pretty hard, that kind of thing can affect your memory."

How had I forgotten that? He was exactly right. I had hit my head pretty hard.

"You're right. Now I really feel like an idiot."

"Don't. As soon as we get back, we'll get you to the hospital for a check-up."

I didn't want to argue, but there was no way I'd be going to the hospital. For what, a twisted ankle? My head didn't even hurt anymore, so I doubted there was any damage.

I closed my eyes and quickly fell asleep.

∞∞∞∞∞∞

I woke a few hours later on the passenger side of a pickup truck. Rain pelted the windshield, and lightning streaked intermittently across the sky.

I let my eyes glide over Alexander. He was wearing a t-shirt that obviously was not his own. It was a size too small and had an enormous smiley face on it. I grinned. He looked like the Hulk on the verge of busting out of his shirt. I held in the sigh that almost escaped my lips. Damn, he was gorgeous.

Gorgeous and confusing as hell.

My mind raced over the events of the day as I tried to make sense of it all. He'd been a real jerk to me, no surprise there. But then he'd taken care of me. He'd caressed my face and carried me through the rain.

What had he meant when he'd said he couldn't be around me? Was it because he wanted to be around me and couldn't? Or that I just annoyed him so much that he couldn't stand it?

I shook my head.

The truth was none of that mattered. I was in a relationship with Ky, so regardless of how tempted I was by Alexander, I couldn't act on it. Maybe that was what Alexander had meant in saying he couldn't be around me. Maybe he knew I had a boyfriend and hadn't wanted to encourage the crush I obviously had on him.

How embarrassing.

My thoughts wandered to the accident and the car I'd seen drive through Alexander. My mind replayed it in slow motion. Alexander's face hadn't shown a moment of fear. Not one moment. It was as if the car hadn't existed to him. As if he were a ghost. The car had flown right through him, and damn it, it had seemed so real. So incredibly tangible. How could it possibly have been my imagination?

CHAPTER ELEVEN
Alexander

"Who is going to be there?" Hannah asked as she twirled her hair around her finger and stared out the passenger side window.

"My dad and stepmother. And my brother, Zane. It's pretty rare when everyone's home. It's a miracle you'll get to meet them all at the same time."

I watched her fidget with her hair.

"You've got nothing to worry about. They're going to love you," I assured her, although if I were perfectly honest, I wasn't so sure.

An image of Gwen's radiant face the day I'd seen her at the church popped into my mind. There was no doubt my family would have fallen in love with Gwen immediately. I shook the traitorous image from my head.

Was this happening too soon? Was it a mistake? I should have waited a few weeks, taken the time to get to know Hannah better and made sure we were compatible before introducing her to my family. But I had gotten impatient.

Damn it. I ran a hand through my hair. I'd never felt this way before. When it came to my love life, I never worried what my family thought. I did whatever I wanted, and they'd always supported me. So why did I care so much now? Could it have been because all my past relationships hadn't meant anything? They'd been just poor attempts at escaping loneliness. I hadn't loved any of them, so I hadn't cared if my family loved them either.

Hell, I wasn't in love with Hannah, either. But I did care about her.

I thought about Zane. If he would only keep his mouth shut and his opinions to himself, this might not end in complete disaster. Eli and Ariel would be polite regardless of their views. But Zane...if he didn't like Hannah, he would say so, and from what I knew of Hannah, it would cause a major scene.

"I'm not nervous." Hannah lowered the visor and checked her makeup in the mirror. She pursed her lips, blowing an air kiss to herself, then smiled at her reflection.

I should have taken her out to a restaurant for dinner.

Hannah's gaze swept over my face. "What is it?"

"Nothing," I lied. "I just remembered something I need to take care of at work. Everything's going to be fine, stop worrying."

"I'm not worried, silly. You were right. Of course, they'll like me." She smiled her biggest smile, that genuine smile of hers that was as rare as it was beautiful. I loved seeing the way it lit up her face and brightened her eyes.

I slid my hand over her knee and attempted to focus on the road as Hannah chattered excitedly.

"I read Eli started Prescott Tech a few years ago, but what did he do before that? I couldn't find anything on the internet."

"You wouldn't find anything on the web because we were pretty boring back then. Just your average middle-class family. He worked as a junior advisor for a small tech company. He used to come home every night and fool around in the garage with his inventions until one day he had a great idea. So he got a few loans and started his own company. Obviously, business went well, and here we are today," I finished, hoping my lie was sufficient.

"What is your family like?"

"My brother is a few years older than me, but we are almost

identical." Her eyes lit up at that, and I almost laughed. "But, he's... how should I say it? He's kind of a player. He's a great brother, though, always has my back. Dad is a workaholic, but when he's not working, he's very family oriented. He's a very loyal and responsible man. Ariel, my stepmother, she's basically the heart of the family. She loves everybody and always tries to see the good in them. She recently started a local charity in town for the homeless-"

"I feed the ducks at my family's farm," Hannah's excited voice drowned out my own. "My grandparents have a farm about five hours north of here. Whenever I visit, I help take care of the animals."

"Really?" I smiled as I tried to imagine Hannah feeling at home around a bunch of farm animals.

She nodded.

"What kind of farm is it?"

"It's a pecan and peach tree farm."

My eyebrows furrowed while I tried to figure that one out. "So... what animals were you talking about?"

"My grandma's Chihuahua. And the ducks at the pond."

I couldn't stop the laughter that burst from my lips. Oh my God, this woman was something else.

She crossed her arms defensively across her chest. "What?"

"I'm not making fun of you, I swear. I just thought when you said you 'take care of the animals' that you were referring to cows and chickens." I laughed. "I couldn't imagine you running around in the mud with your heels and designer clothes. A Chihuahua makes so much more sense."

Her blank expression almost caused me to laugh again, but I held it in. "Come on. You've got to admit it's kind of funny."

Her face softened, and she forced a smile. "Okay, maybe a little." Hannah tapped her manicured nails across the dashboard as I pulled up my driveway. I parked her car, then got out to open her door.

"Thank you," she smiled up at me and leaned in close, her eyes closing as I realized she was expecting me to kiss her. My gaze swept over her flawless face and soft lips. Part of me wanted to lean down and press my lips to hers. But for reasons I couldn't fully explain, it just didn't feel right. Maybe it was too soon. Maybe I was the one nervous about this introduction.

It shouldn't have mattered. It wouldn't hurt anyone if I kissed her. Besides, if I didn't, I knew her feelings would be hurt.

But I couldn't. No matter how hard I tried, I just couldn't force my lips to hers.

What was wrong with me? I bent over and kissed her forehead.

"Come on." I smiled as I gazed into her confused eyes. "You ready to meet my family?"

She nodded. I took her hand and led her into the house and back toward the kitchen where I heard Ariel and Eli talking.

Eli's eyes widened as Hannah entered the room.

"Dad, this is my friend Hannah. Hannah this is my dad, Eli."

Eli took Hannah's hand. "It's so nice to meet you, Hannah."

"Thank you."

Eli raised his eyebrows, but he smiled pleasantly and turned toward his wife. "And this," he wrapped his arm proudly around Ariel's shoulders, "is my beautiful wife, Ariel."

Hannah's smile tightened, but she extended her hand. "Hi."

Ariel took her hand. Her warm voice was such a contrast from Hannah's oddly cold one. "It's a pleasure to meet you, Hannah. I'm so glad you're here."

Hannah nodded her head in response. Her eyes grazed up and down Ariel appraisingly. The silence that followed was awkward. Ariel shifted against Eli's side, her brown eyes staring down at something on the floor.

Eli cleared his throat and looked like he was about to speak when Zane swaggered in.

"Who's the new hottie?" Zane's eyes skimmed up and down Hannah's body twice before settling on her face.

Hannah's demeanor changed instantly. Her eyes lit up, her smile brightened, and she shoved her hand out for his.

"Hannah Kinsley."

Zane's eyes darted to mine when he recognized her name. I gave a slight nod to confirm his silent question, that yes, she was *the* Hannah Kinsley I'd told him about.

Zane's expression abruptly changed from predatory to friendly.

"Nice to meet you, Hannah."

Hannah's face fell.

An awkward silence filled the room once more as everyone stared at their feet. I glanced at Hannah. Her lips were pursed into a pouty expression that marred her face.

Was she really pouting because she wasn't getting the attention she'd wanted? I'd seen children behave better than that. Her behavior didn't reflect well on her. It was so much worse than her usual self-centeredness. She'd been incredibly rude to Ariel. It was as if she'd been intimidated by her. Or jealous. Thinking back on it, she had responded the same way in the car – when I'd told her about Ariel's charity, Hannah had interrupted me to talk about herself. Why would she feel the need to compete with Ariel? As far as Hannah knew, Ariel was my stepmother, so her reaction to Ariel was ridiculous. I had known Hannah was self-absorbed, but this, seeing her behaving this way, was extremely unattractive.

∞∞∞∞∞∞

Dinner wasn't a complete disaster, but it was awfully close. The stress of meeting my family had amplified all Hannah's negative traits. She was insulting and inappropriate the entire meal, and if it hadn't been for Zane, we wouldn't have survived.

Zane kept Hannah talking throughout dinner and flirted outrageously with her. Hannah basked in his attention and became much more pleasant to be around, at least until the meal was over; then her snide remarks toward Ariel became unbearable.

Afterward, I escorted Hannah back to her car, ignored her

attempts to kiss me, and watched as she drove away.

How could I have been so wrong about her? Was she that jealous and competitive with all beautiful women, or was it something specific to Ariel? And how had I not seen it before? She was the exact opposite of Eva. She was childish, self-centered, and rude when she didn't get her way. In hindsight, it was obvious. I had been such a fool not to notice it sooner.

I returned to the formal living room where I knew my family waited for me. Eli and Ariel were in the love seat holding hands while Zane was slouched across the couch with his feet propped up on the table.

"You don't have to say it," I warned them. "I already know."

"It's just..." Ariel hesitated, "she doesn't seem like the right match for you, that's all."

"She's a selfish bitch," Zane's voice boomed across the room. "If we're going to talk about it, we should at least tell it like it is."

"Shut your mouth, Zane." He may have been correct, but I still didn't want him talking about Hannah that way.

"Come on. It's the fucking truth, and you know it."

Yeah, I knew it. It had taken me a while to see it, but now that I had, it was obvious. But even though I couldn't have a romantic relationship with Hannah, I still wanted her in my life. My family would just have to deal with it.

"We have more important matters to discuss." I straightened my shoulders. "I scheduled this meeting so we could discuss the mission, not my love life."

That got everyone's attention. Even Zane pulled his feet off the table and sat up straight.

"Eli, let's hear from you first."

Eli cleared his throat, then stood tall and gave his report. "I've made significant progress with Senator Kinsley. I set up a very lucrative deal between his company and Prescott Tech that will basically put him in our pocket. He doesn't yet know the details of what we want in return, but from his enthusiastic response, I doubt it'll be a problem. When we're ready to ship the supplies to-"

"Don't say it," I admonished him. "You never know who could be outside listening. Just say 'the island.'"

"Yes, sir. When we're ready to ship the supplies to the island, I'm positive I will have his support in bypassing customs."

I hoped Eli was right. We had waited too many years to return to the mainland, and our people were running out of supplies. If this deal didn't work, if Senator Kinsley refused to exploit his position to help us, hybrids like Zane, Ariel, and Eli would suffer. This was all the more reason why Zane's part of the mission was so crucial.

"Good." I turned toward the couch. "Zane?"

Zane swore under his breath before standing.

"I did some research. Edward Tatum, the Verona Beach City Manager, is retiring next year. There will be a special election for his replacement. From what my sources tell me, if I run, it should be uncontested."

That was good news. Zane needed as much experience as he could get if we were going to get him into a position in government where we'd no longer have to depend on the senator.

"Nice work. Now you just need to get out of the house and start meeting people."

"I meet people all the time," he grumbled.

"I'm not talking about the women you bring up to your room every night. You've got to start playing your role. Nobody's going to vote for you if they think you're a player."

"Fine, whatever."

I ignored his insolence and ended the meeting. As everyone began leaving the room, I walked over to Ariel and placed my hand on her arm.

She turned, her sparkling brown eyes looking up to meet mine.

"I'm sorry about earlier. The way Hannah treated you.... That was completely out of line. I had no idea she was going to act like that. I wouldn't have invited her if I had known."

"It's okay. She was just feeling nervous and a little insecure."

"You are too kind, Ariel."

Ariel smiled warmly then turned and followed her husband down the hall.

CHAPTER TWELVE

Gwen

It was the first day of practice, and I still hadn't spoken to Jasper about my part in the play. He had been running around all morning making preparations, and with my sore ankle, I couldn't keep up with him.

Hannah refused to look at me and had ignored me all morning. She just followed Jasper around and pretended to be busy.

It was too bad Ky couldn't have gotten the job as Jasper's assistant. It was the only paid position in the entire play, and he could have used the money.

I saw Ky the moment he entered the backstage area. His clothes were disheveled, his hair still wet from a shower, and it was obvious he'd overslept. Beverly, who was closer to the door, reached him first. I watched as she grabbed him by the arms and shook him violently. I laughed. I could guess what she'd said to him, something along the lines of 'snap out of it.'

"Would you mind telling me what's wrong with him today?" Beverly asked as I approached the two of them.

"Already told you I'm fine. Get the hell off my case."

"What crawled up your ass?" Beverly responded.

Ky sighed and closed his eyes. When he opened them, he looked directly at me. "Are you sure you still want to do this play?"

"Of course she does. Are you mad?" Beverly glared at him.

I knew what he meant. Ky must have read the manuscript Jasper had emailed to everyone. That explained why Ky looked the way he did; he wasn't tired but sick to his stomach with dread. I wouldn't be surprised if he threw up.

"I kind of have to. I need the extra credit to get an A in that class, which I need to maintain my scholarship. Maybe Jasper will let me swap roles with someone. I plan on talking to him as soon as he has a free moment."

Beverly's eyes widened. "Swap roles? Are you kidding? You got the lead role, why would you do that? You love acting. With all the publicity around this play, this could be the break you need to get noticed. Swap roles — Are you out of your mind?" Beverly turned toward Ky. "This is your fault, isn't it? Don't you dare mess this up for her. She's wanted to be an actress since she was eight years old."

Ky hung his head.

"Beverly," Hannah's voice called out across the room. "Jasper is ready for you. You're starting at act one scene three."

I glanced at Ky after Beverly left. He looked miserable.

"She's right, you know. As much as this is going to kill me, I can't hold you back like that. Fuck. I'm playing the role of his best friend. I've got to encourage the bastard." He looked up at me and laughed humorlessly. "I should quit. It might be easier on my peace of mind if I don't have to watch."

Unfortunately, whether he watched or not, this play would test our new relationship. Maybe him being here would help. He would be a visual reminder to myself that Alexander was acting a role for a play and nothing more. I shook my head at the thought. That was so selfish. What kind of person was I to think such things? Ky deserved so much better than me.

We stood in silence until Jasper called my name and told me I was up next. The scene we were practicing was Beth and Nathan's first meeting.

I walked toward the stage and shook off my nervousness.

Jasper clapped his hands. "We haven't got a lot of time to get this right, so let's get to it. This scene takes place at a swanky party. Nathan will be in a suit, Beth, you'll be wearing a dress and heels. We'll deal with wardrobe another day. Nathan the first half of the scene you'll be hanging out around the edges of the stage looking bored. Beth will be dancing with her best friend, Josie." Jasper motioned to Beverly. "This is how the scene begins. Everybody ready?" He paused for any objections. "All right, let's do this." Jasper sat next to Hannah and placed the clipboard in his lap and his arm around her shoulders.

CHAPTER THIRTEEN
Alexander

I watched Gwen from across the stage and allowed the desire I felt to show in my eyes as I followed her every move.

Her hips swayed seductively as she danced at the other end of the stage.

I smiled at the irony that this scene was basically a re-enactment of the night we'd met.

At Jasper's cue, I approached Gwen as Beverly backed away. With perfect timing, Gwen turned, lost her balance, and pretended to fall forward.

Shit, she wasn't pretending!

Between her already sore ankle and her zealousness to make the fall realistic, she had actually fallen. But instead of falling delicately into my arms, she had tripped forward, falling much too quickly to be delicate.

I grabbed her waist. Her momentum spun us wildly around as I pulled her against me. We swung to an abrupt stop, our bodies in a horizontal embrace with hers pressed against the length of mine and her hair falling to the floor behind her.

I opened my mouth to deliver my first line when I faltered. My gaze met hers. I fell into those large emerald eyes, and I was lost. I knew we were being watched. I knew I had lines to deliver. But I didn't care. Those sparkling eyes and soft lips made everything else fade away until all that existed was the two of us. My mind ceased to function. The sensual feel of her warm body intoxicated me. Without conscious thought, my right arm slid down her hips and pulled her closer.

A surprised gasp parted her lips, and everything in me was set ablaze.

My heart pounded in my chest.

A throat being cleared in the distance brought me back to reality.

What was my next line? I was suddenly aware I would lose the part if I screwed this up, and I couldn't let that happen.

In a moment of clarity, my lines returned to me. I rubbed my thumb across her cheek. "Are you okay?"

She nodded. Her chest heaved against mine as her breathing deepened. Unable to stop myself, I brought my lips within an inch of hers.

Fuck, I wanted this woman. My body screamed at me to remove the obstacles separating us. The thin cotton shorts and tank she wore provided little barrier, but I wanted them gone. I wanted to feel the heat from her body and her soft skin pressed against mine. The fire blazing in her eyes said she wanted it too.

She slid her hand up my chest, across my jaw, and up the back of my neck. "My name is Beth."

"It's nice to meet you, Beth. I'm Nathan." We stared into each other's eyes, unmoving. All of the lines for the scene were complete.

Gwen absently drew circles against the back of my neck with her fingertips. The hand I caressed her face with was now rubbing gently across her cheeks, down the line of her jaw, brushing softly across her lips. My heart pounded in my chest as the desire to kiss her overwhelmed me. Just one kiss. I stared ravenously at her lips.

"All right," Jasper yelled from his seat. "We'll stop here. That was fucking hot. Chemistry. That was exactly what we needed. And holy fucking shit, you two have it! We're going to light the stage on fire!" Jasper smiled wide enough to crack his face in half. "I knew you two would be perfect."

Jasper pumped his fist in the air a few times, then took a deep breath. "Good job. But for the first scene, you may need to dial it back a bit."

Jasper turned and addressed the group. "Good practice, everyone. We've got a lot more scenes to cover, but keep up the good work. We'll meet back tomorrow at seven a.m."

I released Gwen. Someone grabbed my arm and yanked me roughly back. Hannah glared at me. "What the hell was that?"

That was a damn good question.

From the moment I'd met her, I'd been unable to evade the pull I felt for Gwen. More and more I realized how pointless it was to ignore it.

But as I stared into Hannah's irate eyes, shame heated my face. All this time I'd pursued Hannah because of this insane idea that she was somehow God's way of giving Eva back to me. I'd made Hannah think I wanted her, yet the reality was, I just wanted Eva. Hannah didn't deserve that.

But what was I supposed to tell her? The truth? I certainly couldn't do it here, and not like this.

So I lied.

"That was acting. I did exactly what I was supposed to do. You heard Jasper, this kind of thing could make or break this play."

She eyed me suspiciously. "Well, it looked real. It looked like you wanted her. What do you say about that?"

"I say that's good acting."

"Hmm." She huffed and crossed her arms over her chest.

I looked at the ceiling in frustration. It was going to be a long night.

CHAPTER FOURTEEN

Gwen

It was even worse than I'd imagined. The moment I walked off the stage, Ky was in my face.

"What the fuck, Gwen?"

He was fuming, his body so tense and his face so red I worried he would burst a blood vessel.

What was I supposed to say? How could I play this off? I couldn't even keep my hands from shaking.

"It was just acting," I lied. "We knew this would happen. We both read the manuscripts."

"Don't lie to me." He paced the room with his fists clenched at his sides.

"Look at me." I waited for him to respond. When his eyes found mine, I continued, "Don't watch practice. None of it means anything, all you're doing is torturing yourself." I walked to Ky and slid my arms around his neck.

He leaned a little closer but stubbornly resisted kissing me.

"A little closer." I pressed my body against his. I smiled when I saw the corners of his mouth start to turn up.

"You know you're not playing fair, right?"

"Did you expect any different?" I asked a moment before his lips found mine. His hands slid around my waist as he kissed me tenderly. It was exactly how he'd always kissed me, but it somehow felt different. The chemistry we normally shared was muted.

Or maybe, I thought as he pulled me closer, *maybe it just pales in comparison to what Alexander makes me feel.*

It was then, in Ky's embrace, that I realized just how screwed I really was.

∞∞∞∞∞∞

I left rehearsal and went to Beverly's for a well-deserved girls' night. It was just what the doctor ordered. We had margaritas, watched movies, and talked about everything but guys. It was the first night we'd had together since Ky and I started dating, and it was over too quickly.

I yawned.

Just a few more miles, and I'd be home. I rubbed my tired eyes as I slowed to a stop at the red light. Home seemed so far away. I could pull over and take a nap on the side of the road. The streets were deserted this time of night. The temptation was hard to resist.

As I waited for the light to turn green, I thought about rehearsal and the insane chemistry between Alexander and me. The fire and passion between us eclipsed anything I'd ever felt. It frightened me. It could ruin things with Ky, the only guy I'd been able to trust with my heart since Wesley.

I rubbed my eyes and looked up. The streetlight went from yellow to red. Damn. I missed my green light. I laid my head on the headrest then tilted it to my left.

I noticed movement across the way. The streets weren't as deserted as I'd thought. I squinted my eyes to find the source of the movement and was able to make out a figure – a man – shifting around inside a small blue car with its engine and lights off. He must've had the same idea I had.

More movement caught my eye. A beautiful woman with silky blonde hair and a denim mini-skirt strutted up to the car and slid into the passenger seat. The old car creaked as she shut the door.

What the hell?

That looked like Ky's car. I leaned forward to get a better look.

The engine started, and they began driving away. I looked up, dismayed to find the light had once again turned red. As the car turned, I got a glimpse of the license plate: 562FE

Yes, it was definitely Ky's car. But who was that woman?

I grabbed my phone and called him.

Please leave a message after the beep.... Beeeeeep.

I looked at the clock on the dashboard. It was two a.m. Ky should have been asleep. Maybe someone had stolen his car. Or maybe he'd loaned it to someone. If I could just talk to him, I knew he'd have an explanation for what I'd witnessed.

The green light flashed. I turned right and headed toward Oliver St. Within minutes, I was pulling into Greenbriar Apartments and parking. I ran up the stairs, around the corner to apartment 5C, and banged on the door.

"Ky, it's me, Gwen." I banged some more. "Please, open up."

I rang the doorbell and tapped my foot. Where was he? I grabbed my phone and tried him again.

No answer.

I opened my purse and fumbled through it, angrily tossing out candy wrappers and random trash until I came upon what I'd been looking for.

A key.

Ky had given me a key to his apartment a few days ago. I shoved it in the lock of the door.

"Ky!"

Nothing. No sound other than the ticking of an old grandfather clock on the wall.

Maybe he's asleep.

I walked through the living room, down the hall to his room, and flicked on the light. His bed was made, and everything was in its place. I slumped down onto the perfectly smooth comforter.

I couldn't believe it. I would never have thought Ky would betray me this way. He was too loyal and good to do something like this. There must have been another explanation.

I reached into my pocket for my phone to text him.

Me: I came by ur apt to c u, where r u?

I waited two minutes.

Five minutes.

Ten.

Tears formed in my eyes, and the room began to blur. I laid back on his bed and curled my legs up to my chest. I didn't know why it hurt so much. I hadn't been in love with Ky, but I cared about him deeply. I trusted him. And all the while, he'd been running around with other women behind my back.

No. Only one woman. Maybe this was the first time. Maybe my preoccupation with Alexander had pushed him away. Was this my fault?

I deserved this. I'd been thinking about another man. How was I any better than Ky? I wasn't. Besides, what had I seen? I'd seen a woman get into his car and nothing else. He hadn't been making out with her. He hadn't touched her. But despite those justifications, the betrayal I felt was real.

I curled tighter into a ball and cried myself to sleep on Ky's bed.

When I woke the next morning, I had a moment of disorientation. I looked around and attempted to remember where I was. Plain white walls and a blue bedspread. This was Ky's bedroom.

Memories of the previous night flooded back, along with the realization that Ky had never come home. He had stayed out all night with that woman.

No.

A sob worked its way up my throat. My eyes watered.

I swallowed hard and forced the emotions down before they could overwhelm me again. I refused to cry over this anymore. I just needed to stay busy.

I looked at my phone. I had already missed rehearsal, but I could still make it to class.

I got to my feet. My stiff neck and back screamed for relief. I rubbed the back of my neck, feeling like I'd aged twenty years overnight.

The normal fifteen-minute drive home took forever. My head pounded with a splitting headache, and my body ached all over. Every minute that passed was torture. I pulled into a convenience store, bought some painkillers, and popped four into my mouth as I got back in my car to drive home.

The rest of my morning wasn't much better. I got a speeding ticket, which held me up on the roadside for almost forty-five minutes. Then, after my shower, I found that my blow dryer was broken. I hadn't done laundry, so the only clean items I had were workout clothes and t-shirts. I had no choice but to go to astronomy with my wet hair tangled around my face wearing yoga pants, an old Beatles t-shirt, and no makeup.

The moment class was over, Beverly pulled me aside and gripped my arms firmly. "What happened? Your eyes are bloodshot. Why have you been crying?" Her fingers tightened.

I told her everything that had happened after rehearsal the night before and this morning. I told her how confused and betrayed I felt. But mostly, I told her about the guilt that consumed me. How my inability to fight my attraction to Alexander may have pushed Ky toward another woman.

"Gwen, stop." Beverly held a hand up. "That's ridiculous. Yeah, you were attracted to another guy. So what? You didn't sleep with him, and you didn't kiss him."

"But I wanted to."

"That's not the point. The point is you didn't cheat. Ky did. That's a big difference. Besides, he told you he loved you. That should mean something." She shook her head. "What an ass. I can't believe he did that to you."

"Yeah, me neither."

"Come on." She wrapped her arm around me. "Let's get out of here. You'll be okay if you miss a few classes. You deserve a break."

∞∞∞∞∞∞

It had been days since I'd last seen Ky, and he hadn't answered his phone or any of his texts. I was on the verge of calling the police when I decided to see if his boss had heard from him.

"Yeah, he called in this morning. He said he was still sick, but he'd be back in a few days. Why do you ask?"

"Just wondering." I left quickly, hoping he didn't notice the hurt expression on my face. All my suspicions had just been confirmed.

At least he isn't missing.

I shook my head in disgust. I shouldn't have allowed myself to cross that line of friendship with Ky. I should have protected myself and my heart from being crushed again. The last few days had strengthened my resolve. I didn't need love in my life. Love made you weak. Love was nothing more than a slow, torturous suicide, and I wanted none of it.

I tossed my purse in my car and flopped onto my seat. I was about to call Beverly when my phone rang.

Ky's name popped up on the caller ID.

What the hell?

Now he decided to return my call? It'd been days. I hit the button to ignore him and started my car. My phone blew up with voicemail and texts, dinging every few seconds.

I had no interest in what he had to say. I refused to read his messages.

Oh shit! I slammed on the brakes.

In my anger, I'd completely missed a stop sign and almost plowed headfirst into a pickup truck. Before I caused any permanent damage, I pulled over in order to calm down.

My phone chimed again, and I involuntarily glanced down.

Ky: SRY I was sick & i cldnt get out of bed

Ky: PLS cmb

My anger flared to scorching levels. That fucking liar! I'd gone by his apartment every day since he'd disappeared. Couldn't get out of bed, my ass! He never even returned home. How could he lie to me like this? He'd said he loved me!

Me: LIAR!!!!

I sent the text and turned off my phone. I didn't want to see or hear from him again.

CHAPTER FIFTEEN
Alexander

I stood bloodied and bruised before the throne, awaiting judgment. To my right stood a tearful Eva, and to my left a furious and indignant Lew. The intensity of my emotions nearly dropped me to my knees. They were tumultuous, shifting with the confusion in my mind. I felt anger, hurt, jealousy, longing, regret, shame, and guilt. I shifted from one emotion to the next, never settling long enough to get a reprieve from their intensity.

Fierce light illuminated and a hush filled the room as God entered and sat on his throne.

"Never has such evil breached the boundary of Heaven. What do you have to say for yourself, Lew?" God's voice, like the sound of thunder, boomed and echoed around the cavernous room.

"Me? I've done nothing wrong!" Lew gestured toward me. "It's that backstabbing bastard over there and that whore of a companion you gave me who sinned. Not me! And Alexias deserved what he got," Lew screamed. Surely, such hatred had never before been witnessed in Heaven.

"We shall see," was God's only reply. "What about you, Eva? What do you have to say for yourself?"

Eva looked at Lew. For a moment, Lew's eyes softened, and the hatred subsided.

"I once loved Lew. He was good to me. But over the years, everything became about him. It was about what he wanted, and I didn't matter to him anymore."

"Lies! You always mattered to me, and even now after you whored yourself out to him, I still love you!" Lew cried in anguish.

"Silence!" God's booming voice sent shock waves through the palace.

Lew dropped his head in reverence.

Eva continued her explanation. "And then I met Alex. He was kind to me. He paid attention to me in a way you never did." She looked to Lew. "And for the first time, I felt loved. The way he looked at me, I didn't want to lose that. So I never told him about Lew."

Eva stared at me, but I couldn't meet her eyes. She was right. I loved her. But not enough to defy God. Not enough to dishonor my best friend. What she'd done went against everything I believed in.

"Alexias? What about you?"

Now it was my turn for confession. But what did I have to confess? "I love her. With every molecule of my being, I love her. But I did not know she was unavailable." I met Lew's gaze. "I swear to you, old friend, I had no idea." I saw his fury light his eyes, revealing his disbelief. "I loved her, but nothing ever happened between us."

"Liar! Someone saw you sneaking off to be together. They showed me. Stop lying!"

"Quiet."

A holographic display of Lew's memories lit up the air before us, showing in detail how a friend of Lew's informed him that he'd seen Eva sneaking off with me. His friend placed both hands on Lew's head and transferred the memories directly into his mind. Images flashed of Eva glancing around suspiciously before ducking off the road and into the jungle, followed closely by myself. Then came images of Eva and I talking. The golden glow that shimmered off our

Who promised you?" Zane sputtered.

"I can't explain it. Something I was promised long ago. I didn't understand it then, but I do now. So I know this will work. It has to."

It had to work. It was the only way.

"Come on. What is this really about?"

I thought a moment and figured, *What the hell?* "I think I've made a mistake."

"You? Make a mistake? I didn't think that was possible."

"Smartass."

Zane smirked. "Seriously, what's going on? Is this about Hannah? Fuck, please tell me this is not about Hannah."

I hesitated once more. "Well, not really. It's about Gwen."

I told Zane the whole story, beginning to end. From Eva to the night I'd met Hannah and Gwen to my current predicament. By the time I was finished, Zane's eyes were wide with astonishment.

"Damn."

"Yeah. So like I said, I think I've made a mistake with Hannah."

"Fuck yeah, you did."

"Zane." I couldn't keep the frustration from my voice.

Zane dropped his head, but when he looked back up at me, there was a wisdom in his eyes I'd never seen before. "Look, Dad. I've never said this, but I know you never loved Mom." He looked at me sharply. "No, don't stop me. I know it's true. I also know you never loved Eli's mother either. You treated them well, and you were loyal and kind to them. But you never loved them. And you've never been happy. After all these years, you deserve some happiness."

"I'm happy," I lied.

"No, you're lonely. And now, with my future as bleak as it is, I'm starting to understand just how much loneliness sucks."

"Your future doesn't have to be bleak. And lonely? Who are you kidding?" I said, trying to lighten the mood. "You've got a different woman in your bed every night of the week."

He chuckled. "I'm not that bad. Maybe every other night. What do you think I am, a man-whore?"

"Seriously? Man-whore should be your middle name. It'd be more fitting than the name I gave you three hundred years ago." We both laughed then fell into a comfortable silence. I poured myself a fresh bowl of cereal and sat across from Zane.

Zane kept his head down, his large bowl of oatmeal remaining untouched in front of him. I couldn't help feeling that all of it was my fault. This plan. This mission. All of it had been my idea. The mission was critical, but Zane's part wasn't necessary. There were other ways to secure our future, but this was the most permanent solution. *Poor Zane.* I would have done anything to switch places with him, but it wasn't possible. Angels couldn't age the way hybrids could. To pull this off, Zane had to force his body to age at the normal rate. He could never let people suspect he wasn't human. In effect, he was shortening his own lifespan by hundreds of years to protect our people. I could never thank him enough.

Zane took a bite of oatmeal. "I checked out the security cameras across the street from our building," he stated, referring to the recent vandalism of our main office. "The twenty minutes of video before and during the vandalism were damaged."

"Everything before and after was there?"

"Yeah. It was fucking perfect except for those twenty minutes. You know what that means?"

"Yeah. We've got a problem." This was not good. Really, really not good. "Check the security vids surrounding the house. Look for anything suspicious. Check everything within the last month." I shook my head. "Damn, that'll take forever."

I stared down at my empty bowl. "Scratch that. I'll write an algorithm that will search much faster." I swiped my left palm through the air in front of me. The virtual computer screen and keyboard I'd designed came to life and hovered in the air.

My fingers flew over the holographic keys. Within minutes, the algorithm would be complete. We would have answers soon.

A cold shiver passed over me. I had a horrible feeling about this. There was no reason for anyone to target us. We'd made sure not to make enemies. Even in our business dealings, we had ensured every deal we'd made was more than generous to the opposing party. So who would intentionally target us? Maybe it was nothing. It was possible that the vandalism was random. It could have been a coincidence that only the twenty minutes of video that could reveal our adversary had been destroyed. I tried to convince myself that it hadn't been anything malicious, but I knew better.

Within five minutes, a chime from the house speakers sounded. I waved my arm through the air, and the screen shimmered to life in front of us. The search was complete. I clicked the file to see the stored video.

A man, about 5'10 and wearing a black hoodie and dark oversized sunglasses, was taking pictures of our house. I watched him pull out his phone and make a call. He dipped his head down as he spoke, so I was unable to read his lips. I started the face recognition software, then sped up the video. He stayed a few hours, snapped multiple photos, then drove away in an old blue Toyota. I paused the video, then adjusted the angle. There it was. His license plate.

The search had taken less than ten seconds, and I couldn't believe my eyes.

No fucking way. That couldn't be right. Zane and I exchanged a look.

"Fuck!" I slammed my fist down on the counter.

Zane ran his hand through his hair. "Damn. I would never have thought it was Ky."

We sat in silence while I weighed our options.

"I'm heading to Gwen's house right now. I can't leave her alone for even a minute. We may have to figure out a way to get her to stay here at the house. In the meantime, learn everything you can about Ky. *Everything*," I emphasized, grabbing my stuff and racing out the door.

It was not long before I found myself in Gwen's backyard, just outside her window. It was the only way to ensure her safety. What if Ky used her to get to us? I couldn't leave her unprotected. I sat in the soft grass, laid my head back, and looked up at the stars. She'd be safer if she moved in with us, but how the hell was I supposed to make that happen?

Since that first day of practice, she'd done everything she could to evade me. She avoided my gaze in class. Skipped rehearsal. She even called the office when she knew I wouldn't be there to call in sick. And damn, I didn't blame her. I'd been such a jerk toward her.

And for what? I'd distanced myself from the first person I'd felt anything for in centuries, all because of a long-lost love. And hell, Hannah wasn't even that.

I shook my head in disbelief.

Gwen could be in danger because of me, and I wasn't about to let anything happen to her. I owed it to her to keep her safe.

I closed my eyes and listened. I heard everything. The crickets chirping. A few dogs barking two streets over. The mini-series that played on the neighbor's television. And soft crying coming from Gwen's room.

Why was she crying?

I almost went to her door, but I knew I couldn't. How would I explain what I was doing?

But damn it, I wanted to know who'd hurt her. I wanted to find who'd made her feel this way and beat the shit out of them. The gentle sobs coming from her room were killing me.

CHAPTER SIXTEEN

Gwen

For the first time in days, I felt relief. I opened my eyes and found that I was finally back on the beach with Luke. The tears I'd been shedding slowed, then stopped.

I had Luke back. I didn't have time for tears. I pulled out of Luke's arms and smiled. I saw the blurry outline of a smile form on his face. He motioned at the sand next to us, leaned over, then did something neither of us had ever thought to do before.

"Are you okay?"

The simple question etched into the sand almost blew me away. All this time it had never occurred to me to find alternate means of communication. Why was that? Was it because communicating with Luke was basically talking to myself? Luke was a figment of my imagination. Someone I had made up in my mind to comfort myself. What kind of conversations could we have? Was the fact that we were communicating a sign that I was finally losing my mind? Should I respond? Or should I resist slipping further into insanity?

I hesitated before responding, "I am now," in the sand beside his question.

I didn't care if I was talking to myself. After everything with Ky, Luke was the only comfort I had. If that meant I was talking to myself, so be it. I'd go with it, taking whatever comfort I could get.

Luke erased my message and created another of his own. "Do you trust me?"

Of course I did.

He pulled me to my feet and led me away from the shore. My bare feet dug into the sand as we strode over the dunes toward a nearby cliff. We hadn't gone far when the sand transitioned to rough pebbles and rocks. Luke stopped, lifted me up onto his back, and carried me the rest of the way.

Soon we were at the top of a cliff overlooking the ocean. But what were we doing? There was nothing up here but a bunch of rocks.

I peered up at the cloudless sky and questioned once again why I would dream of a place so realistic, yet give it a completely fake-looking sky. From this high up, it looked close enough that I could reach up and touch it.

Luke took my hand and led me to the edge of the cliff. My legs shook as I peered over the edge. Holy shit, we were high up, at least a football field length in height. Luke had asked if I trusted him, and I had, but looking at the waves crashing against the boulders below, I was having doubts.

Luke released my hand. Without warning, he dove headfirst toward the rocks.

A silent scream tore from my throat as Luke plunged to his death, his head aimed directly at the jagged boulders below. He was just feet away from the rocks when I decided I couldn't witness it, but just as I was about to close my eyes, his body changed direction. He soared low across the ocean and then shot high into the air.

I couldn't make sense of what I was seeing.

What was happening? Was he flying?

Duh! *Hello, Sherlock, this is a dream, remember?* Apparently even in my dreams, I was an idiot. I berated myself until Luke flew back up and hovered a foot from the edge of the cliff.

Could I do this? Dream or not, it felt real.

Go for it, Gwen.

My fingers trembled as I placed them in Luke's outstretched hand. I gasped when he pulled me to him, and my body glided across the open space over the cliff.

My heart raced, and I shook with fear as I looked down. There was nothing beneath my feet. Nothing between me and the rocks hundreds of feet below.

Impossible.

Luke sensed my fear and positioned himself behind me. He placed his chin on my shoulder and pulled me against him. He took my hands and stretched my arms out to the side.

I looked like a bird. I couldn't help it; uncontrollable laughter burst from my lips, and fear slowly sifted out of me.

When I'd gotten my laughter under control, Luke gave me a swift kiss on the cheek, then gave me silent flying lessons.

As it turned out, flying was easy. Within minutes, I was soaring through the air on my own.

I closed my eyes and breathed deeply as the fresh wind whipped my hair from my face. Adrenaline coursed through my veins as we dove and soared over the ocean. We flew high over a small city, unlike anything I'd ever seen.

I dove, falling faster and faster, laughing at the exhilaration. I flew swiftly between the buildings. I swept quickly to the right, then dodged left as my speed picked up.

It was so beautiful. The buildings sparkled. They reminded me of the Emerald City in *The Wizard of Oz,* except instead of emeralds, the buildings were made of diamonds that threw rainbows everywhere.

I glanced over my shoulder at Luke and realized our time together was almost up. A momentary stab of disappointment pierced my chest. What if I didn't see him again for a while? What if he never came back?

Luke sped up and led me back to the cliff. He grabbed both my hands and pulled me to him. My disappointment vanished.

He placed one hand on my lower back and took my hand with the other. He pulled me close and began slowly gliding us across the air.

Dancing.

We were dancing. There was no music, but I didn't care because Luke was dancing with me.

∞∞∞∞∞∞

Time to stop hiding. I couldn't afford to miss any more school, rehearsal, or work. I felt like such a coward.

Yes, Ky had betrayed me. He had lied and cheated on me. I was sick to my stomach over losing his friendship. But enough was enough. I couldn't lie in bed and cry forever.

For the first time in days, I woke feeling refreshed. Luke had made everything better. The fact that Luke wasn't real.... Well, I wasn't going to think about that.

I got ready and drove to the auditorium. I tried not to think about the fact that Alexander would be there, but no matter how hard I tried to ignore it, my heart raced every time I thought of seeing him again.

Stay strong, Gwen. Don't make a fool of yourself. He doesn't want you, and he probably never did. He wouldn't have treated you like crap if he'd been interested.

I rolled my eyes. After the way he treated me, I was still pining away for him. How pathetic.

I arrived at practice on time and was surprised when Hannah spoke to me. She thought I'd been sick the last few days, and I couldn't tell her the truth. It was too humiliating. And considering our relationship, it was probably better that she didn't know the details.

It was time to start, and I still hadn't seen Alexander. I looked frantically around the auditorium, scanning each group, and wondered where the hell he was.

"Looking for Alexander?" A whispered breath tickled my neck.

I shrieked and whirled around.

Jasper eyed me with an arrogant smirk.

"Jasper." His name came out with a gasp as I struggled to catch my breath. "You scared me."

He laughed. "I didn't mean to. But I must say, you're fucking hot when you're startled. I may make a habit of sneaking up on you."

The adrenaline coursing through my veins gave me a strange high. A sudden laugh burst from my lips. "Thank you. I needed that."

"Anytime," Jasper quipped, then suddenly became serious. "Look, it's none of my business, but are you okay? You've missed a lot of practice."

I didn't want to lie to Jasper, but how was I supposed to answer that? As his lead actress, I could single-handedly ruin his play, and I didn't have a valid excuse for skipping practice.

Jasper must have noticed the look on my face. "I'm not worried about the play, Gwen. Stop worrying about it. You're a fantastic actress. Missing a few practices won't change that. Look, I'm not the most sensitive guy, but I can tell something's up." Despite the harshness of his words, there was genuine concern on his face. "You know you can talk to me, right? Despite my reputation, I'm not a complete asshole."

I looked into his eyes and knew I could trust him. There was just something about Jasper. I felt like I could tell him anything.

"Really, Gwen?" Hannah glared at me. "Is there any guy out here that you're not sleeping with?"

My blood boiled. My hands fisted at my sides. I wanted to rip her pretty little head off, but I resisted the urge. Fighting with Hannah wouldn't solve anything.

I took a calming breath and unclenched my fists. "Hannah, we were just talking."

"Yeah, right." She turned on her heel and stomped toward the stage.

"What's she so pissed about?" Jasper's voice caught me off guard again. I'd already forgotten he was there.

"Everything." I turned and placed my hand on Jasper's arm. "Thank you. For being concerned."

"No problem."

"We need to get started, people." The loud megaphone blaring a few feet away deafened me and redirected my attention. Apparently, Hannah thought she'd take control of things.

Whatever.

I'd ignore her. I didn't want to deal with Hannah's bullshit. What she said was so far off base it was laughable.

Jasper took his seat as I hurried to the stage.

There Alexander was at the other end of the stage, talking to the other actors, completely unaware of me. As I approached Alexander, he laughed at someone's joke, and his eyes scanned the room. He looked right through me as if I wasn't even there. As if I were no more important than a chair.

Fine. I could play that game too.

"Hello, Alexander," I said, my voice as cold and emotionless as I could get it.

"Hey, Gwen." His tone threw me off. It wasn't cold like it had been for the last few weeks. It was friendly, but without the heat from when we'd first met. He had always been either hot or cold, and this neutral response confused me.

I took my place on the stage and waited.

The scene began. Beverly pulled off her lines flawlessly. She had that whole "cool bitchy" friend act down. I had to make sure to compliment her later.

The scene progressed, and before I knew it, the moment I'd been dreading had arrived.

I stalked away from Alexander, pouring the anger and shame Beth felt into the scene. He grabbed me from behind and forced me to face him.

"Beth, please." His words came out with perfect timing. His hold on me was exactly as it should have been. But the fire was gone from his eyes and his touch. His voice lacked the passion that used to saturate it.

His hands gripped my face. His fingers twined through my hair. "Beth, forgive me."

His eyes broke contact with mine and lowered to my lips. "I'm-"

"STOP!" Jasper yelled from his seat. He jerked to his feet and ran a hand through his hair. His agitation was tangible. "What the fuck was that?"

Alexander lowered his head. No explanation was needed. Everyone could see what Jasper was getting at.

"What the hell, Alexander?" Jasper gave him an exasperated look.

"Sorry. I–" he paused. "I don't have an excuse. I'm just not feeling it today. I didn't sleep well."

"Not feeling it? Are you fucking kidding me?" Jasper blew a breath out, then another. He took one last deep breath before raising his hands in surrender. "Fuck it, let's do the next scene. Alexander and Gwen follow me. Now!"

His voice meant business, and the moment he said 'now' everyone jolted into action. I followed Jasper off the stage toward a private alcove in the back. Jasper turned and stared us down.

"I don't give a fuck what happened between the two of you. Just fix it. You got those parts because you were the best actors, but also because you have incredible chemistry." Jasper looked at Alexander. "But this won't work if you keep looking at her like she's your fucking sister. I'm telling you, that was the shittiest acting I've ever had to endure." His eyes flashed at Alexander. "Get your shit together. I don't give a fuck what your problem is." Jasper turned and stomped off.

The silence that followed was stifling. I stared down at my hands, twisting my pinky ring around and around, doing everything I could to avoid Alexander's intense gaze. I twirled the blue diamond, thinking idly about the day Wesley had given it to me. It had been our one year anniversary. He was the first real boyfriend I'd ever had, so I'd had no idea how to handle an anniversary. Should I have made it a big deal, or played it cool? I'd had no clue. I had been so afraid of making a fool of myself, that in the end, I'd pretended not to notice the date. I hadn't even gotten him a gift. I'd been such an idiot. He had shown up at school with a single rose and a beautiful ring box. It wasn't even a real diamond, but it was the most treasured piece of jewelry I owned. I wore it every day.

Alexander shifted uncomfortably before he spoke. "Gwen, I need to apologize. I can't explain my actions, but I know I've been a real jerk toward you. I'd really like for us to be friends if you'll forgive me."

"Friends?" I asked, unsure if I'd heard right.

"Yeah, I think that's a good place to start." A hopeful smile spread across his face as he watched me.

"Okay. Just promise me your asshole days will stay in the past."

"It's a promise."

Slightly uncomfortable, I shifted on my feet. "Well, I need to get out of here." Without waiting for his reply, I turned and left the auditorium, got in my car, and drove home.

CHAPTER SEVENTEEN
Alexander

When I reached Gwen's house, she was already in bed. I listened to her shallow breathing as she fell deeper and deeper into sleep. I put my head back into the soft grass and gazed up at the sky. It was a clear night, and despite the city lights, the stars were on full display. It was so beautiful I could almost imagine I was back in Heaven looking up at the celestial sky. It had been a few millennia since I'd been kicked out, but I remembered it like it was yesterday.

I had been so stupid, lonely, and desperate. I had traveled to Earth, God's most recent creation, on an important mission. But I'd been heartbroken and searching for something to distract me from the gaping hole in my chest after losing Eva. I'd spent years wandering the Earth before I'd caved in to temptation and taken a human female as my wife. Unfortunately, my act of disobedience had encouraged others of my kind to sin as well.

I'd never forget the disappointment on God's face when he confronted me about my indiscretion. I was so ashamed. He had trusted me and made me one of his top leaders. I was supposed to set an example for my subordinates. But instead, I'd failed them.

As a caution to other angels, God ensured our sin would always be remembered. He whispered into the minds of men the words that made their way into Genesis. Our transgression was laid bare for all the world to see. In all of history, there was only one angel who'd disappointed God more than I had. That feeling of failure and the shame of letting Him down was the worst form of punishment, much worse than the penalty He'd imposed.

For our sins, we were expelled from Heaven. Unlike Lucifer, we could visit and enjoy Heaven, but would never be allowed to call it home again. So we made Earth our new home. Eventually, we found an uninhabited island and started our own society, cut off from the rest of the world.

I looked to the sky. It was a stunning tonight. Heaven's sky was breathtaking, but there was never a night sky like this. There were times when it was a deep violet, and the stars twinkled above like diamonds glittering in the light, but it was never truly dark.

It was quiet out, almost eerily so. I listened harder and heard nothing from next door. No television blaring. Nothing.

The only discernible sounds were those of Gwen's heartbeats and breaths. It must have been a pleasant dream. Her breathing was even and her heartbeat slow and peaceful. I wondered if she was wearing those fuzzy pajamas that she loved. I closed my eyes and pictured her curled up in her bed with her long hair tangled across her pillow.

The image stirred a hunger in me. I felt it building up slowly, the desire to see her again. The dark thought swept through my mind that I could go into her room. She would never know. Not only that, but I could better protect her if I were inside, right? The closer I was, the faster I'd be able to respond to any threat. It made complete sense.

I shook the thoughts from my head. Was that the way stalkers justified their actions to themselves? Was I that desperate?

Minutes passed, and my mind kept returning to the possibilities. What would it hurt to go inside? I wouldn't be there to molest her. I was protecting her. It wasn't like I'd watch her get undressed. I would just sit in her bedroom while she slept.

bodies announced our love to the world.

Then Eva's memories flooded our field of vision. Those were painful to watch. They showed how unhappy and lonely she was with Lew and how much she wanted to be with me. Worst of all, I saw how hard she worked to deceive me. How she'd manipulated me to keep me in the dark about Lew.

Then last, my memories were displayed. Those nearly tore me in half. I had to look away. It was too painful to watch the perfect days we'd spent together knowing there wouldn't be another. I closed my eyes as the tears streamed down my face. This was too much. I wouldn't survive this.

∞∞∞∞∞∞

"I need you to add the following to the list: an elektroforesis system, a magnetic stirrer and vortex, a gel documentation system, an autoclave, a refrigerated centrifuge, and a thermal cycler." I glanced over my shoulder as Zane entered the room. "Yeah, I need it asap. Pay whatever it takes. I want it all here by tomorrow evening ... That's right. I want it delivered to the house. I've got a room set up in the basement... I said I didn't care about the cost. Just get it done." I hung up on the head of my research department.

"What's that about?" Zane eyed me suspiciously.

"Nothing." I stared into the bowl of Captain Crunch I'd poured thirty minutes ago. It was a soggy, nasty mess.

"Alex, I'm not an idiot. I know the only use you'd have for that equipment, and we all agreed we wouldn't help the humans with that type of research." Zane watched my face as he spoke before his eyes suddenly lit up with understanding. "No. You know it won't work. I understand why you'd want to do it, but we can't waste that much time and money on something like that."

"It will work." My voice went hard with determination. "I may not have found a way before, but I will now. Besides," I lowered my voice to a whisper. "He promised me."

"He who? What promise? What the hell are you talking about?

Yeah, nothing at all creepy about that.

Regardless of my thoughts, I had already stood up off the ground. I dematerialized, then stepped through the exterior wall of her house.

Gwen's room was smaller than I'd expected. Her twin mattress was covered with a puffy blue comforter. The only other decor was a framed photograph of her and an older couple who looked nothing like her.

I looked to where Gwen slept soundly and smiled. She was exactly as I had pictured her - wrapped in fuzzy pink pajamas and snuggling a stray pillow. She was breathtaking.

I rematerialized and stood against the wall adjacent to her.

I had been such a fool to push her away and a bigger fool to try forcing feelings for Hannah. I should have known better. It was Eva I had loved all those years, not Hannah. Why did it take me so long to realize the difference?

Gwen was beautiful. The thought hit me once again as I leaned over her and reached for a strand of her hair. It wouldn't hurt to kiss her, would it? Just a small brush against her soft lips. Waves of desire crashed through me alongside memories of all the kisses we'd almost shared, how close our lips had come - but we'd always been interrupted. The constant denial of that desire stoked a flame in me that grew stronger and burned brighter every day. If not quenched, that burning desire would surely ignite and consume us both. I could feel it killing me now as I stood there fixated on those luscious lips.

I sat on the edge of the bed and bent over Gwen until my face was inches from hers. My eyes drank in her innocent face. I brushed the back side of my hand across her smooth skin and traced a finger over her parted lips. Just one kiss.

I leaned closer. Temptation had nearly pulled my lips to hers when the sound of a vehicle nearby stole my attention. Adrenaline spiked my blood. My entire body came to attention, prepared at any moment for battle. I listened carefully for every breath, every footstep.

I heard two hearts beating frantically, then shoes connecting with concrete as two figures exited the vehicle.

"What's your problem? Gary is a coworker, nothing more. How many times do I have to tell you that?"

"You need to remind yourself of that because every time he's around, I catch you flirting with him."

Relief washed over me, and my tensed muscles sagged. Apparently, the neighbors had returned and were in the middle of an argument.

I looked back down at Gwen.

What the hell was wrong with me?

I had almost taken advantage of Gwen.

I forced myself from her room before I could make another mistake. I returned to the backyard and once again laid my head in the thick, soft grass.

∞∞∞∞∞∞

It was getting late when we finally made it back to the Verona Beach office. It had been a productive night, the first work night Gwen and I'd had that hadn't been filled with tension. This particular project was the only one that wasn't designed to help my people back home; it was solely for humanity. Its purpose was to provide free and easy communications in third world countries. Free internet access and telephones would make it possible to more efficiently provide emergency services, health service announcements, and aid supplies to the people who needed them most. Out of all of our projects, this was the only one that had nothing to do with profit.

My heart swelled with pride at Gwen's reaction. She was instantly on board, offering whatever help she could give. She even volunteered her free time to work on the project. Her eagerness for the work spurred on my own, and before I'd realized it hours had passed. By the time we'd left Washington, it was one in the morning.

The quiet ride back was a constant struggle. My mind willed me to focus on the flight. My eyes traitorously strayed to Gwen's sleeping form. She had fallen asleep in the jet and looked so peaceful I just couldn't wake her. It was also the perfect excuse to hold her in my arms as I lifted her out of the jet and into the helicopter.

The lights from my building in Verona Beach came into view. I landed the helicopter, turned the engine off, and sat in the dark, watching Gwen sleep. Her head was laid back on the headrest, and her full lips were parted, allowing soft breaths to escape. Long eyelashes caressed her cheeks behind the cute glasses she'd worn. I took them gently off her face and put them up to my eyes.

Huh, no prescription. They were nothing but props. No doubt, she'd worn them in an attempt to look smarter and more professional. I wondered if she realized how damn sexy they looked on her. Probably. I'd bet her friend Beverly had picked them out for her.

Beverly was such a good friend for Gwen. She was loyal, kind, had integrity, maturity, and a great sense of humor. She was also straightforward and didn't take shit from anyone. It was quickly becoming clear to me that Beverly would make an excellent companion for Zane. That is, if he'd ever settle down.

Shit.

I had to contact Zane. I looked at my watch. It was already five in the morning. He'd be asleep, but I had to call him anyway.

" 'Lo," he answered groggily.

"Zane, I need you to meet me at the office. Gwen fell asleep, so I need you to follow me to her house with her car."

"Huh?"

"Come to the office," I repeated, a little impatiently.

"Wait, are you telling me you woke me up to drive Gwen's car so you don't have to wake *her* up? Are you serious?"

"Yes, I'm serious. After all the times I've gotten you out of trouble, you owe me one. Hell, you owe me hundreds," I replied.

"You're at the office? What is Gwen doing there?"

"She's my new assistant. Well, not exactly new. She's been working for me for a few weeks now. And before you ask, no, I didn't hire her. It was quite a surprise coming into the office and finding her there."

"Yeah, damn nice surprise. Why is it the only surprises I get are the shitty ones?"

"You tend to bring those on yourself, Zane. Come on, dude, just hurry up and get here."

It took Zane fifteen minutes, plenty of time for me to rifle through Gwen's purse and get her keys. I carried her gently to my car, although with as hard as she was sleeping, I was convinced I could have shaken her silly and she wouldn't have woken. I put her in the car and reached across her body to fasten the seatbelt. Her perfect lips were right there, and the temptation to kiss her almost consumed me. I leaned in so close I felt the gentle breaths escaping her lips.

"Hurry up. I'd like to get back to sleep sometime tonight," Zane complained behind me.

I kissed her cheek, then shut the door.

"Follow me." I tossed her keys at Zane.

Thirty minutes later, Gwen was tucked in her bed, her lights were out and the doors locked.

"Zane." I leaned against the car and crossed my arms. "We need to talk."

"Oh shit, here it comes." Zane rolled his eyes, for all the world like a rebellious teenager. "What now, Dad?"

"Well, *son*," I responded, "it's about time you started living up to your part in this mission. Besides, you need to stay busy. We can't have you ruining your reputation and destroying the plan, now can we?"

"Just spit it out, I don't need another lecture. What is it you want me to do?"

"You'll be working for Senator Kinsley as one of his aids. The experience will help you with the upcoming election. Also, we've got to get you enrolled in school. You need a degree."

"Can't you pull some strings and make it look like I have one?" Zane's irritation was clear in his voice.

I paused. I hated to concede, but he did have a point. "Fine. I'll probably have to bribe a few people, but we've got to make this work. Our future depends on it, so stop fucking around and stay out of trouble."

"Hey." He waited for me to look at him. "You can give me all kinds of shit about what I have or haven't done right, but try not to forget the sacrifice I'm making. That should count for something."

"It does." I squeezed his arm. "I'm sorry."

I watched as Zane walked away and thought about what I'd discovered tonight. When I'd searched her purse earlier in the night, Gwen's phone had buzzed, and the screen had lit up. I hadn't meant to snoop, but I couldn't help but read the texts that came in.

Ky: Pls 4give me im so sry

Ky: Let me xplain

Ky: @ least tlk 2 me

Ky: i love you

What the hell had Ky done? Whatever it was, it must've been pretty serious if she was ignoring him. I was tempted to hack her phone and read all her texts. It would only have taken a few seconds, but it would have been wrong.

Tomorrow I'd ask her about it.

Yeah right. Like we were such great friends and she'd actually confide in me.

One way or another, that was going to change. I wanted her in my life, so the secrets would have to end.

CHAPTER EIGHTEEN
Gwen

How did I get home?

Sunlight was already filtering through the blinds when a sudden jolt of panic flashed through me. I bolted out of bed and searched for my clock.

Seven thirty.

My body sagged in relief. Rehearsal was scheduled for nine. I glanced down at the bed and couldn't remember getting in it. The last thing I remembered was getting into Alexander's jet.

Determined not to be late, I forced myself out of bed and got ready for the day. By eight thirty, I was getting into my car. I shut the door and put the key in the ignition when I suddenly had the feeling of being watched. I looked around. The sun's rays highlighted the manicured middle-upper-class lawns that surrounded me. The same cookie cutter homes I'd known my whole life evoked a warm, comforting feeling. There was nothing out of place, and I didn't see anyone lurking in the shadows. But I had this strange feeling....

It was silly to let my imagination run wild. Certainly, my unease was a product of the emotional turmoil I'd been experiencing as of late. I shook my head, laughed at myself, and started the drive to the auditorium.

Focusing on the acting career I envisioned in dreams of my

future, I rehearsed the lines for that day's scenes as I drove. Immediately, I found myself becoming distracted. Every scene I was in that day involved Alexander, and just the thought of him caused my mind to go blank.

I drifted to a stop at the red light.

I closed my eyes and imagined my friend John in Alexander's place. *Much better*. I continued the drive to school, rehearsing my lines and gaining confidence that I'd make it through the day.

When I finally arrived, I strode toward the auditorium, head held down. I'd received a text from Ky insisting that we talk at rehearsal.

I increased my pace.

My legs burned from the exertion, but I knew if Ky managed to catch me before I reached the group, I would have no choice but to talk to him. And that was not a conversation that I wanted to have yet.

There he is. I caught his image in my peripheral. He was to my left about sixty feet away. Walk faster, I told myself as I saw him approaching.

"Gwen!" he yelled. "Gwen, please talk to me."

He was catching up. I started to jog, then sprinted the rest of the way. As I reached the door, I flung it open and stumbled forward, falling clumsily to the floor. Everyone turned and stared as I stayed there, on my hands and knees panting.

Ky walked up behind me. "Here, let me help you up." He offered me his hand. I shook my head. I didn't want his help.

He put his hand on my shoulder. "Gwen?"

I shook him off and whispered, "Just leave me alone, Ky."

He pulled his hand back and granted me the space I desperately needed.

I pulled myself to my feet and walked toward the stage. Everyone watched my approach, but it was Alexander that held my attention. I could see the questions forming in his eyes. I saw the moment his expression changed from curiosity to determination.

Just as I reached Alexander, Jasper approached. "Change of plans. Gwen and Alexander, we won't begin practicing the rest of your scenes until next week. You'll be backstage putting together props while everyone else practices." Jasper turned and leaned toward Hannah, placing his hand above her elbow and whispering into her ear. A small hint of a smile graced her lips as he whispered, then with a slight nod, she turned and walked away.

"All right, people, let's get started."

Alexander met my eyes and smiled that sexy lopsided smile of his. "You ready for some arts and crafts?"

I laughed, happy the chill between us had begun to thaw. "Jasper has no idea what he's in for."

Alexander gestured backstage, indicating I lead the way. This was such a bad idea. Acting was the only artistic skill I had. Drawing, painting, and anything else requiring creativity was beyond the scope for me. Jasper really should have asked questions before assigning tasks.

As I passed, Alexander placed his hand firmly against my lower back as he followed closely behind me.

We found the picnic table and the to-do list Jasper had left for us and sat down. Instead of sitting across from me, Alexander sat on the bench beside me, close enough that his thigh brushed mine. He leaned over my shoulder, trying to see the page as I read the instructions. I had just read the first sentence when his chin rested against my neck and his breath tickled my ear. The words on the page began swirling around, and I suddenly forgot how to read.

"What does it say?"

I looked over my left shoulder where his face was centimeters from mine. My breath caught, and I averted my gaze.

"I..." *Focus, Gwen, focus. Read the page.* I closed my eyes and forced myself to forget Alexander was there. I took a deep breath, opened my eyes and re-read the page.

A relieved laugh escaped my lips. Building. Not painting or

drawing or anything remotely resembling creative work. Jasper needed us to build the props. As in, put them together with a hammer and screwdriver. That was something I could do.

Alexander's chest pressed firmly against my back and his chin rested on my shoulder when he spoke softly into my ear, "What's so funny?"

"I thought we were going to have to paint. You know, something artsy. I was so worried. It looks like all we're going to be doing is nailing boards together," I giggled.

Alexander laughed, then got up and prepared to work. I found the pieces we needed to start and placed them in the center of the room. When I finished, I walked to where Alexander had set up a decent work area, complete with hammers, screwdrivers, a sawhorse, and a saw.

"There are a few pieces we'll have to cut. I'll need your help holding the wood steady," Alexander said as he looked at me.

"I can handle that."

"Here, put these on." He handed me a pair of gloves and safety goggles. I did as I was told and watched as he pulled his shirt up over his head. I tried to look away, but my eyes refused to move as they hungrily watched the tight muscles of his bronzed abdomen stretch when he lifted his arms over his head.

Damn.

He tossed his shirt on a nearby counter then turned his attention to me. Sexual tension thickened between us as his eyes met mine.

Alexander cleared his throat. "We should get started." He nodded toward the saw, then put on his goggles. His back flexed deliciously as he leaned over to position the boards for cutting.

I shook my head and focused. This was not the time for distractions. With my luck, I'd lose a finger.

I paid close attention and held the boards steady as he cut. The work was easy, and in under an hour, we were done.

Alexander removed his goggles and went to the vending

machines on the far right wall. He deposited some coins and returned with two drinks.

"Here." He handed me a Diet Mt. Dew.

"How did you know?"

"I pay attention. You always have one when you come to class and at work. I assumed it's your version of coffee in the morning."

"I'm surprised you'd notice something like that."

His eyes grew intense, the blue in them taking on a vibrant supernatural quality. "I notice everything about you, Gwen." His gaze locked on mine, holding me captive once again.

My lips parted to speak, but nothing came out. Things were different. I didn't know what it was, but something had changed between us in the last few days.

"We need to talk." He glanced away, back toward the stage area. "Would you come outside with me so we have some privacy?"

I nodded. "Under one condition." I blushed but refused to back down. "You need to put a shirt on first. I'd hate for you to cause an accident."

A sexy smirk spread across his face as he retrieved his shirt. He held it in front of him and winked. "You sure that's what you want? No take-backs."

I rolled my eyes. Alexander pulled the shirt over his head as we walked outside.

The weather was sweltering; within moments we were both covered in sweat. My shirt clung to me like a second skin.

Maybe we should have stayed inside.

I tripped forward when my foot caught on a crack in the sidewalk, but Alexander's hand flashed out and grabbed me just before I hit the ground.

"You're a danger to yourself, you know that?" He casually slipped his hand in mine. My heart fluttered nervously in my chest. His large hands were warm, and something about the way his fingers curved around mine felt right.

"I know I've already apologized, but I want to say it again. I've been a real asshole to you, and I'm sorry."

"It's okay. As long as you're serious about it staying in the past."

He smiled. "Consider it a promise."

We walked a few steps when he continued. "I know I should have asked you sooner, but I need to know. Are you seeing anyone? I get the impression there's something going on between you and Ky, right?" His voice was calm, but his eyes refused to meet mine. He focused instead on the buildings we passed, his gaze wandering over the shops and the people on the street.

I took a deep breath to steady myself. This was going to be an awkward conversation.

"Sort of. We dated for a few weeks and have been best friends for almost two years. But a few days ago, I caught him cheating on me."

"Damn." He lowered his head a moment before looking at me. "Are you sure? He seemed pretty intense this morning. Are you sure-"

"I saw a barely dressed woman getting into his car with him late one night. I went to his apartment and waited for him. When I woke up the next morning, he still hadn't returned. He disappeared for days and wouldn't answer his phone or his texts. When I went to his work, they said he had called in sick, so I knew his phone was working. Then when he finally texted me back, he claimed he'd been at home in bed sick those few days. It was all a lie."

Tears formed in my eyes. "I went by his apartment every day. Nothing had been touched. He had never returned home."

I paused to catch my breath.

Alexander rubbed my hand reassuringly, brushing his thumb along my knuckles, then spoke in a whisper, as if to himself, "What an idiot."

"I can tell you why." Knowing I'd live to regret it, but suddenly emboldened, I continued, "It's because I wouldn't have sex with

He hesitated. "You always seem fine. I would never have guessed something like that. How did you get through it?"

I almost didn't answer. The truth was too humiliating to confess, but I continued on regardless. "The night after the funeral, I began having these amazing dreams. I'm embarrassed to admit it, but-" I paused and lowered my head. "They were about a guy on a beach. I couldn't hear him or see him well, but in my dreams, he was there for me. I dreamt about him every night, and over time, I fell in love with him."

I looked over at Alexander and was surprised by the look of utter shock on his face.

Great, now he thinks I'm crazy.

"You dream about this guy every night? How long ago did it start?"

"About four years ago. Right after Wesley's funeral. And yeah, it's been every night since, until recently. I know it's ridiculous, but I kind of miss him." I peered over at him again. "Please don't think I'm crazy."

"Oh, I don't think you're crazy." He winked. "I think you're completely insane."

I punched his arm playfully.

"Of course, crazy chicks are hot. So...there is that." He strode a few more steps before he stopped and turned around. "So, are you and Ky really over?"

"Honestly, I'm not sure. I don't trust him, but I haven't officially broken up with him yet either."

He glanced toward the auditorium. "We should head back. They'll be finished soon."

∞∞∞∞∞∞

Ky followed me after practice. He'd had the good sense to wait until Alexander was gone before making his presence known. I'd noticed him first in my rearview mirror. I rolled my eyes thinking of the five calls from him I had ignored on the short drive, but I knew there'd be no ignoring him when I got home.

Sure enough, the moment I parked my car and got out, Ky was right next to me.

"Gwen, please. Just listen to me." He grabbed my arms and forced me to look into his eyes.

I snapped.

The anger I had been holding back the past few days broke through all at once. "Listen to you? Are you fucking serious? What, do you want to tell me again that you were home in bed?"

"Gwen, I-"

"No!" I shoved him as hard as I could. "You don't get to speak. I saw you. I saw that woman get into your car! I tried calling you. I thought someone had stolen your car. But I went to your apartment, and you weren't there!"

His eyes widened in surprise.

"I fell asleep on your bed hoping you'd come home and explain yourself. Do you know what happened? I woke up alone. You didn't return my texts or my calls for days. But you sure as hell called into work. You called them, but not me. How dare you!"

"Gwen, I may not have been sick, but I wasn't cheating on you."

"Then what were you doing?" I paused to catch my breath. "And who the hell was that woman?"

He dropped his head and muttered, "I can't tell you."

"You expect me to trust you? Just like that? Without an explaination?"

His eyes pleaded with me to understand. "It's not that I won't. It's that I can't. I can't tell you."

"Unbelievable." I shook my head.

Ky turned from me, rubbed his hand down his face, and blew out a sharp breath.

What was that? My heart jumped in my chest. I saw a flash of something that couldn't possibly be there.

"Ky, what is that?"

"What?"

"That right there." I grabbed his head and turned it away from me. "There, right there behind your right ear. What is that?" I pointed at the pink mark hidden behind his ear. It was the exact same mark I'd seen on Luke for years.

"It's just a birthmark." He placed his hand over it. "Stop looking at it, you're freaking me out."

"That's not just a birthmark. I've seen that before, it looks like a set of wings. What does it mean? Is it a tattoo?"

"Damn it, Gwen. It's just a fucking birthmark. Stop trying to change the subject. We need to discuss us. Our future. I love you. You've got to believe I'd never cheat on you."

"How am I supposed to believe you? All you've done since we met was lie. About your past, about that birthmark, and about... whatever the hell you were doing last week. And it's not the first time. Apparently, you did the same thing when you dated Hannah."

His eyes widened.

"Thought I didn't know about that, huh? You know what, get out of here. I don't want to look at you."

"But, Gwen-"

I fumbled through my purse until I found the key he'd given me.

"We are over, Ky." I slapped the key into his hand.

"Gwen, please-"

"Go away. I'm not talking to you anymore." I turned and left Ky standing in my driveway.

Hours later, sitting in my living room with a bowl of popcorn, I was still thinking about the events of the day. I knew without a doubt that the mark on Ky was more than just a birthmark. The moment I'd mentioned it, a panicked expression had crossed his face. What was that about? And how did he have the exact same mark that Luke had? I'd never believed in the supernatural, but it had to mean something. It had to be more than just a coincidence.

Was I making a mistake with Ky? Obviously, he was lying to me.

But why? It didn't make sense. It was like he was in the witness protection program or something. His entire life seemed fabricated, but that was impossible. He was only twenty-three years old. There had to be another explanation.

CHAPTER NINETEEN
Alexander

Her smile could light up the sky.

The thought surprised me as I glanced over at Hannah.

The convertible top was down, and a gentle breeze blew her hair from her face. Her smile was genuine, not the calculated smile I'd seen so often. Something about this carefree moment lowered my reservations about her.

"What?" She patted her hair in place.

I smiled at her. "You look so beautiful like that. Not a care in the world."

"Really?" she asked as she reverted to a more familiar well-calculated expression.

"Yeah." I pretended not to notice the change in her expression.

"That's it over there," she exclaimed, pointing to a building off to the left. A pink neon sign for Level Seven hung above the entryway where a long line awaited us.

"Don't worry. We won't have to wait," Hannah stated as if she'd read my mind.

As promised, we bypassed the line and were inside the club within minutes with a private table in the VIP lounge. I was surprised by how nice everything was. The lounge was situated high over the main dance floor with a view of the entire club. Dedicated waitresses roamed the lounge, taking orders and arranging transportation. I ordered a rum and coke, then sat back at my table and enjoyed the music. When Hannah asked me to dance, I refused, choosing instead to keep my eye on the door and wait for Zane. I had texted him as soon as we reached the parking lot, hoping to use him as an excuse to leave early. I knew I shouldn't have agreed to come out tonight, but I couldn't tell her no. By coming here, I feared I'd given her the wrong impression.

I sipped my drink and scanned the club for Zane. Knowing him, he'd get here, hook up with some random chick, and three hours later I'd still be waiting. I shifted my gaze to the small private dance floor in the VIP lounge and watched the dancers grinding against each other, moving in time with the flashing lights and loud music. Everyone here was looking for love of one kind or another, if only for the night. That had been my life for so many years, years in which life had become dull and drained of color and happiness. Drained of everything until recently, when sparks had begun to flicker to life again inside me.

Hannah returned dragging along two newcomers. A smile lit up Hannah's face as her eyes met mine, and she quickened her pace. She bounded up to me, grabbed my hands, and pulled me to my feet. "Beverly and Gwen are here." Hannah practically stood in front of Gwen as she smiled outrageously at me.

"So...how about some dancing?" Hannah gazed up at me. "Please, Alexander, please, please, please..." she begged the way a six-year-old would.

"I ..." My eyes flashed to Gwen's as I searched for the right words to turn Hannah down.

"I'll dance with you." A tall guy who was passing by grabbed Hannah by the waist and pulled her to the small dance floor in the lounge. Hannah started to refuse, hesitated, then flashed a sexy smile in his direction.

Hannah crooked her finger, beckoning him to her, and swayed

her hips to the music. It took all of two seconds to figure out what she was up to. That girl definitely wasn't subtle. As he pulled her to him, she began to grind her hips against his crotch, and all the while her eyes stared seductively into mine. How was it that in one moment I could find her endearing, and in the next, I couldn't stand to be near her?

I turned my attention back to the table, and my gaze connected with Gwen's. Smudged kohl rimmed her emerald eyes. Flashing lights highlighted the contours of her cheeks and sensuality of her lips.

Mmmm...those lips. I wondered what they'd taste like. I bet I could suck on them for hours....

"Ahem." Beverly cleared her throat at the awkward silence. "I'm going to get a drink, I'll be back...." She abruptly turned and walked toward the bar.

Gwen and I stared at each other in silence for a beat.

"Hey," Gwen said shyly after Beverly walked away.

It was evident the ease we'd shared with each other at rehearsal had been replaced with something else. Something that brought a flush to Gwen's face and caused my heart to pound in my chest. Thick sexual tension urged me forward, pushing me to move too quickly, and I struggled to hold myself back from her.

"Hey, stranger," I replied.

"At some point, I'm going to stop being a stranger." She smiled as she took the seat beside mine.

"I sure hope so."

Her face flushed beautifully.

Focus, you'll make a fool of yourself if you keep staring at her like a fucking idiot.

I moved my gaze to the dance floor where Hannah was still dancing. Thankfully, it seemed Hannah had forgotten me and was basking in her new partner's attention.

"There's only one way to fix that. We need to get to know each other. Soooooo...." I tried to think of something clever but ended up settling for bizarre. "What's the meanest thing you've ever done to someone?"

CHAPTER TWENTY
Gwen

How am I supposed to answer that? If I answered truthfully, he'd either laugh or think I was crazy. But if I said nothing, I risked being boring. Besides, hadn't everyone done something mean at some point in their life?

In an attempt to buy some time, I glanced toward Hannah and her ex-boyfriend Bobby. Hannah had practically turned him into her own personal stripper pole, and half the club was watching her.

"Okay.... I once gave my cousin dysentery."

Alexander practically spat out his drink, and I couldn't help but smile at his reaction.

"What?"

"Well, not actual dysentery, but pretty close. You see, I have these two cousins, Christy and Noah. They never got along very well. The night before a family outing, Christy and I gave Noah chocolate Exlax and told him it was candy. Well, apparently that stuff tasted better than we thought because Noah wanted more. Needless to say, Noah spent the entire day on the toilet, and we went on the best family trip we'd ever had."

Alexander began laughing. "Wow, you are evil!"

"Hey, it wasn't my idea! Christy made me, and back then you never went against her. She was scary," I replied, faking a shiver.

"But we sure did have a lot of fun together."

"Anything else you need to confess?"

"Well," I felt rather hesitant to continue.

"Oh no," Alexander prodded. "Don't stop now."

"Okay, me and my cousin-"

"Christy?"

"No, this time it was Sophie. We put blue toilet water in a cup and told my four-year-old brother that if he didn't drink it, he would turn blue."

"Did he drink it?"

I winced. "Every single drop!" I couldn't hold back my smile any longer, and as it grew, I realized I had been grinning non-stop, and my cheeks were beginning to hurt. I tried to relax my face but couldn't. "But again, not my fault. Sophie made me."

"I don't know. I think I'm starting to see a trend here."

"Seriously, that's the extent of my meanness. Those are the only pranks I've ever played. What about you? I bet you've pulled some good ones."

"Of course not." He winked. "I'm an angel."

"Yeah, and I'm Santa Claus," I joked, trying to hide the relief I was beginning to feel. The butterflies in my stomach were still there, but they were gliding around leisurely instead of swarming with an intensity that made me sick.

Beverly returned just in time to overhear me and threw her arms around my shoulders. "Well, if you're Santa Claus, I get the first ride on your lap."

"Ride?"

"Yeah, men don't work that hard without getting something in return. So I get the first ride, even if you are my bestie!"

"I'm a girl," I replied and rolled my eyes.

"I'm sure even Mrs. Claus wouldn't mind a ride now and then." She smiled and wiggled her eyebrows at me.

I pushed her away. "You are disgusting, but I love you."

"You better, you're stuck with me. Besides, you're lucky to have a friend as wonderful as me. Speaking of lucky…" Beverly gestured toward the dance floor. "Looks like Bobby may be getting lucky tonight."

Beverly's face paled. "Oh shit." She glanced at Alexander. "Aren't you and Hannah together?"

"No. We're just…neighbors? Friends?"

"Well, I don't think Hannah knows that." Then, obviously trying to change the subject, Beverly continued, "So Alexander, what the hell possessed your family to move to Verona Beach?"

"You make it sound like such a bad place to live." He laughed and took a sip of his drink. "I don't know. We got tired of the city. Dad thought moving somewhere more rural would be a nice change of pace. We love the beach. Love the peacefulness about it. And Verona Beach is one of the few places in America that combines country living, high-end luxury homes, beachfront property, and," he emphasized with a smile, "hot locals, all in one place."

I rolled my eyes. "Yeah, your dad bought a multi-million-dollar home here because of the hot chicks."

"You laugh, but we all know what motivates men."

"Sex," Beverly and I answered at the same time.

He laughed again. "I was going to say beautiful women, but yeah, sex will do it too."

"Mmm. Sex, my favorite topic."

My eyes darted to a slightly older, brown-eyed version of Alexander strutting over to us, wearing dark fitted jeans and a snug gray v-neck that perfectly accentuated his bulging muscles.

"Hey, hot stuff," he purred as he stepped into Beverly's personal space, took her drink from her hand, and downed it in one gulp.

Beverly's mouth dropped as she stared at him.

He smiled wickedly, lifted a crooked finger to her chin and closed her mouth.

"It's not polite to stare, beautiful."

"Please excuse my older brother, Zane. Apparently, our father failed to teach him any respect," Alexander admonished with a disapproving look.

"Yeah, well. Dear old dad learned to chill out long before you did. What's your problem? You think you're the only one around here who's allowed to get any action?" Zane replied, glancing pointedly at me.

What was that about?

"Zane!"

"Okay, okay." Zane threw his hands up apologetically, turned toward Beverly, changed his demeanor, and affected an English accent. "Please forgive me, m'lady, for I forgot with whom I was speaking. Thy beauty enchanted my wits away from mine head, leaving only my lower head to lead me." Zane winked, then bowed before Beverly.

Beverly, having found her composure, replied, "If thy lower head be thy lead, dear sir, it's no wonder thou behave with such nonsense. With a brain of such size, thou amaze all with thy ability to even speak."

Zane's smile widened. Challenge accepted. "Lovely damsel, if size is the knowledge thou desire, thou will find it speaks quite eloquently in any tongue."

"Zane," Alexander exclaimed sharply. "That's enough."

Zane shut his mouth but continued to smile at Beverly, whose eyes sparkled brightly.

"Alexander," Hannah crooned as she hurried back to our group. "Dance with me, *please*? I won't take no for an answer this time." Hannah grabbed Alexander's hand and dragged him onto the dance floor.

The room was suddenly a furnace. I couldn't stop my fists from clenching as I watched Hannah slide her hands down Alexander's chest as she swayed against him.

Alexander was not a good dancer. He awkwardly moved with the music as Hannah swayed, shimmied, and bounced against him. He shifted from left to right, never even lifting his feet off the ground. It was the white boy shuffle at its finest, but Hannah didn't seem to care, her hands roaming up and down his body.

I looked away, ashamed at the anger and frustration coursing through me, and realized I was alone. Where had everyone gone? I quickly spied Beverly and Zane dancing at the edge of the dance floor. They seemed to be in their own world, staring into each other's eyes, Zane's hands squeezing Beverly's ass while he grinded up against her in a way that was much too vulgar to watch.

I needed a drink if I was going to survive this night. I waved down a waitress and ordered an Amaretto Sour and two jagerbombs. In an attempt to avoid looking at Alexander, I watched Zane and Beverly while I waited for my drinks. Zane looked like he was on the verge of ripping her clothes off right there on the dance floor. From the look in Beverly's eyes, I didn't think she would have stopped him if he'd tried.

What I wouldn't give to be that uninhibited. I could never dance like that, especially in a crowd like this with everyone staring. After a few minutes passed, I watched Bobby return to the dance floor. He grabbed a girl close to Hannah and began twirling, dipping, and grinding up against her, obviously trying and succeeding in getting Hannah's attention. Her jealous side got the best of her, and Hannah began dancing around Alexander like a woman possessed.

How much more of this could I take?

I downed my drinks, slamming the last shot glass down onto the table, then made my way onto the dance floor. Not bothering to look for a partner, I threw back my head, closed my eyes, and swayed my hips to the slow, hypnotic beat. The music was erotic, the beat vibrating through my body. I felt the alcohol kick in as my muscles loosened and swayed.

Large hands slid around my waist and pulled me back against a hard, muscular chest.

"Hey, stranger."

Alexander.

I stilled as his warm breath whispered across my neck.

We stood motionless amongst the throng of writhing bodies.

His fingers trailed up and down my sides in maddeningly slow circles, up my ribcage, then slowly down to my hips, up further, then down again.

The music pulsed around us. Violet lights flashed against the gyrating bodies. All I could feel was the teasing of his fingertips, the hardness of his chest as it pressed into me, and the warmth of his breath on my neck.

My body hummed with pleasure.

Soft lips grazed my shoulder and skimmed up my neck.

"What-" I gasped as his teeth tugged at my ear. "What are you doing?"

"I thought," he teased, "I was dancing with you."

His lips brushed my neck again, and I shivered.

"This," I dropped my head back onto his shoulder as his fingers made another round up my sides, "is not dancing."

"Isn't it?" he breathed into my ear.

Alexander spun me around and jerked my body against his. His chest was crushed against mine. His hands gripped low on my hips.

And then he began to move.

His arms pulled me tight as he moved to the sensual beat of the music. His hips rolled against mine, and I gasped.

I had never been so thrilled to be proven wrong. Alexander wasn't a bad dancer. He was fucking amazing.

Alexander's forehead lowered to mine as he slipped a hand possessively around the back of my neck. His indigo eyes, just inches from mine, blazed with a fiery intensity.

He moved to the rhythmic beat. Every vibration of the music and every roll of his hips had his hardness rubbing slowly between my thighs and driving me insane.

My grip tightened around his shoulders. My nails dug through the soft fabric of his shirt and into the bulging muscles beneath.

Hunger flared in his hooded eyes.

"How about this?" he growled. "Is this dancing?"

He ground against my hips in the most delicious way.

"No," I hissed.

His lips parted as he leaned forward. The world spun wildly around me. I couldn't breathe, and the throbbing between my thighs pounded as I anticipated his kiss.

Alexander's hand slid up from my neck and twined through my hair. His hand suddenly fisted and jerked my head back.

I gasped.

Chills shot from the roots of my hair down my spine. His grip tightened, pulling my head back and forcing my mouth open as he lowered his parted lips to mine.

But not all the way. He remained just barely out of reach. Taunting me. Teasing me. My inhale became his exhale. Our mouths mimicked our bodies as he tortured me with his hips.

I begged him to kiss me. I strained against his grasp and struggled against his hold, desperate to seal my lips to his. My body screamed for release. Demanded it.

Temptation, desire, need, and want coursed through me, feeding my frustration. I couldn't take much more. It was already too much.

The music changed, shifting the atmosphere along with it. A popular song with an upbeat tempo blared from the speakers. As the dancers around us moved to accommodate this change, we remained wrapped around each other in a heated embrace.

Alexander's hand stayed tangled in my hair, his lips a breath away from mine. Then slowly, so very slowly, that hand loosened and slid down around my waist. He gathered me to him and nestled his face into my neck. His body trembled against mine as we stood motionless on the dance floor.

A moment passed.

His grip remained firm.

"You okay?" I could barely breathe the words as I gasped for air.

He groaned into my neck as he squeezed me tighter against him.

Drunken dancers bumped and jostled us. Another song started. Silent, unmoving moments passed between us before he tilted his head to the side and brushed a kiss against my cheek.

His warm breath heated my hair as he murmured something unintelligible, then released me.

His assault on my body had destroyed my equilibrium. My knees gave out, and I stumbled forward.

"Little too much to drink?" he asked with a laugh that didn't match the fire in his eyes.

"Yeah," I managed as he slid an arm around my waist. When we reached the table, everyone was ready to go. I paid my bill and followed the group toward the parking lot.

I walked a few paces behind, alone and confused. Alexander had released my waist the moment Hannah came into view and glared at us. With nothing more than an apologetic glance, he went to her. She smirked, then wrapped her arm around Alexander's and pulled him ahead of the group.

Beverly and Zane were all over each other. They kissed and groped as they walked, bumping into parked cars and traffic signs. Following at the back, I retraced my steps through the night.

What the hell had happened? One minute Alexander was all over me, in the next he was rushing to Hannah's side. Why would he do that? He'd said they weren't together, but he sure as hell had acted guilty when Hannah had glared at us.

I shook my head.

I should have known better. That man was a player who enjoyed toying with my emotions. I knew that, yet still, I'd let him seduce me again.

"Motherfucker!"

Zane jerked away from Beverly and sprinted across the lot. A string of curses flew from his mouth as he circled a bright red Ferrari. He ran his hands across his face and through his hair.

What was wrong with him? In the low lighting, it took a moment to see what he was going on about.

Holy shit. Every single tire was slashed. Glass was littered across the asphalt from the windshield that had been busted out. Massive dents and scratched paint covered the car.

Alexander swore.

"Yeah." Zane knelt beside his mangled car. "Why the Ferrari? Why couldn't they have waited till I drove the damn Jeep?"

Zane jerked to his feet.

"Shit, shit, shit, shit!" Each word grew louder as Zane tightened his fists and paced around his car.

"Zane, chill. I'll take care of it." Alexander pulled out his phone and punched in a number.

"Can we ride with you?" Alexander asked Beverly while waiting for whomever he dialed to pick up.

"You can ride with me," Hannah said hastily.

"No. Beverly and Zane are the only ones who haven't been drinking." Alexander looked to Zane. "You drive Hannah home in her car. Beverly, would you mind giving the rest of us a ride?"

Beverly's eyes flashed to mine. "Yeah, sure."

Hannah's face dropped, and I swore she almost stomped her foot. When Zane took Hannah's keys, she pursed her lips but didn't protest.

"Damn." Alexander pocketed his phone. "They're not answering. I'll have to call a tow truck in the morning."

"What about the police?"

"I'll give them a call once I get home. I know a few officers at the station. They'll take care of this without us having to hang around all night to give a statement."

With that, Alexander hopped into the passenger side of

Beverly's car, leaving me in the back seat by myself.

CHAPTER TWENTY-ONE
Alexander

The equipment I'd ordered had finally been delivered to the house. For some reason, they had been unable to procure everything in the time I'd requested, but at least it was here now.

The research I planned would hopefully map the differences between human and hybrid DNA. Angels lived forever and didn't age. But when they conceived with a human, the resulting DNA combination gave hybrids an extremely long life. Hybrids aged at a much slower rate than humans, allowing them to live for thousands of years. What I wanted to accomplish was to first find which particular gene was responsible for this extended lifespan then devise a way to manipulate it in human DNA. If successful, I might actually stand a chance of having a real relationship with Gwen.

To begin my research, it would have helped to have a sample of her DNA. I looked up from my perch at the foot of Gwen's bed and gazed at her sleeping form. Now would be the easiest time to get it. I got up and crossed the room.

Damn, she was so beautiful. I stood at the edge of her bed, captivated by her. She was curled away from me, facing the wall. Even that partial glimpse of her took my breath away. What was it about her? Like a siren's call, I was drawn to her against my will. The desire I felt for her ran deep. I yearned for her at a cellular level. I felt it in my bones.

And it went well beyond the physical. There was so much more to Gwen. I'd seen glimpses of it over the past few weeks. There was a quality in her I couldn't explain, a strange mixture of kindness, selflessness, forgiveness, strength, and a certain groundedness that pulled me in.

I stood enthralled by her. My eyes were glued to her innocent face. My mind was completely blank. A strong emotion surged through me. It swelled within me, threatening to burst from my chest. I couldn't contain it. I couldn't breathe as it ravaged my insides.

What is happening to me?

My hands shook as I pulled out my phone and called Zane. He'd have to watch over her tonight. Something was wrong with me.

But I needed that blood sample first. My eyes swept over her. It was just a little blood, I reminded myself. She wouldn't even feel it.

"No!" her soft voice called out. "Luke, where are you? Why aren't you here?"

Who the hell is Luke?

Was there another guy in her life I wasn't aware of?

Damn it.

I had to get the hell out of her room. I'd get the blood sample later.

CHAPTER TWENTY-TWO

Gwen

Despite Beverly's reassurances, I felt horrible.

Once again, Alexander had left me feeling rejected like a toy taken out and played with to pass the time, then put back on the shelf when he was bored. I was sick and tired of it. If he couldn't decide between Hannah and I, then Hannah could have his sorry ass.

I was an emotional wreck. I hated the rejection that washed over me every time I thought about that night. I hated the tears running down my cheeks. But no matter how hard I tried, and no matter how irrational I knew it was, I couldn't stop them.

Knock, knock, knock.

What now?

"Gwen, open up, it's me." Ky's determined voice was muffled through the door.

I wiped my eyes with the back of my hand then flung the door open with too much force. Ky took a cautious step back. "Gwen?"

"What do you want, Ky?" My response would have been harsh if not for the sob that followed.

It only took a moment for Ky to take in my tear-stained face and weak voice. He pushed his way into my house, shut the door, and pulled me to him. He didn't ask what was wrong; he just held me tightly and let me cry.

I couldn't help it. I cried until I couldn't anymore, until my body didn't have any moisture left. Ky held me through it all, and as much as I hated to admit it, it was a relief to have him with me.

Ky rubbed my back as he held me close, and after a few minutes, I began to calm.

"I need to freshen up. I'll be right back."

I left Ky and went to the bathroom. I blew my nose and splashed cool water on my face.

I patted my skin dry, then ran a brush through my hair.

When I returned to the living room, Ky was resting comfortably on my couch, shoes off, feet propped up on my coffee table. It would have been so easy to forget everything that had happened and return to how we'd been a few weeks ago when everything had been perfect between us. The thought was tempting. Being with Ky felt so comfortable and safe like a warm pair of pajamas. But I couldn't forget how he'd betrayed me.

"What are you doing here?"

"I wanted to talk. You refused to speak to me before, so I gave you space to think. But now you need to hear me out."

I walked to the couch and sat next to him. Out of habit, he reached over, twined his fingers around mine, then laid both our hands against his thigh.

I sighed. It was undeniable how effortless it was being with Ky.

He straightened and cleared his throat. "I love you, Gwen. I've been in love with you from the day we first met. There's nothing in the world I wouldn't do for you. You have to know it's true. You can't deny it. So why can't you believe me when I tell you I wasn't cheating? I would never cheat on you, Gwen." His eyes met mine with a fierce intensity.

"Then what about-"

"I can't tell you where I was during the time I was gone. All I can say is that I've been doing some investigation to find my family."

That got my attention. "You told me your family was dead. You said you didn't have any family."

"It's a long story. The information is dangerous, and I've already told you too much."

I nodded. As crazy as it sounded, a small part of me believed him. Or maybe I was just lonely and needed to fill the gaping hole in my empty life. I scooted closer and laid my head on Ky's shoulder.

We sat in amicable silence for a few moments. Ky's warm hand around mine was comforting. I looked at him, noticing again how stunning he was. Images of the times we'd spent together flashed through my mind. The first night he'd kissed me. That sparkle in his eyes the first time he'd told me he loved me. That damn sexy smile of his. My heart swelled as the memories surfaced but plummeted when I remembered all the deception.

After everything that'd happened, how could I ever trust him again?

He stared straight ahead, lost in thought. His strong angular face was the type dreams were made of. Fantasies to be more exact. It had been a constant battle keeping other women away from him when we'd been together. Not that he'd noticed. He was completely oblivious to anyone but me.

"I'll try." The words escaped my lips before I thought them through.

His eyes pierced mine. A slow smile spread across his face. "What did you just say?"

"I said I'd try. To believe you, that is. But just as friends. I'm not promising anything, but I'll try."

CHAPTER TWENTY-THREE
Alexander

What the hell is this?

From Gwen's backyard, I listened to Ky drive up Gwen's driveway and knock on her door. What was he doing here? Was he here to hurt her? Or was he trying to get her back?

Note to self, have Zane research Ky's background immediately.

"Give me a minute. I'm almost ready."

She was expecting him? The gears in my mind ground to a halt as I stood dumbly in Gwen's backyard.

She wasn't supposed to trust him. They were supposed to be over. And hell, I'd thought we'd started something the other night at the club.

Had my actions not made it clear that I wanted to be with her? I'd thought I'd been pretty obvious. But then again, there was Hannah. Always forcing herself between us.

Everything suddenly shifted into focus, and I saw how the events of that night would have looked to Gwen.

I groaned.

Fucking Hannah.

The way she'd grabbed me and monopolized my attention hadn't gone unnoticed. And she'd done that shit on purpose.

I'd played right into her game. Hell, I'd made it worse after

Zane's car was vandalized by being so aloof.

I'd been so focused on scanning the area and trying to figure out who was fucking with us that I'd completely ignored Gwen.

And now Ky was back. The guy that had hidden outside and taken pictures of my home.

Damn it.

I'd only left her alone for a few hours the day before. Ky must have talked to her then.

Stupid, stupid, stupid. I didn't know what the hell I'd missed, but it was obvious she wasn't angry at him anymore. Were they just friends, or had they gotten back together?

I felt my blood pressure rise. Was he getting closer to her so he could hurt her? So that he could hurt my family? The thoughts rolled around in my mind, worsening as the minutes passed.

Gwen finished dressing and got into Ky's car. Within seconds I was in my car and following them from a distance. I left the radio off and listened in on their conversation. When their car turned right on Adams Street, I heard Ky ask, "Did you get the email about the changeup?"

"Yes," she answered tightly.

What changeup?

I hit the autopilot button I had installed and pulled up my email.

"I think it'll be interesting," Ky snickered. There was something in his voice that I didn't like.

What is he talking about? I scrolled down, found the group email Jasper had sent out the day before, and began reading. Jasper had made some changes to the play to shake things up a bit. As I read the new manuscript, I felt my blood pressure rise. Apparently, Jasper thought Nathan needed competition. So now, Nathan's best friend, the character played by Ky, was going to pursue Beth as well.

This play was getting too fucking real for comfort.

Damn. I could play it cool and act detached to a point, but there was no fucking way I'd be able to sit by and watch Ky making out with Gwen.

I slammed my fist down on the armrest. There was a loud crack as the plastic shattered.

Fuck it. If Ky thought he could use this play to seduce her, he'd have the competition of a lifetime. *Game on.*

"Gwen, do you think—"

"Don't push me. I said I'd think about it."

My head shot up. What was she going to think about? She couldn't be thinking about getting back together with him. They must have been talking about something else. Obviously, they'd had a conversation in the short time I wasn't with her yesterday.

From now on, either Zane or I would have to be with her every minute of the day. Ky was dangerous, and I couldn't leave her unprotected.

I spent the remainder of the ride memorizing my new lines and trying hard not to think about how Ky would soon be kissing Gwen.

CHAPTER TWENTY-FOUR

Gwen

Ky was enjoying the change of script a little too much. He talked about it nonstop in the car, and then again in the auditorium when he smirked at Alexander. Apparently, Ky was under the delusion that Alexander was interested in me. He hadn't yet figured out that Alexander didn't care.

Before I could start dwelling on Alexander again, I forced myself to refocus on the play.

Jasper had really outdone himself. The stage looked fantastic. The moonlight illuminating the "rooftop" looked so real I couldn't figure out how he'd accomplished it.

I closed my eyes, took a deep breath, and focused on getting into character.

I was Beth. Things were going downhill with Nathan. Nathan's best friend Ethan had asked to speak with me and led me to the rooftop for privacy.

I gasped in an astonished breath as I walked onto the stage. I looked up, admired the non-existent stars, then glanced out over the romantic dinner setting that Ethan had set up.

"Oh, my–" I paused trying to look flustered. "You just wanted to talk, right? All this isn't for me.... This is a mistake." My voice faded off as I looked at Ky.

His eyes begged me to listen. "Beth, I did want to talk. I wanted to tell you that I've fallen for you." His words hit me hard. These were the same words he'd said to me not long ago.

"I love you, Beth. You're my world. Please." His beautiful brown eyes pleaded with me, and I knew he meant every word. "Choose me."

My heart squeezed in my chest at the hurt I knew I was causing him.

I looked away.

"I don't know." I shook my head. "This isn't a good idea."

"It's a great idea," he whispered.

He grabbed my hands, jerked me roughly into his arms, and crushed his lips to mine. And just as Beth was scripted to do, I pushed Ky away. But when he persisted, I allowed myself to melt into his kiss.

∞∞∞∞∞∞

I was relieved that rehearsal was over. It was early, yet I felt utterly drained. I wanted to go home and curl up in bed. There'd been too much going on lately. I'd spent a majority of my life avoiding drama, and now I was immersed in it.

"Are you ready?" Ky asked as he motioned toward the door of the auditorium.

When I nodded, he grabbed my bag and headed for his car.

Something had to change with this whole guy situation. It was getting ridiculous.

And painful.

Rejection stung more than I'd ever given it credit for. I had thought Alexander felt something for me. Attraction if nothing else. But now...well, I could see I was completely wrong about there being any mutual attraction between us. He'd just been playing a game to see how long he could string both Hannah and me along.

I glanced at Ky as he navigated downtown Verona Beach. That kiss during practice had been amazing, but that didn't make it enough to erase the past. Ky would never be more than a friend, and this whole thing with the play wasn't fair to him. He needed to accept that things were over between us.

I allowed my gaze to drift up over his profile, noticing once again how handsome he was. It certainly wouldn't take long for him find someone else. I just hoped he would find someone who would treat him right.

Ky glanced over his shoulder to pass the car in front of us, and I caught a glimpse of that pink birthmark I'd noticed before.

I knew it was the same mark Luke had, but that was crazy. Luke was just a dream. He wasn't real. But I'd noticed that mark behind his ear years before I'd ever met Ky. That had to mean something, didn't it?

Luke and Ky *were* similar. They had the same birthmark. Luke's face had always been too blurry to truly make out, but it could have been Ky. They were close to the same height, though Luke seemed to be leaner. And Ky didn't have a golden tattoo.

What was wrong with me? Why was I looking for an excuse to make more out of our relationship than there was?

"We're here."

I looked around and saw that we were parked outside Mercury Technologies.

Ky leaned over the armrest. Was he trying to kiss me? It was one thing to do it for the play, but this was different. I had no intention of getting back together with Ky. Yet for some reason, my words stuck in my throat, and before I knew it, his lips were brushing gently across mine.

"Have a good day at work. Call me when you get out."

I scrambled out of the car, horrified at what I'd allowed to happen.

What was wrong with me? Why had I given Ky false hope like that?

A hysterical laugh nearly escaped my lips when I realized I was leaving Ky to go work with Alexander. Jumping from the frying pan straight into the blazing hot fire.

I closed my eyes and took a deep breath.

I could do this. I needed this job.

But damn it, I couldn't work so closely with Alexander. Between his mercurial mood swings and my foolish infatuation with him, I was bound to get hurt.

Maybe I'd get lucky tonight, and he'd have an out-of-town meeting. Then I'd be able to stay behind and take care of the paperwork in peace.

The office was empty when I arrived. Even Bonnie, the daytime secretary, had gone home.

I went to Alexander's office and sat at his desk. I was surprised I didn't find much work to do. In fact, it looked as if there hadn't been any work piling up in all of the days I'd been gone.

"Enjoying yourself?"

I jumped out of Alexander's seat. My face reddened as I peered up at Alexander.

"Just doing my job." I leaned over and logged off the computer. "I've been gone a few days and expected to be flooded with work, but there's nothing. What have you been doing this week?"

He placed a hand over his heart. A dimpled smile spread across his face. "Gwen, are you worried about me?"

My heart fluttered, and I had to remind myself not to fall into his trap again.

"No." I clenched my fists and ignored the magnetic pull. "I'm just doing my job."

He studied me a moment before his posture straightened. "Chad Powell in the Atlanta office took over for me the last few days."

Alexander sat at this desk, logged into his computer, and printed out a few documents.

"Here. These are Chad's. Go through them. Make sure everything is documented, and let me know when you're done."

I snatched the papers from his hand and left his office.

If I just focused on my work, maybe I could forget Alexander was here. I bent over the papers and got down to business.

This Chad Powell was meticulous. I couldn't find a single error in his work. I poured over his papers and checked every detail. There was a lot to go through, much more than I'd expected. It took nearly three hours to complete everything. By the time I'd finished, my back ached, and my eyes hurt from the strain.

I went into Alexander's office without knocking and handed over Chad's paperwork. Alexander shook his head, motioning toward the filing cabinets across the room.

I hated filing, but I dutifully crossed the room and did my job.

"It looks like you forgave Ky."

I didn't answer.

"Are you getting back together with him?"

"That's none of your business." I slammed a cabinet shut, then opened the next.

Why couldn't he leave me alone? He'd barely spoken to me all night – why would he decide to use the last twenty minutes of my shift to screw with me?

"Gwen."

I refused to face him. Refused to engage. I wouldn't play his games anymore.

"Gwen. Are you getting back together with Ky?"

I tried to ignore him, but then I found myself wondering –

Why does he even care?

"You're jealous," I spoke the words in awe as the thought occurred to me.

"Yes," he whispered, sending a thrill through me. "Are you getting back together with Ky?"

"I don't know." I shrugged. "Maybe."

When he didn't respond, I thought the conversation was over. I grabbed the next file and-

I felt his presence behind me. His warm breath tickled my ear as the heat from his chest radiated into me.

"You don't want Ky."

"Yes, I do." I could barely get the lie out as my heart thrummed loudly in my ears. "And I enjoyed kissing him today, too."

His chest brushed my back as he towered over me.

I hated the way I shivered at his closeness. Hated how I yearned for his touch.

I could almost feel his lips against my skin as he whispered, "You're lying."

I denied it with a shake of my head.

"Is it his kiss that leaves you breathless? Is he the one who makes you so drunk with desire you can't see straight?" His voice was low and seductive. Each word whispered over my skin in a sensual caress.

"Tell me, Gwen," he growled into my ear. "Does his kiss do that?"

"Y-Yes," I breathed through trembling lips.

I gasped as he grazed my neck with his teeth.

His warm breath caressed my skin. I was drugged with anticipation.

I wanted his lips on me. I wanted *him*.

"No." His head shook gently. "He doesn't evoke a tenth of the passion you feel for me. Right now." He pressed a lingering kiss against my jaw. "And I've barely even touched you."

A breath I hadn't known I was holding came out in a huff.

He stepped away and cool air chilled my backside. My body revolted against the sudden loss and swayed as it regained equilibrium.

Alexander walked back to his desk and pulled out a pen.

His focus shifted seamlessly to his work as if he'd merely taken a momentary coffee break.

Humiliation flared brightly as I realized he'd played me again.

My muscles tensed and heart pounded with adrenaline. I was infuriated at my traitorous body's response to him, at how easily he made me look the fool.

That bastard.

I stepped forward. "You-"

Just then, Ky strode into the office and gave me a strange look.

"Hey," I said as casually as I could. "I've got about ten more minutes if you want to wait in the car for me."

Ky didn't move. He stared at Alexander.

No. They stared at each other, neither one willing to back down.

The tension in the room skyrocketed, and I shifted uncomfortably.

"Alexander, I'll finish these tomorrow."

I didn't wait for his response as I dropped the papers on his desk, grabbed Ky's arm, and dragged him outside.

We had only been in the car for three minutes when Ky broke the silence. "What the hell was going on back there?"

I pretended to search for something in my purse. "What do you mean?"

Ky gave me a look that clearly said, *Who do you think you're fooling?*

"I was just filing some paperwork."

"Yeah, if that's the case, then why did you look like you were about to take his head off?"

I shook my head and smiled. "It was nothing. Just a disagreement about some paperwork. Don't worry about it."

The rest of the ride home was made in stark silence. Ky focused on the road, deep in thought, and I did my best to forget the last few minutes I'd shared with Alexander.

Did he get off on screwing with my head? Flirting with me, then pushing me away?

I clenched my fists as I remembered that sexy smirk he'd flashed me. I wanted to slap it right off his face.

Calm down, Gwen.

The last thing I needed was for Ky to notice how pissed off I was. He didn't need any more reasons to hate Alexander.

The moment we pulled into my driveway, I reached for the handle to get out. "Thanks, Ky."

He grabbed my hand as he leaned toward me. His lips were an inch from mine when I blurted, "I can't."

I jumped out of the car and ignored the hurt expression on Ky's face.

Guilt washed over me as I dashed up the drive and through the front door, but Ky should have known better. I'd told him we were just friends.

Even so, I felt horrible. Ky was my friend, and I was hurting him.

Not for the first time, I wondered what was wrong with me. Why was I still drawn to Alexander? He constantly pushed and pulled me. Went for Hannah one minute and me the next. Why was I so physically attracted to a man who would treat me that way? And why was it I could easily ignore all that Alexander did, but I couldn't overlook what Ky had done? Despite the fact that Ky was clearly hiding something, I believed his insistence that he hadn't cheated. And yet, I still couldn't get past his deception. I still couldn't rekindle that spark.

Minutes later, I stood in front of my bathroom mirror and studied my reflection. Somehow, I'd expected to look different, that the turmoil inside me would reflect on the outside. But the same face I'd looked at for the past twenty-two years stared back at me, completely unchanged.

∞∞∞∞∞∞

I'd missed Hannah's friendship and felt horrible about the resentment I'd harbored for her recently, so I was pleased when she invited me over this afternoon. Maybe this was the first step toward repairing our relationship.

We were sitting in her bedroom getting ready for the party she was throwing. I had a date meeting me, a date Hannah had set up without asking me, and she wanted to make sure I looked good. Shane was a decent guy. He'd had a crush on me since fifth grade but had never dared to ask me out. The poor guy must have thought Hannah was doing him a favor. But I knew the truth. Hannah was still trying to get with Alexander and thought Shane would distract me. Too bad she didn't know I was no longer interested.

I needed to hurry. Technically, the party had started about thirty minutes before, but Hannah and I weren't quite ready yet. She'd picked out my outfit. Ultrashort cut-off jean shorts, a white cufflink shirt buttoned only half way up to show off my cleavage, and brown cowboy boots. My long strawberry blonde hair was braided down my left shoulder.

"I look like I just stepped off the set of a country music video."

"Yeah. You're the hot chick in the video the guys are always singing about!" Hannah responded, laughing as she adjusted her cleavage and pivoting in front of the mirror to make sure 'the goods' were adequately covered. "Besides, you're from *Georgia*. You're supposed to look like a cowgirl."

"Yeah, when I was in kindergarten. And obviously, you've never been to Atlanta. Not many cowgirls there, or anywhere else in Georgia, for that matter."

Cowgirl or not, I had to admit, I looked pretty hot. Not 'Hannah' hot, but definitely enough to turn a few heads. Regardless, the moment I opened my mouth to speak, I knew I'd ruin the whole sexy facade. I sighed as I applied my mascara.

My phone buzzed. It was Shane. "Hannah, that's Shane. I'm headed downstairs to meet him."

"Okay, girl. See you in a few. I'm almost done," she replied, putting a few finishing touches on her makeup.

Walking down the staircase, I couldn't help but admire the beauty of Hannah's extravagant home. Even after all these years, the place still took my breath away. I personally didn't care for the modern style furniture and decor, but the sheer size and luxury were enough to make me green with envy.

I reached the bottom of the staircase, walked to the poolside bar, and ordered my usual Amaretto Sour. I took a seat while I waited. There were well over a hundred people here, but I quickly spied Shane hanging at the other end of the deck with a few jocks, re-living a recent victory.

"Gwen."

I turned towards the masculine voice and saw Jasper walking towards me from the pool wearing nothing but black board shorts. He was even hotter than I'd remembered, with blonde hair, aquamarine eyes, and the body of a god. He could've been Brad Pitt's hotter, younger brother, assuming such a thing were possible.

"Jasper." I met his eyes, trying hard not to notice the water dripping down his muscled chest. "What are you doing here? It's not very professional to party with your cast," I teased.

He stepped closer so that he towered over me. His bare chest brushed mine as he whispered in my ear, "Fuck professional. I'm a hands-on kind of guy."

My heart stammered in my chest.

"Come on, babe. Everyone knows I party." He stepped back and brushed his golden locks off his face, flexing an impressive bicep.

Feminine voices called to Jasper from the pool. He glanced casually over his shoulder. "Well, I guess I'll see you around, Gwen."

He caught my eye before he turned to leave. "By the way, that was impressive acting the other day. You keep that up, and you'll have the audience as hot for you as Alexander is." He paused thoughtfully. "Or the director, for that matter." His eyes burned into mine before he turned and walked away.

Once my mind began to function again, I threw back my drink and mentally chastised myself. What was wrong with me?

I need a distraction from all the hot men in my life.

Five minutes later, I was standing by the pool listening to Shane with a fake smile plastered on my face, wishing I'd never agreed to this date. I didn't know if he was nervous or what, but spending time with Shane was getting on my last nerve. His first lousy joke was forgivable, earning him a courtesy laugh, but unfortunately, Shane took my laugh as encouragement to tell an unending barrage of corny jokes.

"Oh, I've got another one. You're going to like this. Why don't you play poker in the jungle?"

Kill. Me. Now.

"Hmm, I don't know." I gave up, praying he didn't know any more jokes.

"Because there are too many cheetahs!" he laughed loudly. "Get it? Cheetahs!"

I wanted to roll my eyes. Why had I agreed to this?

Oh, that's right, because of Hannah.

I hoped after a few drinks, he'd pass out, but my luck was never that good. More likely, I'd be stuck with Shane all night. "I need a bathroom break," I said as I strode away.

CHAPTER TWENTY-FIVE
Unknown

How was I going to get Gwen away from that idiot Shane Martin? How had she ended up with him anyway? I'd thought for sure Alexias would have invited her. He'd been staring at her all fucking week. Everyone could see how much he wanted her; even Hannah wasn't completely oblivious to that fact. The only person who didn't see it was Gwen. That girl was fucking clueless.

Alexias Prisco. Wow, how the mighty had fallen. Never thought I'd see old Alexias acting like such a little bitch. Too afraid to be a man and take what he wanted. I figured I'd do my old friend a favor and move things along for the little pansy ass.

I watched as Gwen left her date and walked into the house. Now was my chance.

"Hey, Shane, what's going on?" I walked over and slapped my hand against his back. "How 'bout that game last week...?"

I continued to talk nonsense while I stared into his eyes and sent my true message deep into his subconscious, giving him a set of orders that his weak mind would be incapable of ignoring. Shane's eyes glazed over, and he stumbled away from me, toward the bar.

That was almost too easy. Persuasion rarely worked on the strong-willed, but with weak minds like Shane's, it was like taking candy from a baby. I couldn't have found a better tool to snap Alexias into action.

Alexias had always had a hero complex. Maybe tonight after the big save, Prince Charming would finally make his move.

CHAPTER TWENTY-SIX

Gwen

I went inside hoping to find Hannah when my phone rang. It was Beverly. I was so grateful to hear her voice.

"I'm glad you called, I desperately need a distraction. When will you be here? You're on the way, right?"

"Date not going so well, huh?" She laughed into the phone. "You need to listen to me more often. I told you not to go out with him. You guys have zero chemistry."

"Why aren't you here yet? I need you to save me from my bad decisions!"

"Don't I know it! But sorry, hon, it's going to be a while before I get there. So until then, you're on your own with comedy central."

"You think you're funny, don't you?"

"I'm fucking hilarious, and you know it," she replied, laughing. We talked for another twenty minutes as I intentionally dragged out the conversation to avoid going back to Shane.

Beverly knew me too well. "Gwen, you've procrastinated enough. Get back outside. I'll be there as soon as I can. Love ya."

I ended the call and walked the long corridor that led back to the party. Again, I found myself staring in amazement at the size of the house. I bet playing hide and seek would have been a blast here. I took my time walking back, imagining all the crafty hiding places I would use.

I was immersed in these thoughts when a hand reached out from the shadows and grabbed my arm, jerking me inside a dark room and slamming my body against the wall. A bloodcurdling scream erupted from my throat. My heart pounded frantically in my chest and ears, blocking out all other sounds. My attacker, shrouded in darkness, had both my wrists pinned above my head with one hand while his other slid up between my thighs. The strong smell of liquor enveloped me, throwing my senses into a crazed panic.

I opened my mouth, but my scream was cut short as my attacker's lips assaulted mine, forcing the taste of cigarettes, whiskey, and rancid breath down my throat.

"Come on, baby. Don't act like you don't want me," he murmured against my lips.

Oh, my God. I know that voice!

"Help!"

CHAPTER TWENTY-SEVEN
Alexander

Where is Gwen?

I was sure she'd be here. I sipped my beer and scanned the area. Under other circumstances, I'd be having a blast. Great music, free drinks, and beautiful women had always been my downfall. And yet tonight, none of it held my attention. Gwen was all I could focus on. There was just something about her I couldn't ignore, and I was tired of trying to stay away.

It was Gwen I had been meant to meet that night at the fundraiser. She was the one, I could feel it.

Except for that whole thing about her still technically having a boyfriend, though after overhearing their conversation the other day, I really couldn't tell.

A fucking boyfriend. Part of me didn't care. I'd fight for her. Besides, Ky was a cheating bastard, and she deserved better. Not to mention the fact that he was the shady son of a bitch who'd been stalking my family.

And who the hell was this Luke character Gwen had been dreaming about? I'd asked around, and as far as I could tell, she didn't have any friends by that name.

I tapped my fingers impatiently against my beer bottle, hoping Gwen would appear soon.

I needed to talk to her. To tell her how I felt in case I hadn't made it clear.

Made it clear? The only thing I'd made clear was that I wanted to get into her pants, and while that was definitely something I wanted to do, it was not all I wanted from her. I needed to tell her that.

But it seemed like anytime I had a chance to be with her, something or someone got in the way. Usually Ky or Hannah.

Hannah seriously needed to move on. I couldn't seem to make her understand that while I cared about her, it was not the way she wanted. She just wouldn't take no for an answer.

I scanned the area again and finally caught a glimpse of Gwen walking around the pool. Good Lord, she was the hottest thing I'd ever seen. Perfectly sculpted legs, rounded hips, and an ass that bounced with each delicious step.

So fucking hot. I couldn't take my eyes off her. It took every ounce of my self-control to stop myself from charging over there, ripping her away from the dickhead she was talking to, and having my wicked way with her right in front of everyone.

I shifted in my seat and tried to force the image of my fantasy from my mind. This was not the time for that.

Twenty minutes later, I sat in a lounge chair after a long, well-needed dip in the pool. My body was relaxed, and my head felt clearer.

What was wrong with me? Whenever Gwen was around it was like everything was amplified, every emotion so much more intense. In all my years, I'd never felt anything so powerful, and my body had never before responded without my mind's consent. For the first time in my life, I wasn't sure if I could trust myself.

Everything about Gwen made me want her. From her quiet intelligence to the patience and kindness she showed everyone around her. I loved the way her face flushed, and how tongue-tied she got when she gazed into my eyes. Absolutely adorable.

What was that?

An almost imperceptible noise caught my attention. The faint sound drew me out of my reverie. It was a sound that sent shock waves through my body and had me racing toward the house. It was a scream only loud enough for my sensitive ears above the noise of the crowd, and it belonged to a voice I could never ignore.

Gwen cried out for help, louder this time.

As I raced toward her, my heart nearly stopped.

CHAPTER TWENTY-EIGHT
Gwen

"Shh…" He pressed a finger to my lips. "You don't want to ruin our fun, do you? Of course not. You wanted this. Why else would you have agreed to go out with me? I'm going to give you what you've been wanting." He chuckled, his hot breath wafting across my face. He removed his hand from my thigh and began undoing his belt buckle.

How could I have been so wrong about someone? I had to get to get away from him.

"Help! Somebody help me, please!" I yelled once more. With the loud bass from the party music and the shouts from the crowd, I was losing all hope of anyone hearing me. I struggled to free myself, knowing it was no use. Tears poured down my face. A sob ripped past my throat, violently shaking my body. I couldn't believe this was actually happening.

Shane shook me, banging my head against the wall as he released my hands to grip my neck. I couldn't breathe. I grabbed at his hands. I tried to pry them off of me to no avail. The harder I fought, the stronger his grip became. I was on the verge of passing out.

This was it. This was the day I would die. I always assumed I'd die an old lady asleep in my bed. Never once had I imagined I'd go out like this.

As the last bit of my vision blacked out, something miraculous occurred.

Oxygen filled my lungs. Shane's body was ripped from mine and slammed against the adjacent wall with a loud boom. My body crumbled to the floor as I gasped for breath.

"Keep your damn hands off of her!" shouted a voice I'd recognize anywhere. "Don't come near her again. Don't talk to her. Don't even think about her, or I swear to God, I will fucking kill you."

Alexander threw Shane out the door and into the hallway wall with such force that Shane was knocked out cold. He then turned away from Shane's lifeless body and switched on a nearby lamp, bathing the room in a subtle yellow glow.

Alexander was seething. The anger radiating off him was almost tangible. He closed his eyes and took a few deep breaths. Within seconds, his hands unclenched and relaxed.

Alexander closed the short distance between us. Sadness and concern colored his eyes as he took in my tear-stained face and red-rimmed eyes. He gently took my hands in his and helped me to my feet.

"Gwen..." He reached for my face but hesitated. His eyes met mine, begging permission.

I nodded.

His outstretched hand moved to gently brush my cheek. "Oh, Gwen..."

The care with which he touched me and the gentleness behind it was too much to bear. Tears burst forth, and sobs racked my body. Alexander pulled me roughly against him in a tight embrace just as my knees gave out. He held me effortlessly, his body a shield to the outside world, keeping me safe and warm as tears poured from my eyes.

"It's going to be okay, baby," he soothed me, placing gentle kisses on my forehead and cheeks. "I've got you."

My tears slowed as Alexander lavished soft kisses upon me, relaxing me and warming my body with his strong embrace. My tears stopped long before he released me. He leaned back, his bare arms still wrapped securely around me, and gazed into my eyes.

He had the most amazing eyes. Deep blue irises that appeared to glow from within. Such a striking contrast with his bronze skin and black hair. My eyes wandered down, taking in his broad shoulders and perfectly chiseled chest and abs. I noticed for the first time the thick tattoo artistically covering his right chest and shoulder and wrapping down around his right bicep. The design was like that of a metallic breastplate with intricate hieroglyphs etched into the metal. It gave him the appearance of a fierce warrior.

A fierce, sexy, badass warrior...that was currently staring down at me and waiting for a response.

Oh shit. What did he just ask me?

"Yeah. You're okay." He laughed affectionately as he released me from his grip.

"What?"

"We've really got to work on your vocabulary, babe."

"*We?*" I shook my head. "What?"

"Stare much?"

"Hmm?" I mumbled, again distracted by his half-naked body. Seriously, what was wrong with me? It was like I'd become this sex-obsessed maniac.

And after what had just happened...

The enormity of it all hit me full force. If Alexander hadn't shown up, I would have been raped. I could have ended up dead.

Oh, my God.

My mind raced at the possibilities, and all of a sudden, I couldn't breathe. The world faded away as my trembling knees weakened.

"Whoa." Alexander's warm arm wrapped around me and held me up. His soft eyes met mine, and I could see in their watery depths a familiar tenderness, an emotion hiding deep inside that I wasn't ready to acknowledge, that I wished I hadn't seen. Somehow in this moment, I felt safer than I ever had, and yet a flash of fear swept over me.

Love.

I couldn't have seen love in his eyes.

No. It was stupid to even think it.

I quickly erased the idea from my mind and snuggled into Alexander's warm arms.

∞∞∞∞∞∞

I almost didn't recognize the image reflected back at me in the bathroom mirror. Most of my hair had been pulled from my braid and was mushed against my forehead and shoulders. Thick black rivers streaked down my cheeks from bright red eyes. My shirt was ripped and missing buttons, and I suspected the dark shadows across my neck were the beginning of what would become very noticeable bruises.

I couldn't walk out of the party like this. I turned on the faucet and scooped water into my trembling hands.

Another sob escaped.

No.

No more tears. I needed to be strong. I splashed my face with water and began removing my ruined makeup.

I scrubbed harshly, leaving my face clean, yet red. I opened the cabinets below the sink. I knew Hannah kept backup makeup in every bathroom of the house in case of an emergency. Well, this sure as shit qualified. I pulled her hidden makeup bag out. Unfortunately, her foundation didn't match my skin tone, so I opted for just mascara and lip gloss.

Retrieving a towel, I dried the sweat from my hair as much as possible, then I brushed and re-braided my hair into place.

My eyes were still red, but at least I no longer looked hideous. I didn't see any marks on my neck anymore. *Huh*, it must have been dirt.

Now I had to figure out what to do about my shirt.

"Alexander, are you still there?" I asked loudly through the door.

"Yeah. Is everything all right?"

"Umm...I need a new shirt. Would you ask Hannah for one, please?"

"Here, take mine. I went back to the pool and got my stuff while you were cleaning up. Crack the door open, and I'll slip it in." I did as he said, then shut the door. I removed my shirt and shoved it in the trash, never wanting to see it again.

I slid Alexander's soft cotton t-shirt over my head and took a deep breath. He had the most intoxicating scent. It was a very fresh, masculine smell. I closed my eyes and breathed it in until a disturbing thought snapped my eyes open again.

Shane.

I still had to deal with Shane.

Suddenly, I felt his hand sliding up my thigh. Smelled the whiskey on his breath.

No!

I clenched my teeth and squeezed my eyes shut.

Just take deep breaths.

I calmly thought through the steps I needed to take. Unless he had awoken, Shane would still be lying on the floor in the corridor. I had to call the police and file a report. I couldn't let him get away with this.

But I didn't want to deal with this tonight. I didn't want to think about it.

I rubbed my hands over my face, overwhelmed. I took a few minutes to calm down, gave myself a pep talk, then left the bathroom. The moment I opened the door and Alexander saw my face, he snapped upright. "What? What's wrong?" He took a worried step toward me.

I released a strained breath. "I just realized I'll be spending the rest of my night at the police station. And I just want to forget about the whole thing."

Alexander smiled.

"Your wish is my command," he exclaimed with a bow. He slid his arm around my waist and led me back toward the party. "I made a call while you were in the bathroom. My family has friends on the force," he winked, "you'll have a restraining order effective tomorrow morning. He'll only spend tonight in jail, but he will have a charge of assault on his record. *And* you won't have to deal with the police."

"How-"

"Doesn't matter how. I took care of it." Alexander stopped walking and looked me in the eye. "But if you want that fucker to fry, just say the word. I'll make it happen. Whatever you want."

The intensity in his eyes was almost frightening. If I asked, I believed he would personally see to it that Shane got more than he deserved.

"No, that won't be necessary."

We walked down the corridor and into the main living room before Alexander spoke again. "Oh, and Gwen." He waited for me to look at him. "Call me Alex from now on. We are friends, after all."

"We are, are we? Are you sure this time?"

His arm tightened around my waist as he laughed. "I'm positive."

Hannah, who had been flirting with Jasper, zoned in on us the instant we walked through the patio doors.

My grin dropped. Even from a distance, it was easy to see that her playful expression had changed to something much less friendly on spotting us.

I looked up at Alex. "You're here with Hannah?"

Alex's smile never faltered. "Well, she invited me, if that's what you mean. But then again, it *is* her party. She invited everyone here."

"You know what I mean."

"Gwen." Alex abruptly stopped walking and faced me. "I want you to listen to me very carefully. I am *exactly* where I want to be." His tender gaze held my mine as a warm feeling spread over me.

"Gwen!"

I looked behind me in time to see Beverly saunter up and slide her arm around my waist. "Hey, chica! Sorry, I got here so late. Traffic was a bitch! Oh," she glanced over at Alex with a surprised look on her face. "Hi."

Alex nodded.

"So, where's the jester?" Beverly asked, looking around for Shane.

Alex's face darkened as he opened his mouth to speak, but I beat him to it.

"He went home. He said something about feeling sick." The words rushed out of my mouth. "I guess it's my lucky night after all."

Alex gave me a strange look but remained silent.

Beverly's eyes narrowed. "Gwen, why are your eyes red? And why are you wearing someone else's shirt?"

"It's been a rough night, and I don't want to talk about it right now. If I promise to tell you later, will you let it go?"

Her icy blue eyes studied me a moment. "I guess I could agree to that," Beverly said grudgingly.

I hated not confiding in her right away, but despite the warm feeling from my moment with Alex, the night's events were still freaking me out. My hands were trembling, and my knees were still weak. "I'm sorry. I'm going to call it an early night. It's been a little too much excitement for me."

"No." The word burst from Alex's lips. Beverly and I both turned to stare at him.

"No?"

"You shouldn't be alone. Didn't you mention your parents are out of town? You'll be safer with me. You'll stay at my house."

My jaw dropped, and my eyes widened in surprise. I didn't know what threw me more, the fact that he wanted me to stay with him, or the way he'd stated it like it was a predetermined fact instead of a question.

Unable to speak, I stared into his eyes. I knew Alex was concerned for me, and his invitation was innocent. But I couldn't help but imagine it was more. All the little hints from the past few weeks flooded back to me. The desirous stares, the steamy flirting, the intense passion on stage, and then coming to my rescue tonight. Why had I been so unsure of him? How many more ways could he have spelled it out for me?

"Stop overthinking this and come home with me," Alex pleaded when I didn't respond.

I hesitated just a moment before nodding in agreement.

Alex turned to Beverly, who stood by silently trying to decipher our conversation. "Follow us in Gwen's car so she'll have it in the morning. Zane will give you a ride back to the party."

"No problem."

One look at Beverly's face, and I knew it was taking everything she had to keep her mouth shut. Alarm was etched into her eyes as she followed us out.

"Beverly, I'm okay. Don't worry."

She nodded her head, acknowledging my words, but I knew she didn't believe them. Not knowing what happened was clearly killing her, but like the great friend that she was, she gave me the space I needed.

∞∞∞∞∞∞

I gazed speculatively at myself in the mirror. I eyed the two-piece silk pajamas Alex had given me and wondered if I should put my own clothes back on. These were nothing like the pajamas I normally wore, and I felt self-conscious knowing Alex would see me in them.

Although I had to admit, Ariel's borrowed pajamas looked good on me. The shorts showed off my toned thighs, and the cut of the top showed off my breasts without making me look cheap.

Then again, how could anyone look cheap in something like this? The silk fabric was exquisite. The way it caressed my body was pure heaven, and its burgundy color looked rich against my tanned skin. *What would Alex think?* I pivoted in the mirror, scrutinizing every inch of my five-foot-four frame.

Stop procrastinating! I shook the tension from my shoulders, opened the bathroom door, and entered the adjoining bedroom.

The room was dark, save for a small lamp next to the bed that offered a dim glow. A gentle ocean breeze blew in from French doors opened to an oversized balcony.

"Wow." I walked toward the beautiful ocean view, mesmerized. I placed my hands on the concrete balustrade that looked out over the sea. Light from the full moon reflected off the rough waves below. The fresh breeze blew my hair from my face.

Beautiful.

I closed my eyes and breathed in the salty air.

"Peaceful, isn't it?"

I barely heard Alex's voice above the roar of the waves. I turned and opened my eyes.

Alex stood bare-chested, clothed only in loose pajama pants. My body reacted instantly to him – to the way the light and shadows defined the hard muscles of his chest and abs, the way his pajamas hung low on his hips, the way fire burned in his eyes as he stared into mine. Desire raged through my body. The overwhelming feeling drowned out the embarrassment I'd have otherwise felt.

We stood in silence, devouring each other with our eyes.

The darkness that shadowed his haunted eyes couldn't hide the struggle behind them. Restrained desire sharpened his features as his hands fisted at his sides. Every muscle was pulled tight.

My hands trembled. I didn't know what to do. My body yearned for him with a desire I couldn't explain, but I didn't know how to do this.

I averted my gaze and flushed at the thought. I was a virgin. Why would he even want me? Would I even know what to do? Would he be disappointed afterward? My sudden doubts squelched the desire building in me.

"Alex?"

Understanding shone in his eyes. His posture relaxed as he took the last steps between us, gripped my hand, and led me back into the bedroom.

"You need to rest." He began moving the sheets and blankets on the bed. "I put a glass of water on the nightstand for you." He held the covers and indicated that I get in. "You see that door to the left? That's the guest bedroom for this suite. I'll be sleeping there. I'll leave the door open, so if you need anything at all, let me know."

"Whose room is this?"

"Mine," he replied with a tone that implied, *Of course.*

"I can't take your room. I'll stay in the guest room." I attempted to get out of the bed but was gently pushed back down onto the pillows.

"You can. And you will." He leaned over and placed a gentle kiss on my cheek. "Good night, Gwen."

CHAPTER TWENTY-NINE

Alex

What a fucking night.

I laid in bed, watching as the ceiling fan above me made another leisurely revolution and wondering if I'd ever fall asleep. I was exhausted, but every time I closed my eyes, I remembered the sound of Gwen's scream and felt the terror that had shot through my body, followed by the rage I'd felt when I'd seen Shane's hands on her. I had wanted to kill him, torture him, tear his flesh from his bones. It was a mercy he got knocked out when he did. Otherwise, I may not have been able to stop myself. And poor Gwen. She'd looked so frightened and frail. Just seconds from completely falling apart.

It was only when I'd left her in the bathroom and called the police to get Shane that I'd discovered the horrifying truth. Shane had been manipulated by one of my kind. "Persuasion" was what we called it. When a human had been persuaded by an angel, there was always a telltale sign left behind, and once I looked for it, it was plain as day.

This was much worse than Gwen knew. Much worse than even I'd suspected. My home was the only place safe from the others. Somehow, I had to convince Gwen to stay here for a while.

As time crawled by, my body relaxed, and I finally drifted off to sleep.

Flashes of memories flickered in my mind. Random dreams too faint to remember floated just beyond my reach. In this hazy state of awareness, a particular memory surfaced.

Blood and sweat poured down my face as I strode across the gardens. I ran up the stairs, into the palace, and bypassed the guards.

"Sir, wait. Sir, He's not seeing anyone...." The voices trailed off as I hurried past, ignoring them. The information I needed to relay couldn't wait. I moved as swiftly as I could through the palace, then tripped over my feet when I realized I didn't know where He was.

I noticed a guard down the corridor and yelled, "Where is He? It's urgent."

"He's in the creation room, but He doesn't want to be disturbed-"

I didn't wait for the guard to finish. My patience was finally gone, and I ran down the corridor to the last room on the right, flung the door open, and rushed in.

"I have important news..." I was out of breath, and my words came out in huffs.

"I know," was His very calm reply. Despite the size of the cavernous room, I didn't have to search for Him. His light shone with such intensity that He was impossible to miss.

Of all the rooms in the palace, this one was the most incredible. It wasn't as beautiful as the other rooms; not one jewel was encrusted into its ceiling, and not a single piece of art adorned its walls. In fact, the walls in this spherical room were plain white. A platform circled the outside, while the center appeared to be a bottomless pit. In the midst of the room hovered innumerable universes, all expanding and increasing in size, pushing and stretching the boundaries of Heaven.

I followed the platform around to the other end of the room. The vastness and diversity of the universes were incredible. Their only constant was their universal compliance with the laws of physics.

There He is.

I slowed as I reached Him. We stood in silence as His newest creation came to life, the universe slowly expanding before us. I watched as matter spilled out from its center, rapidly expanding outward. Gravity pulled atoms closer and closer together, swirling in brilliant clouds of gas. I saw stars form then die in massive explosions, sending metals and gases further out. Asteroids formed, then planets. Orbits formed around respective stars. In what was but minutes to us, millions of years passed in that young universe.

I watched in fascination as galaxies formed and rushed outward.

"They all start out the same," He began. "The types of life I create for each universe are different, but the basics don't change. All except for this universe. This one shall be unique. It will be exceptional in many ways."

I leaned forward and studied it. Nothing about this particular universe jumped out as being anything other than the norm. "How so? It looks like all the others."

"The difference isn't in the construction. It's in the life that will be created there. They will be given freedom unlike anything experienced in all the multiverse. They will have the capacity for extremes beyond any ever encountered. The darkest of evil, and the greatest love."

"Why? Why would you create a place with such potential for tragedy?"

"It is a mystery." His voice was contemplative, but I wasn't fooled. We both knew it was for me to consider. He never did or said anything without reason. Was this a mystery that I was to uncover? Was I to have any part in this new universe? And if so, what part would I play?

"You are correct about the tragedy," He continued, "but only from tragedy can something uniquely beautiful be created."

Yet another mystery.

From what I'd seen in the multiverse, nothing good ever came from pain and suffering.

"By more freedom, what do you mean?" I asked. "People in all the multiverse and in Heaven have the choice to either obey or disobey. How would this universe be different?"

"In all previously created universes, the life created was constructed with DNA that made them less susceptible to sin, and my presence in these universes enhanced the effect. That's why it's incredibly easy to be obedient in Heaven where my presence literally saturates the air."

"Are you saying you would intentionally corrupt their DNA and then remove your presence from them?" My voice was incredulous.

"No," He answered. "But they will choose that path for themselves."

"I don't understand-"

"As I said, it is a mystery."

A supernova exploded in a brilliant display of color and light – intense white flashes followed by pinks, purples, and blues.

"What will it be called?" I asked quietly and motioned toward the universe.

"The planet of concern will be called Earth."

"Just one planet?" For the second time in under a half hour, I was shocked.

He chuckled. "No. There will be trillions of planets, millions of which will have their own unique life forms. Some of which will be more advanced than even the Earthlings. I just meant that Earth alone would be unique."

I stared deep into the new universe. I doubted this "Earth" had even been created yet, but I looked anyway.

I focused in on one particular galaxy that was swirling around and around like a clock. As I watched, it grew larger and larger until it took up my complete field of vision, and I was being sucked into its core. Darkness and light swirled around me at a dizzying rate. Screams sounded in my ears. The sound of millions of souls being tortured sent terror through me as darkness completely enveloped my sight.

When clarity finally came, it wasn't millions screaming, it was just one. Gwen. Confusion fogged my mind, but my body shot out of bed and flew across the room with determination. Only a second had passed when my mind caught up to what my body already knew.

Gwen was in trouble.

I ran out of the guest room and into my room where Gwen was sleeping. I threw open the door in time to see her thrashing arms knock the blankets off her body as she screamed.

A nightmare. It was just a nightmare.

A sigh of relief escaped my lips, and my shoulders relaxed.

"Gwen." I gently shook her arm.

Bam!

Her left fist swung out and clocked me right between the eyes.

"Shit."

My eyes watered, but I ignored the pain and continued shaking her arm. She jerked away and screamed louder, the sound sending chills up my spine.

I'm making it worse.

Understanding came swiftly. By grabbing her arm, I'd become a part of her dream, and she was trying to get away. I instantly released her.

I leaned over and whispered into her ear. "Gwen. It's me. Everything's okay, sweetheart." I repeated that mantra over and over as she slowly relaxed. Her screams stopped, the jerking of her hands slowing until the room went quiet.

I was about to leave when Gwen's eyes fluttered open.

"Alex?" Fear and trepidation laced her timid voice. "Please don't leave me."

I looked down at her. Moonlight from the open balcony doors cast her face in a silvery sheen. Her long blonde hair tangled wildly across the pillow beneath her. No makeup marred her flawless face. She was breathtaking. The only detraction from her beauty was the fear evident in her sparkling green eyes and the trembling of her delicate fingertips.

I couldn't leave her. So against my better judgment, I pushed the blankets back, climbed into bed, and pulled her against me.

CHAPTER THIRTY

Gwen

Cuddled in Alex's arms with the filtered sunlight illuminating the massive room and the cool ocean breeze blowing in from the balcony, I assumed I was still dreaming.

At some point in the night, we'd rolled onto our sides, and he was spooning me. As much as I knew I shouldn't take advantage of the situation, I couldn't pass up this opportunity to really look at him.

I moved slowly, silently twisting around to face him, watching his face for any indication he would wake up. I cocked my head to the side and perused his peaceful face. Insanely long, black lashes fanned across his chiseled cheeks. His full, pink lips contrasted deliciously with the five o'clock shadow that'd grown in overnight. He had the perfectly smooth, tanned skin that models only dreamed about.

God, he was beautiful.

And he was so much more than that. He was intelligent, thoughtful, and kind. Of course, he was also unpredictable and moody. But his other attributes more than made up for it. He made me laugh, gave me butterflies on a daily basis, and most of all, he completely astounded me with his generosity. The charity project he was working on was amazing. Alex was going to make a difference in the world, and he'd be so easy to fall in love with.

Love? Where the hell had that thought come from?

Both times I'd allowed myself to care about someone, I'd been hurt. First by Wesley, and then by Ky. And while the relationships had felt great at the time, the pain that had followed had been crushing. I couldn't go through that again. Love caused nothing but grief.

But lust? Yeah, I could handle that.

His arms suddenly tightened around my waist and pulled me roughly against his body. My chest was flush against his, but his chin jammed against my forehead and pushed my head back at an awkward angle. I stared awkwardly at his neck, unable to move my head from the position I was in. I was so close to him that my eyes crossed.

Great, now what do I do?

I couldn't fall back asleep because of the awkward position my neck was in, and I sure as hell couldn't wake him up. My only option was to wiggle out of his grip.

If I could just slide my body down a few inches, his chin would no longer be pushing my head back. I bent my knees and attempted to drag the rest of my body down, but as I started to move, his weight shifted so that if I continued to move, I'd end up kneeing him in the crotch.

Damn. I was left with no choice but to lie still and hope he released me. With a little luck, it wouldn't take long. I closed my eyes and allowed my mind to drift off.

Waking up next to a man instead of alone in my bed was a definite first. It was quite a nice surprise too and gave my body this crazy high that I never wanted to come down from. I loved the way his arms felt around my waist and the way his hard chest felt against mine. He even smelled wonderful. Not the funky smelly breath and body odor I would have expected first thing in the morning.

As I enjoyed his warmth, it occurred to me that it was going to be incredibly awkward when he woke up.

What would I say? I barely knew him. Would he regret staying the night with me? He had probably only stayed out of obligation, and the moment he woke up, he'd realize what a mistake it had been. A kiss would have been acceptable, normal even, given all the flirting between us. But this was intimate. The way he held me in his arms, it was the way lovers held each other, and we'd never even been on a date. We'd never even kissed. I needed to get away from him before he woke.

The ache in my neck intensified. My head was pressed back so far, I could barely move.

If I could wiggle downward just a few inches, I'd get some relief. I tried again and was able to shift down about an inch. My face was still firmly pressed into his neck, but the position had improved. I listened to his steady breathing for a moment, then resumed my descent.

Almost there. I shifted on the bed.

"Mmm," Alexander grumbled.

No, no, no. Please don't wake up.

I froze in place and waited. I heard nothing but the sound of his steady breaths.

After a few tense moments, I wiggled down the remaining distance until I was finally able to move my head forward.

Ahh. Sweet relief.

Alex shifted restlessly, his arms tightening around me and pulling me against him as he thrust his hips into mine.

My eyes rolled back, and I sucked in a breath. The feel of him against me, with nothing between us but his thin cotton bottoms and my silky pajamas, was indescribable.

He mumbled in his sleep as his hand slid from my waist down to my hips.

Oh, my God! He must be dreaming.

His hips thrust forward yet again. A throbbing between my

thighs, a sharp intake of breath, and my racing pulse prevented any further thought. Alex's hand fisted my silk shorts, pulling them tight against my thighs.

The doorknob turned, and the door shoved opened. Zane strode in wearing nothing but a pair of black boxer briefs. "Alex, you up yet...."

Alex's eyes flew open, and his body stiffened. His gaze shifted to mine just inches away, and his eyes widened.

"Oh shit." The words flew out of his mouth almost instantly.

"'Bout damn time," Zane muttered, leaving the room with a sarcastic smirk on his face.

"Fuck." Alexander released his grip, then scrambled to get away from me and out of bed.

"Gwen, I..." He paused and ran his hands through his hair. "I'm..."

My face was in flames. It was as worse than I'd feared. Shame and remorse were evident on his face. Regret colored his voice. I couldn't handle it; I threw the covers over my head and hid.

"Your clothes are on the dresser," his cold voice informed me before the door slammed shut.

My chest tightened. He wanted me to leave. He might as well have been telling me to get the hell out with his last words.

I had to get home, now. I couldn't stay here, and I couldn't chance seeing him in the hallway. I threw on my clothes, grabbed my keys, and slipped out of Alex's home unnoticed.

My car was easy to find, parked at the end of his driveway. I threw myself into the vehicle and drove away as fast as I could.

The moment I stepped through my front door, I let the tears I'd been holding back slip down my cheeks. I was so confused. My emotions were all over the place, and while the tears fell, I tried like hell to pinpoint exactly what I was feeling.

I was ashamed. I was embarrassed. But where the hell was this internal turmoil that had me crying like a damn baby coming from?

CHAPTER THIRTY-ONE
Alex

Once again, I was outside Gwen's house, staring up at the stars, and thinking about how I'd screwed things up. In less than a weeks' time we'd gone from almost getting together to me being relegated back to the friend zone.

Hell, I'd be lucky to even be in the friend zone. Right now, she just might hate me, and I didn't have a damn clue what to do about it.

Why had I reacted like a jackass that morning? Fuck, it had felt so good waking up with her tangled around me. It'd been years since I'd woken up that turned on. Then I'd freaked out when I'd remembered she was a virgin. I'd been trying to protect her modesty, but I'd probably ended up making her feel rejected, as if I hadn't wanted to take her right then and there. Damn, if she only knew how much I'd wanted her.

This wasn't over. One way or another, I would win her back.

My phone buzzed in my pocket.

"Hello."

Zane's voice came through loud and clear. "We have a problem."

"What did you find?"

"Kyle Harper doesn't exist. At least not the twenty-three-year-old that lives in Verona Beach. There was a thirty-five-year-old named Kyle Harper from San Diego that died five years ago. Interestingly, he had the same social security number as the Kyle Harper we have here."

"Oh shit."

"Yeah."

We sat in silence contemplating the implications. Obviously, Ky was hiding something. But what? "Did you use the new facial recognition technology on him?"

"Just started the search a few minutes ago. It hasn't found anything yet."

"Let me know as soon as it does."

I hung up the phone and resigned myself to the fact that I wouldn't be sleeping for the next few nights. Not that I needed the sleep, but it sure felt nice.

I sighed.

It was going to be a really long night.

∞∞∞∞∞∞

Ring.... Ring.... Ring....

The sound of Gwen's phone surprised me. I glanced at my watch. Who would be calling Gwen at four in the morning?

"Hello," Gwen's groggy voice slurred.

"I need your help," Beverly's voice frantically blared out of the phone.

I sat up and listened intently while Beverly explained that her parents had been in a car accident while vacationing in Europe and were in the hospital in intensive care. Beverly needed Gwen to give her a ride to the airport.

"Of course. I'll be there in twenty minutes." The moment she ended the call, Gwen sprang out of bed and rushed to the bathroom. Five minutes later, she was out the door and in her car.

I followed as closely behind as I could without attracting her attention and watched as she picked up Beverly and took her to the airport.

I wished I could do something to help, but there was nothing to be done.

Besides, what mattered was Gwen's safety. Regardless of how bad I felt for Beverly, I couldn't dwell on it. Someone, another fucking angel, was out to hurt Gwen. For what reason, I couldn't fathom, but I'd be damned if I was going to stand by and let it happen. And when I found out who it was, there would be hell to pay.

CHAPTER THIRTY-TWO

Gwen

If I could get through today, I'd be okay. A few more days and the weekend would be here, and I would finally have some time to sort through all the conflicting emotions I was having.

Once again, Ky insisted on driving me around. I wasn't sure how I felt about that. Every time I looked at him, I remembered the heartbroken look in his eyes from when I'd stopped him from kissing me.

I hated hurting him. Maybe trying to stay friends wasn't the best idea.

Ky was shocked when I told him about Beverly.

"Yeah, she left early this morning. She said she would call when she lands."

"What happened?"

"I don't know much, just that they were in an accident. It must have been pretty bad, they're in intensive care. She said the authorities contacted her, both her parents are unconscious." I sighed. "Mr. and Mrs. Shultz are like family to me. I hate being stuck here knowing they're hurt."

"I'm sorry."

There wasn't much to say after that. I couldn't shake the depressed feeling I'd had since I'd gotten her call.

We rode the rest of the way in silence. As usual, Ky got us to school on time, then walked me to class.

When I sat at my desk and noted Beverly's empty seat, I wasn't sure I could deal with her absence. Everything about the last few weeks had felt off, and now with her gone, it was unbearable. I counted the hours on my hands, and then again. My heart sped up when I realized just how much time had passed. I should have heard from her by now. She had a layover in Newark. Her flight would have landed hours ago, and she had promised to call.

I pulled out my phone and dialed her. It went straight to voicemail. That wasn't like her. I'd try her again in a few hours.

Finally, the part of the day I wasn't entirely dreading arrived. Rehearsal. It was getting more and more awkward by the day because of Ky and Alex, but I still loved the thrill of acting. The excitement of performing and the rush that came from being someone else for a few moments was addictive.

Today's practice was a lot like our last one. Alex and Ky took turns glaring at each other across the stage. I had more scenes where I had to kiss Ky that he took full advantage of. Each kiss was sensual and enticing. They were everything a kiss should be. But like before, there were no fireworks.

The play was coming along well, which was great considering our first performance was a little over a week away. Yet we still hadn't practiced the most controversial scenes. I'd done my best to avoid thinking about it, but very soon I'd be getting extremely cozy with Alex.

I scanned the room and found Alex and Hannah on the other side, deep in conversation. He had his hand on her arm comfortingly, but Hannah looked pissed. I was sure if I looked close enough I'd see steam billowing out of her ears.

I looked around the auditorium and caught Ky talking casually with Jasper, so I walked over to them.

"Hey, Jasper."

"Good practice today, Gwen," Jasper replied.

"Thanks."

"If you've got a minute, I need to talk to you in private."

I glanced at Ky, then nodded and followed Jasper outside.

Jasper's eyes pierced into me. "Are you sure you're able to do this?"

"What do you mean?"

Jasper took a step forward, bringing him well within my personal space. Against my will, my heart sped up. My eyes skimmed over him, noting how his snug t-shirt accentuated his broad chest and biceps, and how his designer jeans fit just right. My eyes traced back up his body to meet his amused eyes.

The smirk on his lips told me I'd been caught checking him out.

He took another step closer, close enough that I could feel his breath on my face.

"We have a problem," he whispered. He gently trailed a finger down the side of my cheek and across my lips, spreading fire along my skin.

"What?" The words fell breathlessly from my lips.

"The way that gorgeous skin of yours blushes at the slightest touch." He smiled and took a step back.

My body sagged in relief.

"That's what concerns me, Gwen. Your innocence."

"What are you saying?"

He leaned his hip against the building and crossed his arms. "You're not ready for next week. With you being a virgin and all—"

"What makes you think I'm a virgin?"

A low chuckle told me he wasn't buying it. "I've been with a lot of women. Trust me, I know a virgin when I see one." He shrugged. "Nothing to be ashamed of. But there are some pretty steamy scenes, and you've got to deliver. Are you sure you can do this?"

"Yes."

"But can you perform on stage with Alexander while you're still with Ky?" He waited a moment before continuing. "And are you going to be able to perform those scenes without a fight breaking out between Ky and Alexander?"

How was I supposed to respond to that?

"Alex and Ky won't be a problem. Ky and I broke up, and Alex doesn't like me like that—"

Jasper raised an eyebrow. "Are you serious? Alexander looked like he was ready to claw his own eyes out when you kissed Ky."

Yeah, right.

"And you and Ky have broken up, but I'd bet it was not his choice. Am I right?"

"Maybe."

"You do realize that after practice on Monday, Ky's going to want to maim Alexander, right?"

I didn't answer. How could I? He was right, at least the part about Ky being pissed. I needed to have a talk with him about this before the issue exploded in my face.

"Don't worry. I'll take care of it. I won't let them ruin your play," I told Jasper with more confidence than I actually felt.

"I don't give a fuck about them. I'll take care of their asses if they get out of line. I just want you to be prepared. And you might want to practice before our next rehearsal."

"What's that supposed to mean?"

Jasper leaned in close. His eyes sparked with mischief. "Those sex scenes. You might want a little practice. So you'll be prepared."

My eyes widened and my heart raced.

Jasper winked. "I wasn't offering, Gwen. Stop looking at me like that. I'm just saying, it wouldn't hurt."

"Um, thanks?"

He flashed me another one of his heart-stopping smiles. "You're welcome. And, Gwen, I really am your friend." He grabbed the phone out of my hand and put his number in it. "If you ever need someone to talk to...." He tossed it back and returned to the stage.

Well, that was nice, I thought, as I headed back toward Ky.

"Hey," Ky said as I reached him. "Something came up, and I can't drive you to work tonight. I called you a cab, it should be outside soon."

The look on Ky's face told me something was up.

"What's wrong?"

"There's a problem at my apartment building that I've got to take care of. I'll see you tomorrow, okay?"

"Okay," I replied, unsure of what else to say. Ky turned and brusquely took off toward the exit. I gathered my things and headed for the changing room. Ky never acted like that. He was obviously lying to me again. But why?

I was getting sick and tired of this crap. I slammed the door behind me, changed into my work clothes, and sprinted outside, praying the cab was still waiting for me. I breathed a sigh of relief when I saw the car sitting on the curb with the engine running.

∞∞∞∞∞∞

That night, work wasn't half bad. Alex spent the night in his office with the door shut, which was completely out of character for him, but it allowed me to do my job in peace.

I finished typing up the report I had been working on, signed off my computer, and rifled through my purse. Where the hell was my phone? I began emptying my purse to find it.

I had removed a majority of the contents when I remembered exactly where my phone was. The last place I'd used it was in Alex's office, so it was probably sitting on his desk.

I groaned. I really didn't want to talk to him, but I stood and reluctantly walked to his door.

His voice was muffled through the walls, but his irritated tone was evident. Indecision over whether to risk interrupting him froze my body in place, and my fist hovered at the door.

"What?" His loud voice boomed through the walls and startled me, causing me to fall clumsily on my butt.

"Ow," I mumbled as I climbed to my feet.

"How the hell did this happen? How can an entire shipment disappear?"

I reached for the door.

"Well, figure it out." The silence that followed was cut short by the slamming of his phone.

What in the world was going on? I'd never heard him talk like that before.

I slowly opened the door. "Alex? Is everything okay?"

He jumped at my voice, then looked up at me with those disarming eyes. "Sorry. What did you say?"

He was looking at me, but I wasn't sure he really saw me.

"Is everything okay?"

He closed his eyes and took a breath. "No." He opened his eyes and smiled up at me. "But it will be."

I scanned the top of his desk, and sure enough, my phone was on the far corner where I'd left it.

"I'll give you a ride home," Alex said as he watched me grab my phone.

"I can call a cab."

"Gwen, I'm driving you." His tone left no room for argument, so I shoved my phone into my purse and followed him out the door.

Alex's car was the exact opposite of Ky's. It was a bright red high-end sports car with all the perks. He opened the door for me, and I slid into the seat. I sighed as I slid my fingers longingly over the smooth leather.

Alex joined me on the driver's side, pushed a few buttons, then started the car. We practically glided over the road.

"What kind of car is this?" After I asked, I realized what a stupid question it was. "Never mind, it wouldn't matter anyway. I can't tell the difference between a Chevrolet and a Ford."

He shook his head.

"It's not either of those, is it?"

He laughed. "Not even close." Alex glanced at me. "Look, Gwen, I had an ulterior motive for driving you home tonight."

I glanced down and fidgeted nervously with my hands in my lap, wondering where this conversation was headed.

"I hate the way things have been between us. That morning you left my house, I wasn't angry at you. I'm sorry I gave you that impression."

The sincerity in his blue eyes was easy to see, but his words weren't what I needed to hear. The problem wasn't that I'd thought he was angry, it was that he wasn't interested in me at all. I had felt so ashamed and rejected. But how could I tell him that? How could I explain I was ashamed of my attraction to him, that I felt foolish for assuming the feeling was mutual? I pressed my lips together.

We glided to a stop at an empty intersection. Alex placed the car in park and reached across the seat. His large hand engulfed mine.

"I know you thought I didn't want you. That is the farthest thing from the truth. I wanted you so bad it hurt." His intense eyes met mine. "I still do."

He ran a hand down my cheek and caressed my face. "I want to be with you, Gwen."

"I...." My heart raced. It was hard to breathe. "I..."

He smirked and raised an eyebrow at me. "Well?"

When he looked at me like that, I couldn't think. I knew there was a reason I should say no, but for the life of me, I couldn't remember why.

"Okay." The answer slipped from my lips just as the light turned green. Alex put the car in drive and that sexy-as-hell grin of his appeared. "It only makes sense for us to be together, considering you can't stop having all those dirty thoughts about me."

"I do not." I turned toward the window to hide my flushed face.

"Boyfriends and girlfriends don't lie to each other, Gwen."

A smile so wide it hurt spread across my face.

Girlfriend? I was his girlfriend now? It sounded impossible. I couldn't believe that all this time he'd wanted *me,* and it hadn't been my imagination or some stupid game.

Then I remembered something that dampened my mood.

"What about Hannah? I always thought something was going on between you two."

"I won't lie to you, Gwen."

My heart sank.

Oh, damn. Here it is. I braced myself as I awaited his explanation.

"For a while, I thought I had to be with her."

He thought he had to be with her? What does that mean?

"Because of your families?" I asked.

He nodded. "Something like that. But there was never anything there. No chemistry. The whole time we were together, I was thinking about you. It wasn't fair to Hannah. She's a good girl. She deserves to have someone who wants her, but that isn't me. I told Hannah a few days ago that we couldn't see each other. She didn't take it well, but at least she knows. But you need to know that I plan to keep Hannah in my life. We've become friends, and I care about her. Please, tell me you accept that."

He wanted to stay friends with Hannah? God, that was a hard pill to swallow. The past few weeks Hannah and I had drifted apart, but I still cared about her. Part of me still wanted her friendship, but the idea of Alex spending time with her made me uneasy. I knew Hannah wouldn't give up on him. She could have five other guys in her life, but she'd never let me win.

I found myself answering Alex the way I had Ky.

"I'll try."

Alex's eyes searched mine. A broad smile stretched across his face.

I smiled back, and he winked.

"God, you are such a flirt!" I accused.

Laughter burst from his lips. It was good to hear. The sound of his voice was music to my ears, and his laughter so much more so. It was impossible not to laugh with him.

"So now that's settled, what d'you say we have some fun tomorrow?"

"Where are we going?"

"It's a surprise. Now go." He motioned to the door, and I was shocked to find we had already pulled into my driveway. "I'll be here at two."

"Wait." I stopped just after I'd closed the door behind me.

He rolled down the window. "Yeah?"

"I have plans with Ky. I won't be home until four. Can you pick me up then?"

His eyes darkened. He opened his lips to speak, then snapped them shut. His brows furrowed, then with a determined look, he said, "I don't think you should be spending time with Ky."

Anger flared, bright and hot. "You want to stay friends with Hannah. Well, I don't want to lose Ky either. I'll make sure he knows about us, but I won't just drop him from my life."

"Whoa. It's not like that." He hesitated for a moment, then said, "Ky is dangerous. Trust me, you need to stay as far away from him as possible."

Unbelievable.

"I'm going home now. Don't bother picking me up tomorrow. I won't be back in time. We can get together another day."

"Gwen—"

"Sorry, I can't hear you," I said childishly as I stalked up my drive and went inside.

I was so tired of all the drama.

I walked inside and dropped my stuff at the door. I needed some serious downtime. I wasn't much of a drinker, but if I were, I would've had a few drinks and passed the hell out.

Instead, I took my comfort from vanilla ice cream. I went to the kitchen, pulled a bowl from the cabinet, and filled it to the top with my favorite brand. I cut up a handful of strawberries and was tossing them on top when Spyder began rubbing his furry little body around my legs.

I picked him up. He purred as I rubbed under his chin, and I cuddled him to my chest. He made himself comfortable as I carried him to the living room and dropped to the couch.

I shifted him so I could get my spoon to my mouth.

Mmm... I felt the drama and stress of the day melt away. I knew one day this habit would come back to bite me in the butt, but right now I didn't care.

I ate until I'd consumed the entire bowl, then fell asleep, cuddling with Spyder and my favorite blanket on the couch.

∞∞∞∞∞∞

I woke snuggled into my favorite blanket on the couch. I stretched, pulling my arms and legs as far as they could go.

I got up, showered, brushed my teeth, then ate breakfast. I was about to take a bite of my Apple Jacks when my phone buzzed with a text.

Ky: U ready? Picking u up in 15

Me: yeah where r we going?

Ky: drag strip, big race, rmbr?

Me: sry i 4got. ill b ready

I finished my breakfast and was about to put on my shoes when I remembered to feed Spyder. I walked back to the kitchen and filled his bowls.

"Gwen?" Ky walked in unannounced. "I've been outside knocking for the last five minutes. You didn't hear me?"

"Sorry, I've been distracted."

I went to my room and called Beverly. It went straight to voicemail. I checked and found she hadn't been on any social media. As a last resort, I checked my email and found nothing. This was not like Beverly. Something must have happened.

When I returned to the kitchen, Ky had helped himself to a bowl of cereal. He glanced up from his bowl, and that rare but brilliant smile of his stretched across his face.

"I thought you were ready to go," I said as he scarfed down his breakfast.

He quickly finished off the rest and replied, "I am."

He turned and led me toward the door, then to his car. When I got in and put on my seatbelt, I came to a decision.

I had to tell Ky that Alex and I were together now. It was only fair. And hopefully, it would convince Ky that things really were over between us.

CHAPTER THIRTY-THREE
Gwen

The first thought that came through my head when I woke was, *Thank God it's Monday.*

Who the hell thinks crap like that? Oh yeah, that would be me.

The reason...Alex.

Today we'd finally practice the kissing scenes. And tomorrow... the sex scene. But while a part of me couldn't wait for rehearsal to start, the other part hated the idea of our first kiss being fake.

I hadn't spoken to him since the night before I went to the races with Ky. I'd had good reason to be angry. Ky may have been an ex, but he was also my friend. And there was no way he was dangerous.

But even so, I may have overreacted a little. I just hoped Alex hadn't changed his mind about us.

I shook my head. I should have gotten his phone number, and then we'd have been able to talk before the kiss.

I showered, brushed my teeth twice, then drove to the school auditorium. From the looks of the parking lot, I was the last to arrive, but according to the clock, I was still ten minutes early. Apparently, I wasn't the only person looking forward to practice today.

I strolled inside and sought out Alex. I found him standing left stage, talking casually with Jasper, and dressed and ready for our next scene. And damn, he was something to see. Tight acid-wash jeans hung low on his hips. The strategically placed rips accentuated his muscular thighs. His broad chest and biceps were on full display with that tight white tank clinging to his perfect skin and narrow waist. He was barefoot, standing in that relaxed, sexy way of his; he was downright sinful.

My gaze skimmed slowly over his lean, sensual body, and for a moment, I had what I could only describe as an out of body experience. Images flashed through my mind. I watched myself on my knees, sliding that tank slowly over those firm abs, kissing my way up his body. My body yearned for his. I watched as I ripped the tank off him, and then the strangest desire overtook me. My mouth tingled and the tips of my teeth itched as my eyes drunk in his perfection. I watched as I jumped into his arms, wrapped my legs around his waist, then sunk my teeth into the firm muscles where his neck met his shoulder. He groaned as my teeth scraped against him. God, the rapture of his tight skin and taut muscle between my lips made my eyes roll back. He was like a tender piece of steak, and I couldn't get enough. My lips searched out his muscular neck, sucking and biting and breathing in his masculine scent.

As if sensing me, Alex's head turned and his hypnotic indigo gaze smoldered into mine, pulling me back to the present and causing my breath to hitch. The heat from his gaze combined with that vivid fantasy threatened to set me aflame.

Jasper shook Alex's arm. Alex tore his eyes from mine, and I huffed in relief as the sexual tension drained from my body.

I gathered my wits as I walked backstage to change into my costume and look for a mint. There was no way I'd allow our first kiss, real or not, be ruined by bad breath. I opened up the supply cabinet, and in the very back found a bag of red peppermints. *Perfect.* I popped one in my mouth and pulled my costume off the rack.

My costume was similar to Alex's. Acid cutoff shorts that quite frankly were too short for my taste and a thin white tanktop — without a bra. I hadn't gone without a bra since I was ten years old. My 34C boobs just didn't allow it.

I couldn't believe I'd agreed to this.

I dressed quickly and looked in the mirror. The tank was totally see through. There was no way it would go unnoticed. And the underside of my butt literally hung out the back of my shorts.

I groaned. I looked like a freaking hootchie. I took a very slow, deep breath, summoned up my courage, and stepped out of the changing area.

"Smoking hot," Aria, our sole makeup artist, exclaimed as I sat in her chair.

"Thanks." I crossed my arms over my chest and waited while Aria smeared black sludge across my face and body. This particular scene was placed in a garage, where Alex and I worked together fixing cars. I assumed the black sludge was supposed to be oil.

"What is that stuff?"

Aria smiled. "Oh, that's my secret recipe. It looks nasty, but it'll wash off easy enough. It won't stain your clothes, won't burn if it gets in your eyes, and," she paused and placed a gooped up finger in her mouth, "it tastes delicious."

"Ew."

"Come on. You've got to at least try it."

"No, thanks. But kudos on that whole easily washable thing, that couldn't have been easy to figure out."

She smiled again as I slid out of the seat.

From the distance came Jasper's deep voice. Apparently, whatever acting he was watching wasn't up to par, because every other word was "fuck."

I giggled. That man was hot as hell and filthy as sin. If he ever decided to stop being a man-whore and settle down, whoever snagged him would be one lucky woman.

Yeah, right. Jasper Mills settle down? Not in a million years.

I stepped onto the empty stage. My internal chatter had distracted me, and the nerves I'd expected to feel weren't there. Before I could overthink the upcoming scene, I ducked under the car and signaled to Jasper that I was ready.

Lying under our prop car, wrench in hand and pretending to work, I waited for Alex to enter the stage.

"Beth, we need to talk."

"We're done talking. Go away, can't you see I'm busy?" I made my voice as harsh as I could, imagining how hurt and deceived Beth would feel.

"Beth, it's not what you think-"

"I don't want to hear it. You lied to me before, and you're lying to me now." A strangled sob I'd been pretending to hold back escaped.

"Beth, please. Just hear me out."

I pushed myself out from under the car and strode across the stage, away from Alex.

Alex's voice lashed out, a strong note of authority reverberating through the auditorium. "Stop."

I halted. My hands were fisted at my sides. Tears streamed down my face. The anguish Beth felt rolled through me. Overwhelmed me. My chest heaved as silent sobs racked my body.

"Look at me," Alex's distant voice commanded.

I shook my head and refused to turn around.

Not a sound was made, but I knew he was right behind me. My body pulsed with awareness, the new connection between us hummed with desire. Firm hands gripped my shoulders and gently forced me to turn and face him.

His eyes caught mine and a blast of heat slammed through me.

"Baby," his sensual voice caressed my ears. He could make love to me with that voice, hypnotize me and make me do crazy things. My body involuntarily swayed toward him.

"I didn't want to lie to you. I was forced to." His hands made lazy circles down my fingertips and around my palms as he talked. He began explaining away the lies, but his voice faded out. Nothing existed but the feel of his hands caressing my arms and face and the searing heat in his eyes as his gaze swept over me.

Alex took a small step forward and erased every scrap of distance between us. His chest and thighs pressed into mine as he towered over me. Waves of desire rolled through me as his eyes lowered to my lips.

Hot holy hell.

He brushed a thumb across my bottom lip. Without thinking, my tongue flicked out and grazed his smooth finger.

He sucked in a harsh breath then jerked me hungrily against him. His hard body molded deliciously with mine, as his mouth came crashing down on my waiting lips.

The kiss was far from gentle. His hand gripped my face as his tongue brushed mine in rough, ravenous strokes. Blinding waves of passion overwhelmed me, and the world spun drunkenly at the taste of his lips. His strong arms lifted me with ease, and I instinctively wrapped my legs around him.

All rational thought ceased as I wrapped my arms around his neck and pulled him closer. My eyes rolled back when he gripped my hips and yanked them so harshly into his I could feel his arousal.

When I gasped, Alex caught my bottom lip between his teeth, and his growl vibrated through me. His grip on my hips tightened into a bruising embrace. He sucked my lips into his mouth, grazing his teeth across them. His tongue ran deliciously against mine. He alternated between biting and sucking my lips and tongue until the world spun around me. I moaned as he ground his pelvis against mine. Over and over, his lips, his tongue, and his body assaulted my senses. My legs tightened around his waist. He thrust against me once more, and my entire body exploded in intense, blinding waves of pleasure. A strangled cry escaped me as an orgasm tore through my body.

His warm breath tickled my skin as he placed slow sensual kisses up my neck and muttered his apologies. "I never meant to lie to you, Beth."

Beth? My eyes fluttered open and took in the bright stage lights and theater curtains above. Awareness shocked me out of my sexual haze.

Oh shit.

Alex was still kissing my neck as the stage lights dimmed and the curtain came down. Alex stilled, his lips frozen in place at my neck, his arms wrapped tightly around me. His only movement was the rise and fall of his chest against mine as he took in ragged breaths.

After a few tense seconds, his grip loosened, and a gentle chuckle escaped his lips. "You don't play around with this acting stuff, do you?"

Before I could give my mortified response, the entire auditorium was inundated with whoops and catcalls. The sounds echoed through the massive space.

Alex chuckled and whispered in my ear, "I think they're asking for an encore."

Unable to speak, I lowered my legs from his waist.

Alex kissed me gently on the cheek then muttered, "Why don't you get changed? We'll talk later."

I nodded, then stumbled to the changing area and closed the door. *Holy shit.* I leaned against the closed door for support. That was so intense I'd forgotten we were on stage. My face flushed as I realized how it must have looked. How was I going to walk out of here? How was I going to face everyone?

The door opened, jostling me forward as Aria walked in.

"Oh my gosh. That was so freaking hot."

I couldn't face her, but I nodded my head and started removing my clothing.

"You are an amazing actress. You should, like, be on Broadway or something," Aria gushed. "Of course, performing with Alexander probably isn't a hardship. He is such a babe."

Aria's words calmed my nerves.

"Yeah, I guess it could be worse."

"As far as I can see, it couldn't get much better. That boy is fine!"

Maybe it wasn't as bad as I thought. Apparently, everyone thought I was acting. Nothing to be embarrassed about, right?

I said goodbye to Aria and grabbed my purse with my still trembling hand.

Jenny Henson stopped me at the door. "Gwen, I wanted you to know I'm taking Beverly's place as Josie, your best friend."

They were replacing Beverly already? She'd only been gone for...holy crap. I counted the hours in my head. A wave of panic washed over me as I realized I still hadn't heard from her.

"Oh, don't worry." Jenny mistook my expression. "I've been memorizing my lines the past two days. I'm ready," she assured me with a smile.

"Of course. I'm sure you'll do great." I smiled and pushed down the wrenching in my gut. Why hadn't I heard from Beverly yet? My mind began contemplating all the things that could have happened. Cell phone battery dead? No way, she kept a backup battery with her whenever she traveled. Maybe she was too busy taking care of her parents? But she'd been gone for days, she would have had time to call.

My heart rate sped up. Plane crash? What if her plane had fallen out of the sky, and her body was somewhere in the Atlantic? No, a plane crash would have been all over the news, I would have heard about it by now. Then another, more horrifying thought – What if she had been abducted at the airport and was being held captive, or worse, sold into sex slavery? I'd seen a documentary about that. It was a possibility.

I began to hyperventilate, and the edges of my vision began to blackout. Someone had kidnapped my best friend. She was probably being tortured or raped right at that minute. My knees weakened and then collapsed beneath me. Through my darkening vision, I was vaguely aware of the ground rushing up to meet me, but I didn't care. I welcomed the darkness that enveloped me and prayed I'd wake to find it was all a dream.

∞∞∞∞∞∞

Beep.... Beep.... Beep....

I awoke to the soft sound of a rhythmic beep.

What was that awful smell?

I opened my eyes and took in the drab grey walls of the dimly lit room. I was on the floor, stationed between two hospital beds, with nothing but a blanket between myself and the cold, hard floor.

What is going on?

I stood and looked at the patient to my left.

I gasped. My hand flew to my mouth as I realized it was Mrs. Shultz. Her head was heavily bandaged, and her face was covered in bruises, but it was definitely her.

I looked to my right. Mr. Shultz wasn't much better off; his face was a patchwork of black and blue bruising. Poorly installed stitches ran in stretches across his forehead and cheeks.

The sound of footsteps alerted me, and I spun around to find a pale blonde man in a lab coat entering the room.

"I'm Gwen Adams, a friend of the family. Can you tell me how they're doing?"

The doctor ignored me. He strode to Mrs. Shultz's bed, pulled a syringe from his pocket, and injected it into her IV bag. Wordlessly, he walked to Mr. Shultz's bedside and did the same.

"Please, just tell me-"

The doctor turned to leave, and as he did, his white lab coat swung open, giving me a brief glimpse of the gun tucked into his pants. Instinctively, I reached out to grab his arm but found no resistance as my hand traveled right through him. He walked out the room unscathed and completely unaware of my presence.

What the hell is going on?

A loud alarm blared behind me, then another alarm sounded with it.

A doctor and two nurses ran into the room and readied their equipment.

"Clear," the doctor yelled before pressing the pads into Mrs. Shultz's chest. Her body jolted, but the monitors remained flat.

No. This couldn't be happening. I sunk to the floor, and tears streamed down my face as I watched the doctor unsuccessfully work to save Mr. and Mrs. Shultz's lives.

My chest heaved, and I struggled for air as the truth of the situation hit me.

They had been executed. The man that had come in a few moments before hadn't been a doctor.

He was an assassin.

I felt my world tilt and swirl as the images blurred around me. The last sound I heard was Beverly's terrified scream.

"No!"

∞∞∞∞∞∞

"NO!"

I sat up with a start, heart racing and completely out of breath.

"Gwen?" Alex knelt on the floor next to me, his hands gently cradling my face. "Calm down. Everything's okay."

I couldn't listen. I brushed his hands aside and scrambled to my feet. I yanked my phone out and called Beverly.

The number you've dialed is outside its coverage area. Please check the number and try again at another time.

The robotic voice infuriated me.

"Damn it," I yelled in frustration as I jammed my phone into my back pocket.

"Gwen." Alex's commanding voice pulled my attention. "What's wrong?"

I paced the room as Jenny, Alex, and Jasper waited for my

answer.

"It's Beverly. I haven't heard from her. And I've got this sinking feeling something's wrong."

Jenny spoke up. "She's probably been too busy to call. I'm sure you'll hear from her soon."

"Where's Ky? Maybe he's heard from her." The sudden thought filled me with hope.

Alex pressed his lips together and lowered his head.

Jasper looked away.

"What?"

Jasper cleared his throat. "Ky stormed out of here during that last scene. I haven't seen him since."

Oh crap. *Ky.*

Alex put an arm around my shoulder and led me outside. "Everything will be just fine. I'll have someone find Beverly for you. I'm sure she's just had her hands full, don't worry."

His words reassured me, and I was surprised to find that I trusted him, that deep down, I somehow knew he'd always keep his word to me. And if anyone could find Beverly, it would be Alex.

I took a deep breath, then slowly released it. I knew I was overreacting, but I couldn't shake this strong sense of foreboding.

I shook my head harshly, hoping to physically force the thoughts from my mind. I would focus instead on the amazing guy walking next to me. *My boyfriend?* God, even in my own mind, that sounded like some insane fantasy. How could this impossibly sexy, wealthy, intelligent man want someone as ordinary as me?

I reached my car and turned to face him. The sun was rising in the sky behind me, casting its brilliant rays directly into Alex's stunning eyes – the same deep blue eyes and sooty black lashes that haunted my dreams.

"Do you wear contacts?" Surely, that color couldn't be natural.

His lips twitched suspiciously for a moment. "Do I need contacts? I don't know, maybe. I am having a really *hard* time seeing you."

Alex's eyes smoldered with a predatory gleam as he stalked toward me. He erased the space between us and pressed my backside firmly against the car door, effectively caging me in as both forearms rested on either side of me. The heat of his body slammed into mine. The stretch of that thin shirt across his broad shoulders and those tight biceps around me took me back to that fantasy I'd had before practice. I licked my lips and flicked my eyes up to his.

It took everything in me not to move as he lowered his face to mine.

He squinted his eyes. "Hmm. Is this really Gwen?"

He moved with deliberate slowness as his lips skimmed across my cheek and down my neck, close enough that I could feel his warm breath against my skin. He didn't touch me. He teased me with his closeness. Left me breathless with his warmth.

A shiver of pleasure ran down my spine as he inhaled deeply and whispered against my neck, "It certainly smells like Gwen."

His lips skimmed over my skin again until they hovered over my own parted lips. I could taste his minty breath, could feel the heat from his body radiating into me. He ran his tongue slowly across my bottom lip. It was warm and wet, and I found myself panting in desperation.

He pulled my lip between his teeth and growled, "It certainly tastes like Gwen."

He pulled away, and his heated eyes met mine. My chest heaved as I leaned against the car; my breaths came in embarrassing gasps.

He crossed his arms over his chest and took an arrogant step backward. His cocky smirk taunted me. "But I can't be sure it's really Gwen because I just can't see her without my contacts. Besides," he shrugged, "the Gwen I know, she likes to dry hump me when I kiss her."

"Hey!" I reared back and smacked his shoulder as hard as I could.

Mortification suddenly overwhelmed me. I turned my back on him, grabbed my purse, and nervously searched for my keys. Anything to keep from looking him in the eye.

"Gwen."

I ignored him and continued fumbling through my bag. *Where were those damn keys?*

Alex grabbed my bag and pulled it from my hands.

I huffed. Unable to face him, I stared at the asphalt.

Alex stepped in front of me and took my hands in his. "Gwen, look at me." His voice was as gentle as I'd ever heard it. His right hand cupped my cheek and forced my eyes to his.

His intense blue eyes softened as they focused on me. "Gwen, I'm sorry."

I was so mortified. How would I ever be able to look at him again? I couldn't. I shook my head and tried to pull away from his strong grip.

"Not going to happen, Gwen. I'm not letting you go. Please look at me, you have no reason to be embarrassed."

"Yeah, right," I mumbled as my gaze shifted to the auditorium behind him.

He forced my eyes to his. "Don't think for one moment that I don't lose my mind every single time you touch me."

What?

I blinked in confusion, and Alex continued, "Don't be embarrassed about being attracted to me. I'm not." He leaned over and placed a tender kiss on my lips.

The kiss was chaste, but when his warm lips lingered on mine, my chest swelled with warmth.

"See. Everything's okay." He took my hand once again and smiled that perfect smile of his.

Unable to speak, I nodded weakly in response.

"So," Alex continued, his tone implying a change of subject, "since we seem to have skipped a few steps, how do you feel about backing up and spending some time with me tonight?"

"You mean like a date?"

"Yeah, a date."

I thought about it for a moment. I loved the idea of spending time with him, but I was so emotionally drained that all I wanted to do was crawl onto my couch and hang out with Beverly.

But Beverly wasn't here. I felt my worry for her start to build again, but I pushed it down before it could spiral out of control.

I glanced up at Alex. His easygoing smile made saying no to him impossible.

"Sure, what time?"

His smile widened. "I'll pick you up at eight."

He handed over my keys, got me in my car, and shut the door behind me. He waved as I started the car, but before I could drive away, a realization hit me.

"Where are we going? I need to know what to wear."

A humorous glint lit his eyes. "As far as I'm concerned, you can go naked."

"Very funny."

He winked as he turned to walk toward his car. "Dress comfortably. See you tonight."

∞∞∞∞∞∞

Hannah was waiting in my driveway when I got home. Her black hair was slicked back into a tight ponytail. Her milky complexion and bright red lipstick worked to accentuate the angry scowl plastered on her face.

This was not good.

Obviously, she had been at practice and hadn't liked what she'd seen. From the look in her eyes, I could tell she was about to let me know just how much she hadn't liked it.

I parked my car and reluctantly walked over to her.

"So," her voice lashed out at me, "are you going to tell me that was just acting?"

"Hannah-"

"No! Just shut your damn mouth and listen."

I exaggerated pressing my lips together, which seemed to piss her off even more.

"Keep your filthy hands off my man, you dirty whore."

Okay, that was it. I'd tried being nice to Hannah, but that shit stopped now.

"Wait just one fucking minute. Weren't you the one that was all for turning this into some twisted contest between the two of us? And dirty whore? Really? Please remind me, who is it that's been sleeping around with every guy in town? Was that me? I didn't think so." I paused for emphasis. "And by the way, he's not your man. He's mine. We made it official a few days ago."

Hannah blanched.

"He wants to be with me, not you. So back the fuck off."

"You..." Hannah's face had reddened like a volcano ready to erupt. "You fucking bitch."

She got right in my face and continued, "You stole Ky from me. You manipulated him and everyone around us into believing you were this perfect fucking angel, and now you're doing the same with Alexander."

Hatred flashed behind Hannah's honey-colored eyes as she pushed a finger into my chest. "You are going to pay for this, bitch. Both of you."

CHAPTER THIRTY-FOUR
Gwen

I'm going on my first real date with Alex.

My hands shook as I skimmed my closet for the perfect outfit. Despite what Alex had said, I couldn't wear just anything. Whatever I chose had to be perfect.

My hand brushed the soft silk of a violet blouse I'd bought at the mall with Hannah the year before. At the thought of Hannah, my hands clenched around the fabric. Anger coursed through me. She'd claimed I'd stolen Ky from her, that I had manipulated him. Her words were so far from the truth it was ridiculous.

Determined to forget about Hannah, I pulled the silk blouse from my closet and held the fabric against my skin.

No, definitely not. I tossed the top on my bed and returned to my browsing.

Why was I so nervous? We'd had our first kiss, and we'd even technically "slept" together; yet, looking down at my trembling hands, I knew none of that mattered. He could kiss me a hundred times, and I'd still feel like this. There was something about him that affected me in ways I couldn't explain.

I went to the kitchen for the only thing I knew that could calm my nerves. A few minutes later, a small snack in one hand and a glass of wine in the other, I returned to my room with renewed determination.

Alex had said to dress comfortably. I reached into my closet and pulled out a simple dress. It was a white cotton dress that hung casually off my shoulders – the most comfortable piece of clothing I owned that wasn't pajamas.

I took a large gulp of wine, then placed the glass on my dresser. I removed my clothes and slid the dress over my head.

Not bad. I turned in the mirror, checking every angle. The color highlighted my tan, and the soft fabric was feminine and flirty. Looking at my reflection, I wondered why it'd been so long since I'd worn it.

Satisfied with the dress, I walked to the bathroom to apply my makeup. As I crossed the threshold, I noticed Spyder playing under my foot a moment too late. I threw my leg out and shifted my weight to miss him, then realized my mistake as I fell forward, dangerously fast toward the bathroom vanity. There was a loud crack, then a bright flash of light before everything went black.

∞∞∞∞∞∞

Darkness enveloped me. Blurred images flickered through my mind like a strobe light.

A beautiful, young blonde stood outside a brick building and argued with someone on her phone. She brushed her long, silky hair away from her face as the wind blew its strands haphazardly.

"He's the one, Ky. Don't you get it? This could change everything for us-"

She huffed and stamped her foot.

"Damn it. This is more important. You can't let your emotions get in the way-"

She slapped her hand down on the brick.

"But Jebad-" She paused and lowered her head.

I furrowed my brow. There was something strangely familiar about her blurred image. Had I seen her somewhere before? I was almost sure I had.

The image faded out, replaced quickly by darkness.

Nothingness.

Time no longer existed. It could have been seconds, it could have been days, and then another vision illuminated my mind.

This image was blurrier than the first, but I quickly made out the backside of a man. He was massive, at least six and a half feet tall. He wore black slacks, and the sleeves of his fitted white dress shirt were rolled to his elbows, showing off muscular forearms. A black tattoo snaked its way out from under his right sleeve. The blackened color was so dark it seemed to suck the light from the air surrounding it. His vibrant blonde hair was cut short but gelled fashionably. I imagined if he turned around, his face would be as stunning as the rest of him. Yet, there was something undeniably evil about this stranger.

Movement caught my eye, and as I looked past the massive man, I was shocked to see Hannah's smiling face. Her large amber eyes sparkled in the light, filled with adoration as she stared up at him.

She reached up and cupped his face. Her ruby lips whispered to him as she pulled his lips to hers and wrapped her arms around his neck.

I watched in horror as two black claws, and a serpentine tail shot out the man's back.

His arms held her captive as his scaly claws ripped the flesh from her bones. Blood splattered the white walls. Her agonized screams seared my mind, as he laughed and laughed.

This time when the image began to darken and fade, I slumped in relief. The stark emptiness replaced the horror. The silence erased the screams.

∞∞∞∞∞∞

I sat up slowly, my foggy memory trying to decipher how I'd ended up on my bathroom floor. I glanced down at the white dress I was wearing and vaguely remembered my date with Alex. I jerked my head toward the clock I kept above my dresser and winced. I reached my hand up to the back of my head, where throbbing pain radiated from my skull.

I must have knocked myself out.

I stood up and walked to the kitchen. Getting a glass of water and some medicine in my system were the first things on my list. The second, I wasn't exactly happy about, but I needed to cancel my date with Alex. I couldn't go out tonight. I could barely see straight.

I dialed the number Alex had texted me earlier that day.

"Gwen?"

"Hey..." I paused, wondering how I was going to cancel. I should have figured it out before I'd called.

"Gwen, are you okay?"

"Well..." I tried to think of a clever excuse, but the pounding in my head prevented that. "I can't make it tonight."

There was silence over the phone, and for a moment, I thought he'd hung up on me.

"I'm coming over." His determined voice left no room for arguing, and honestly, I didn't have the energy for it.

I agreed, then hung up the phone. I unlocked the door so he'd be able to get in, then laid down on the couch and prayed for relief.

A soft knock woke me. I heard the door, then felt the soft breeze against my skin. I knew instantly that it was Alex by the intoxicating scent – some strange mix of mountain forests, rushing water, and fresh open fields – that filled the room. I inhaled deeply.

Seconds passed, and then the edge of the couch dipped as his weight settled and his warmth seeped into me.

There was some shuffling, then Alex's warm hands gently adjusted my body as he slid behind me on the couch. He pulled my back against his chest and wrapped an arm around me. He laid there with me in silence, tracing small circles up and down my sides.

"Baby, what's wrong?"

"My head is killing me." I barely got the words out.

"Is it a headache?"

Unable to think, I tried to shake my head, then groaned in pain.

Taking another shaky breath, I answered. "I tripped and hit my head."

Alex's chest rose and fell behind me, the soft fabric of his shirt caressing my skin.

"It's going to be okay." He gently brushed a strand of hair from my face. "Just close your eyes and rest. I'm sure you'll feel better soon. You took something for the pain, right?"

"Yeah."

He snuggled in closer and pressed a gentle kiss to my aching temple as I drifted off to sleep.

CHAPTER THIRTY-FIVE
Gwen

My eyes fluttered open with the most amazing sense of well-being. I felt terrific, better than I had in a long time. I peered over my shoulder at the magnificent man wrapped around me.

His blue eyes gazed into mine.

"Good morning, sunshine," he teased with a playful smile.

I bolted up and searched for the clock.

He chuckled as he lifted himself up. "It's only seven o'clock." He laughed again at my panicked expression. "PM."

I exhaled, my tense shoulders slumping in relief.

"How are you feeling? Better?"

My brow furrowed. "I feel great."

"You still up for going out tonight?"

I was surprised to find that I was. I felt absolutely fantastic, like I could jump up and run a marathon.

"Yeah, I think so." I ran a hand through my disheveled hair, and my cheeks heated. "But I've got to finish getting ready."

"You look great to me."

I stood and glanced back at Alex. He was dressed casually in designer jeans and a light blue t-shirt. The snug shirt was stretched tight across his chest and almost ripped at the seams around his biceps. Casual or not, this man was dressed to turn heads. My eyes drank him in, absorbing every fine detail, from his trim waist up to his broad chest. He defined sex appeal; it rolled off of him in waves. The energy in the room shifted as my mind dwelled on all the delicious things I wanted to do with him. A desperate, animalistic need took over me. I moved closer, itching to have his skin against mine.

Alex's eyes burned with intensity as he stared up at me. His hands dug into the couch as I felt another wave of heat blast through me.

"Gwen, you should finish getting ready," Alex's strained voice pierced through my consciousness.

No. There was a strange supernatural pull from his body on mine. I couldn't fight it. I didn't want to anymore. I wanted my clothes off, wanted his body enveloping mine. Our eyes met, and suddenly I was on fire. I could barely breathe. His eyes burned brighter, their intensity flashing in the darkening room.

"Gwen, go. Now."

The urgency in his voice finally broke through the haze. I turned, stumbled to my room, and slid down the closed door as I wondered what the hell I was doing. My heart pounded, and my body ached for him. Part of me wanted to rush back and beg him to take me right there on the family couch. He had an irresistible pull, and I was powerless against it.

I rose up on shaky legs, wobbled to the bathroom, and started the shower.

The cold water was like a slap in the face. It snapped me back to my senses, and I found myself wondering what the hell was going on with me. I was a virgin, for heaven's sake. The farthest I'd ever gone was making out with Wesley after a football game, and we'd only barely gotten my top off before my parents had found us. Where were these intense desires coming from?

I thought about my wonderful Wesley, and my heart ached. I missed him so much. It didn't matter that I had only been a teenager;

he had been the love of my life. He had been everything to me, and the thought of wanting someone else more than him, even if only on a physical level – it felt wrong.

Deep down, I knew it was illogical. I knew it was possible to feel intense lust without love. But if I'd loved Wesley the way I'd thought I had, shouldn't I have wanted him sexually just as bad, if not more? Shouldn't he have been the one to consume my thoughts? Shouldn't he have been the one to drive me to distraction with his presence?

I cut off the water and glanced toward the door. Alex was behind that door.

A strange sadness settled over me. Alex was kind, generous, and funny. He also was intelligent, protective, and sexy as hell. He was everything a woman could ever ask for, and then some. And he deserved so much more than I could give him.

His actions toward me this evening were the actions of a man looking for something more. Something I didn't want to look at too closely because it scared me.

He wasn't going to find what he was looking for in me.

My thoughts depressed me, but despite everything, I got dressed and blow dried my hair. I brushed on some mascara and applied a coat of lip gloss.

When I was finished, I found Alex exactly where I'd left him, waiting patiently on my couch.

∞∞∞∞∞

This is not at all what I expected, I thought as I gazed up at the star-filled sky.

After we'd left my house, we'd driven straight to the office, which had confused the crap out of me, but Alex had absolutely refused to explain. It was when we boarded the helicopter that I had begun to get nervous. At that point, I'd practically threatened his life if he dragged me into a fancy restaurant dressed the way I was.

He hadn't taken me anywhere that would embarrass me. Instead, he'd flown us to a private island owned by a friend of the family. The island estate was about thirty miles offshore, according to Alex, and it was the most beautiful place I'd ever seen.

Instead of the fancy ordeal I'd imagined, our dinner had been fruit, wine, and cold sandwiches he'd prepared ahead of time. We ate under a beautiful white pergola lined with twinkling white lights. With the gentle ocean breeze and stunning view, it couldn't have been a more perfect night.

Sitting beside Alex, overlooking the ocean, I was so relaxed I could have taken a nap. I glanced at Alex and could see he felt the same.

"Tell me. What does your future look like, Gwen?"

I small huff escaped my lips. "I wish I knew."

I had no idea what I wanted to do with my life. I loved acting but knew making a career of it wasn't practical. And I'd changed my major so many times that although I refused to admit it, there was no way I'd graduate on time.

"The truth is, I have no idea what I want to do with my life. I don't even know if I want to stay here in Verona Beach or if I want to travel. My parents are never home, so once we graduate, and Beverly and —" I stopped myself before I said Ky's name. "Once Beverly graduates and moves away, there'll be nothing keeping me here."

"Is traveling something you'd want to do?"

"Well, yeah, if I had the money to do it. But it's going to take all the money I've got just to finish college, so realistically, traveling is out. I guess I'm kind of stuck here."

Attempting to shift the spotlight from myself, I asked, "What about you? Where do you see yourself five years from now?"

A dark shadow crossed his face, then his eyes flashed to mine. "I'm not sure. I know where I'd like to be. But the choice isn't mine."

"What, does your dad try to control your life?"

"No." He paused, then muttered under his breath, "But my father does."

What the hell does that mean?

If he hadn't looked so serious, I would have thought it was a joke. Instead, it was like a strange riddle that only he knew the answer to. I waited for him to start laughing and fill me in.

Alex cleared his throat awkwardly.

"Do you like to read?" I asked in an attempt to change the subject.

There was a flicker of a smile before he answered. "Not the same books you do, but yeah, I love to read."

We both laughed as we remembered that day on the beach.

I playfully smacked his arm. "Those aren't the only books I read."

"Oh, yeah?"

"Yeah. In fact, that was the first romance novel I've ever read."

"I hate to break it to you, princess, but that was not a romance novel." He eyed me with a smirk. "That was what you call erotica, not romance."

I rolled my eyes. "Is there a difference?"

He wiggled his eyebrows. "In romance, the characters may end up having sex, but in erotica, the sex itself is described. In detail. It's like the difference between a rated R movie and porn."

"Oh." My cheeks flushed.

Apparently deciding to have mercy on me, Alex changed the subject. "So, if erotica isn't what you're into, then what is?"

"I like to read just about anything. Science fiction and fantasy are my favorites, but I also like mysteries and non-fiction. Basically anything but self-help books."

"Why fantasy and sci-fi?"

I shrugged. "Because the real world is so boring. Why would I want to read about ordinary, everyday life? I live it every day. Sometimes I just want to escape reality."

Alex nodded, and his expression grew morose. "Yeah. Me too."

I watched him a moment and wondered what was wrong. I

reached out and took his hand in mine.

"Are you okay?"

"Yeah."

Alex stood and pulled me to my feet, lacing his fingers through mine and leading me toward the beach.

It was a magical night. Stars twinkled like diamonds above. Moonlight glittered across the waves. A gentle breeze brought over the fresh scent of the ocean and blew my hair from my face.

We stood, hand in hand, listening to the crashing roar of the sea. Alex shifted in front of me and pulled me close.

His eyes never left mine as he cradled my face in his hands, and his lips came down tenderly on my own. My mouth parted, and his tongue stroked mine in long sensual sweeps. His enticing scent swirled around me, as he rubbed his thumbs against my jaw and pressed slow drugging kisses against my lips.

The wind picked up, whipping my dress around my legs, but with Alex's warm arms around me, nothing else mattered. All I saw and all I felt was him. His warmth surrounded me, his scent called to me, his lips weakened my knees.

His kiss deepened, becoming more urgent. His hands pulled me tighter, squeezing me to him.

He smothered my gasp as he covered my lips once more.

"Gwen." He breathed my name between kisses.

I couldn't speak as I clung to him. My world spun. I couldn't see. I couldn't think. He owned my senses.

With one last lingering kiss, he released me and pressed his forehead to mine.

His eyes closed and he took a deep, unsteady breath as he traced a finger over my eyes, down my cheek, and across my lips.

Then, as if it were the most natural thing in the world, one arm slid around my back and the other low at my hips, as we began dancing to the sounds of the ocean.

His muscular chest pressed into mine as he held me in his arms.

A feeling of rightness washed over me as we swayed and dipped under the stars.

∞∞∞∞∞∞

"Mom?"

I rounded the corner to the kitchen, following the mouth-watering aroma of pancakes and bacon.

My mom faced the stove, spatula in hand, watching pancakes bubble on the skillet. Her short black hair was pulled up into a spiky ponytail.

I looked enviously at her five-foot-two, ninety-five-pound frame and wondered not for the first time why I couldn't have gotten her looks.

She turned, her chocolate brown eyes flashing to mine. "Hi, honey. You're awake!"

She dropped the spatula and hugged me fiercely.

I closed my eyes and enjoyed the warmth of her embrace.

"I missed you." I squeezed her tightly. "When did you get home?"

She turned off the stove, wiped her hands, and faced me. "We got home last night about ten o'clock."

"Last night? But I didn't see the car."

She nodded. "It's in the garage." She waved away my questions. "Don't ask, it's a long story. The real question is, when did *you* get home last night?"

"Um..." I tried to come up with an excuse.

A knowing smile spread across her amused face. "Did you and Ky finally get together?"

My brain nearly sputtered to a stop. "W-What?"

She smiled. "Oh, honey, I know I wasn't around that much, but it was obvious to everyone how Ky felt about you. So...?"

I shook my head and struggled to keep the smile on my face. "No, Mom. We dated for a while, but things didn't work out."

She pursed her lips and placed a few strips of bacon on a plate.

"Well, why not?"

"It's a long story, Mom."

She waited a few moments before conceding. "Okay, okay. I can take a hint."

We both took a seat at the table.

I took a strip of bacon and popped it in my mouth.

"So, who is he?" She smiled knowingly. "Come on, honey. If you weren't with Ky last night, then who were you with until three in the morning? Are you seeing someone? Please, you have to tell me."

The eagerness in her sparkling eyes was hard to ignore.

"Yeah." A shy smile spread across my face. "There is someone."

She wiggled excitedly in her chair, and I was suddenly overwhelmed with emotion.

I stood up and threw my arms around her. "I've missed you so much, Mom."

She squeezed me harder. "I've missed you, too." She brushed a tear from her cheek. "I'm sorry we're gone all the time, honey."

"I understand. I know you have to work."

She shook her head. Her sorrowful eyes met mine. "No, you deserve so much better from us. I hate how we've left you by yourself all these years." She grabbed my hands in hers. "One day, you will understand why things had to be this way."

The expression in her eyes and the inflection in her voice told me there was more to what she was saying below the surface of her words.

"Mom, what-"

She shook her head and swiped another tear away. "Never mind me." She straightened in her seat, and her smile brightened. "So, tell me about this guy you're dating."

I smiled as I thought about last night and the kiss Alex and I had shared. I remembered the emotion in his eyes just before his lips had touched mine. My heart tugged in my chest. Somehow, for the first time in years, I finally felt ready to take the next step. I wasn't afraid anymore.

"Oh, that good, huh," she squealed. "Tell me, tell me!"

So I told her everything. I started with how Ky and I began dating. She was so excited until I got to the part where he'd betrayed me.

"Oh, my. I would never have thought-"

"Yeah, me neither."

"Okay, so you met this new mystery guy after you broke up with Ky?"

I shook my head. "Actually, I met him at the beginning of the summer. He was at the senator's fundraiser. His name is Alexander Prescott."

Orange juice sprayed from her lips as she choked.

I patted her back and waited for her coughing to stop.

"Did you say his name is Alexander?"

"Yes." I paused at her shocked expression. "Mom, are you okay?"

She ignored my question. "Do you like him?"

"Mom! Stop trying to change the subject. What's wrong?"

"Nothing is wrong. I just tried to inhale my juice and ended up choking on it. But I'm fine. So, do you like this guy or not?"

I looked into her speculative eyes and wondered what was going through her mind. Something was bothering her, but she was hiding it from me.

"Well?"

"Yeah. I like him."

"Like who?" My dad's baritone voice boomed through the kitchen.

"Nobody, Dad."

He grabbed a plate from the cabinet.

"Um, Dad." I paused and gathered my courage. "I need to ask you something."

"Shoot," he replied as he took the seat next to me.

"Did you call in a favor to get me a job at Mercury Technologies?"

He furrowed his brows, and his blue eyes met mine. "What?"

"When I interviewed for the job, Mr. Grimes told me I had good recommendations. I assumed you called in a favor. Was it you?"

"No. You asked me not to get involved, and I respected your wishes. Sorry, sweetheart."

Huh, if my dad didn't do it, then who did?

Buzz...

I lifted my phone and looked at the incoming text.

JASPER: play canceled due to bunch of fucking ninnies, someone complained to the Dean

What?

I looked at the text again. It was a group text, sent out to the entire cast.

The play was canceled?

Buzz...Buzz...Buzz...

It was Alex.

I waved to my parents as I left the kitchen and went to my room.

"Alex, you got Jasper's text?"

"Yeah. Can't say I'm surprised. You've got to know Hannah or Ky would do everything they could to stop this play."

He had a good point. After yesterday's practice, I could imagine either one of them pulling a stunt like that.

"By the way, I need to ask you something," I said, then hesitated.

"Gwen?"

I wasn't sure why, but I was suddenly reluctant to ask.

"Gwen?" Alex asked again.

"Did you tell Mr. Grimes to hire me?"

He laughed into the phone, and my face burned. "You sounded

so serious, you had me worried for a second. Trust me, I wish I could take credit for hiring you. But, it wasn't me."

If it wasn't Daddy, and it wasn't Alex, then who recommended me for the job?

"Gwen, I made a few calls and found out Beverly's flight got delayed. She ended up in Italy for half a day, but she's fine. From what I've been told, she made it to the hospital, but communications there aren't the best."

"What about her parents? Did they tell you anything?"

"No details, but they did say her parents were expected to make a full recovery."

I blew a slow breath from my lips as tension I hadn't realized I'd been carrying slipped from my shoulders. "Thank you."

"No problem, babe."

I grinned.

"Since we don't have rehearsal today-" Alex started.

There was noise in the background. Alex's voice was muffled when he said, "Yeah, just give me a minute," then more clearly into the phone, "I'm sorry, Gwen, I've got to go. Oh yeah, I almost forgot, we'll be flying out of state tonight for a meeting. We'll probably be out late."

"Okay. I'll be ready."

I said a quick goodbye to Alex and left my room, but when I returned to the kitchen, I found my mom carrying a suitcase toward the door.

"Mom." I looked at her luggage. "What's going on? I thought you'd be home a few days."

"I know. I'm sorry, honey. Something came up."

Something always comes up, I thought bitterly.

Dad rushed by, his arms loaded down with bags, and his face pinched with worry.

My eyes shifted between my mom and dad. Something was wrong. They never worried like this.

"What's going on?"

Mom's distressed eyes met Dad's for permission. Dad shook his head.

"Honey." My mom placed her hands on my arms. "Everything's going to be okay."

"What's going to be okay? I don't understand what's happening. Why do you both look so worried?"

She lowered her head and closed her eyes. The silence stretched awkwardly between us.

"Mom?"

She squeezed her eyes tighter. "I can't do this anymore."

"What-"

She threw her arms around me and held me tight. "I love you so much, sweetheart. There's so much you don't know. So much we can't tell you. And I am so sorry for that."

"Mom, you're scaring me. What's going on?"

Why were there tears in her eyes? Why were her hands shaking?

"Oh, honey." She wiped a tear from her cheek. "I'm just a little emotional right now because I miss you. Please don't worry, I'm just being silly."

She pulled me into another hug and kissed my cheek. Before I could argue, she grabbed her bag and headed for the door.

"Dad?"

He stopped mid-stride, dropped his bag, and wrapped me in a warm embrace. I couldn't remember the last time my dad had hugged me.

"Don't worry about us," he muttered gruffly. "Just take care of yourself while we're gone. I love you." He placed a swift kiss on my forehead, and within seconds, they were both out the door.

I stood staring at the door in shock. The suddenly quiet house seemed larger and lonelier than ever before.

What the hell had just happened? It was like a whirlwind had blown through and swept them away.

I walked to the window and watched as their red Prius pulled out of the driveway.

What could have happened to make them act so strangely?

I returned to my room and fell limply across my bed. I stared up at the ceiling and tried to ignore my parents' odd behavior. I'd given up on understanding them years before. They were too unpredictable. There were moments when they seemed genuinely concerned for me, and then other times they took a completely hands-off approach to my upbringing. The constant back and forth always left me with feelings of whiplash.

I turned my head toward my nightstand and reached for the photograph of my family. I ran my fingers over the wooden frame and thought about the day the picture had been taken. It had been the only family vacation I could remember us taking, and we'd had a blast.

I ran my fingertips across our smiling faces and wondered if we'd ever experience that again.

∞∞∞∞∞∞

We were flying back from a meeting we'd had to attend in Maryland.

I watched Alex from my position in the passenger seat, and warmth flooded my chest. His handsome face was studying the night sky as we flew high over the earth.

I spoke into the headset he'd given me. "Alex?"

A smile spread across his lips. "Hey, I thought you'd fallen asleep over there."

"No." I blushed. "I was just thinking."

"What were you thinking about?"

"Nothing," I lied. "How much farther do we have?"

"About twenty minutes. Everything okay?"

I felt my lips curve up into a smile. "Everything's perfect."

It was quiet as Alex focused on the journey. I gazed outside, noticing the lack of illumination below. It took me a moment to realize we were flying over a dense forest.

"Gwen?"

"Yeah," I answered, wondering why Alex was suddenly speaking so softly.

I heard him exhale, then barely speaking above a whisper, he said, "There's something I've wanted to talk to you about."

Nothing but silence followed.

I fidgeted nervously with my hair.

After a few moments, when he didn't continue, I coaxed, "What is it? You can tell me anything."

Silence again.

I twirled my hair around my finger as I stared at my lap.

"It's not a big deal, but-"

Weee-ooo-weee-ooo-weee-ooo...

A loud siren erupted through the cockpit.

"What the fuck?" Alex suddenly became very animated. He flipped two switches, then tapped on a gauge above his head.

He slammed his hand against the console. "Fuck!"

I didn't have a clue what was happening, but whatever it was, it was bad.

Alex's head dropped back. He seemed to contemplate the ceiling for a moment before he sprang into action again.

He reached across the console and flipped another switch, then punched in a few keys.

He turned to me and took my arms gently.

"Gwen, there's an issue with the engine. I've got to step outside and take a look at it." His voice was so calm, and his hands rubbing up and down my arms were so soothing, it took a moment for the meaning of his words to filter through to my brain.

"O-Outside? What? What does that mean?"

He rubbed a hand across his face. "It'll be okay. I've just got to take a look at the engine. All right?"

I nodded.

Alex grabbed the door, then suddenly stopped and turned to me. Before I could speak, he'd cupped my cheeks between his palms and crushed his warm lips to mine. The kiss was harsh and demanding and ended as quickly as it had begun as he jerked away and threw open the door.

Wind whipped wildly through the cockpit. The loud roar of the engine overpowered the static of the headsets.

I watched helplessly as Alex stepped out onto the landing skids and slowly inched toward the engine compartment. Watching him out there, dangling hundreds of feet above the ground, had my heart racing in my chest. Just one wrong move, and he'd fall to his death.

I searched the cockpit. Why the hell didn't he have parachutes? What he was doing was dangerous. I looked back out my window. Alex had shimmied along the outside of the chopper toward the back, and I could barely see him.

Knowing I'd regret it, I unbuckled my straps and slid over to the open door so that I could see better. The wind was fierce, almost enough to blow me down. I grabbed the handhold adjacent to the door.

I looked back outside, but Alex was gone.

Oh, no.

I gripped the handle tighter and leaned out over the opening.

Alex suddenly appeared in front of me, his haunting blue eyes inches from mine. Before I could speak, he wrapped his arms around my waist, then flung us both over the edge to our deaths.

My stomach dropped. The darkness below rushed up to meet us, swirling around us in a rush of wind that stole my breath. Through the horror, a part of my brain tried to comprehend what Alex had done.

A loud explosion deafened me. Orange flames burst through the night, traveling faster than we could fall to escape them. I felt the searing heat of the flames as they approached.

No.

I watched in slow motion as flames plumed out from the explosion, growing closer and closer, the heat building in intensity.

Then something miraculous happened. The flames wrapped

around us, enveloping us but not touching us, as if we were surrounded by a protective shield. Then, all at once, the falling sensation ceased, and we were suspended high in the air, engulfed in flames that were not consuming us.

What the hell is happening?

I trembled in Alex's arms and watched as the chopper fell from the sky in pieces. The bright light from the explosion faded away until all that remained was the moonlight reflecting off our suspended bodies.

My heart raced.

"A-Alex?"

"Shh. It's okay, baby. Just close your eyes." His soft voice beckoned my heart to relax.

"But-"

"Shh. I promise I'll explain. Just let me get us home first."

I nodded and squeezed my eyes closed.

What was happening? My mind couldn't make sense of what I'd seen, what I was still seeing. Why hadn't the flames burned us? Why hadn't we fallen to our deaths? How were we still in the air?

I clung to Alex as my whole body shook. Wind whipped my hair around us. I slid my eyes open, peeping over Alex's shoulder. Darkness prevented me from seeing much, but it was evident we were rapidly moving through the air. A wave of panic overtook me, and I slammed my eyes shut as tightly as I could.

As the minutes passed by, I recounted all the times something strange had happened when Alex was around. Like that day I'd seen a car drive through him. Or how he'd always shown up when I had been in danger or hurt.

The wind slowed, and I felt my feet being lowered onto solid ground.

A voice echoed in my mind as if from a great distance. "Gwen? Gwen?"

My mind slowly focused on Alex's voice.

"Are you okay?" Alex's warm arms released me, then he reached back and pried my fingers from his back.

"Alex, what...?" My voice faltered. "What the hell happened out there? I feel like I'm losing my mind."

I glanced around. We were standing on the balcony outside his bedroom. "How did we get here?"

Alex took my elbow and led me inside. "I'll tell you everything, but let's get inside first and sit down."

CHAPTER THIRTY-SIX
Alex

Damn it.

I watched Gwen sip her water and shakily take a seat on the edge of my bed. Her wavy blonde hair fell across her face as she stared down at the drink her trembling hands could barely hold.

Every moment that passed, I grew angrier. Whoever had done this was going to pay. There would be no mercy.

It killed me that I couldn't figure out how they'd managed to plant a bomb inside the engine compartment. It was sheer luck the culprit had accidentally clipped the tube that eventually sounded the alarm. If not for that mistake, Gwen would have surely been dead right now.

Dead.

Whoever had done this was going to pay. If it were another angel, I'd make sure he suffered in agony for eternity.

My eyes roamed over Gwen, and I felt something inside my chest tighten. Oxygen was sucked from my lungs as a shock wave rocked through me.

How had I not seen it sooner? I knew I'd felt something, but this was more than *something*. I had no idea when it had happened, but somehow, I'd fallen desperately in love with this girl.

I observed her carefully now, cataloging every detail, every perfection, every flaw. She was everything to me, and it was this final admission that brought relief flooding through my body. A weight lifted from my shoulders.

Holy shit.

I ran a hand down my face.

I had to tell her the truth. But how the fuck was I supposed to do that?

I closed my eyes a moment before glancing at her trembling fingers. "I'm not who you think I am."

Gwen's head lifted. Her eyes stared deeply into mine.

"My real name is Alexias Prisco. Alexias means 'defender of mankind,'" I paused. "Where I come from, everyone's name has a meaning."

She stared down at her cup. "Where are you from?"

I cringed but answered honestly. "Heaven."

Her eyes darted back to mine.

I held my breath as I awaited her response, but when she didn't speak, I continued. "Gwen, I know this is going to be hard to believe, but I'm an angel."

Her eyes widened. "An angel? Like God, Satan, and the Bible kind of angel?"

"Yeah."

She hesitated a moment. "Are you a good angel, or a fallen angel?"

If she hadn't looked so damn nervous, I would have laughed.

I took her shaky hands in mine and looked her directly in the eyes. "Gwen, I am not a fallen angel."

"So...you're a good angel?"

I laughed humorlessly. "Not exactly. But I'm still on good terms with God. I assume that's what you mean."

Gwen stood and paced the room. "What about your family? Are they angels too?"

"Yes," I answered quickly and then clarified. "Actually, they're hybrids. Half human, half angel."

She stopped pacing. Her vibrant green eyes were wide with astonishment. "That's possible?"

"We really aren't that much different from you."

"Oh."

I expected her to question me more about that, but instead, she asked another difficult question.

"How old are you?"

I didn't want to freak her out, but I wouldn't lie to her.

"I can't tell you how old I am in Earth years because I honestly don't know. But I can tell you I was born many millennia before Earth was created."

She dropped to the bed. Her long blonde hair fell across her face, hiding her eyes from me.

She looked so fragile sitting there, and all I wanted was to hold her in my arms and comfort her. She'd been through so much, and I wished I could take it all away. But I knew Gwen needed space right now.

She nodded her head and distractedly twirled her ring around her finger. "So all this time, you've been lying to me."

"Not the whole time. And only when I had to."

She took a deep breath and straightened. "If you're an angel, then why all the drama with Hannah and me? Shouldn't an angel have more important things to do?"

"Gwen, I already told you, I'm not a great angel."

I saw a flicker of a smile before she continued. "Tell me the truth. Why were you with Hannah? Was it really because of her family?"

I huffed and rubbed my hand down my face. How was I supposed to explain this?

"Alex, just tell me."

I nodded. She deserved the truth.

"You're right. I wasn't honest with you about Hannah."

Gwen sucked in a breath.

"Hannah resembles someone I once loved a long time ago. So that night at the fundraiser, I thought meeting her was fate. I believed she was the one I was supposed to be with."

Gwen's beautiful eyes lowered and refused to meet mine, but I wasn't having it.

"Gwen. Look at me."

It took a moment, but her eyes slowly lifted to mine.

"I thought I was supposed to be with Hannah. But it was you that I was drawn to. It was always you that I wanted. And I kept pushing you away because I thought I had to be with Hannah. But every time I went out with her, I was thinking about you. Then one day, I realized that you were the one I was meant to be with, and that I'd been such a fool for pushing you away for so long."

Gwen's eyes lowered, but a small smile crept across her face. She hesitated a moment, then her face flushed. "I have another question."

"Whatever you want to know."

"Do you have superpowers or something?"

I struggled to keep a smile off my face, knowing Gwen was freaked out and trying to stay serious. "No. We don't have superpowers." I thought a moment. "Well...not exactly."

Her questioning eyes searched mine.

"We have certain abilities that humans don't have, but I wouldn't call them superpowers."

"What would you call them then?"

This wasn't something I'd ever had to explain before. "It's all based on science. It's in our DNA. Calling it a superpower makes it sound like magic."

I was surprised when a small grin appeared on her face. "Haven't you heard that quote by Arthur Clark, 'Magic's just science we don't understand yet?'"

Damn, I love this girl.

I finally let the smile I'd been holding back spread across my face. "Yeah, I guess you're right."

Her smile brightened, and she finally stopped shaking. She licked her lips. "What kind of superpowers do you have?"

"Well, obviously I can fly-"

"I wondered about that. I didn't see wings. Why don't you have wings?"

How could I explain it? "I have wings, I just don't always choose to let them show."

"So, they're, like, invisible? Unless you let them be visible?"

"Yes."

"Why didn't the flames burn us?"

Knowing she was going to have a lot of questions, I answered quickly. "I wrapped my wings around us, protecting us from the flames."

"Oh." She looked thoughtful for a moment. "What else can you do?"

"I have the ability to heal wounds-"

"Wait." She placed a hand on my thigh. "Do all angels have the same abilities?"

I stared into her emerald eyes and shook my head. "Do all humans have the same talents?"

I waited a moment for her to process my words. "We have different abilities, just like humans. Our skills are usually tied to our personalities. There are a few gifts we all have in common, such as flying and healing. The mechanism for the healing is different from angel to angel, but the ability is almost always there. For the most part, angels' abilities are very different. Most angels have anywhere from two to five unique abilities."

She looked at me strangely. "Mechanism?"

She always focused on just the wrong thing. "By mechanism, I meant how and what we can heal."

"So...?"

This is going to get interesting.

"Alex, tell me," she insisted, her earlier reservations apparently gone. "How do you heal someone?"

Oh hell, why not?

"Whenever I need to heal someone..." I paused, not sure if I wanted to continue.

"Tell me!"

"Okay, fine," I huffed. "When I heal someone, I have to kiss them."

She blanched. "Why would you have to kiss-"

"It's just the way it is. Like I said, our abilities are tailored to our personalities. Since all angels can heal, and God didn't want us running around treating every ailment, he put limitations on us. These limitations were based on personality. Mine is that I have to kiss the affected body part."

Her eyes widened. "You don't like kissing people?"

I chuckled. "I don't like kissing guys. There was once a time when I was a soldier. I guess God didn't want me running around healing my fellow soldiers. He'd probably see that as an unfair advantage in battle."

"Oh." She paused a moment, and I could almost see the gears turning in her head. "Have you ever healed me?"

"Yes."

She waited, her wide eyes questioning me.

I sighed. "The other day, when you hit your head."

She looked down at her hands and began twirling around her ring again. "Is that the only time?"

I looked to the ceiling in frustration.

Fuck.

I hadn't wanted to bring it up. She didn't need to think about that night with Shane ever again. But I'd promised myself I'd be honest with her.

"No," I answered reluctantly. "I healed you the night Shane attacked you." I cringed as I remembered the bruises around her neck. "There were a few other times, but they were minor."

I shifted on the bed to face her, and it was then that I saw it in her eyes.

Overload.

It was becoming too much for her. She'd had enough for the night.

I knelt in front of her and took both her hands in mine. "I think that's enough for now."

She nodded.

"We'll talk in the morning. You can sleep here. I'll be in the guest suite next door."

I kissed her gently on the forehead and left the room.

The moment the door shut, a cold determination took over. My face hardened as the plan formed in my mind. I pulled my phone from my pocket and called Zane as I headed out of the house.

"You still keeping an eye on Ky?" I asked the moment he picked up.

"Yeah, he's at Scooter's over on Westlake Drive." He hesitated. "What's going on?"

I jerked my car door open and jammed the key in the ignition. "That fucker is going down tonight."

"Alex, what the hell are you talking about?"

"Just go to the house and keep an eye on Gwen. She should be asleep in my bedroom. I'll explain as soon as I get back."

Despite the rain, the drive to Scooter's took half the normal time. My anger urged me forward, the speedometer gliding well past ninety.

I was consumed with rage. My brain locked down. All logic ceased.

I was going to kill him. Human or otherwise, I didn't care. He was going to die tonight for what he'd done.

The parking lot was almost empty. I pulled the car into the first available spot and jumped out. Long, angry strides took me quickly inside.

I found him instantly. He was sitting at the bar with his back to the door, but I knew it was him. My world went red.

Within seconds I'd reached him. Without warning or thought, I grabbed the back of his head and slammed his face into the bar with enough force to crack the wood.

His head wobbled back and blood poured from his busted nose, but his drunken eyes sharpened. "What the fuck-" Recognition lit his face. Without warning, he burst up from his seat and tackled me to the floor.

I didn't avoid his hits. Quite frankly, I needed the pain of his fists smashing into my face to deal with what had almost happened to Gwen tonight. I embraced it knowing I was about to unleash a whole fucking shit ton of pain on this bastard.

His fists rained down on me. I shifted, then rolled, taking him with me. I swung over and over again. Each punch pounded his head into the concrete floor. A sick satisfaction filled me with each loud crack. Blood covered my fists. Mine, his, I didn't fucking care.

It wasn't enough; it didn't release the rage crushing my chest. I planted my feet, grabbed him by the throat, and threw him against the adjacent wall. There was a loud crack and an eruption of shattered glass around us.

A fist out of nowhere connected with my ribcage. The breath was knocked from my lungs.

Fuck. He was stronger than I'd thought.

I grabbed his head and slammed it forcefully into the wall behind him. In the background, I heard distant voices yelling. I didn't care. I slammed another fist into his bloodied face.

Hands grabbed me from behind and violently jerked me back.

My red-tinged vision began to clear, and I was suddenly aware that I was being handcuffed.

I looked up from the concrete floor to the officer who was currently handcuffing Ky.

"You have the right to remain silent. Anything you say can and will be used against you in a court of law. You have the right to an attorney. If you cannot afford an attorney...."

Ky was lying face down on the concrete in a similar position as me. I was disappointed to note the bastard was still conscious.

What the fuck?

Any man who could take a beating like that wasn't human, which meant he was either an angel or a hybrid.

The rage that had begun simmering down came rushing back to the surface.

I knew it.

I'd known the whole fucking time he was bad news, and now it was confirmed.

∞∞∞∞∞∞

"You did what?" Zane yelled through the phone. I explained as much as I could with an officer monitoring my call and glanced at the clock.

Damn it.

My five minutes were almost up.

"You fucking idiot!" Zane exclaimed. "Ky couldn't have sabotaged that helicopter. You performed maintenance on the damn thing yesterday, and you would have noticed a fucking bomb in the engine compartment, right?"

"What's your point?" I glanced at the clock again.

"I've been following Ky for the past two days. He's been nowhere near it."

Fuck.

I let that sink in, then realized I didn't give a shit. That fucker needed an ass beating.

"Just get me out of here. They won't let me out until morning, so send someone to pick me up at seven. And keep an eye on Gwen.

We still don't know who's behind this."

I slammed the phone down and turned toward the uniformed officer.

"This way."

He led me down a long hall to a single empty jail cell.

I glanced around, surprised that there was only one cell.

Just fucking great. Unless there was another room hidden somewhere, we'd be stuck in here together.

The keys clanged as the jailer pulled them from his pocket and fiddled with the lock.

"In you go."

I stepped inside the small space and eyed the single toilet, rusty water fountain, and concrete bench.

"Put your hands through the bars."

I did as I was told, and the handcuffs were quickly removed from my wrists.

I took a seat on the cold bench, leaned back against the wall, and stared up at the ceiling.

Gwen could have died tonight, and that would have been my fault. If I had just checked the engine first, or if I had thought to install security at the top of the building, none of this would have happened. After the vandalism we'd had a few weeks before, we'd had top-of-the-line security installed all around the building and hired night guards to patrol the area. It had never occurred to me to secure the top of the building against another fucking angel that could fly up and bypass all our security measures.

I should have thought of it. I was the one who thought of everything. It was the reason I was in charge of my people. Because I didn't make mistakes.

Well, I'd made a huge fucking mistake this time. And it had almost cost Gwen her life.

Not to mention the mistake of attacking Ky.

I bent over and put my head in my hands. I could have murdered someone tonight. I could have become a real killer.

Wait a minute...

I straightened, confused. Despite the fact that Ky couldn't have sabotaged us, he still wasn't human. I knew that for a fact. So what the hell was he doing? He must have been up to something since he'd been spying on my family.

Footsteps echoed down the hall, slowly getting louder.

Ky was brought in. His face was cleaned up, and he'd obviously had some first aid administered.

"Are you two going to be a problem?" the officer asked with a distrustful tone.

"No," I answered honestly.

Ky still looked pissed, but gave a grudging, "No."

The officer removed Ky's handcuffs, then turned and left.

Ky's left eye was nearly swollen shut and already a startling shade of purple. His lip was swollen and busted open on one side. Yet despite his innocence, I didn't feel an ounce of guilt.

He took a quick appraisal of the room, then walked to the bench and sat right next to me.

Brave bastard.

He stared straight ahead as he spoke, "I'm not sitting on the cold ass floor just to avoid your fucking ass."

"Didn't expect you to."

We sat in silence for a few moments. What the hell was I supposed to say to him? *Sorry?* I didn't fucking think so.

"Coward."

I jerked my head his direction. "Come again? You might want to re-think that, asshole."

"You are a fucking coward. Who the hell sneaks up on someone and slams their head into a bar without so much as a fucking hello? You know, I've wanted to kick the fucking teeth out of your head from the moment I saw you." He paused, then lowered his voice as he said again, "Fucking coward."

I couldn't deal with his shit anymore. "Who the fuck are you? I know you've been spying on my family."

His eyes widened.

"And I know you're not human either."

I could see the internal war waging on his face before he finally answered. "So you really are him?" He shook his head in disbelief. "I was never sure. We'd done everything to check into your background, and everything always came back legit."

He looked at me. A new appreciation shown in his eyes. "You're good. We had our best hackers trying to dig up dirt on you, trying to invalidate your 'story.' And they came up with nothing. Couldn't find a shred of evidence that you weren't who you claimed to be."

My fists clenched at my sides, and I forced the question again through my teeth. "Who the fuck are you?"

The idiot ignored me. "You're the infamous Alexias Lukas Prisco." He shook his head. "I can't believe it."

My fingers twitched impatiently. I was about to lose my shit, but I kept my mouth shut, and waited for him to explain himself.

"I'm a hybrid. My mom was a human, my dad an angel. Maybe he knew about me, or maybe he just didn't give a shit. I don't know, and I don't fucking care. All I know is since Mom died, I've been stuck on this fucking planet completely alone."

He stared up at the ceiling.

I wasn't satisfied. None of that explained why he'd been looking into my family, or how he knew my real name. I was about to voice these thoughts when Ky continued.

"But then I found others like me. Hybrids who'd been abandoned by the angels who created them. We formed our own small communities and have been quite happy up until the last forty years. With technology being what it is, it's getting harder and harder to forge social security numbers and identification. My people are practically starving."

Finally, he turned toward me. "Over the years, we heard stories about a safe haven for hybrids. A place where we didn't have to hide our identity. A place where no one goes hungry."

"What's that got to do with me?" I was stunned. How the hell had our secret gotten out? As far as I was concerned, no one knew about our island.

Ky's look told me he wasn't fooled. "I was working multiple jobs trying like hell to provide for them when I ran into Hannah." He slapped his hand against his leg. "She was the spitting image of Eva. And I knew, I just knew that eventually, you'd show up. So, I took a huge gamble and used up every bit of our savings and enrolled in the local college. Just to find you."

I was speechless. What could I say to that?

Ky continued. "Let me be clear. I do not like you. But I'm putting my feelings aside for the greater good."

"Believe me, the feeling is mutual." I let my head drop back against the wall. "How many of you are there?"

"There are multiple communities throughout the world. Ours is called Thonis, and we have fifty-three members. We're based out of Orlando and have periodic meetings."

"Thonis?"

"You know, like the ancient underwater city."

I grinned, thinking of all the good times I'd had there. "Yeah, I know it."

"So, will you help us?"

"I'll need to meet them first."

Ky nodded, then leaned over on his elbows and placed his head in his hands.

I saw a small smudge I hadn't noticed before.

What the hell?

I bent over to get a better look. A pink birthmark in the shape of a set of wings mocked me along with a set of symbols:

αδελφή ψυχή

The distinctive mark of αδελφή ψυχή was behind his ear. A dark, sinking feeling settled in the pit of my stomach.

No.

Dread filled me. It seeped out of my pores. I was suddenly drowning in it.

No!

It was a mark meant as an omen of love and happiness, and it had just destroyed any chances for my own. The first ray of sunshine I'd seen in centuries was immediately snuffed out.

αδελφή ψυχή literally meant "soulmate" and appeared on the body of an angel or hybrid after they kissed the one God intended them to be with. The mark would fade unless the "unity" ceremony was performed. There were cases where angels chose to carry out the unity ceremony with someone who wasn't their soulmate. But because of the ceremonial promise to be together forever, the mark would then appear, branding them forever. The fact that Ky had the mark could only mean....

"Are you in love with Gwen?"

"Yeah, from the moment I first saw her." His response was quick and sure.

Fuck.

Gwen was intended for Ky.

Fuck.

I jerked to my feet and paced the room. The walls closed in on me as thoughts swirled through my mind. Was history repeating itself? Could this possibly be happening to me again? First with Eva. Now Gwen.

Why?

What about me?

What about my happiness?

I gripped the bars tightly and contemplated ripping them from the walls. I growled into the empty hallway.

Damn it. He'd promised me! I hadn't been perfect, but I'd done everything He'd ever asked, and this was how He repaid me.

I lifted my eyes to the ceiling, knowing He would hear, and vehemently whispered, "This is fucking wrong, and you know it."

"Dude, what the fuck are you talking about?" Ky's voice surprised me. In my frustration, I'd forgotten he was there.

"Wasn't talking to you."

His quizzical look went unanswered. He could think I was nuts. I didn't care.

I had to figure out what to do about Gwen. She wasn't meant for me, and I...

I would have to do the right thing. Like I always did.

"How about I meet them tomorrow morning?" I asked.

"What?"

"As soon as they let us out of here, get in touch with Thonis and call an emergency meeting. We're only a few hours from Orlando. We could meet tomorrow morning. I can't make a decision of this magnitude without meeting them first."

Ky shook his head. "It's too soon. I don't have the authority to call a meeting of that scale. But I can talk to our leadership about getting a meeting set up."

I nodded. It made sense that they would be cautious.

We sat a few moments, lost in our own thoughts before Ky's quiet voice broke the silence. "Thanks, man."

I nodded.

"No problem."

CHAPTER THIRTY-SEVEN

Gwen

I stretched languidly on the plush mattress and sighed. I could get used to such luxury. My muscles were as relaxed as they'd ever been. I felt like a cat purring and stretching in the sun.

Oh no, Spyder! I'd forgotten about him. The poor guy was probably starving.

My eyes blinked open, taking in the massive bedroom around me. It wasn't the first time I'd slept in Alex's bed, but it still felt foreign to me.

I glanced at the dresser, and sure enough, a set of clothes had been set aside for me today.

So very thoughtful. How many guys thought to do stuff like that?

I climbed out of bed, picked up the bundle, and inspected it. He'd even thought to get me underwear and a bra. Well, that was awkward. I wasn't about to wear Ariel's panties.

I looked at the delicate fabric and noticed the tag hanging from it. They were new. Upon closer inspection, the bra was new too.

Wow.

I went to the bathroom to change and again was shocked to find a new toothbrush had been left out for me.

I smiled. He had indeed thought of everything.

I dressed, brushed my teeth, and decided to find Alex. I had a ton of questions I hadn't gotten the chance to ask him the night before.

I went to the guest room he'd been sleeping in. It was empty. The bed was made, and everything was perfectly in place. It was as if he'd never been there.

Where is he?

With nothing else to do, I figured I'd give myself a tour.

I opened the bedroom door, peered down the hallway, then stepped out and closed the bedroom door behind me.

The last time I'd been here, I'd been too traumatized to notice anything. And last night we'd landed on his balcony, so I hadn't even had a chance to see the damn hallway.

Landed? The word seemed crazy in the light of day. Had we actually flown home? Had he really confessed to being an angel?

An angel, like the kind they talked about in church? Alex may have been a good guy, but he was certainly no saint. And absolutely nothing at all like the angels I'd always heard about.

Satan was an angel.

The thought crept into my mind, but I squashed it. Alex was not evil. But he wasn't exactly good either.

How did I even know he was telling me the truth? It was far more likely that I'd imagined the whole thing.

I shook my head. Those were thoughts I could leave until later. Right now, I just wanted to relax.

I strolled down the wide hallway and admired the ample artwork that decorated the walls. I wasn't an art aficionado, but to my untrained eye, they were quite beautiful. I leaned over one that caught my eye. It was an intricate piece, a painting of an ornate snow globe that held within it a magnificent island surrounded by the deep blue sea. A brilliant city glittered in the background. The spray of waterfalls misted the area, giving it an ethereal quality.

I reached out and traced the delicate strokes, enjoying the contrast of colors and admiring the shimmering paint. It was stunning.

As I admired the painting, I felt the strangest sensation that I'd seen it before.

"Like the painting?"

I small shriek escaped my startled lips. I spun around and found Zane gazing at me, obviously amused with my response.

I clasped my hand over my pounding heart. "You about gave me a heart attack."

He smirked but didn't respond.

I turned back to the painting. "It's beautiful. Who's the artist?"

"Luna Prescott."

Prescott? "Is she family?"

"I'd say so." He laughed. "She's Alex's twin sister."

Twin sister? Alex had a sister?

"Where's Alex?"

Zane shrugged. "Taking care of a few things. You want a tour?"

What the hell?

"Sure, why not?"

∞∞∞∞∞∞

At first, I believed Zane's lie that Alex was just taking care of business. But after hours had passed and he still hadn't returned my calls, I realized the truth.

He had changed his mind about us.

Again.

He was pushing me away.

Again.

I plopped down on my couch, grabbed the remote, and began flipping through the channels.

I could have been wrong. It wouldn't be the first time I'd come to the wrong conclusion. But why else would he avoid me?

Maybe he was busy. It was possible. He could be on a business trip with Eli.

But if he were, I'd have known about it. I had access to his schedule, and there wasn't a meeting scheduled for today.

A more obvious reason for his distance was that he regretted telling me the truth. The truth that I still had a hard time wrapping my head around – that Alex was an angel. How was that possible?

And the whole thing about his family being hybrids, how did that work? How could his father and brother be hybrids if he was supposedly a full angel? And apparently, he also had a twin sister that he'd never mentioned.

And what were angels doing around humans anyway?

My eyes widened.

When I'd asked Alex how old he was, he'd said he was older than the Earth itself. But he only looked twenty-three. It made sense that he wouldn't age, but that meant that his background was fake. His whole family would have had to have moved around often enough to prevent people from noticing. Which made the question all the more important.

What are they doing here?

Ding....Dong...

I jumped up and raced to the front door.

My foot caught the edge of a rug in the foyer, and I stumbled as I flung the door open.

Breathlessly, I glanced up into Ky's brown eyes. A wave of disappointment washed over me.

"Oh, Ky. Hey."

He furrowed his eyebrows and nodded. "Yeah, it's me. Don't be too disappointed."

"No, no. I'm just-" I placed my hand on my chest and tried to catch my breath. "I just thought it was someone else."

He shook his head. "Yeah, I got that."

We stood in awkward silence.

I didn't know what to say to Ky. I'd thought we were fine after I'd told him I was dating Alex, but he'd been avoiding me since our last practice.

I understood why. Knowing I was dating Alex was one thing, but seeing us kiss had to have been quite another.

Ky's eyes scanned down the length of my body before returning to my eyes. He shrugged unapologetically, then motioned toward the door. "May I come in?"

"Yeah."

I stepped aside and followed Ky to the couch. I clicked on the lamp, then sat opposite of him, intentionally creating space between us as I pulled my legs under me.

His dark brown eyes searched mine, looking for something we both knew he wouldn't find.

Light illuminated his tortured face, and that was when I noticed the bruising.

"Ky, what happened?"

"It's nothing."

I knew from the determined look in his eye that no coaxing from me would get him to talk about it.

"Gwen." He licked his lips and dropped his eyes. "Are you sure about Alex? Is he really who you want to be with?"

I nodded. I cared about Ky, but even if Alex hadn't been around, I wouldn't have taken him back. I couldn't trust him anymore.

"I can't be with you, Ky. It has nothing to do with Alex, and everything to do with how you've lied to me."

Ky's hands clenched. Anger flashed through his hardened eyes.

"I'm sorry-" I started, but Ky put his hand up to stop me.

He pulled his phone from his pocket and typed out a quick text before dropping it on the coffee table between of us. "Gwen." He stood and brushed his hands down his legs. "Fuck!"

I jumped in my seat as his voice echoed through the room.

Buzz.....Buzz.....

I reflexively looked to his phone at the incoming text.

ZEBADIAH: it wsnt esy bt I gt it

Who the hell is Zebadiah? I knew all of Ky's friends, and I'd never heard of him.

"Who's that?"

Ky snatched his phone up and shoved it in his pocket. "Nobody."

Anger at being lied to again pushed me to respond. "Get out," I snapped. "Get the fuck out of my house, and don't come back."

His eyes met mine. There was a flicker of something in his eyes, and then it was gone, replaced by cold resolve.

"Fine."

CHAPTER THIRTY-EIGHT

Alex

Ky had given me the phone number to contact Thonis. Their leader was a woman named Adah, and she was expecting my call.

I was shocked that there were so many hybrids living on the mainland. I'd thought the only hybrids were the ones created by my fellow angels and myself.

How had this happened? Where were the angels who'd created them? And why hadn't the wayward angels been exiled like we had been? It didn't make sense.

Either way, Thonis needed my help, and I needed to call them.

I stared at the phone in my hand. I knew I had to take care of this as soon as possible, that it was important, but regardless of the immediacy of the situation, I couldn't push the damn call button.

All I cared about was Gwen and the fact that she was lost to me forever.

If I only had the power to slow down the clock. I'd slow time to a crawl. Slower and slower until it halted completely. Then I'd be able to think, and I'd figure out how to survive letting her go.

And what about her? How could I do this to her after all the times I'd pushed her away and toyed with her emotions? I had been such an asshole to her, and damn it, I'd promised her it wouldn't happen again.

This wasn't fair.

God had sworn that He had someone special picked out for me. My soulmate. He'd told me it wouldn't be easy, but I would find her eventually. And I had waited so long.

When Gwen had told me about Wesley and then about her dreams of the island, I'd known she was the one. Between the scar on her wrist and her inability to see the guy in the dream, I knew. For the last few years, I'd had the same dreams. An absolute beauty met me every night on the island. I couldn't see her face, but I knew in my heart that she was the one. I'd fallen in love with the girl of my dreams.

All those years I'd thought they were just dreams. When I'd realized my dream girl was Gwen, I'd understood that I'd developed a latent ability. It was exceedingly rare, but occasionally an angel could develop an ability centuries after maturity.

But why her? Why had I tapped into her mind, across hundreds of miles, if she wasn't my soulmate?

Anger coursed through my veins and I wanted to hit something.

I tried to relax the tension in my shoulders. Hitting someone wouldn't make me feel better. But a bottle of scotch just might.

I turned the car on autopilot and called Zane.

"Yeah?" Zane's bored voice boomed out the speakers.

"Zane, are you still watching Gwen?"

He huffed. "Dude, what's your problem? I swear she's called your number at least a hundred times today. Why haven't you answered?"

"Why do you care?"

"Because when you didn't answer, she started questioning me. I don't like lying for you. And she was driving me nuts, asking questions I wasn't sure I could answer. When I didn't say anything, it pissed her off. So she went home. And now, because you were being such a fucktard and not answering your phone, I'm stuck hanging out in her backyard while she sleeps."

"Are you done yet?"

"Do you plan on giving me answers?"

I swallowed back the despair and forced the words from my lips. "I can't see Gwen anymore."

There was a moment of silence as Zane absorbed my words. "Why the fuck not?"

"I just can't be with her." I shook my head at the words I never thought I'd say. I'd only just realized I was in love with her, and already I had to give her up.

My hands tightened into fists. "She's got to get back together with Ky."

Zane's voice was incredulous. "What the hell are you talking about? Ky? The guy we've been investigating? The man who's been spying on us? What the fuck?"

My anger boiled over. "He's her fucking soulmate!" I yelled into the phone.

I breathed deeply and waited for his acceptance.

"Fuck that," he responded without an ounce of sarcasm.

What? "What did you just say?"

Zane huffed into the phone. "I said, fuck that. I don't give a shit who's soulmate she is. You love her, right?"

"Yeah, I love her."

"So, fuck that whole soulmate bullshit, and get the girl you love."

"And what, go against God? Are you insane? Zane, just stop. You know I can't entertain those thoughts. This discussion is over."

∞∞∞∞∞∞

I went to the garden and plopped onto a seat.

The bottle of scotch I'd purchased on the ride home accompanied me, and I lifted it to my lips –

A warm tingling sensation crept up my back. My skin shimmered with light.

I felt His presence before I heard His deep familiar voice in my mind.

"My son."

The gravity of the moment rocked me. I hadn't heard from Him in over a century, and still, His voice had the power to ravish my insides. Elation and anger swept over me in equal parts. They devoured me. Had I not been sitting, I would have fallen to my knees.

I gathered my strength. I held tightly to the rage I felt until I was strong enough to respond.

"Don't," I forced the word through clenched teeth. "You claim you love me, yet you torture me. I can't...I can't deal with this right now. Please leave me be."

There was a moment of silence before I felt His sadness wash over me and His presence slowly drift away.

I wiped a tear from my eye, then laughed. What the hell did He have to be sad about? I was the one miserable and alone.

I lifted the bottle to my lips again and let the liquid burn its way down my throat.

How the hell could I ever think there would be something good for me in this world?

I took another gulp and opened the text that Ky had sent me earlier that day. It had the contact info for the leader of Thonis. I dialed the number and waited.

On the third ring, a loud feminine voice answered harshly, "Yeah."

"This is Alexander Prescott. I'm trying to find someone by the name of Adah."

Her voice lashed out from the phone, "And who exactly are you, Mr. Prescott?"

I glanced at the phone. Had I dialed the wrong number?

"Sorry, wrong number." My finger was on the "End" button when I heard her speak again.

"I need authentication of who you are, Mr. Prescott."

It suddenly made sense. This Adah was a smart woman. It was wise to be cautious.

"Ky gave me your number. Is this Adah?"

"You must prove yourself first, Mr. Prescott. Tell me the name of your heavenly lover."

"She wasn't my —"

"*Tell me her name.*"

I sighed. "Eva."

"And tell me, who is your second in command?"

Interesting. She had no way of knowing the truth. Regardless, something about her no-nonsense tone had me dropping my guard.

"On this particular mission, that would be Eli Prescott."

"Mmm hmm." She made a sound of approval. "I am Adah. Supreme Chief of Thonis. Ky told me to expect your call."

"Ky explained your predicament," I told her. "And I do in fact have a safe place, but I'll need to meet with Thonis before I can make a decision. I mean no disrespect, but I have to ensure the safety of my own people first."

"I understand." I heard the shuffling of papers in the background. "How about Tuesday, three weeks from now? That'll give my people time to prepare."

"Perfect. We can set the time and place later. It was nice talking to you, Adah."

"Alexander, wait." I was surprised she used my first name. "There's more. We know the whole story behind you and Eva, and why you're here. We also know about Hannah."

What else did these people know?

"We had Hannah tested, without her knowledge of course, and she is without doubt a human. You understand, with the astonishing resemblance between them, we had to be sure."

I hadn't thought of that. All this time I'd just assumed Hannah was human. I had the equipment in my basement to do the testing myself, but it had never occurred to me.

"Alexander, are you still there?"

"Yeah, sorry. And call me Alex."

"I'll call you Alexander."

I laughed. "Okay, Alexander it is."

"Alexander, there's something else. We've been monitoring the area, and the last few months we've seen a disturbing increase in the number of fallen angels. I don't know what's going on, but I've got a bad feeling about it."

There was silence on the line, and I almost thought she'd hung up on me when I heard her sigh.

"Alexander, I know how that must sound to you. But I can tell you this. I follow my intuition for a reason. It's saved my life many times. And I'm telling you, I have a terrible feeling. Please be careful."

CHAPTER THIRTY-NINE

Gwen

It'd been three days, and I hadn't heard a thing from Alex.

A feeling I'd hoped to never feel again gripped me. Rejection's fingers slipped tightly around my throat, choking me, dragging me under the water.

My chest ached as I gasped for breath. The familiar feeling of an oncoming panic attack had my heart hammering.

No, not again. I couldn't deal with this.

I summoned my strength.

I wouldn't let this beat me. Not this time.

I sat on my couch and closed my eyes. A few deep breaths later, the tightness in my chest had subsided. The anxiety had fled.

Only raging anger remained.

I grabbed my phone and called Alex, knowing full well he wouldn't answer.

Leave a message after the beep....

"You liar! You promised you were done jerking me around. We've gone on one fucking date, and you've already done it again. If your plan was to break up with me, it's done. We are done. I'm tired of this shit. And by the way, you are a fucking coward for not having the balls to tell me in person."

I wouldn't waste another moment upset about that asshat. If he didn't have the time to speak to me, I wouldn't waste mine pining over him. I refused to be one of those girls.

If only Beverly were here. I'd have given anything to hear her voice, to get her outrageous yet somehow perfect advice, and to have her sarcastic comments making me laugh. I needed a friend right now.

I pulled out my phone and scrolled through my contacts, then paused.

My thumb hovered over Jasper's number.

He'd said I could call him, and he'd certainly seemed sincere.

No. Jasper was the ultimate player. He wasn't looking for a friend.

I pushed my phone into my pocket and grabbed my keys.

In no time, I had my car's engine revving, and I was flying down the highway.

I needed to get Alex out of my head. I turned up the radio and sang along with everything I had. I imagined myself on stage, performing for a live audience. I put everything into the vision, and soon I'd forgotten my problems.

I sang and danced as I sped down the highway. I was belting out "Bitch" by Meredith Brooks when I pulled into the parking lot of Horizons Mall.

I parked the car and smiled at the complete transformation of my mood. The burden on my shoulders had lifted, and I had a little extra pep in my stride.

This little trip was exactly what I needed.

I put my keys in my purse and sauntered to the food court. I was starving.

I scanned the court in approval. It was refreshing to have so many choices. Quite a nice change from Verona Beach. There were at least ten restaurants to choose from, and I narrowed it down to either Chinese or pizza.

"Definitely pizza."

I jumped at the male voice that whispered in my ear and spun around.

Jasper Mills stood inches away looking devastatingly handsome in tight jeans, black boots, and a grey henley. His blonde hair contrasted with his shocking aquamarine eyes. My eyes drifted down, appreciating the way his snug clothing accentuated his muscular frame.

Oh, my.

Jasper cleared his throat and my eyes flashed up to his.

His eyes sparkled with amusement.

Yeah, I'd just been caught checking him out. Again.

Instead of teasing me, Jasper stunned me when he took my arm. "Come on. Let's get some food."

Ten minutes later, we were still standing in line at the Pizza Shoppe.

"I'm sorry."

Jasper raised an eyebrow. "What the hell for? It's not your fault these people are slow as fuck."

"Shh!" I glanced at the workers. The last thing I wanted was for them to spit in our food.

My eyes shifted to Jasper, but he was no longer paying attention. He was watching three teenage girls across the food court. We couldn't hear their words, but it was obvious what was happening.

Two girls confronted another smaller girl. Their hands were on their hips, and nasty sneers were plastered across their perfect faces. They were beautiful. Probably eighteen or nineteen years old, looking like they'd just stepped out of an Aeropostale catalog. With their golden hair and perfect makeup, they could easily have been models.

The third girl was the exact opposite. Her ill-fitted clothing was worn and tattered. Her auburn hair was tied back in a messy bun, and her oversized glasses slid down her nose as she stared at the floor. She stood stiffly with her bag gripped tightly in front of her while the bitch twins took turns berating her.

Without a word, Jasper left my side and strode confidently across the court. As he approached, the girls stopped talking and stared at him with wide eyes.

Jasper took the brown-haired girl's bag, leaned over, and kissed her cheek.

Her face reddened, and a shy smile spread across her face.

Jasper slipped his arm around her waist. Hell, the poor girl needed it, she looked like she might pass out. The two blondes' eyes bugged out, and their jaws dropped as they watched Jasper leave with the other girl.

I smiled smugly. I doubted they'd be harassing her again.

The guy across the counter cleared his throat. Apparently, it was my turn to order.

Should I order something for Jasper?

I figured if he didn't return, I'd take the extra pizza home for a snack.

I ordered two slices and a soda, then went to the outside pavilion to eat.

Jasper found me five minutes later. He adjusted his chair to face me and stretched his long legs along either side of me. He leaned back in that lazy, relaxed way of his and began eating.

The sun was setting behind me, throwing its orange rays directly onto Jasper. For the first time, I really studied him.

He was beautiful. He had the square jaw, high cheekbones, and flawless skin any model would kill for. The deep blue-green of his eyes glowed in the orange sunlight.

And that body. *Mmm.* That body was downright sinful. He obviously spent hours in the gym but didn't have the grotesque musculature of a bodybuilder. He had the long, lean muscles of a competitive swimmer. He was by far one of the hottest men I'd ever seen.

Maybe even hotter than Alex.

Nope. I wasn't going to think about Alex. As far as I was concerned, he no longer existed.

Determined to distract myself, I focused again on Jasper. It was no surprise that women flocked to him. With that face and body, not to mention the whole bad boy vibe he had going on, he was irresistible.

But definitely not for me, I reminded myself before I let my mind go *there*. The last thing I needed was another player.

Then again, this player had just protected that young girl.

"That was really sweet of you."

"Sweet?"

"Yeah, you rescued that girl."

"I wasn't rescuing her." He huffed as if I'd offended him.

I waited, expecting some sort of explanation.

"What?"

I stared at him.

Jasper put his pizza down and looked me in the eye. "I wasn't defending her. I was stopping them. There's a difference."

"Okay, then. What's the difference?"

"The difference is I don't go around trying to be a fucking hero." He took a huge bite out of his pizza. "I just can't stand bullies."

I almost laughed. Jasper thought he was such a badass, but I was beginning to realize it was a load of crap. No matter how much he protested, he had saved that girl from those bitches. In my book, that made him a hero.

CHAPTER FORTY

Alex

What the hell am I supposed to do now? I clenched my fists as I watched our stock price fall lower and lower. We were losing thousands by the second, and there was nothing I could do to stop it.

The explosion at our Miami plant was nationwide news. What had at first been thought to be an internal failure was now being considered sabotage. It was early, but an investigation was already underway to find the culprit.

Thank God we'd had a rare malfunction that had shut the plant down for the day. Otherwise, we'd have had a few hundred dead employees as well.

Damn.

We had other facilities, but this particular plant was the one that could provide us with consistent funding for the foreseeable future. It meant fewer trips to the mainland and possibly extended the length between trips.

But now? Fuck, I wasn't sure how to fix this.

Bzzz....Bzzz....Bzzz....

My phone buzzed in my pocket.

It was Gwen.

Again.

I felt like absolute shit every time I ignored her calls, but I couldn't help it. I couldn't be with her, but I also couldn't let her go. The end result was that I was completely avoiding seeing her. If I didn't see her, I wouldn't have to act — and I wouldn't have to tear my own damn heart out.

I shook my head in disgust.

Ky had been right. I really was a coward.

My desk cracked under my fingers. I couldn't take this. It wasn't fair.

My anger was fueled by the images that flashed through my mind. Images of Eva and Gwen. Both flaunted before me, and both unexpectedly ripped away.

An inferno released within me. My vision tinged red. Rage consumed me, fueling the intense energy inside that was bursting to get out. I needed a release. Without thinking, I gripped the edges of my desk and threw it against the wall. The desk exploded in pieces, chunks of drywall and wood scattering around the room, but it wasn't enough. Nothing would ever be enough.

Fuck this shit. I was done.

The good, law-abiding Alex was gone.

"Fuck you!" I yelled toward Heaven.

Zane was right. I didn't give a shit about anything else. I was getting Gwen back.

Anger simmered in the background of my mind as I formulated a plan.

I thought back to our one and only date. Remembered the way her soft body had felt against mine as we'd danced under the stars. Remembered the way her eyes had sparkled and that shy smile had turned up the corners of her lips as she'd gazed at me.

My heart lurched forward in my chest.

I wouldn't give up on her. It didn't matter what it cost me. I would find a way.

But how would I convince her to trust me after the way I'd ignored her again? I couldn't just apologize. I had to do something big.

It took some effort, but after an hour, a decent plan started to form. Hope blossomed in my chest for the first time in days.

Bzzz.....Bzzz.....Bzzz

Was it Gwen?

My shoulders slumped when I saw Zane's name across the screen. A moment later, a text came in.

ZANE: Answer your fucking phone asshole this is important

What is it now?

I called him. "What?"

Zane's panicked voice got my attention. "Gwen is gone."

"Explain."

"I followed her to the mall in Valda, Florida. That's about twenty minutes from Verona Beach. Anyway, I followed her to the mall, and she went to the food court to eat. She ran into Jasper, and they decided to eat outside. I couldn't follow because they were the only ones out there, and they'd notice me. So, I stood inside the glass doors and watched them. Then I got distracted for a moment –"

"Distracted?" My voice lowered to deadly levels. I was seconds away from losing it.

Guilt colored Zane's voice. "Yeah, there was a woman..."

"You lost Gwen over some random –"

"It doesn't fucking matter right now, Alex. What matters is that when I looked back up, Gwen and Jasper were gone. Their chairs were turned over like they'd been yanked out of their seats. I checked the parking garage to be sure, but Gwen's car was still there. I think ...*Fuck*, I hate to say this, but I think they've been abducted."

CHAPTER FORTY-ONE
Gwen

Everything was blurry as the world swirled around me.

Where am I? Who am I? Questions I couldn't answer or make sense of drifted like fog through my mind.

Flashes of memory faded in and out.

A wonderfully gorgeous man with golden hair and eyes like the Caribbean Sea smiled at me.

Was he my boyfriend?

Was he my lover?

When I looked at his warm smile, I felt....

I wasn't sure how I felt.

His face lit my vision for a few beautiful moments before fading away into darkness.

A strong sickly-sweet smell invaded my senses and overpowered the darkness. I retched as memories of pain shot up my spine. My back slammed into something cold and hard. Darkness. The fog jumbled it all together.

Voices drifted in and out. An unfamiliar voice echoed through my mind, "...tie her wrists. We don't want them getting away..." Everything morphed together.

Nothing made sense.

My eyes blinked open, and foggy light shone as if through the end of a tunnel. My head lolled to the left. The world spun wildly. My insides twisted, and the taste of bile coated my throat.

I wanted to move, but my limbs were too heavy, and a crushing weight pinned my chest to the floor.

I sucked in labored breaths as blurry images hovered above me.

This was too much.

I closed my eyes in surrender. The darkness pulled me down as the world spun and spun around me.

∞∞∞∞∞∞

Ow.

My head was killing me. I felt my heartbeat pounding in my head with every pulse.

I blinked up at the dingy room around me.

Where am I?

My face was pressed into a cold, damp floor as I struggled to keep my eyes open. Plain concrete walls surrounded me. Was I in a basement? The lack of windows and the single dimly lit bulb overhead led me to believe so.

How had I gotten here?

I struggled to remember, but all I got were blurry images. A woozy feeling nearly overwhelmed me at the memory of something overly sweet entering my nostrils. There were flashes of Jasper's smiling face. Flashes of the mall.

Come on, there must be more.

The memory of a van pulling up next to us, three men in black jumping out.

Oh, my God.

I attempted to sit up and fell painfully on my side.

I glanced down. My wrists and ankles were bound in front of me by tight cables.

My heart raced. I began hyperventilating as I realized what had happened.

I had been kidnapped.

Everything began to fade when a pained groan startled me.

I'm not alone?

I was on the verge of passing out, but I calmed my breathing. Color seeped back into the world around me. My heart calmed, and I finally had the energy to move around. I slowly rolled over to see who was behind me.

I gasped.

There was a large shirtless man on the floor. His torn back faced me. Blood trickled and smeared across the bruised skin. His arms were secured behind his back. Cables dug harshly into his wrists where blood congealed in an ugly black mess.

I wiggled closer and gently tried to wake him.

"Hey, are you okay?" I struggled against my restraints. "Hey." I brushed my fingertips against his arm. "Are you awake?"

A deep groan emitted from him, and then he rolled to face me.

No!

Jasper's face was streaked with blood, his lips bruised, and his left eye was swollen shut, but I recognized him instantly.

"Jasper! Oh, my God. Say something, please."

His good eye blinked rapidly, then focused on my face. "Gwen? Is that you?"

I reached to touch him but hesitated. Almost every inch of his skin was covered in bruises, with patches of swollen flesh that flushed red.

What had they done to him?

A sob worked its way up my throat, strangling me.

"Gwen?" Panic entered his cracked voice. "Did they hurt you?"

"No." I hiccupped. "I just woke up a few minutes ago." I struggled to calm myself, but the tears kept coming. "I-I don't remember anything. How did we get here?"

"I only remember bits and pieces." He groaned as he shifted onto his back and slowly pushed himself up against the wall into a seated position. He motioned for me to do the same.

The moment I leaned back against the wall, my muscles cried out in relief. "Tell me what you remember."

Jasper nodded, then grimaced. "Five guys jumped out of a van and grabbed us."

"I only remember three."

He shook his head and answered slowly, as if each word stung his cracked lips. "They chloroformed you pretty quickly. That's why your memory is messed up. I managed to take down two of them before they got to me, that's why I got the beating I did."

I reached up my bound wrists and wiped a tear from my cheek. "How long have we been here?"

"I'm not sure, at least a few hours."

"Do you know why they took us?"

Jasper closed his eyes. "I really hope I'm wrong, but I think they may be trying to blackmail my father. I'm sorry, Gwen, you shouldn't even be here."

"Why would they blackmail him?"

"For money? He's a wealthy man. I don't know anything for sure, but it's the only thing that makes sense."

I cringed as I stared into Jasper's guilt-ridden eyes. "It's not your fault, Jasper."

He shook his head and closed his swollen eyes.

"Yeah," he responded sadly. "It probably is."

∞∞∞∞∞∞

The door slammed open. Three men in black hoods stormed in. The military efficiency in their movements was apparent as they came to a sudden stop in front of us.

They had strong muscular builds. The man to the left was massive, at least six-and-a-half-feet tall. The smallest man, by far the runt of this team, was at least five-feet-ten-inches with a wrestlers build. The one in the middle was as still as a stone statue; he didn't even seem to breathe.

"Just the male."

"What about the female?" Runt questioned.

Behemoth, the one who towered over the others, shook his head. "Only as a last resort."

Runt and Stony grabbed Jasper and dragged him from the room.

Jasper jerked out of their hands and landed hard on the concrete floor, face down.

Stony laughed. "Not too bright, is he?"

Runt smiled as he and Stony lifted Jasper and headed again for the door.

"No! Please! Please, stop! Don't hurt him!"

My cries were ignored.

The cold floor sucked all the warmth from my body. Tears streamed down my face. My lips trembled. Time crawled by as I waited for Jasper's return.

The door creaked open, and I looked eagerly toward it. Behemoth strode out and across the room until he towered over me. My fingers trembled as I held back a sob.

He squatted and leaned menacingly in my face. "If you don't fight back, I can make this a little more comfortable for you. We got a deal?"

I looked warily at the masked man, not sure if I believed him and not sure if I wanted to cooperate.

What I wanted was to kick his teeth down his throat, but more than that, I needed to survive.

I nodded, and he pulled a knife from his pocket and flipped it open.

I jerked back, waiting for the moment when he changed his mind and stabbed me instead. He leaned forward and swiftly cut the cables around my ankles.

"You'll behave?" His eyes caught mine in warning.

"Y-Yes."

He brought the blade to my wrist. "If you try to escape, there will be consequences."

I nodded.

With a flick of his wrist, the cables were cut.

I rolled my wrists and stretched my fingers.

Behemoth reached into a bag I hadn't noticed and pulled out an old blanket and small flat pillow.

"Here. Now, I'm going to leave you here, unbound. But if you cause any problems, you'll regret it. Understood?"

Again, I nodded my head in agreement.

He motioned to the far corner of the room, where a large cardboard box lay on its side.

"On the other side of that box is a toilet. If you do anything stupid, I will remove that box, and you will lose your privacy."

"What about Jasper? What's going to happen to him?"

He ignored my question and crossed the room. As he left, I did my best to see what was on the other side of the door.

A tall staircase raised upward to a single door. My heart sank in despair. I had hoped to get a better layout of our captivity, but from what I could see, there was only one way out, and it led directly into the hands of our captors.

My hands went cold as ice.

No one would even notice we were missing, not for a few days anyway. We'd been abducted from the mall on Friday. There were no classes to attend over the weekend. No practice. No work. Beverly wasn't around to question my absence. Ky was avoiding me almost as much as Alex had been. And Jasper was such a loner, I doubted anyone would be looking for him.

I let my head fall back on the hard wall behind me. We were completely and unquestionably screwed.

I heard a loud thud above me.

Muffled voices drifted through the floor.

"Hold him still…"

Bam.

There was a short skirmish upstairs followed by cursing.

I held my hands over my ears and waited. Hours seemed to pass as I prayed for Jasper's return, hoping like hell they hadn't killed him. I was certain by the loud banging and groans above that he was being tortured.

Every blow gutted me. Each tortured sound had my body racked with sobs.

I didn't know how long it took, but eventually, my body succumbed to exhaustion, and I fell into a fitful sleep.

∞∞∞∞∞∞

"Luke?"

I lifted my head from the warm sand and pulled myself onto my elbows.

I looked around the deserted beach, but Luke was nowhere to be found.

I smiled.

He would show up eventually. He always did.

I wiggled my toes happily in the sand as the waves lapped over my feet. To my right, a seagull was tapping its delicate legs in the water and fluttering its wings. It was beautiful. Maybe I could stay here in my dream forever. Wouldn't that be wonderful?

The sky began to darken in an eerie way as if something had passed in front of the sun. I gazed up to the cloudless expanse above as a dark shadow moved slowly across the sky.

What the hell?

A soft tap on my shoulder drew my attention from the anomaly.

Luke.

He threaded his fingers through mine, then pulled me against him in a desperate embrace. His arms circled around me and squeezed the air from my lungs.

I patted his back comfortingly as he held me tight. He held me like his life depended on it. Like he hadn't seen me in years. I could barely breathe.

A strangled gasp slipped past my lips, and his arms abruptly released me.

He stepped back, slipped a hand into his board shorts, and pulled out a small phone.

He typed a message into the phone and handed it to me.

LUKE: are you ok?

I nodded my head. Of course I was okay. What a silly question.

LUKE: i will rescue you. tell me everything you know about your captors. do you know where they're holding you?

This was ridiculous. I didn't want to waste my escape from reality discussing this. I slipped my arms around Luke's waist and leaned in to kiss his cheek.

Strong hands gripped my shoulders, and for the first time ever, Luke pushed me firmly away from him.

LUKE: this is important. where are they keeping you? we don't have much time

He thrust the phone in my hands.
Fine.
I'd play along, but I wouldn't like it.

ME: i don't know. they always wear masks. i've only seen three of them, but i hear more upstairs. i have no idea where we are.

I felt faint vibrations, and everything around me faded as I began to wake up. Luke pulled me to him. His lips descended on mine...
"Gwen."
My eyes fluttered open.
Jasper was lying beside me, his wrists shackled together by zip

ties.

"Jasper, are you okay?"

"Depends on your definition of okay," he rasped.

I leaned over him and wrung my hands in frustration. Anywhere I touched him would hurt. All I would do was cause him more pain, but I had to do something.

"What can I do, Jasper? What do you need me to do?"

His lips trembled, his body shook, but before he could answer, I knew.

I grabbed the blanket and wrapped it around his shaking shoulders. I guided his head onto the pillow, then slid down behind him and wrapped my arms around his waist.

There was a slight hiss when my skin made contact with his, but after a few moments, his breathing evened, and he drifted off to sleep.

CHAPTER FORTY-TWO
Alex

I was going to go out of my fucking mind. It'd been days since Gwen had vanished, and we'd found nothing.

And after my first attempt, I hadn't been able to make contact with her again. Why couldn't I control the dreams? The one time I'd been able to talk to her, I'd gotten nothing. I didn't even know if she was still alive.

I did everything I knew to do. I hired private investigators, hacked security videos, and bribed mall employees. I'd even involved Ky, who had been more help than I cared to admit. But still, we'd found nothing.

Where could she be? The thought repeated over and over in my head like a broken record. I had to find her. And one way or another, whoever was behind this would pay with their lives.

My phone rang. It was the office, and I almost ignored it.

"Hello."

"Mr. Prescott, I just wanted to let you know you have a package to pick up."

"Okay," I replied, annoyed I'd even bothered to answer. "But from now on, just have Joe deliver everything to the house."

"Joe didn't deliver this one. This wasn't from a normal carrier."

Alarm bells went off in my mind, and intuition prickled up the length of my spine.

"Who delivered it?"

"Some kid, he said to make sure you got it. It's been sitting on my desk since yesterday."

Damn it. "What did he look like, Bonnie?"

"Well...he was young. About your age actually, but not nearly as handsome as you."

"Bonnie," I growled. "What did he look like?"

"Oh sorry, Mr. Prescott. Okay, he was about five foot nine and really skinny. He had light brown hair and brown eyes." She paused. "Oh, and he was wearing a red hoodie."

This was getting me nowhere. I remembered the security cameras I'd installed weeks before.

"Thanks, Bonnie. I'll be there in a few minutes."

I had the momentary impulse to rip off my shirt and fly to the office, completely bypassing all the speed bumps and traffic that would slow me down. I was on the verge of doing just that when I glanced toward the window. The brilliant sunlight pouring in mocked me. Sometimes I hated the sun.

I grabbed my keys and ran to my car. The engine revved, and within seconds, I was speeding down the highway toward the office.

In half the standard time, I was parking my car in the company parking lot and jogging up the front steps.

I flung the glass doors open wide, ignored the pleasant greeting of the receptionist, and bypassed the elevator. I ran up the stairs three at a time until I reached my floor. I shoved open the door and stopped abruptly at Bonnie's desk. Her startled eyes went wide, and her mouth opened, but I didn't have time for her questions.

"Bonnie, where is that package?"

Her face flushed as she eyed the jogging pants and t-shirt I was wearing.

"Bonnie!" My voice lashed out at her. "Focus. Where is that package?"

"O-Over here." She reached behind her and grabbed a manila envelope off her desk.

I grabbed the package from her hand, went to my office, and locked the door. With a flick of my wrist, the blinds were closed, and I was alone.

I looked down at the thin package in my possession. My hands shook as I held the first piece of evidence. I didn't know how to feel. This could be my only opportunity to find Gwen. But if this package was what I thought it was, it would only mean bad things for her.

Gwen needed me, I remind myself. Refusing to dwell any longer, I ripped the envelope open and pulled out the single typed page.

I TOOK YOUR MONEY

NOW I'M GOING TO TAKE

YOUR GIRL

Images of the Miami plant engulfed in blue flames flashed through my mind. Temperatures of more than five thousand degrees had incinerated almost everything. The facilities had been ravaged, the destruction so devastating nothing had been able to be salvaged.

And now they had Gwen.

Ice crystallized in my veins, and a chill ran up my spine. I stared down at the words before me, and for the first time in my life, I felt genuine fear.

CHAPTER FORTY-THREE
Gwen

I huddled in the corner while I listened to the pummeling taking place above my head.

They had dragged Jasper upstairs again almost an hour before and had been beating on him ever since.

How much more of this could he take?

I worried my ring around my finger, wincing at every thud, and praying they'd release him soon.

Every day since we'd been taken here they'd brought him upstairs and tortured him. We'd never been given any demands or asked any questions. Jasper thought his father was being blackmailed, but there was no evidence of it. They'd never asked about his father nor taken any videos of us to send for ransom.

They just seemed to take pleasure in hurting him.

It was the same three captors every day. They continued to wear the black masks, but I knew it was them because of their distinct builds and personalities. Behemoth was the kindest of the three and the obvious leader of the group. Stony rarely spoke but had a keen eye and watched me like a hawk. Runt was the most vicious and temperamental of the group. His icy blue eyes never failed to send shivers down my spine.

The days blurred together, and hopelessness set in.

We didn't know why they were keeping us, and they gave no indication that it would ever stop.

A loud thud sounded above me, pulling a sob from my ragged throat.

I heard the *thump, thump, thump* of their footsteps down the stairs. It was a sound I'd become accustomed to. The door swung open. Runt and Stony tossed Jasper into the room. The loud thud and limpness of his body caused something inside me to finally snap.

I rushed at my captors, forcing all the energy I had into my weak legs, and tackled Runt to the ground. Not thinking, I slammed my fists into his masked face, swinging as hard as I could, relishing in the feeling of finally fighting back.

Strong hands gripped my arms, and before I could respond, I was flying backward. I was slammed forcefully into the wall, my breath knocked harshly from my lungs.

"Stupid bitch." Runt's icy eyes flashed with hatred. He ripped off his mask and sneered at me. I should have feared the hatred burning in his cold eyes, but I was beyond fear.

He stalked toward me, the rage on his face evident.

The moment he was within my reach, I lashed out. I slapped him hard across the face, and the diamond of my ring tore a jagged path across his cheek.

He raised a hand to the blood drizzling down his face. His look of surprise momentarily masked the hate. He rubbed his cheek. Bright red blood smeared across his face as his eyes narrowed.

Pain exploded across my face as his fist materialized out of nowhere. My feet flew out from under me, and my back hit the concrete with a painful thud.

Runt rushed toward me. His fist was cocked back, ready to deliver another blow, when Stony grabbed his arm. "Let's go."

Runt struggled against his friend. "Get off me. That fucking bitch deserves it."

"We follow orders," Stony reminded him, his grip tightening on

Runt's bicep.

"I know." He yanked free of his buddy, then leaned over me.

I flinched, waiting for the blow that would end me.

Instead, he reached for my hand, ripped the ring from my finger, then backhanded me smartly across the face.

"You need to fucking listen," Stony growled as he grabbed Runt and forced him from the room.

My ring. The asshole had taken my ring. The ring Wesley had given me, one of the few things I had left of him. *That bastard!*

I looked to where Jasper was lying on the floor. I crawled to him and rolled him onto his back. They'd really done a number on him today. Blackened blood from days past was caked thick on his skin, contrasting gruesomely with the bright red from his fresh wounds.

"Jasper?" I caressed his face.

The door swung open, and Behemoth entered the room with a tray. I positioned myself between him and Jasper, praying they weren't coming for him again.

Behemoth ignored me entirely and placed the tray on a table in the corner of the room. He nodded once in my direction, and just as quickly as he'd entered, he was gone.

I returned my focus to Jasper. New bruises were forming on his cheekbones, and fresh blood seeped from his split skin.

A pained groan escaped his lips, and it felt like my heart was breaking all over again.

I went to the small table where they'd left our daily rations: a plate of bread, a bowl of soup, and a dirty glass of water. Not enough for a small child, much less two adults.

I grabbed the food and water and walked back to where Jasper laid. Placing everything on the floor, I sat down and guided Jasper's head into my lap.

This was my fault. All these bruises, the ribs that I knew had to be broken. They were all because of me.

They hadn't attempted to hurt me until a week into our captivity.

The first time they'd tried to take me, Jasper had lost it. He'd fought back with more energy than I'd known he had. Every time they'd tried to pull me upstairs, he'd fought them off until eventually, our captors decided to give him the daily beatings they'd planned for me. Instead of hurting him once every day, they did it twice, and nothing I said to Jasper would change his mind about it.

I sat there like I had so many times before and sang while I stroked his face and arms. I waited until he was ready to eat, then forced both our rations into his cracked lips. I traced my finger over his swollen eyelids. His once beautiful face had become unrecognizable.

My hands grazed over his shoulders and down his chest. He shivered beneath my fingertips, and I jerked my hand back.

"No," he croaked. "Don't stop. It feels...nice."

I smiled and ran my fingers across his cheek.

My stomach growled. I couldn't remember the last time I'd eaten. I'd been able to fool Jasper into thinking they brought me food when he was upstairs.

I focused on Jasper and ignored the pain in my belly.

Help had to show up soon. We wouldn't survive much longer.

CHAPTER FORTY-FOUR

Alex

"That's all you've been able to find?" Ky's exasperated voice pissed me off despite my similar feelings.

"Yeah. The guy who delivered the package was offered a hundred bucks to drop it off at my office. He said he had no idea who the guy was that offered him money, didn't even see his face because he was wearing a pirate mask."

"Did you look at any of the security videos, find out who this masked man was?"

"We did. There were hundreds of people running around in pirate masks that day. It was the Pirates' Booty Festival, so every idiot in town was out there. And at the location where they met, there were no cameras. I have no way of figuring it out."

"Damn it."

I didn't know what else to do. It seemed we'd exhausted our options.

I paced around Ky's cluttered apartment and tried to think. We had to be missing something.

I stopped at a small desk in the corner of Ky's living room. There were two glass flasks, rubber tubing, test tubes, and a Bunsen burner sitting next to a stack of papers.

"What's this?" I asked as a sliver of suspicion crept up my spine.

Ky shook his head dismissively. "Just some equipment from a chemistry lab I took last semester."

I fingered the papers on the desk. They were filled with notes and formulas.

Ky slammed his hand down on the stack. "Focus, damn it. We've got to find Gwen."

I sighed. He was right, I needed to focus.

"What about you?" I motioned toward his phone. "Were your contacts able to find anything?"

His hands fisted at his sides. "No."

"Anything at all? The smallest clue could help."

"I told you. They haven't found anything," he answered.

"All right. Look, I'm going to go back to the mall to talk to more people and see if they remember anything."

"I'm coming with you." The determined look on his face stopped me from arguing.

"Let's go."

∞∞∞∞∞∞

Searching the mall again was a complete waste of time. Plenty of people had noticed them – Gwen's beauty attracted attention – but no one had seen the moment they'd been attacked.

I ran my hands through my hair.

"We're going to find her," Ky assured me.

It was strange how this whole ordeal had made me see him in a different light. I still didn't like the fucker, but he wasn't the complete asshole I had taken him for.

We walked through the mall, headed for the exit. I watched the hundreds of people milling around and wondered how it was possible there were no witnesses. There were literally people everywhere. There was a girl with her feet in the water fountain, talking on her phone. I spied an old lady in Spencers holding up a disco ball. The place was swarming with people. How could Gwen and Jasper have been taken with all these people nearby? Hell, there was even a military couple looking at rings in the jewelry store. I could hear them talking to the sales clerk, asking, "How much can I get for this?"

Idiot. It's a jewelry store, not a pawn shop.

I froze.

One of the men held a blue diamond ring in his hand. A ring that looked exactly like the ring Gwen wore every day.

An odd sensation swept over me.

I stopped walking and took in every detail. Both men sported military buzz cuts and wore black boots. One of the men had an angry scratch down his left cheek.

"What?" Ky demanded.

"That's them. They're the ones that took Gwen."

I grabbed Ky's arm as he attempted to take off in their direction. He swung around violently, arm cocked, ready to pummel me, but as much as I appreciated and agreed with how he felt, we needed to know where they were going.

"We have to follow them to Gwen. After that, we'll take turns beating the hell out of them."

Ky lowered his arm and nodded.

We kept our distance, eventually making it back to the car and following their black SUV out of the garage and onto the highway.

The highway gave way to back roads that curved and twisted through the woods. There was nothing for miles and miles but trees.

"Ever feel like you're a pawn in someone else's chess game?" Ky's question surprised me.

"What?"

"You know, like someone's constantly fucking with your life, and you're helpless to stop it."

That sounded oddly accurate.

I smiled. "I've felt that way every single day for the last fourteen thousand years."

The SUV half a mile in front of us turned left. I followed,

carefully keeping a good distance back.

Out of the corner of my eye, I saw Ky shaking his head.

"Fourteen thousand years? Holy shit."

I agreed. Holy shit was right. And every day of those fourteen thousand years, I'd been alone. Yeah, I'd had an island to manage. I'd had friends and family. I'd even been married a few times over the years, but I'd never found true love. Never had a real partner in life.

I wanted all of that with Gwen. Soulmate or not, she was the only woman for me. I had to get her back.

"What are your abilities?" I asked, and immediately, I could tell my question surprised Ky.

"I'm not sure what you mean."

"All angels have individual abilities, as do hybrids. The abilities don't manifest until their twenty-third birthday, but they all have them. Abilities that are unique to them, things only they can do. For example, some hybrids have wings — it's rare, but it happens. What are your abilities? We need to figure out how best to utilize them."

Ky shrugged. "Honestly, I don't know. Other than slowed aging, I didn't know we had special abilities, so I never tried to figure it out." He paused. "Are you sure hybrids have special abilities?"

"Yeah. But that sure as shit isn't helpful now. Even if we figured it out, you wouldn't be practiced enough to be useful." I paused thinking through a plan. "Well, at least I know you can take a punch."

Ky smirked. "Yeah, I can deliver one too. Don't forget that."

Yeah, he sure as hell could. It'd been a long time since someone had hit me that hard. My jaw had hurt for hours afterward.

Damn it. I suddenly remembered that Zane was out of town running an errand for Eli, and I had no backup.

"So if you don't have abilities, please tell me you have some fighting experience."

Ky nodded. "Yeah, I used to be a soldier. I've fought in Vietnam and World War II. I'll be fine."

Good. At least I wouldn't be going in without help.

The SUV slowed and pulled onto a dirt pathway to the right. I slowed to a crawl, hoping to stay undetected, only turning onto the path when I was sure we wouldn't be seen.

I wished I'd driven the Hummer as we bumped along the uneven path through the brush and stray tree limbs. The trail seemed to go on for miles, and the SUV was no longer in sight.

We rounded a sharp corner. In the clearing ahead sat a large estate. The three-story stone house was surrounded by a ten-foot concrete wall topped with razor wire. It looked like a cross between a prison and a medieval castle.

I backed the car up until we were out of sight.

Ky began to speak, but I shushed him.

I closed my eyes and pushed my hearing out as far as I could. I could hear the uneven thump of thirty different hearts beating. "There are thirty people inside."

I listened for more. There was a television playing a rerun of *Friends* and the loud roar of a washing machine spinning.

"Jasper, I'm sorry," Gwen's weak voice crooned.

Relief washed over me. "She's here. Jasper's with her."

"Can you pinpoint exactly where they are?"

"Not exactly. I'm not sure why, but everything has an echo. All I can tell for sure is that they're here."

We crouched toward the ground, heads low, and snuck quietly through the open landscape toward the wall.

We needed a plan. I sure as hell didn't want to get Gwen killed by doing something stupid.

But there was no way to plan for this. I didn't know the layout of the estate. I had no idea who had abducted her or why. I scanned the area once more, searching for motion detectors or security cameras I could hack into.

No such luck.

I shook my head in disgust. I had absolutely nothing to base a rescue off of.

We reached the wall, and I turned to Ky.

"Based on what I can hear, there are three stories and an underground basement. There are thirty men on the premises. I can't prove they're human, but there's nothing to indicate they are angels or hybrids. Still, watch your back. We both can enter the first floor, you take the second, and I'll take the basement. The first one to find her gets her out and doesn't look back. Agreed?"

Ky nodded, then motioned ahead. "Unless you plan on flying your fairy ass over the wall, I don't know how you intend to get through this. The concrete is at least a foot thick and has a patrolling guard with a rifle."

I rolled my eyes at him.

I listened intently again for a heartbeat and quickly found the guard patrolling the inside of the wall. The moment he was across from us, I punched my arm through the wall, grabbed his neck, and jerked him through to our side. Blood sprayed, and a bloody mangled heap hung from my clenched fist.

"Damn." Ky's eyes went wide. "If you can do that, what the hell do you need me for?"

"Because if the police find a pile of bodies like this, it'll look suspicious. We have to make it look like a human fight." I dropped what was left of the body in a heap, punched a bigger hole in the wall, and stepped through. "Let's find Gwen."

We strode across the yard and pressed our backs against the stone exterior. Ky reached for the door, but I jerked his hand away.

"What?"

"Shh." I placed my finger to my lips and motioned with my hands at the two guys with guns just beyond the wall.

Ky nodded once and waited for my lead.

I took a step back, then kicked in the door, quickly kicking the rifle from one asshole's hand, then throat slamming the other to the ground with a loud crack.

I turned to check on Ky and found him struggling in a headlock with the first guy. His face was turning red, and I was about to intervene, but Ky shifted his legs and knocked his opponent off balance. He rotated his hips and spun around, pulling him into a tight arm-bar and forcing his opponent to his knees. Ky's knee came swiftly up to meet the guy's face, instantly jamming his nose up into his brain. Ky dropped the lifeless body to the floor.

"Not bad."

Ky smiled.

A deafening crack boomed through the room. I was thrown face down on the floor. Pain ripped through my left shoulder.

"Fuck." Ky dropped to the ground, grabbed a stray pistol, and fired behind me. There was a loud thud as a body fell to the floor near my feet.

I rolled onto my back and looked at my ravaged shoulder. Blood spilled, and muscle lay exposed from the one-inch hole where the bullet had exited.

"Holy shit. Are you all right?"

I staggered to my feet.

The wound would heal within an hour, but the blood loss would weaken me.

I ignored the searing pain. "I'm fine. Let's keep moving."

I scanned the room. To our left was a staircase heading up. "You take that direction. I'll take care of this floor and check out the basement."

Ky nodded and shoved the captured Beretta into his jeans.

"Remember, if you find her, get her the hell out of here. Got it?"

Ky's eyes met mine before he nodded again, then he headed for the stairs.

CHAPTER FORTY-FIVE

Gwen

The sounds of shots being fired woke me. I looked at the ceiling, not knowing if the sounds above were our salvation or our doom. I glanced down at Jasper's bloody face in my lap. I hated waking him, but if the opportunity came to escape, we needed to be prepared.

"Jasper, wake up. Please wake up." I shook him gently as the firing above became louder and more frequent.

Getting desperate, I began to shake him vigorously. "Jasper, wake up."

One bloodshot eye opened. His voice cracked when he spoke. "What is it, Gwen?"

"Guns are going off. Maybe it's the police. They could be rescuing us."

That got his attention. He sat up laboriously and groaned.

"We need to get ready." He stumbled to his feet and got against the wall behind the door. "Gwen, I want you to hide over there in the corner."

"I'm not about to hide while you risk your life."

"Just do it. We don't have time to argue. Do you want to get out of here or not?"

"Fine," I grumbled and did as he said.

My heart raced as we waited. The shots and yells above were

becoming fewer and fewer.

Suddenly, the door burst open, and the last person I'd expected to see came rushing in.

Alex.

My emotions warred within me. Staggering relief at being rescued. Awe that Alex cared enough to come for me. Icy fear that he'd hurt me again.

Alex's striking gaze met mine and time stood still.

Alex's face was streaked with blood and sweat, his clothes were torn, and his hands were stained red. He was every bit the warrior I'd imagined him to be.

His sultry eyes captured mine in a scorching embrace.

"Fuck." His voice was anguished and pained. He rushed toward me, his bloody hands gripping my face, and before I could speak, his lips were on mine.

It wasn't a sweet kiss, and it wasn't one born out of desire. It contained all the emotions swirling behind his tortured eyes. I could taste the anguish and desperation in him. The feelings of helplessness that mirrored my own. And most potent of all, there was love.

Bam!

Alex jerked away from me in time for us both to see Jasper punch a guy who was inches from stabbing Alex in the back.

Three more men came down the stairway and Alex shoved me against the wall.

I held my breath as one of the men lunged at Alex, his knife perfectly aimed at Alex's chest.

"No!" I watched the knife enter Alex's body.

Nothing happened. There was no blood, no resistance. No pained cry from Alex's lips.

Alex grabbed the man by the throat.

"H-How?" he gasped as Alex's grip tightened.

Alex didn't answer as he slammed his fist into the man's face.

I heard a scuffle behind me and turned. Jasper was struggling with Runt. I saw a flicker of color as someone entered the room from the door behind them.

No, it can't be.

I'd been in captivity for too long. I had to be hallucinating.

CHAPTER FORTY-SIX

Alex

The last two captors were in our grasp. Mine had a knife, which was laughable considering it would go right through me.

There was no longer any point in trying to hide what I was. Jasper had seen enough to figure it out.

Jasper had the other captor in a headlock. It was surprising that despite his injuries, he was quite a good fighter. For a human, at least.

Jasper snapped the guy's neck at about the same time I'd finished off mine.

"Not bad." I motioned toward the body on the floor.

Jasper staggered then slid slowly to the floor. "Thanks, man."

Finally, it was over.

I wiped the sweat and blood from my face just as I heard a feminine voice clear her throat.

I turned slowly in the direction of the voice, praying my intuition was wrong.

Hannah stood behind me, one arm wrapped tightly around Gwen's shoulders, the other holding a syringe to her neck.

Hannah's head dropped back, her long black hair swaying as she laughed wickedly. "You should see your face right now."

"Hannah, what are you doing?"

"It was always about Gwen, wasn't it?"

I inched toward her. "You don't want to do this, Hannah."

She raised her eyebrows quizzically. "I don't? Really? Oh, I think I do."

Gwen struggled in Hannah's arms, trying unsuccessfully to shake her off.

I just had to get a few feet closer, and then I could pull the syringe from Hannah's hand before she could inject it.

I edged forward as I looked into Gwen's panicked eyes.

"You always wanted her, your precious Gwen. I was nothing to you."

"Hannah-"

"Oh no," she chided as she stepped back. "Don't come any closer." She slid the needle into Gwen's neck, and her thumb hovered over the plunger.

Gwen gasped and stilled in Hannah's arms. Her emerald eyes pleaded with a look that would haunt me forever.

"Well, I found someone better. Someone who wants me. And now," she paused as a smile spread across her face, "now, you can't have Gwen or me."

Her thumb pushed down the plunger, and the purple liquid injected smoothly into Gwen's neck.

"No!"

"Oh, by the way," her sparkling eyes met mine, "thanks for finding her for me, you made this oh so easy."

Gwen's eyes drifted closed, and she slumped in Hannah's arms.

Hannah released her, dropping Gwen to the floor like a rag doll.

"You stupid bitch." I stepped forward.

She lifted a hand to stop me, an arrogant smile forming on her lips. "I wouldn't do that if I were you. You see, I'm the only one who has the antidote, so you can't touch me," she smirked. "For someone so smart, you can be so stupid. And so easy to manipulate." Hannah dropped the syringe.

The high-pitched clink of the glass as it cracked on the concrete floor momentarily drew my attention.

Hannah's hair fanned out behind her as she spun and ran up the stairs.

If she thought that would save her, she was out of her fucking mind. I would torture the information out of her before I let her get away.

I ran up the stairs after Hannah.

"Alexander!"

I glanced over my shoulder. Jasper stood over Gwen's supine body.

Gwen!

I ran to her and threw myself on the floor. When I lifted her into my arms, her head fell back loosely, her eyes closed.

"Gwen?" My voice sounded frantic to my own ears. "Gwen!"

"What the fuck was in this?" Jasper was looking at the glass pieces of the syringe coating the ground.

My eyes flashed up the stairs in the direction Hannah had gone. I faintly heard her opening the front door.

"Is it done?" A masculine voice asked her. A voice that sounded too much like Ky's.

"Of course, babe," Hannah answered cheerfully.

That lying bastard!

I couldn't believe I'd trusted him. My mind flashed back to all of his strange behaviors. He'd always had a plausible excuse, and I'd believed him.

Damn it. He had been behind everything all along.

Ky's loud laughter snapped me into action. I was going to kill him.

I laid Gwen down and rushed up the stairs. Ky would pay for this. They both would.

I made it up the stairs and halfway across the living room.

"Alexander!" Jasper yelled from behind me. "Gwen's having a

seizure!"

Fuck!

I ran back down to the basement and threw myself again on the ground next to Gwen's convulsing body. Foam bubbled out of her mouth, her back arched, and then she suddenly went completely limp.

Oh, no. I couldn't hear her heart.

I kissed her. Nothing happened. I kissed her chest, her arms, every place I could think of, but nothing happened. Nothing fucking happened!

Why isn't this working? Why isn't this healing her?

"What are you-"

"Shh."

I couldn't heal her. My healing ability must have only worked on injuries. How had I not known that until now? With that realization, I began doing the only thing I could think of.

CPR.

With each compression, I became more desperate. She couldn't die. I couldn't live without her. Not anymore.

Nothing happened. I continued compressions. One, two, three...then breathe. One, two, three...then breathe. One, two, three... Over and over again. Her lifeless body taunted me.

Again.

One, two, three....

It wasn't working.

I dropped my head back and screamed in frustration. Tears mixed with blood as they poured down my face.

I can't lose her. God, please. I'll do anything you ask if you save her. I'll even let her go if that's what you want.

With renewed determination, I began chest compressions again. One, two, three....

Jasper grabbed my arm to stop me and I flung his hand away.

"If value your life, you will not try to stop me again."

Jasper sat back and rested his hand on her limp arm. He bent over and whispered in Gwen's ear. "After all we've been through, you're not going to give up now. You're stronger than this."

Again, I placed my hand on her chest to start compressions.

Gwen's eyes suddenly fluttered open.

∞∞∞∞∞∞

This was my fault. If I had just followed my heart and pursued Gwen from the beginning, Hannah would never have done this. But I'd been stupid and selfish and delusional, thinking I'd somehow gotten Eva back.

But how could I have known? Not in a million years would I have imagined Hannah harbored such hatred for Gwen.

And then there was Ky. After all that anger and jealousy, we'd finally found some common ground. We had banded together to save Gwen. We'd fought and bled together. He'd even earned my grudging respect.

His feelings for Gwen had seemed genuine. He'd played his part well.

I shook my head in disgust. To think I'd actually trusted that backstabbing bastard.

The worst part was that the evidence had been staring me in the face the whole time, but I'd listened to his lies and believed him. I'd allowed myself to be fooled, and now Gwen was paying the price.

After I'd carried Gwen to the car, I'd gotten another surprise. Sitting on the dashboard on the passenger side had been a folded piece of paper with a word written in Ky's handwriting:

Checkmate

I'd called Zane as soon as I'd seen the note. He'd driven to Ky's house and verified the handwriting was indeed Ky's. He'd also found that all of Ky's clothing was gone.

Despite Jasper's objections, I'd taken Gwen to my house instead of the local hospital. Along the way, I'd explained to Jasper who I was, and that I was much more capable of taking care of Gwen than the doctors were. He'd agreed but insisted on coming along.

We walked through the door of my basement, and I laid Gwen down on the couch before tossing Jasper the first aid kit.

Jasper scanned the room with approval. "You've got a full laboratory here?"

I nodded.

"And you're sure we shouldn't take her to the hospital?"

"I'm positive. I'm much more knowledgeable and have better sterilization equipment."

Jasper motioned to my bloody shoulder. "What about you? That wound needs stitches."

"That wound was completely healed twenty minutes ago." I pulled the bloody shirt from my chest and tossed it in the trash. "You should clean up. It's going to be a while before I get any test results back. If you go back up the stairs, Zane's room is immediately to the left. You're about the same size. You can borrow some of his clothes and take a shower."

Jasper nodded and limped out of the room.

I walked to Gwen's side and crouched at the edge of the couch.

Her skin was deathly pale, and her trembling lips had taken on a bluish hue. I'd test her blood in a moment, but from the looks of her, it appeared she was suffering from cyanosis. It was a condition that resulted from a lack of oxygen in the blood. Any number of poisons could have caused it, anything from cyanide to carbon monoxide to heavy metal poisoning. Hell, it didn't even have to be a poison. Viruses could have caused it, but there were none that worked this quickly.

I brushed a strand of hair from Gwen's sweaty forehead and whispered in her ear. "I will fix this."

I kissed her cheek, then went to the sink and sterilized my hands. I grabbed a latex tourniquet and a syringe before returning to

Gwen's side.

"This will only sting for a second, sweetheart."

I slid the syringe in, removed the tourniquet, and watched as blood filled the tube.

As soon as I was done, I put a sample of her blood on a slide and slipped it under the microscope.

I stared at the computer screen in front of me.

No fucking way.

I adjusted the focus then glanced back at the screen and hung my head.

"What? What the hell is that?" Jasper asked as he entered the room.

"That," I motioned to the screen, "is Gwen's DNA."

"Is it supposed to look like that?"

"No." I rubbed a hand roughly down my face. "This is not good."

"Why?"

"I've just...I've never seen anything like it. Whatever they've given her, it's altered her DNA. Look here." I pointed at a spot on the screen. "You see this section right here?"

"Yeah."

"Normal DNA doesn't look like that. Hell, even angel and hybrid DNA don't look that bizarre."

I figured I might have better luck examining the leftover poison from the syringe they'd injected her with and extracted the few residual drops of solution from a glass shard of the syringe I'd pocketed from the floor. I placed half of the drops on a slide and the other half in the spectrometer.

I took the slide and placed it under the microscope. Putting my eye to the black ring, I took a peek at what was killing the woman I loved.

I stared at the specimen a long while. *What the hell?*

"Do you know what it is?"

"Fuck." I slammed my hand down on the table.

"What? What is it?"

I shook my head in dismay. I didn't have a fucking clue what I was looking at. Where the hell would Hannah have gotten something like this? There was nothing else like it in the world.

The spectrometer finished its work, and I ran the remaining tests even though I knew I'd find nothing.

How the hell was this happening?

This...whatever it was, it was going to kill Gwen.

"So how do we cure her?" Jasper's eyes fixed on mine.

I hated the words as they left my mouth, "We can't. No medicine on Earth could cure this. And at the rate she's deteriorating, I'd never discover a cure in time."

Jasper grabbed my arm. "You can't give up."

"I'm not giving up." I jerked his hand off me. "I just need a moment to think."

I stalked up the stairs and headed for the garden. The small tropical garden was full of ferns, palms, and orchids; it resembled so much of my home and calmed me when nothing else did.

I sat on the ground, leaned against a lemon tree, and closed my eyes. I took in a slow deep breath and savored the fresh ocean breeze. I imagined Gwen's healthy skin glowing in the sunlight and her broad smile beaming up at me. Wind blew her golden locks around her, and her emerald eyes sparkled brightly in the sun.

A strong gust of wind rustled the ferns and leaves above me. A lemon fell, bounced off my shoulder, and rolled a few feet in front of me. I gazed at the bright yellow peel of my favorite fruit.

That's it!

I jumped to my feet, raced down the stairs to the basement, pushed the door open forcefully, and grabbed Gwen.

"I know how to save her."

"I thought you said there wasn't any medicine for this."

I ran up the stairs, not bothering to check if Jasper was

following. "There isn't. I'll explain later. We need to go right now. Run to Zane's room, grab enough clothes for both of us. He's got extra toothbrushes under the sink. I'll get something for Gwen. We leave in ten minutes."

Moments later, we were racing down the highway. The path I'd set for us was one never traveled before, but I didn't care. All that mattered was that Gwen survived.

Once she was saved, I'd have to figure out who was really behind all of this. The bombing of my helicopter and facilities and the production of this poison were beyond the abilities of Ky or Hannah. Someone else had to be the mastermind behind it all.

But who?

∞∞∞∞∞∞

As I drove, I blocked Jasper's never-ending questions from my head. I was agitated, twitchy, and irritable, and taking my frustrations out on Jasper wouldn't accomplish anything.

I had to figure out who'd done this to Gwen. Who had the motive and necessary resources to pull it off? Hannah and Ky had obviously been working with someone, but who?

Mile after mile passed as the sun drifted over the horizon. The darkness brought sleep to Jasper, and his incessant questions finally ceased.

The quiet sounds of the road calmed me. Slowly, a faded memory made its way to the surface of my mind.

Judgment had been passed down. And as always, God had been just. But that knowledge didn't remove the sting from the punishment.

It had been decided that Lew could make himself a home in the universe of his choosing, but Heaven could never be his home again. Eva would be taken from him, sent away by God to an undisclosed location and prohibited from seeing Lew. The punishment served two purposes. First, to punish Lew for his hatred. And second, to punish Eva by separating her from me.

As usual, God decided to speak with us individually after sentencing. I sat in the banquet hall awaiting my turn to enter the throne room. Eva was called first, and despite my reservations, I pushed my hearing out so I could eavesdrop on their conversation.

"But why? I love him."

There was silence for a few moments, and then Eva's voice again: "But it's not fair."

I realized then that God knew I was listening in. He hadn't stopped me from hearing Eva's part of the conversation, but He had kept me from hearing His responses.

Interesting.

"But what about the baby? You can't punish the child because of my sin."

There was some shuffling, then the sound of Eva sobbing.

"Thank you," she gushed. "Thank you so much."

There were a few muffled sounds, then a guard entered the banquet hall. "Sir," he saluted me. "He will see you now."

I returned the guard's salute and strode through the archway and into the throne room.

As always, it took my breath away. The cavernous room boasted gold walls accented with platinum crown molding. Diamond chandeliers glittered overhead. A sparkling body of water covered the expanse between the entrance and the throne.

The throne itself was surrounded by seven blazing lamps and four cherubim and was made of the purest sapphire. Its deep blue hue glittered across every surface in the room.

Above the throne, a luminous emerald rainbow blazed brightly. Behind it, the twenty-four chief assistants sat in gleaming obsidian chairs.

Most brilliant of all in this dazzling room was God himself. He sat on the throne and shone with the most intense white light. His body was the outline of a man but had the appearance of a sparkling gem.

His overwhelming presence dropped me to my knees.

"Rise, my child." His voice reverberated through me like thunder.

I lifted my head and watched as He rose from His throne and stepped out onto the water. The water rippled and glimmered with each step as He walked across its surface.

I dropped my head as He approached. "My Lord."

He placed a hand on my shoulder. My arm tingled and hummed with the most incredible sensation.

"Alexias, this conversation is private." He motioned to the others in the room. "No one can hear me but you."

I nodded in understanding.

"Through all this, you have remained innocent of wrongdoing. Yet I feel the excruciating pain you're experiencing. I know how this has affected you."

It was true. This ordeal had pained me like nothing else had before. My heart ached in my chest, and it hurt to breathe.

"I make this promise to you so that all will know my glory. That promise is this: you will find your soulmate one day. You will share a love so strong it will alter your world. Your path won't be easy, and it won't make sense, but you must be patient."

He turned to leave.

"W-Wait! Please, my Lord. Is that all? That's all you'll tell me?"

I couldn't see His face, but I could feel His smile. "Yes, my child. That is all."

In His usual fashion, He'd left me mystified.

When I left the throne room, I waited outside and leaned against the wall. Again, I stretched my hearing out and listened in, knowing God would stop me if He wanted to.

"It wasn't my fault —" Lew's voice was unexpectedly cut off. There were a few moments of silence before Lew spoke again.

"Will I ever see you again?" Lew's distraught voice saddened me.

"Yes," God's voice boomed. "We will see each other again. But you must turn from this destructive path you've set for yourself. It will do you no good."

"But I love her —"

Ten minutes of silence followed before Lew finally stepped out of the throne room.

Lew ignored me until we were both out of the palace and entering the gardens. "Where is she?" he demanded. "Where is Eva?"

I shook my head. "I don't know. They already accompanied her out."

"What?" Lew yelled at the same time two guards came out of the palace to escort him.

"Get your hands off me," he ordered as the guards gripped his arms and tried to force him toward the portal out of Heaven.

I watched my friend with regret as he struggled with the guards.

How had he become so consumed with anger? It must have started long before this event.

I walked toward the guards and commanded them to wait. Being the good soldiers they were, they stopped immediately and held Lew steadily between them.

"Lew, please —"

"No." He struggled against the guards, and his eyes blazed with hatred as he glared at me. "This is all your fault. You took Eva from me. You will pay for this."

"I am your friend, Lew —"

"No!" he yelled. "Don't you dare call me Lew. We are no longer friends." His face contorted into a mask of hate before he spat, "From now on, you will call me Lucifer."

......to be continued in **<u>Genesis (The Infinity Series, Vol. 2)</u>**

Genesis (The Infinity Series, Vol. 2)

The unthinkable has occurred. The love of Alexander's life was dying. Every moment pulled her away from him. Every second brought her closer to death. And he'd do anything to save her.

Even if that included treason.

Even if it included defying the God he'd sworn to obey.

In a race against time, Alexander set out on a new mission. To scour the multiverse for the three gatekeepers who blocked the way to the only cure.

For all upcoming books, deleted scenes, and bonus material visit my website at
www.bellamywestbayauthor.com

Acknowledgments

I'd like to thank my husband and son, for being patient through all the hours that went into the writing and editing of this book. Thank you to Ana Grigoriu for the absolutely beautiful book covers and website design. A special thanks to John Fox at BookFox for all your advice, and fantastic editing skills -- you were amazing. A big thanks to my beta readers: Amanda, Brit, Julie, Katie, and Kim. But most of all I'd like to thank Leigh, without your encouragement this novel may never have seen the light of day. Thank you.

CPSIA information can be obtained
at www.ICGtesting.com
Printed in the USA
LVHW03s1443091018
592979LV00002B/418/P